# Lady Lazarus

# Lady Lazarus

## Debrah Martin

Published by IM Books

www.debrahmartin.co.uk

© Copyright D. B. Martin 2017

LADY LAZARUS

ISBN 978-0-9933613-7-1

# Chapter 1: Lady Lazarus

The bottle said *Take two with liquid*. Little magic pills if you took them the right way. Little mind-bombs if you didn't. That was the way they'd been described to her. She culled the white powder from two of the capsules and sprinkled it into the coffee. Drifting from the kitchen back into the hall, avoiding the lounge, she called out,

'I've made us coffee.'

She lingered there, in front of the mirror at the bottom of the stairs – a great elaborate monstrosity like the one in the hall from her childhood days. She imagined … and shivered. That was then. This was now. Here. And she was now, here. About to … She realised then she was holding her breath. She let it go in a small perfunctory rasp and studied herself more closely in the mirror. She looked relaxed, but inside she was coiled tight. To distract herself she mimicked birdsong under her breath; Jenny Wren's melodic tune or a swallow's swooping call – but the birdsong mutated into an ugly caw so she stopped and counted to control her breathing instead. Nerves were getting to her. It had better be soon or she would need those little magic pills herself.

The lounge door opened behind her, and there she was; her alter ego. She was carrying both mugs of coffee and already sipping one of them, cool and commanding, like she'd been ever since Jay.

'So …' Her alter-ego came to a halt alongside her in front of the mirror.

Their two faces stared back at them, one defined and determined, the other diffuse, pensive. Waiting. The same. And that wouldn't ever change. Jay gave them no choice but to play out the same old routines, the same old miseries. Which mug had she chosen? Ah, the one with the little mind-bombs. Cup, sip, slip; slipping slowly with each sip. Fate had decided for them, then. This was meant to be. She took the other mug with a gesture of thanks.

'So,' she agreed, eyeing her counterpart with the poisoned chalice of

1

coffee, mimicking the same tone.

'What now?'

'Can we not compromise?' She tried to make it sound the natural solution, obvious.

'Compromise? How?'

'Make this the last time like this.' She remained facing the mirror, watching the reflection in it. The reflection stared back suspiciously at her, still sipping coffee.

'The last time?' the reflection asked, eyes narrowing – no, squinting to focus. The little mind bombs had begun to burst.

'As we are now,' she explained. She sounded so calm – how could she? She cupped her hands tightly round her own mug to stop herself grabbing the poisoned one, throwing it to the floor, confessing her sins – like she'd always done. Until now. 'I'll show you how I do it. Everything. That's what you've always wanted, isn't it?'

'Really?' The reflection's eyes widened, then squinted again. 'After all this time? Why? What do you get from that?'

She began to marshal words, explanations, persuasion – but it wasn't necessary. The eyes were already glazing over, losing focus, body slumping – becoming as *she* had been all this time. Spineless. The little mind-bombs had completed their work. And so fast. No turning back now.

'Freedom,' she replied instead, so quietly she wasn't sure she was even heard. 'I want my freedom, so I have to give you it too.' Then louder, 'does it matter? If it's what you want?'

'What I want ... But ... You seem ... You're ...' A frown. Trying to quantify the change. 'Different. More like ... me...'

*Now* she took the mug – before it fell – cutting across the bewilderment; biting back her own sense of disorientation at how things were changing.

'Maybe I am. And you are like me. So, we shall be we. I'll show you how to fly too, if you want to?'

'Fly?' So slurred. 'But you said that was impossible. That was why Jay couldn't ... didn't ...' The usually strident voice was a shadow of itself. Unsure, confused.

'Not impossible,' she cut across the objection, pulse racing and heart hammering against her ribs. She clenched her hand into a fist and it shattered and re-formed. A good trick – one of the best – but just a trick by comparison to what she was about to do. *But careful – you won't be able to do any of it afterwards. Not for real.* That empty stare was starting to get to her. 'It was impossible *then* but I've learnt how to now. I can show you, if you want me to.'

'I ...' head swaying on her neck like a flower on a stalk. 'I feel odd – weightless.'

For a moment, her heart felt like it had stopped. She couldn't. No! She couldn't do this ... Hesitation trickled down her spine at the realisation of what it would mean. But, then, she'd always known what it would mean, right from when she'd first had the idea.

'Like you could fly?'

'Like I could fly. Yes ... Yes!'

But there was still Jay; always there, lurking behind those staring eyes, greedily gleeful that at last ... Her heart kicked back into rhythm. She shrugged doubt away.

'Then you will. Follow me.'


And she had. All the way upstairs and the waiting window; open and coquettish. Should there be a note? But then what would it say? And it would take time to compose. No, they could all just assume. And it was time now – before the mind bombs dissipated. She led the way across the room, pushed the window wide and climbed up onto the sill, cramming herself into one half of the open space.

'Come on,' she called over her shoulder. 'Come and see how the world looks from here.'

'But ...'

'It's alright. You won't fall. You're going to fly.'

'OK,' the merest doubt hanging in the dulled voice.

Squeezed hard against the window frame and they rubbed shoulders in the cramped space. Together, they looked down over the emptiness below; the hard, grey slabs and cold winter morning. Her heart pounded.

'Ready to fly then?' she prompted.

'I don't know how ...'

'You do. Just think about what you want to do and you'll do it.'

'But I can't ... not like you ...'

She shaved the edge from her voice and forced encouragement into instead. 'Just try it. Think. Hard. Put the wish into your head and desire it.'

Blank eyes squinted into the distance and then back at her. 'I am, but ...' Vacant eyes, vacant mind. The little mind bombs had all exploded now. Time to self-destruct, but she couldn't. Her mind had already done so. She would have to push the button for her to start the countdown sequence.

'Shall I help you?' she asked. Kind. How they should have been to each other but for Jay.

'Yes.'

The gratefulness, the thanks in the inflection of that affirmative – oh God! She almost broke then, but no. This was just a shell of a body, she reminded herself as she peered sideways at the nodding, vacuous head. A Lady Lazarus in the making.

'I'll think it with you, then.' She put her arm around the hunched shoulders and filled her head with the idea. 'Now say it aloud with me too,' she prompted, squeezing the hunched shoulders. 'I want to fly!' she called aloud. 'Come on.'

'Alright. I want to fly,' the echo quavered like an undernote to her descant.

'Again! I want to fly.'

'I want to fly…'

'Now together, and think it too. I want to fly!'

'I want to fly,' they chorused, and their voices rang out even as far as the trees on the hill in the distance. 'I want to fly …'

She paused just long enough after enunciating the words before pushing hard against knotted muscle and tense sinew. The drag of gravity would have taken them both but that she had hooked her other arm through the crack between window and frame. She steadied herself against it and pulled back, watching the falling body tumble after the echoing words. It twisted mid-air as the woman desperately attempted to grab at something – anything – to stop her fall, but the ground was already too close. Eyes not vacant now, but full of surprise, then fear. That tense knot of muscles in her back were only now registering the imprint of the hand that had pushed her, even as hope faded from her mind and her plummeting body met the harsh, grey ground.

'Goodbye, Jay,' she murmured, sadly. 'Goodbye, Roseanne.'

She turned away and climbed back in from the window ledge, carefully avoiding looking down at the crumpled white and red figure lying on the stone slabs two floors down. A fly flew in the open window, droning lazily past her before she pulled it shut. It landed on the edge of the mirror on the small dressing table at the end of the bed. She exclaimed irritably and wafted it away, but proximity to the mirror caused her to pause and study her reflection again. Just hers, this time. Yet, was there a wisp, a shadow there, maybe? She squinted at the pinched white face staring back at her in the mirror.

'No!' she exclaimed. 'I am Lady Lazarus. Only me.'

# Chapter 2: Grant

There was a fly stuck in the room, trying to escape. He hated flies. He opened his eyes, squinting to locate the culprit. The buzz became more insistent. Close by. No, just the alarm clock, on repeat. Darwin Grant slammed his hand down on the annoying buzz. He peeled his tongue from the roof of his mouth where it seemed to have stuck overnight and cleared his throat. Silence returned, apart from the clock's gentle tick.

'Ummm,' he grunted appreciatively. He rolled onto his other side and drifted again. He was warm and his head was full of nothing. He floated comfortably on the emptiness of everything, luxuriated in it; that momentary waking sensation where everything is a blank – fresh; a page waiting to be filled before the day rushes in and fills it with responsibilities and necessities and worries. An empty page, slowly filling with words. It took a while to focus on why that idea palled. Ah. Stacey.

He rolled over and took in the patchy off-peach walls of the bedroom. The colour Stacey had chosen before she'd buggered off. Like puke. He'd always thought the colour looked like puke. Someone, a niece or a cousin, had once overfed their baby apricot custard at some do he'd been at – maybe even his own wedding – and the baby had thrown it up all over the white damask tablecloth. It had been exactly that colour when it came out.

'Story of my life,' he grumbled to the puke wall.

And he shouldn't have polished off that second bottle of red last night because now he was fully awake he felt ready to puke too, nicely accompanying the mother of a headache that went with it. He lay perfectly still, waiting for the nausea to pass and reluctantly allowing the nothingness to fade away and be replaced with what lay ahead for the day. The monthly Inspector's meeting – even though he'd been bumped from the privilege of calling himself Detective Inspector after the fiasco of the Riggs case. And another bollocking, no doubt, when they found out

6

that the monthlies still hadn't been completed from last month and here they were already into December and another set of them should have been started. That would be the first thing. Then the open cases. Then another round of recriminations over the Riggs case. No comeback over his last shot across the bows there yet, though – the little piece he'd passed on to his successors – and the press. Fat lot of good that it had done. He sighed and rolled flat onto his back. Although the bollocking surely wouldn't be long in coming anyway. The leaked facts had been in Friday's *Aldwych Daily*; just a paragraph, next to an appeal for some recent local suicide's friends and relatives to come forward. Poor kid. Just a paragraph in a local rag and then forgotten, both of them. Neither had made the news big time. That had been more concerned with the spotting of some ex-local porn film starlet at one of the seedier nightclubs in town. Said a lot about priorities, that – the lost and lonely less important than self-promoting wastrels. He thumped his fist against the mattress in frustration. And the bloody ceiling was still looking patchy – even after three coats of apricot white to keep Stacey happy. "I refuse to sleep in a bedroom that's a wreck, even if the rest of the place is," she'd said, toe pawing petulantly against the floor like she did when she was going to throw another paddy at him. At least the ceiling wasn't puke-coloured, waiting to drip down on him if he let his imagination run away from him … like Stacey had. Jesus, he hated this place with its eighties flocked wall paper, chipped paintwork and ill-fitting antique pine kitchen – almost as much as he hated his life. Nevertheless, he'd have to face the antique pine kitchen before he could even down a black coffee to get him going.

'Antique, my arse,' he said aloud. Puke walls, floral wallpaper and dilapidation. "Needs updating," the estate agent had said. 'Needs bloody demolishing,' he'd replied – but too late. He'd been coerced by Stacey by then. Before she left.

He rolled onto his side and threw back the covers. The rush of cold air made him shiver. And the central heating didn't work as of two weeks ago – the day Stacey had left. Grant planted his feet on the ground and dug his toes into the pile of the carpet. The bedroom was the only room with decent flooring Enjoy. Puke peach again, though, unfortunately. Pulling his bathrobe around him he shuffled around the room until he could find something to put on his feet. His outdoor shoes were the nearest to hand. Who gave a toss that he looked like a prat in a bathrobe, half-dressed for the outside and half-dressed for bed? There was no-one here to see any more. He plodded downstairs, the nothing of the early-morning blank page rapidly filling with miseries. The tiles on the roof were still rattling, the doormat was littered with envelopes that looked like bills and there were three messages on his phone. One from Stacey.

*"You are feeding the cat, aren't you?"*

'Fuck off,' he said to it. 'Oh wait, you already have. The cat has too.'

*"Your next payment for your card ending in 5354 is now due ..."*

'You can fuck off too. That's her card, not mine.'

*"Voicemail has a new message for you."*

He checked voicemail. It was the Super's PS.

*"Detective Sergeant Grant, Detective Superintendent Carter-Rowles would like to see you in his office at nine am sharp on Monday."*

It had been left on Friday at eight o'clock in the evening. Carter-Rowles' way of showing he was dedicated to the job, and his PS was dedicated to him, no doubt. Had he not checked his phone all weekend? He couldn't remember. Judging by the number of empty bottles stacked by the sink, probably not. So maybe it hadn't been the second bottle last night that had caused this mother of a hangover. He found the newspaper article from Friday. It had to be about that – even though it didn't mention his name; only that *a detective* had continued to pursue the case until it had been proven to be murder. He glanced sadly at the plea in the article alongside for relatives of the suicide to come forward. Bloody shame that. She'd only been in her twenties too. Pretty name too. Roseanne. He teared up. This was ridiculous! His sense of loss was out of all proportion to his total lack of connection to an unknown woman – just a suicide; but still ...

He needed coffee. It was going to be a grim day.

'Wonderful,' he said to the empty coffee jar. It would have to be tea, and the milk was off. That, he did remember from yesterday.

He took his mug of black tea into the lounge. At least it was bright in there. The estate agent had boasted how it faced east. 'The sun rises in the east," he'd said jauntily. "Lovely and bright in the morning.'

'Yeah, and dark as fuck in the evening,' Grant added under his breath. He stared out of the front window at the untidy front garden, the fence, leaning at an obscure angle inwards towards the house as if hoping for support that wouldn't come. He put his mug down on the window sill and tried to pull the sash window more firmly into place in an effort to stem the draught he could feel whistling in round the frame. The bottom edge splintered as he applied pressure, puncturing the fleshy part of his left hand. 'Shit!' He examined his hand and the jagged splinter now piercing it. At least it wasn't his right hand, but this place was a death trap. Why the hell had Stacey wanted them to buy it? Renovating it to its full glory was a pipe dream – something for the experts or the dedicated to tackle, not reluctant amateurs like them. And come to that, why the hell had he agreed? He yanked the splinter out and sucked at his palm as he picked up his coffee mug with the other hand. He moved across to the latest pile of papers that had accumulated over the weekend on the makeshift desk next to the window. The names were all as familiar to him as his own now – yet he knew none of them.

'Ghoulish,' Stacey had said. 'The past is the past.' He pictured her there, leafing through his close-handwritten pages as she always did when she'd wanted to really get at him, waving them around like a script from her drama group. 'What's the point of raking over old crimes when you'll probably never find the culprits? My God, this one goes back to the Dark Ages.'

'1536, Robert Pakington. First handgun death recorded in London.' The response was automatic – and regretted immediately.

'Exactly – the Dark Ages. What does it matter now who killed him?'

'It matters because someone *did* kill him – whenever it happened. It matters to me. And one day I might find out.' Then he'd taken the sheaf of papers carefully back off her – as he always did – before she dropped them and they created their own haphazard pattern on the murky brown carpet. He really ought to number the pages with Stacey around, interfering. Except of course, now she wasn't.

'Shame you don't spend as much time researching a holiday for us – or new windows.' Then she'd flounce off, like she always flounced off – been flouncing off for years.

He patted the weekend's work. Nothing concrete – but a germ of an idea. Not about Robert Pakington – she was probably right there. Too long ago. But the 2013 baseball bat murder in Bosham – the Christmas house sitter; maybe there was something there to pursue – and it would be the third anniversary of her death soon. There was a point to that.

Distantly, from the kitchen, he heard his phone ring. He stumbled back to the dingy pine of the kitchen, stubbing his toe on the way. It was another message. A reminder. The Super's office at nine am – sharp. That meant it was important and it was now eight-thirty. It would take twenty minutes to get to the nick, even in good traffic and he wasn't even dressed. He was going to be late. He sighed, thinking about the late lamented Robert Pakington whose murder would probably forever remain unsolved, no matter how long he researched it, and a twenty-something with a pretty name who'd thought life was so bad she might as well leave it. Yes, it was going to be a grim day.

# Chapter 3: Erin

The world had ticked on, but it was still a hard, grey surface, and she, crushed against it. She tried to push it away but it pulled her closer, pinning her to it as she called out in protest. Trapped – trapped again. Had she failed, after all?

'No!' she tried to shout, but the constriction in her throat made her choke. All around her the hard, grey world was screeching and buzzing as shadowy figures rushed at her.

'Stay calm, Erin. You've had an accident'

'But Roseanne…' she pleaded with them before she remembered with a sharp rush of exhilaration, and the dark pulled her back into its depths again.

# Chapter 4: Beringer

Even the sleek sophistication of his minimalistic office and reception left him hollow today. He'd hoped to beat Jenny in by half an hour, feeling virtuous that for once she wasn't already there, neat and professional, whilst he dragged himself in for another day of monologues from his patients and monotonously similar replies from him. After all, there was no warm female body to keep him in bed currently ... but there she was, bright and early, radiating efficiency, handing him the stack of morning post as usual. And there he was taking it from her with his polished urbane charm – as usual. God, it never changed. And to make it worse today, Sykes had published another paper and it was garnering even more attention than the last one.

Sykes had been the village idiot at university, whilst he, Michael Beringer, BMBCh (Oxon), had been the golden boy – destined for great things. Now Sykes was the golden boy and he was the village idiot, albeit living in a very comfortable village full of expensive leather furniture and expensive leather-look clients. What had gone wrong?

He took the morning's post into his office and closed the door. The room's view cheered him slightly. It was magnificent – and he was lucky to have found it; added an edge of distinction to the location. Who else could visit their shrink and enjoy such a breathtaking view at the same time. He stood for a few moments, admiring his acquisition. Rolling hills – bleak at the moment, but in spring and summer they encompassed astonishing hues of green combined with the acid yellow of rape or the burnished gold of wheat. Sumptuous. A fitting backdrop to his slick but tediously boring daily routine. The routine that was about to get started again in less than twenty minutes. Did it make it all worthwhile? If the fee was right, maybe. He laughed without humour.

He turned off the intercom and scanned Sykes' paper. Nothing exceptional or particularly ground-breaking, but moving the world of clinical psychiatry on a notch where he merely repeated the same old practices with the same old people day in, day out. He needed something new. Something to bring some excitement back into his life – maybe inspire him to get back on the professional conveyor belt again. He should write another paper. He was well overdue one. But on what? And who could he use as a research subject? He leaned back into the plush leather of his chair and enjoyed the way it moulded itself to him. It had been the most expensive chair in the showroom. That was one of the main reasons he'd chosen it – that and the fact that it had the same give as a woman's body. If his mind had to atrophy on a daily basis at least he could enjoy some pleasures of the flesh whilst it did so, especially since those pleasures were temporarily curtailed by the absence of a suitable structure – apart from the chair – to supply them now Clarice had taken off and taken her expensive but accommodating body with her.

'Mr Beringer?'

He looked up from Sykes' paper, now crumpled where he'd twisted it whilst his mind had been wandering. His receptionist was at the door, peering timidly round it.

'Sorry, Jenny. You wanted something?'

'Your intercom is off and your first patient is here. Mrs Young.'

'Ah, yes, Mrs Young – neurotic anxiety and repression. A wonderful start to a Monday.' He could hear the sarcasm in his voice but for the moment he didn't care.

The receptionist looked at him nervously. 'Should I send her in, or …?'

'No, no. Send her in. The day must begin and so must the psychoses – such as they are.'

'Oh, and by the way, have you seen the note I left you about the police.'

'Police?'

'Yes, they want to talk to you about *that death*.' Her voice dropped to a hushed whisper, loud enough only for him to hear. He could almost see her inwardly grimacing.

'Death?'

She nodded. 'Yes, the article in the paper?'

'Ah,' he struggled to recall which article she was referring to. 'One of ours? You have denied all connection and told them we don't share patient information, haven't you?'

'Yes, I have.' She looked over her shoulder and turning back to him, hissed, 'But apparently they have to talk to you as a matter of routine since she was in your care.'

'Oh.'

'Shall I tell them to send someone over later? They are very insistent.' He drummed his fingers on the desk as he considered the best response. 'Mr Beringer?'

'Yes, yes, I'm thinking.'

'And sorry, but Mrs Young is getting a bit agitated,' now the receptionist's grimace wasn't merely inward but spread all over her face.

He pictured the long arm of the law invading the oasis of calm in reception – possibly even coming into contact with the likes of Mrs Young or others of her ilk. He sighed, fiddling with the Sykes paper again. The grand slam ground-breaking paper and professional elevation would have to wait for another day, or another year – or another lifetime. He puffed out his cheeks and shook his head.

'No, too close to the other patients. I don't want them spooked. Tell this policeman he can catch up with me on my rounds at the hospital later on today. It won't matter there. They're non-paying. Tell him the wards I'll be visiting – ward twenty-four might be best. They're usually quite quiet unless there's been a new admission. Is there anything I should know about it? Press coverage or anything?'

'No, just that she jumped. Better go. Mrs Young is getting agitated. I'll send her in.'

Just that she jumped? Habitual boredom left him in a rush of adrenalin and anxiety. He opened his mouth to ask who but the receptionist was already closing the door softly behind her. Damn! Rapidly he reviewed which of his patients could have been a potential jumper. He couldn't think of any. Sad, neurotic and desperate maybe, but all tenaciously clinging to life – and him. Damn again! It would have to wait until later now when he could take Jenny aside without anyone else around and get the full report. He swept the Sykes article and the morning post into the top drawer of his desk, just as he spotted the newspaper, Jenny, no doubt, had included for him to read, peering out from under the pile. *The article in the paper*... The door opened again and he pinned his psychiatrist smile in place.

'Mrs Young,' he rounded the desk to greet the bone-thin woman with the nervous walk and hunched shoulders. 'Now, what shall we talk about today? The usual or something different? Some exciting adventure you'd like to go on? No? The usual then. Do make yourself comfortable whilst I collect my notes.'

He slipped back round to the open drawer on the pretext of collecting pad and pen as his patient settled herself on the edge of her chair. The newspaper was still standing proud of the pile of post. Jenny had helpfully ringed the article. The name sent a shock wave through him. Roseanne Grey. Christ! Now she was quite a different matter ...

# Chapter 5: Grant

'One of yours, apparently?'

'Regrettably, Roseanne Grey was my patient, yes.' The speaker was tall and thin; aquiline, Stacey, would probably have called him – she and her drama chums. Grant rued the day she'd signed up to that screenwriting course now, even though he'd encouraged it to get her off his back about working late so often. There might have still been a Mrs Grant to nag him instead of the carefully hidden pitying looks he was treated to at the nick – and the solicitor's bills. Grant slapped the thick manila folder on the desk and wished it was Stacey underneath it, feeling the force of the slap, anyway. He signalled to the PC outside to fend off the ward sister. He hadn't finished with this one by a long chalk. He'd been told by the Super to deal with it, and by God, he would, but in his own way. Never liked suicides.

'Suffering from?' Grant sat back in the ward sister's lumpy NHS issue office chair and prepared for a game of cat and mouse. The room was small and overfull, bursting with files and papers. Just like the NHS, Grant thought sourly. Too much paper and not enough people. Bloody shrinks. Never said anything if they could get by with saying nothing – not even the ones who gave evidence *for* them in court.

'I'm not at liberty to say, I'm afraid.' The handsome mouth twisted into a charming but clammed-shut smile. *He was bloody enjoying himself – the bastard! And this was a suicide!* Now all he wanted to do was wipe the smile off the shrink's supercilious face. Grant fiddled meaningfully with the manila folder on the desk.

'I give you liberty,' he said smiling equally smoothly. The Christmas tree lights flickered off and back on again. It made him want to laugh, wondering if the plug for them was the one in the socket nearest him. He could even duplicate one of those 'aha' moments by switching the lights off and back on again himself whilst he shut this smarmy bastard down. Childish, admittedly, but satisfying. 'Or that could be replaced by more

16

than just a polite request.' He ignored the Super's last words about focussing purely on clearing cases and hitting targets and added, 'since we don't definitely know she jumped. She might have been pushed. Might have been attacked first, even.' Why the hell had he just said that?

'Murder?' Smarmy psych leant forward abruptly, knocking one of the branches on the Christmas tree and making the baubles bounce jauntily.

'That's generally what pushing someone out of a second floor window amounts to, if there's solid stone to land on below.' He couldn't help the embellishment developing or the sarcastic edge creeping in. The bloke deserved to be shaken up a bit, self-satisfied bastard! Stacey would have told him off for being judgemental, but Stacey wasn't here – and nor were her playwriter pals, specifically not the other aquiline bastard she'd run off with.

'My God...' the psych looked genuinely shocked, then edgy – cagey. Grant observed him more carefully. Not quite the reaction he'd expected. He sat up straighter and stopped thinking about fiddling with the lights. 'But why – who?' The psych's eyes had narrowed. 'What do you know?'

A defensive attack? Grant automatically parried. You never attack unless you have something to defend – and now he was into it, he simply couldn't help himself. Apart from which, Beringer was nervous...

'Well, that would probably be giving the game away at this stage but let's say there are suspicious elements we need to investigate further. That means we would like to see all your patient notes on her, doc.' The emphasis on the 'doc' didn't go unnoticed by smarm-face.

'I'm a mister, actually,' Beringer replied with mock modesty. 'I'm a consultant psychiatrist so I've lost the doctor in favour of mister. Funny kind of reverse kudos we operate under.'

'OK, *Mister* Beringer, we will be needing to see your patient file for Roseanne Grey. Is it here or do you have a private practice?'

Something inside him was flashing off and on like he'd imagined doing with the fairy lights. The Super would have his guts, but it was too late now. Oh well, make the bastard squirm a little, *then* close it all down if there was nothing. At least he would have paid more than lip service to investigating the woman's death. How sad was it to just rubber stamp it as suicide and file her away, otherwise?

'Yes, I do, and that's where I saw her – nowhere else. And you *could* see her file, but only with a warrant. Patient confidentiality.' He hesitated. Grant waited. The bloke was desperate to find out more. You could smell it – policeman's nose they called it. 'But if *you* could tell me a bit more? I might be able to help put some flesh on the bones of what is really pretty much a routine case of disassociation following trauma.'

'Disassociation following trauma, eh?' Grant feigned deference. They just couldn't help it – could they? These arrogant know-it-alls.

'Yes,' Beringer leaned back expansively in his seat, setting more of the Christmas tree baubles swinging. 'Fairly common with anyone who's spent some time in ITU or in a coma. When they wake up, patients often claim to have experienced strange after-life experiences or met people who have already died or don't even exist.' Grant sat mouse-like. The psych was in full-flow now; bring it on! 'Sometimes they even claim to see themselves. They also talk about voices they've heard and often re-evaluate their whole life as a result of a near-death experience. Salutary for anyone, I would say. It can also be partly due to the side effects of the type of drugs sometimes employed when patients need to be kept unconscious – because of brain swelling and that sort of thing. It's a toss-up which is worse – the brain's natural response to trauma or the brain's unnatural response to chemicals.'

'So did Roseanne Grey claim to hear or see someone then?'

'Did I say she did?' The smarmy face looked less smarmy, freezing automatically into professional blandness.

'You said she was a routine case, then you described a routine case.'

Beringer eyed him. 'I described a generic routine case, not a routine case that was Roseanne Grey.' He smiled charmingly, recovering.

'But you're implying she was *like* your generic routine case? Or was that all just for show and you can't even remember her?'

Beringer frowned. 'Of course I remember her,' he snapped. 'What she saw was herself – or possibly the self she imagined from before the accident, urging her on, I suppose. Or maybe the self she wished she still was after the accident. But that's common too, as well as losing confidence in oneself, which is why people often closet themselves away out in the sticks with only a cat for company.'

'She did that too?' Grant smiled to himself. *Only saw her at your private practice? Tripped yourself up there, haven't you? Not so clever now.*

'Again, Detective Sergeant, I only said in general that is a common reaction.'

'Oh, so you *don't* remember her then? Duty of care and all that a bit lacking then – a suicide case you can't even remember.'

'You're deliberately misunderstanding me, I suspect.' Beringer's

18

smile spread all the way across his face. Grant could almost imagine him wagging an admonitory finger at him, like you would someone who was teasing you.

'Oh, I don't think so, *Mister* Beringer. I get the impression you don't want to tell me anything about her because you probably didn't take much notice of her until now – hence all the blurb about generic cases. I don't want generic cases. I want Roseanne Grey's case. Unless of course it's the reverse of that and you knew her rather too well ...'

'Most certainly not!' Beringer straightened his shoulders as if shrugging off Grant's aspersions. 'I went to her home only once, and then purely because she'd seemed a little unsettled at our last appointment and she was in need of new medication. Things had been somewhat erratic with her appointments just beforehand so I thought it might be a good idea to make sure all was still well with her. I take my duty of care very seriously, thank you.'

Grant cocked his head to one side. 'Oh? Erratic with her appointments?'

'I'd had chickenpox of all things, Detective Sergeant – courtesy of my receptionist's children. It's not a nice illness to have as an adult, I can tell you.'

'No,' Grant smothered his grin. *Shame it didn't pock-mark you*, he thought, looking at the smooth brow, the handsome regular features and the clear, sharp blue eyes, currently observing him with animosity. 'And was it? Well, I mean – since she died afterwards?'

'Apparently, yes.'

'Apparently?' This time he allowed himself a small sardonic smile at his victim's expense. 'I'm beginning to think you have no idea who this woman was, even if you did go to her house to take her happy pills. Apparently all right, generically routine – and then she jumps out of a window? Doesn't make sense, does it? Kind of case insurance companies make a fortune out of with negligence claims.'

Beringer pursed his lips. 'Apparently in that there were no indications to the contrary. I have very full records of her state of mind and her behaviour beforehand so there is no question of negligence or anything else, Detective Sergeant Grant.'

Grant rejoiced. This man was rattled. He was going to enjoy this. Rattled usually meant imprudent.

'So I can see her file, then?'

'I'm afraid not. That's confidential.'

'Or you're worried there might be something in it. Something odd – like she was going to jump?'

Beringer's smile twisted his face into a sneer, quickly hidden. 'The only odd thing in her file would be that she could see herself.'

'Ah. That she could see herself? But can't we all see ourselves? Isn't that normal?'

'Not without looking at ourselves, Detective Sergeant.'

'Oh, right. Not normal at all. So she was crazy then? But you gave her happy pills to sort that – despite erratic appointments with her? Without knowing her then current state of well-being – and then she jumped?'

'No, by no means. And no-one is crazy, Detective Sergeant. Sometimes we suffer chemical imbalances in the brain and that can cause conditions such as depression, psychosis, bipolar disorder and so on. Sometimes trauma to the brain can cause permanent damage or re-routing of synapses to bypass areas of trauma, and again this can cause what seems to be a mental disorder. But what is normal? Only an arbitrary line we've decided on that suits each of us. What's normal for one person is entirely abnormal for another and – '

'OK, I get it. No need for a brain drain class. She was suffering from some kind of chemical imbalance then?' Grant pulled the manila folder back towards him. 'And that was the reason for the happy pills – even though you hadn't seen her recently? And then she jumped ...'

'I had seen her recently – I'd seen her only that afternoon ... And I really shouldn't say anymore because of – .'

'Patient confidentiality,' Grant finished for him, testily. 'I know. So what did you find when you went to see her?'

'Nothing. Nothing at all. Like I said. She was – fine.' Beringer stopped abruptly. Grant waited for him to continue, but he didn't – not in that vein, anyway. 'Detective Sergeant, what makes you think she was attacked or pushed?'

Grant rubbed his hand across his lower face. The Super really would have him if he wasn't careful, but now his instincts were alerted his other instinct was to keep what had alerted it all to himself. This psych might be an arrogant ass, but he was also too clever and too smooth to be trusted. That might be because he reminded Grant of the bastard Stacey had slipped away with, of course. He'd been tall and charming, with a pretty face and no beard to speak of too. The reverse of Grant, in fact, and his permanent five o'clock shadow and deep gouge in his left cheek where some arsehole with a bottle had taken umbrage when Grant was still just a young copper pounding the beat. He'd have to do something though or Beringer would clam up completely. Opportunism got the better of professionalism.

'See for yourself,' he said pushing the manila folder back across the desk and flipping the cover open. The image of the broken and twisted body was uppermost. Beringer picked it up and studied it, face impassive. He put it down on the cleared area of desk top next to the folder and picked up the next photograph in the file. At first glance it was just a series of dirty brown splotches on a twisted sheet, edges blurring and mushrooming into each other. Beringer frowned.

'And what is this?'

'Her bedlinen. Blood and saliva-stained probably. Obviously been involved in some kind of tussle too from the way it was screwed up.' Grant mentally crossed his fingers. Showed he could do just as well as that arsehole playwright Stacey had run off with. Just use a bit of imagination …

'Not rape too?' Beringer's face twisted anxiously.

'Don't know – we haven't got the autopsy report back yet. It's not impossible though.' Grant improvised with what he could remember of the folder. 'The garden gate was left open, there was debris all over the grass and the kitchen looked like it had been trashed – things all over the place, stinking fish scattered all over the counter, pools of water all over the floor and the washing-up bowl thrown down in the middle of it. Almost like someone started washing the floor and then gave up and just trashed the place.'

'What happened to Sammy?'

'Sammy?'

'The cat. Absolutely doted on it. She'd never have deliberately abandoned it.'

Grant's ears pricked up – out of the mouths of babes and unnerved shrinks …

'Well, you know cats. Bestow a favour on you when they want to and piss off when they don't. No sign of it, anyway. I thought you'd only been there once.'

'I had, but she talked about it – .' Grant clearly looked disbelieving. 'No matter. But are you sure the signs are that she was attacked? Not just disorientated.'

'I didn't say she was attacked. I said she could have been.' Grant studied him, mind starting to sift and turn over hitherto apparently

irrelevant evidence. 'We'll have to wait and see what Forensics turn up –
and the autopsy samples, but disorientation? Any particular reason why?'

'No, no – not at all. Like I said …'

'She was fine?'

'Yes.' Beringer looked down at his hands.

'OK, well, thanks. I'll bear it in mind.' Grant surprised himself by
realising he actually meant it. Bloody psychs – they always got under
your skin. He wondered if the bloke Stacey had run off with had ever
studied psychology.

The WPC appeared at the door again, making urgent signals, followed
immediately by the ward sister before the signals could be translated into
any meaning. The ward sister pushed past the WPC and flung the door
wide with customary health official dominance. The taut cocoon of
Christmas tree, forensic images and testosterone was invaded by a mix of
antiseptic and boiled greens.

'Whether you'd finished or not, Detective Sergeant Grant, you have
now. I need my office back.' Sister waited imperiously by the door and
Beringer assisted by ushering him out. Grant joined the WPC in the
central ward area, by the nurse's station, straining to hear what the sister
was saying to Beringer above the bustle of the ward itself.

'Sir,' the WPC began.

'Shut up, I'm *listening*,' he said tersely. In the background the hum of
the acute admission section of A and E signified the hospital's engine was
still whirring – albeit inefficiently, alongside the buzz of alarms and the
squeak of unoiled trolley wheels.

'… RTA victim who's wanting discharge. Head-on but remarkably
unhurt and conscious now too. There's still the possibility of some brain
swelling, but unlikely. Thought I'd get you out of there though, since as it
looks like she could fall within your domain, Mr Beringer.'

'Thank you, Sister. You're my very own Florence Nightingale.'
Beringer turned on the sunshine for the Sister and she basked in it. 'Why
might she be in my domain though? She doesn't sound too seriously
affected.'

'Well she was probably just hysterical from shock but she was going
on about seeing angels when she was coming round – or at least someone
in white flying out of a window. Isn't that your speciality?' She winked at
him.

'Ah! Well, usually it's devils,' he winked back, 'but I'll take angels
any day if they're available. Interesting possibility though.'

*Someone in white flying out of a window?* Grant sidled alongside.

'Anything I should know?' he asked pointedly.

'Detective Sergeant, you're still here? No, nothing for you to worry about at all.' Beringer turned his back on Grant and addressed the ward sister again. 'What's the patient's name?'

'Well it certainly isn't what she called herself when she came round!'

'What was that?' Grant and Beringer both asked simultaneously. Grant positioned himself in between the ward sister and Beringer. She eyed him irritably. 'Look, I'm police,' he added. 'If she was an RTA, there'll be a file on her soon enough anyway. I'll merely be adding to it, that's all.'

'Well,' she looked uncertainly at Beringer. He shrugged. 'Alright. It sounded like Rowsan, but it was very garbled. She'd been intubated until just before we brought her round so her throat would have been very sore.'

'Interesting.' Beringer sounded dismissive but Grant noticed his small start to attention. 'Well, let's see how she does leading up to discharge.' He turned and eyed Grant with irritation. 'Now, is there anything else you need me for Sergeant Grant?'

'*Detective* Sergeant Grant,' Grant growled. 'And I'll let you know.'

Beringer nodded and loped away towards the corridor, his long-limbed body duplicating the lean, clean look of his face. Grant watched him sourly until he turned the corner. Why was it that all the handsome bastards were bastards? He rounded on the ward sister.

'So what *is* this patient's name, by the way?' Grant asked. 'I'll check the file's in order when I get back.'

She breathed down her nose at him like a fiery brood mare. 'Matthews,' she said. 'Erin Matthews,' and whisked away, skirts rustling officiously.

'Are we all done now, sir?' the WPC asked cautiously, sidling up alongside Grant. 'Only I'm off duty in five minutes.'

'What's your name again?' he asked, juggling names and cases in his head so he didn't forget.

'WPC Atkins, sir.'

'No, I mean your Christian name.'

'Josie, sir. I was allocated to you yesterday by Detective Superintendent Carter-Rowles – to clear up the old cases.'

'Yes, I do remember as far back as yesterday,' he said, mouth compressing into an acerbic half-smile.

She bit her lip. 'Shall I put this one down as sorted?'

'No. You just make sure it's on the books.' Still she hesitated. 'Go, go on!' he flapped his hands at her. 'Go back to the station and get it written up.'

'What as, Guv?'

'Suicide but may be suspicious. Leave it open. Make sure it's listed for inquest. Give us some time to check it out for a bit longer.'

'OK,' she looked uncertain.

'Go on then,' Grant prompted. She looked as if she was about to say more but they were split apart by the arrival of the drugs trolley. Grant flapped at her again and she left, small face waif-like under her cap, and heavy blue wool uniform bulking out what was more like a will-o-the-wisp than a force of the law. 'And tomorrow, you're out of uniform if you're on my team,' he called after her. 'I hate uniform.'

She tipped a salute at him and disappeared round the corner of the corridor, leaving Grant pondering what he'd done. Absent-mindedly he watched the drugs trolley meander past the central nurses' station. One of what would once have been an object of desire for him scrawled a name against a bed number on the white board behind it. Her badge said Nurse Oji and the whiteboard allocated an Erin Matthews to Bed 4 in Side Ward 2 of Ward 24. His mind wandered back to the conversation he'd had with the Super only the day before. Not really a conversation, a command – which he was already disobeying.

*'No more special cases, Grant, do you understand? I expect my detectives to detect, not play Sherlock Holmes. You're not above being bumped back to uniform, and you bloody well will be if you don't get your head down and your arse in gear. Be warned.'*

*'But the Riggs death was a murder, sir.'*

*'Yes, but not perpetrated by the one you so publicly accused of it – and who took the flak for that? Me, whilst you buggered around accusing all and sundry except the murderer himself. And now you want to take the credit for it?'*

*'Sorry, sir.'*

*'You will be if I have to clean up any more of your messes. This isn't one of your little research projects. This is now and this is current. Look at the facts, apply the facts, act on the facts and wrap it all up fast. I've even given you extra help to do that, God help me! I've given a list of the cases that need wrapping up to Carly, but here; you can practise from scratch on this one. But don't think of it as one of your precious cold*

*cases just because it's been hanging around for a few days already. It's only a suicide ...' He turned, 'Oh, and Grant, spruce yourself up. You look like something the cat's sicked up.'*

Only a suicide? He hated it when someone said 'only'. Maybe it was. But what about the forces that had driven a young woman with everything to live for to give up on life? What about the sheer bloody desperation that had made her decide it wasn't worth trying anymore? Just recently he'd started to understand how that felt himself and there was no 'only' about it. And now that, out of sheer bloody-mindedness, he'd made a case for *only a suicide* to be something else to the shrink, he'd started to convince himself too. The shrink had been uneasy too ...

# Chapter 6: Erin

'And you're sure you're Erin Matthews?'

'Yes,' Erin replied impatiently. That damn hallucination as she'd come round; would they never leave it alone? All she wanted to do was get away – away from the bustle of the hospital. To find some peace. To find herself again. That was her problem – there was no peace here day or night to just be still and silent. Even now, in the 'quiet room', the sounds and smells of the hospital invaded. Indelibly imprinted on her, it seemed – the alarms, the intern's off-key whistling, the distant sound of a phone ringing, the smell of wet dog from the cleaner's mops, spreading more dirt than they whisked away. They cocooned her here, an unwilling butterfly on the verge of freedom, not quite able to unfurl her wings and fly away until all the stages of transformation had been observed.

'I'm sorry but I have to go through the discharge routine with you before you can go.' The little staff nurse seemed genuinely sorry. She was one of the more thorough ones, and kind – when she wasn't rushed off her feet.

'It's all right. I understand. I just want to get home. I've had enough of hospitals to last me a lifetime.'

'Of course,' the little nurse sounded sympathetic. 'Just got to fill in these discharge papers and make sure your follow-up session is booked with Mr Beringer, and then you can go away and forget about us.'

'Mr Beringer?' She had to consciously suppress her agitation. 'Another neurologist? I thought I'd been given the all-clear?'

'No, Mr Beringer's a psychiatrist. We always refer patients who've had a spell in ITU and have suffered head trauma to him. Call it grounding yourself before getting back into real life again. It's an odd experience being in ITU. You're not fully conscious some of the time, yet your brain is still picking up messages and storing information which you remember later, but out of context. He helps you sift the real from the imaginary and put it in its correct place.'

'Well, it's very kind of you but I don't need to talk to a psychiatrist – I've already told all of you that several times. More than that, actually – I *won't* talk to a psychiatrist.' She could feel her mouth setting in the thin line it took on when she was being truculent. Jay had called it the thin line no-one dared cross when he was being amusing. Amusing hadn't happened often towards the end, though. Deliberately she closed her mind off to Jay and all the Jay-things she didn't want to think about. Not for the moment, anyway. This was one problem she hadn't anticipated.

'Erin,' the nurse reached across and patted her hand kindly. 'You may not want to talk to anyone, but you do *need* to talk to someone. Do you remember the accident?'

'Of course I do,' Erin bristled.

'Then, you'll remember that it's claimed you deliberately drove at the other car in the collision. If they push it, they could bring charges against you – attempted murder, even. If you talk to Mr Beringer, they can't do anything until he discharges you.'

'I didn't try to murder them,' Erin stared, open-mouthed, at the nurse. 'It was … I couldn't … I don't remember,' she said finally, 'but it wasn't attempted murder.' They sat in silence, surveying each other. 'I don't need to talk to anyone,' Erin added after a while.

'And the other person?'

'The other person in the crash? They survived didn't they?'

'Yes, they survived, but ...'

'And they were on their phone when they were driving. That's illegal.'

'Yes, true, but you also drove straight at them. They know they're on a sticky wicket themselves, so there might not be any charges from them against you, but the police may still investigate. But I didn't mean them. I meant the other person you kept talking about when you came round.'

'Who?' Her fingertips prickled. She pretended ignorance.

'Roseanne.'

'I'm not Roseanne,' Erin bristled at her.

'I didn't say you were,' the nurse looked surprised. 'But you were very confused.'

'Well, I'm not now,' Erin replied stonily. 'And I don't know why I was talking about anyone. It must have just been a weird dream. Lots of your patients must get weird dreams.'

'Yes, they do. It can be a by-product of being in and out of consciousness, but you came round telling us about this person in fine detail, so … Well, it's not just a by-product in this case – put it that way. Maybe something deep in your subconscious? Your neurological consultant's opinion is that you should have some sessions with Mr Beringer, just to sort it all out for yourself before you get on with living. Mr Beringer agrees.'

'Well of course he would,' Erin could hear the sarcasm in her voice. 'But I don't want to be psychoanalysed just to keep the boys in jobs. I decline and I accept full responsibility for whatever flows from that. Can I sign my discharge papers now and go, please?'

'I don't think you've understood properly, Erin. It's a condition of your medical discharge that you have at least one debrief session with Mr Beringer. You won't be discharged otherwise.'

'I won't be discharged? Why not?'

'It's an obligation that's placed on us as your health care provider. You must be physically and *mentally* fit to be discharged into your own care. I'm sorry. It's for your own good.'

'So if I don't agree to see a shrink, I'm classified as of unsound mind simply because I was in a road accident and a bit confused when I came round?' She could feel her cheeks flushing and her heart starting to pound with that familiar combination of anger and dismay that Jay had regularly produced in her towards the end. Still trapped – even now.

'Not unsound. Just possibly in need of care,' the little nurse fiddled awkwardly with the bottom right-hand corner edge of the discharge papers attached to the regulation royal blue clipboard they all seemed to carry around here. She looked up anxiously at Erin, eyes almond-shaped and imploring. 'And you need to eat better. I know the food here isn't good, but still.' Oji touched Erin's bone-thin arm. 'That's another reason to accept help,' she added cautiously. Anger was replaced by pity. Erin wondered how the little nurse – Oji it said on her badge – had drawn the short straw and had to deal with this particular discharge. 'He's a nice man, Erin,' Oji added, 'and apparently very good at what he does. He's certainly got a wonderful reputation, anyway. It will be fine, you'll see. He'll help you. Get you back on track.'

'So I have to be helped whether I want it or not?'

'To be discharged …'

Erin considered that. *OK, enough protestation then. Give in gracefully and get out of here.* Her heart stopped pounding and steadied to a rhythmical beat again. She could feel her face softening as the idea took root – the sapling of a plan … She found herself saying, 'and freedom is all, isn't it?' a thin-lipped smile twisting one corner of her mouth. 'Oh, it's OK, I'm not getting at you.' And she wasn't, she marvelled. She actually wasn't. It was as if someone had un-stoppered a hole in her feet and all the animosity and belligerence that had been building in her at the thought of being *ordered* to be counselled and *forced* to remember Jay and all his clever little manipulations had drained out through the hole. She didn't have to do either. That was all in the past. She was Erin and she merely had to agree and it would be fine, like Nurse Oji said. This man knew nothing about her, and nor did he need to, other than what she chose to tell him. 'When do I have to see him?'

'In about fifteen minutes?' Oji suggested, face breaking into a child-like beam of gratitude. 'Just to be introduced and get things underway. He has a free session then and you could go home straight afterwards if he thinks all is satisfactory with you.'

'All is satisfactory?' Erin repeated whimsically. Yes, all would be satisfactory. 'OK, I'll see him in fifteen minutes and all will be satisfactory,' she said quietly. The figure shifting in and out of view behind Oji nodded agreement. She'd always wondered what it would be like looking at her doppelganger – or something like that, Erin mused; and now she knew. She looked at the white business card Nurse Oji had given her. *Mr Michael Beringer, Consultant Psychiatrist,* it said. A doppelganger was definitely not something one would tell Mr Michael Beringer, Consultant Psychiatrist, about or things would certainly *not* be satisfactory … But she could deal with this. She was more than up to dealing with Mr Michael Beringer, Consultant Psychiatrist. She smiled to herself. Oh yes, and there might even be advantages to this. In fact, the more she thought about it, it couldn't be better. The possibilities were immense.

# Chapter 7: Grant

Grant shuffled the folders that were spread, chaotically, across his desk. The file that ended up on top would be the one he pursued today, whatever the Super said. That was how he felt – how he often felt these days since Stacey had gone – like it was too difficult to decide for himself. The room was a dingy beige – the same as his mood, and the file that ended up on top was the Grey case, beating to the winning post by miles the robbery and insurance fraud cases the Super had marked pointedly with post-it notes saying 'check and close down'.

The woman who'd jumped – or was she pushed?

He pushed it listlessly to one side. It was the one that would get his attention first but still he couldn't get any enthusiasm up for anything today – not since reading the solicitor's letter that had arrived that morning. Grant v Grant, it stated. The adversarial Grant (Stacey) wanted the defensive Grant (him) to put the marital home in such a state of repair that it could be sold and the proceeds divided as the first step towards mutual disentanglement. Mutual disentanglement? There was nothing mutual about it at all! Or maybe there was now. He spread his legs out under the desk and leaned back in his chair. The backrest bent back too far and the wheels got stuck on a ruck in one of the carpet tiles. How could you have a ruck in a bloody carpet tile? You could if they were regulation police issue, dun-brown, coffee-stained, muck-speckled and grime-laden. Or as shit as his marriage had turned out to be – now being disentangled – come to think of it. In fact, it was also precisely what his life felt like currently: a ruck in the carpet.

He puffed out his cheeks and manoeuvred the chair and its recalcitrant wheels onto a smoother area. To take his mind off Stacey and mutual disentanglement he picked up the folder for the Grey case. Probable suicide the Super had said. Probable? Or maybe not. The more he thought about it, there were the makings of something else. Suspicious, certainly – if only because of the shrink's refusal to help and his uneasiness. Murder, maybe – except there were no suspects. No one had been near or by for days – apart from the shrink. The woman had become a recluse since her accident. The only person who had any regular contact with her had been Mr baby-faced-charmer-Beringer. But he had a cast-iron alibi so, despite how much pleasure Grant would have got from being able to bring him in on suspicion, there was no cause for suspicion. That was a shame. He'd like to see that smarmy bastard squirm – him and all the other smarmy bastards who preyed on women. He corrected that; preyed on vulnerable women, lonely women, women whose husbands were too busy working … He pulled himself up short. Don't cross the line, he reminded himself. It was what old Joe Ruskin had taught him when he was still in nappies, the baby of the squad – not the one supposedly heading it, under threat of demotion or not. The case had been a suicide too, the deceased a sixteen-year-old, much like Ruskin's own daughter – missing for six months by then. The similarities had been uncanny. The two girls had even gone to the same school, been bullied, depressed and subsequently run away, except DS Ruskin's daughter had – happily – turned up a couple of months later, pregnant but alive, in a squat near Paddington. Ruskin had been beside himself with worry, though, throughout the case, yet no-one would have known – except Grant. He'd seen Ruskin studying the case notes late at night, hollow-eyed. He'd been the one Ruskin had confided in – despite his rank and inexperience.

'But never let it get personal,' he'd added afterwards. 'There will always be people and cases that will bug you. That you'll see likenesses to your own mess in. The trick is to remind yourself they are cases, not *your* case. Never let it get personal, no matter how you feel about it in here.' He'd thumped his chest. Yeah – but Ruskin had died from a massive coronary a year later – too much feeling inside and not letting it out. What was that if not personal?

And Grant had done it anyway – he'd let it get personal about one too many cases, with one too many speculative accusations; letting it out, instead of keeping it in until he was sure, and look what had happened. Angela Riggs had happened, and all the speculative accusations had come right back at him. She'd been down as a suicide too, initially. What was it with suicides? He'd been bloody lucky the Super had decided not to throw him to the wolves then, but the Super was right, and Joe Ruskin had been right. Keep it in check. Keep his pet projects, as the Super called them, outside of his job. Robert Pakington and companions were for the weekends, not weekdays. Keep it all in, check it and close it down as soon as you could.

Grant toyed with the folder, about to close it, precisely as instructed, but the photograph of the dead woman slipped askew from the other papers. Someone hadn't fastened it in place properly. He studied it. But actually, this still felt personal. Not because of a similarity, but because he felt sorry for the woman who'd survived a head-on collision which had then taken her into therapy, only to top herself barely a few months later. What kind of luck was that? The kind of luck he had at the moment! Only a suicide, the Super had said. Only. Did he know what it felt like to be *only*? He rifled through the folder and found a photograph of the woman as she'd been before she jumped. It was an old employee ID photo, about three years out of date; round-faced and smiling. Roseanne Grey, twenty-six, single, no close family, no boyfriend – or none that had come forward, and seemingly no friends too, or maybe they simply hadn't come forward either. That was odd in itself. An apparently happy woman with nobody in her life but a cat – according to her shrink. Maybe he should backtrack a while – past the accident and see what her life had been like before. Who was part of it then? He picked up the phone on the corner of his desk, shuffling the rest of the folders to one side so he could focus solely on the Grey case file. The rest of the no-hopers on the Super's list could wait – at least until the end of the week when he would be required to report in on them. Targets. They were the Super's problem for the time being, not his.

The phone buzzed into life and the team's PA came on the other end, nasal and bored.

'Yes?' It wasn't quite rude, but it certainly conveyed her irritation with being summoned when she was on what she would call her lunch break. Grant would have called her whole day a lunch break, fat Fanny Adams that she was.

'Carly, who's on roster this afternoon? I've got a job for them.'

He waited for the usual response, a heavy sigh and then Carly's flat nasal twang outlining Monday's roster. A fly buzzed against the window pane, drowsy with the heat of the office yet still keen to get outside into the frost that hadn't yet cleared from this morning. Maybe the Met boys were right for once and there would be snow this Christmas. It certainly looked grey and sullen enough outside, but that could also have been the grime on the windows.

'Josie, Steve and Archie, but Archie's in court on that fraud case so you can't give him anything extra to do. Then he's on leave. He's going

32

to Tenerife for Christmas – all right for some …'

'Thanks,' he cut her short, refraining from telling her what he gave his team to do was none of her fucking business.

'And Steve's wife is about to drop, so he's out getting extra nappies and stuff.'

'If she's about to drop, he should have already got bloody nappies!' Then he cursed himself for letting her aggravate him enough to draw a response.

'*Extra* nappies,' she corrected him. 'It's nearly Christmas and he didn't want to get caught short.' She sounded triumphant.

'He already has, with a kid on the way,' he spat back. Memories of Stacey and her 'it would have been different if we'd had children…' soured his mood even more. 'What about the WPC – what's her name? Josie, yeah, Josie, then?'

'Oh her? She's on a long lunch – present shopping. It *is* nearly Christmas. Goodwill to all men and all that.'

'So it's nearly Christmas? So fucking what? Forget it! I'll do it myself. When Steve gets back with his nappies and Josie with her festive abundance, tell them they're to have cleared all the Blues by the time *I* get back.' The Blues – all the nuisance reports that mounted up over the course of the month – the other special gift of the Super to him to make him get his finger out. Time-wasters in themselves, they all had to be followed up, finalised and filed whether they were an abusive phone call from Mickey Mouse or a confession from the next serial axe murderer. They were hated by all and sundry. A fitting reward for long lunches and nappy fetishes. The fly buzzed away from the window and made a pass in front of him, narrowly missing his nose. He swatted it away and knocked the dregs of his coffee mug into the waste bin. 'Shit!' he hissed under his breath.

'And when will that be?' Carly sounded cool and disapproving. 'I'm not here to cover for you, you know.'

'When I'm back!' he snapped back and slammed the phone down. *Don't let it get personal.* 'I'm not,' he announced aloud. 'I'm just doing what nobody else around here seems capable of doing.' The fly ricocheted off the window and did another run past him. This time it was personal and his swinging arm batted it across the room to bounce off the half-open filing cabinet. 'Bloody flies. Why are there bloody flies in here in the middle of winter? Don't they know they should be hibernating?'

He retrieved the now empty mug from the bin and set it back on the desk. Its contents settled into a blossoming sludge as they soaked into the rest of the paper debris in the bin. It reminded him of the dirty brown marks on the bedclothes in Roseanne Grey's bedroom. Forensics should be back by now. They'd had plenty of time. He picked up the phone again. This time the response was crisp and efficient before he could say a word himself.

'Forensics. Alice Richards speaking.'

Where fat Fanny Adams Carly was the image of slothfulness, Alice Richards was the essence of efficiency. Grant smiled. Ah, that was better; then the instinctive reaction was tempered with unfortunate association. He hadn't had that much to do with Alice Richards, but still she'd unwittingly already changed his life. She'd provided the second opinion forensic report on the Angela Riggs case at his behest, indicating it could be murder after all, not suicide, and they'd met a couple of times at work socials. The latter was the more relevant of the two facts, since he'd already decided the Riggs suicide wasn't, and launched himself onto self-destruct before the autopsy report had even arrived. For the last social, Stacey had deigned to join him – a retirement do, just before Stacey had retired him. Ironically, she and Alice had met at it and hit it off like long-lost lovers, whilst he'd kept his distance. Stacey had talked to Alice for longer and more animatedly than she'd talked to Grant in years. By the end of the afternoon, Alice Richards had probably known more about the woman Grant was married to than Grant had found out in years. A coffee meeting had followed, from which a shared love of literature had transpired, then the book club she'd gone along to with Alice as a result of that conversation, and then ... then, it was the old, old story from there. Stacey had progressed to a screenwriting class and then to the screenwriting class tutor – not that he could say that was Alice's fault. It was Stacey's – and maybe his. And at least Alice appreciated what Stacey called 'that ghoulish old stuff – his cold case research. That had been the one thing that had temporarily halted the quick-fire ping-ping conversation between Stacey and her. She was fascinated by the unsolved deaths of the past too.

'Re-opening history, I call it,' she'd explained enthusiastically. 'But where you want to solve the crime, I want to crack the forensics to solve the crime. We should put our heads together sometime.'

Yeah, now Stacey wasn't around to make faces at him and scatter his hard-won research, maybe they should. He pulled his face into the semblance of a grin even though Alice Richards couldn't see it. Stacey had told him people could hear your body language in your voice. Probably crap, but nevertheless …

'Hi Alice, Grant here.'

The hesitation lasted less than a second. 'Oh, hello, Darwin. How are you? And your research on the Pakington case?'

He laughed ruefully. 'No great shakes, but I'll keep trying. I'm concentrating on a different one now though – a more current one. I'll tell you about it when you have a moment, if you like?'

'Good for you. How can I help now?'

'I wondered if you had the results back for that stain on the bedclothes in the Roseanne Grey case?'

'Roseanne Grey? Is she a case?' There was a pause. 'I mean, I know *who* you mean, but I thought she was already classified as a suicide. We've really just sort of inherited and kept her because no-one's instructed otherwise yet. She was brought in weeks ago, but nobody's claimed the body yet. She really should go to the Coroner for a verdict before Christmas. I think they might have put another appeal out though, so they can push that on and arrange for a local authority burial. Let me see what I can find for you.' The other end of the phone went quiet. Grant, chewed on a fingernail while he waited. Alice Richard's voice came back strong and warm the other end of the phone. 'Interesting that. It's possibly not her blood on the bedclothes – the deceased's, I mean – but it's so close, it's only a question mark, not a major mystery. We assumed the blood stains were hers originally because when we did a direct comparison with the bloods in her medical records, they were the same, but oddly, the markers in the sample from the body are slightly different. They have less whereas the blood on the covers has more. Interesting, huh?'

'Extra markers? You mean she'd ingested something and it had gone into her bloodstream before she fell but worn off by the time she had?'

'No, markers are always present in our blood – they're our genetic blueprint, if you like. And you can usually match them precisely which is how we match identities from different specimens. But in this case, it's debatable. Although the genetic patterns look basically the same, the bedclothes samples seem – let's say – enhanced. Subtly different.'

'You sure?'

'Well, we've done two comparisons now. One just as part of routine confirmation of identity – she was pretty smashed up from the fall, and we haven't managed to track down any dental records yet. That was inconclusive – similar enough to be acceptable but not absolutely identical. But that can happen due to contamination and so on, of course, and there wasn't really any debate about who she was anyway. Then we found that she'd had the usual battery of tests done on her when she was admitted after an RTA a few months back, so we were able to do a direct comparison with them too. We did. In the body blood samples, the markers are merely like shadows – suggestions. In the ones from the RTA, they're quite clearly defined, and slightly distorted, but the blood stain on the bedclothes and those in the notes retained from the RTA are definitely from the same woman.'

'So what does that mean?'

'I don't know – contamination maybe, like I said – or gene therapy, possibly. Not drugs though. With drugs it would show up as a substance, but transient. These markers aren't transient – they're very switched on.'

'Gene therapy? Who could have been doing that to her?'

'I don't know – and I didn't say that was what it is. I just suggested it as a possibility that would explain a change in blood markers – or an enhancement of them.'

'The only therapy our girl was in was with a shrink called Beringer.'

'A psychologist?'

'Or psychiatrist – they're all the same, aren't they?'

'Not exactly.' He could hear the smile in her voice, laughing at him and his prejudices, but not in the way fat Fanny Adams did – or Stacey. With gentle indulgence. Maybe Stacey had been right then? You could see body language in sound. He liked the sound Alice Richards made, anyway. In fact, he liked Alice Richards; he liked her a lot from the smiley voice all the way down to the appreciation of the same thing that intrigued him, even if Stacey called it weird and morbid. 'A psychiatrist deals with mental health issues with a more medical or biological methodology in mind. A psychologist deals more with finding the source of a problem and dealing with it behaviourally. They both mind-manipulate. Which is your guy?'

'Which is more of an arsehole?'

Her laughter was rich and appreciative. 'Probably depends on the individual,' she replied. 'The blood stain on the bed covers wasn't enough to suggest any kind of attack though, really. Maybe more a small injury before the main trauma – a small cut perhaps? But we probably should retest in view of them not quite matching completely. There was also quite a high concentration of drugs in her system.'

'Drugs? She was high?' Grant felt disappointed. So she was just another suicide after all then.

'Prescription drugs, not heroin or anything like that. The kind of drugs prescribed for pain relief, mainly. Maybe a residual treatment routine left over from the RTA. We requested a list of prescribed drugs from the hospital but they're not on there. But if she was seeing a psychiatrist, they might have prescribed something new for her. It wasn't approaching an overdose, but the levels were high. There were traces of the same drug in some coffee dregs from one of the mugs in the kitchen. Presumably she ingested it that way. Do you know what treatment she was having?'

'No, he's claiming patient confidentiality.'

'Well, I suppose she has been designated a probable suicide so it's not mandatory … Oh, I see the status is actually suspicious death now. Your doing?'

'Well … if she was high when she jumped – even on prescription drugs – someone's got some responsibility for that, haven't they?'

'Maybe. It would depend what and how the medication was prescribed and monitored – if it needed to be.'

'Yeah, well, my bet is our good doc doesn't want anyone poking their nose in his files because he was dishing out happy pills without checking on what the lucky recipients did with them.'

'You'd have to prove that,' she reminded him gently. 'And it would still be suicide anyway. Pain relief medication isn't generally regarded as narcotic, even though it can have that effect. Why do you think her death is suspicious?'

'Dunno,' he said. And that was true – it was probably just his gut and Angela Riggs and that 'personal' feeling, but nevertheless … Plus now he'd got to do something with it since he'd told Josie to record the case status as under investigation. There was a pause, and he could hear the hesitation in Alice where he'd heard the smile before.

'How are things with Stacey, by the way?'

'They're not.'

'Ah.'

'But it's OK.' Even though it wasn't. Or was only maybe becoming OK.

'Well, if you need an ear to bend …' He imagined her shrugging, gently impartial, and wasn't sure what to say next. It was tempting and he liked Alice. He liked Alice a lot – but in that way? And so soon after Stacey? And they worked together … He was probably wasting an opportunity but hell, he was good at that.

'Can you send over the details of those blood tests?' he asked, awkwardly. 'I'd like to have a better look at it all – and the drug stuff.'

'Of course,' she replied. The hesitation had gone from her voice now, but the smile remained. 'And we'll do some repeats to double check.'

'Thanks,' he said, not sure whether he was really thanking her for the blood results or the invitation or for her understanding of his refusal of it. All of it, probably.

He put the phone down. So, the Roseanne Grey who'd jumped out of the window was the same but different from the Roseanne Grey who'd collided head-on with a car only months previously? And she was stuffed full of prescription drugs. More curious details to add to the unusually blank personal life she had, according to everyone they'd managed to talk to – namely Beringer, her GP and the one neighbour who lived close enough to report the open window and the body on the ground below. The cat, when they found it, wouldn't count, unfortunately. If animals could talk … He searched through the personal history details at the back of the folder and found Roseanne Grey's previous job and address history. Well, there was one explanation for the lack of friends – she'd moved to that isolated place a short while after being discharged after the RTA. Another odd thing, considering most people felt the need for localised support, not increased isolation, after a major trauma like that. She'd even changed her job – gone from being one of a team of up-and-coming interior designers at some swanky design consultancy to temping – admin jobs.

'Who were you, Roseanne Grey?' he asked aloud of the photograph of the smiling young woman, staring gently back at him from wide trusting eyes, red bandana jauntily encircling a mop of luxuriant brown curls and an apple-cheeked face in the old employee ID photo. A backyard kind of girl; one who'd wear dungarees and a check shirt at weekends, bite her nails as regularly as she bit on apples and not be noticed in the crowd. Almost a tomboy, but not quite. One of the WPCs had found the photo tucked into the corner of her mirror, as if to remind herself that was who she was looking at. The broken white doll puppet lying in a pool of her own blood in the photo he placed next to it made him shiver. 'And what caused you to abandon your life?'

# Chapter 8: Erin

She assessed him objectively even as he assessed her. So what do we have here, they could have been saying to each other. He was tall, commanding. Even sitting down, he gave that impression. Good-looking too. And he knew it. She disliked him instinctively, and yet... He looked too like her image of Jay to like him, but not at all like Jay when he spoke.

'It's been a tough few weeks for you.' He sounded sympathetic although his eyes were still evaluating. His eyes were blue – like Jay's – but kinder.

'I survived,' she shrugged. What was he noticing about her? The thin face – malnutrition or disgusting hospital food, emphasised by the lack of flesh on her where before she'd had rounded edges? The fingers twisting the strand of rough-cut brown hair between them, over and over until it formed a tiny knot to trap her in? *Stop that. He'll assume you're nervous.* The wide mouth and high cheekbones that Jay always said made her look excitingly Slavic, or waif-like, or a bitch – depending on the mood? She'd been at pains to hide them before, cover them in pasty flesh. But now – yes, now, she would be that bitch. The reverse of what she'd been. It went well with the role.

'Did you expect to?'

Ah, the first loaded question – and so quickly!

'I didn't expect anything either way. It just happened.'

'In that case, are you glad you survived?'

Now that was more difficult to answer without getting caught out. His eyes had narrowed too. Not just evaluating now; guarded.

'Why would I want to be dead?'

'I don't know,' he replied gently. 'That's for you to tell me about, perhaps? Shall we talk about that?' He waited for her reply. 'We have to talk about something,' he prompted. 'It's in the contract,' he added, winking.

Her hackles rose but she controlled the instinct to get up and walk out.

'There's nothing to tell. In fact, I keep telling everyone there's nothing to tell.'

She sounded exhausted, but she could hear the catch in her voice. She hoped he couldn't or he'd know she was anxious. He might be smooth and lazy, but she suspected he could be smart too.

'There is. About the accident. You drove straight at another car.' He paused again. 'It's a miracle that neither of you were badly hurt given it was head-on. I'm told there was no obvious fault with your car that might have affected steering or brakes and the other driver – *the victim* in police parlance – made a statement to the effect that you deliberately drove straight at him.'

Erin watched the dust patterns settle on the floor. Don't react. If you don't react, he can't tell anything from what you say or don't say. She could see her doppelganger in the dust patterns. Not actually *see*, just imagine-see; the woman who'd deliberately put her foot on the accelerator. The woman who'd seen the BMW as it approached – the same model and colour as Jay's would have been – who'd imagined what it would be like if she just drove straight at him. It would all be over – all sorted, anyway. And it had provided good cover for the waiting game, but that also meant she had no option but to continue to play out the scenario now. And then it had been too late and the car seemed to have taken on a will of its own. After that it had all happened too quickly to see anything but the shock on the other driver's face – that frozen Munch *Scream* face, still clutching a mobile phone to his ear like a telephone line to God as they impacted. Or maybe she'd blacked out before they impacted?

She touched her forehead before she could stop herself; the place that had found the soft cushion of the airbag, but somehow unfortunately also punctured it and found the hard rim of the steering wheel too. It had been broken glass, they'd speculated when they'd interviewed her. Broken glass from the windscreen. Unusual for a windscreen to crack like that but the forces of speed and velocity were still often a law unto themselves. Luckily, she'd added silently. They hadn't got it either. The other car had mounted hers and rolled over, ending in a ditch the other side of the road, the driver still screaming hysterically into his phone when the emergency services arrived. One phone call he wasn't ever going to forget. Lucky he wasn't being prosecuted, but that was why his statement hadn't been enough to bring charges against her, it seemed. Unless it was really deliberate? Who really was the dangerous driver? Her or him? The police hadn't wanted to test it out, it seemed – not without a psychiatrist's report to back them up, anyway. The irony almost made her hysterical with laughter.

'Is it still too raw?'

She played dumb. He was, after all. Make him spell out what he wanted to know and then she'd tailor what she said accordingly. 'What?'

He gestured to her hand, still touching her temples, skin still puckered and rough where they'd sewn her up. 'Is it still too raw?' he repeated.

'That's an odd word to use. Sore, maybe.'

'And raw. Any incident in our lives that results in trauma – physical or emotional leaves us raw. Hence, is it still too raw?'

His face was kind. Not like Jay's at all, now she came to think of it. It was just that they were both tall and handsome and had blue eyes. The temptation to tell him how she felt was almost too much to resist. But she wouldn't. That wasn't part of the contract. Only talking – or pretending to.

'It will heal,' she replied.

'Erin?' It had a touch of the plea-bargain to it, but she wasn't playing that game. 'I'm not here to judge but to help. You know that,' he continued when she remained silent. 'There have been many times in my life when things have been raw too. The wounds heal, but they leave scars. Some obvious, like the scar on your forehead. Some hidden, but just as painful. Just like the medical staff here sewed up your forehead and healed your physical injuries, I'm here to help heal the injuries that no-one else can see. Call me your personal band-aid, if you like.'

That made her laugh, and the laughter was a release. She hadn't laughed in such a long time and although this was hardly funny, it convulsed her nonetheless. He laughed with her, apparently enjoying the joke as much as she was, or maybe the fact that he'd made it.

'Laughter heals too,' he added, when she'd finally calmed down. He was right. There was a lightness inside her she hadn't known before – a lightness filled with laughter gas. And still he hadn't got it. She marvelled at his myopia. 'But I need to understand to be able to help.' She risked looking up and got caught in his gaze. It was intense, determined, perplexed. She got the point it was making.

'I guess you do,' she agreed. 'OK, it was a bad day. Something had happened recently that I hadn't anticipated and I was still caught up in trying to rationalise it. It wasn't intentional. I was just suddenly hurtling towards another car and the guy in it had his phone in the air and this face on him like …' She made the face at him. 'I knew then we were going to crash but he was heading straight for me too. Too busy with his phone to pay attention to the road perhaps? Anyway, it just happened. I didn't mean to hurt him at all.' And that at least was true – not him or her: Jay.

'What was it you were thinking about – the bad thing that had just happened?'

'Can I go yet?'

'No. Not yet. You've just told me you'd had a really bad day because something you hadn't anticipated had just happened and that led to the crash. I probably need to know what first – in case there might be another crash if I allow you to be discharged.'

'Allow me?' she narrowed her eyes at him.

'Allow you,' he agreed, still smiling kindly.

'You're saying I'm a danger to others as well as myself?'

'Aren't you?' he made a face expressing regret. 'I'm sorry. I didn't mean that to come out sounding so harsh.' He seemed to mean it. 'But you understand why.'

'I do, but it won't happen again.' They fixed eyes, like two rutting stags locking antlers.

'Why not?'

'Because I don't suppose I'll have the same kind of bad day again.'

'And why is that?'

She sighed. He was really pushing it, and he knew it, but he also had the upper hand for the moment. Allow her to be discharged. Or not. He was studying her intently. A thought struck her – one that she'd had before but in another context. He *was* studying her, but without understanding. OK, give him something to study whilst she adjusted who had the upper hand. There was no harm in telling him about Jay – a little bit. Give him something to hang his questions on and make it satisfactory all round. The past was the past now anyway. She summoned Jay to mind and he stepped up to the mark like he always did – tall, dominating, determined – invincible.

'The man who'd been in my life for what seemed like forever had just ended our relationship.' *Oh come on, so tame!* her doppelganger taunted. Elaborate. He'd got you to the registry office and then dumped you. He'd got you to sign over your home into joint names and then dumped you. He'd got you pregnant, told you to get rid of the baby and then dumped you. Or that time he just dumped you – for a younger model. Anything like that would do. OK, it was all tame by comparison, but it would keep

Mr Beringer, Consultant Psychiatrist, happy. She picked one of the themes at random: dumped for a younger model; that would do for starters – and it wasn't untrue either. She elaborated on it, of course, venomously, whilst she monitored Beringer's reaction.

'Wow! That is a bad day,' he agreed, eyeing her cautiously.

'So can I go now?'

'Well …' he hesitated. 'Is that all?' Christ he was greedy! Why fix his target on her when she had little of interest to focus on, really? Unless …

'For now.' They locked antlers again. This time he took the point.

'OK, I can understand why you might not want to talk about it just yet, but can we make a pact, and *then* you can go, temporarily?'

'A pact?' *Temporarily?* Now he was really pushing it too far.

'That together we'll make sure you don't have that kind of bad day again?'

'How can you make sure of something like that? You can't control what people do.'

'No, but you can control how they react to it. You could have the worst day in the history of time, but how you react to it will make it either the end of the world or the just the end of another day.'

'If you feel bad, you feel bad,' she shook her head.

'If you feel bad, you feel bad, but the bad feeling can be contained and managed.'

'You want to drug me.'

'God no! I don't believe in drugs unless someone needs drugs for something like a specific chemical imbalance.' *Liar!* 'I don't think you have that but I do think you might be severely depressed – and don't take that the wrong way. We all get depressed from time to time. Sometimes it's bad, sometimes it's not so bad. It's always not so bad if we have mechanisms in place to deal with it. I'd like to show you some of those mechanisms, that's all.' He looked sympathetic but she could see the scheming lurking in his eyes. 'I want to help you.' This wasn't going to be a one-stop chat. He was in it for the long haul – and yet he hadn't got it. So why?

'And?'

'That's all. And all we have to do is talk about what you're ready to talk about, when you're ready to talk about it and you'll pretty much work out how to help yourself by doing that. Sound OK?'

She cast a glance at her doppelganger. She was shaking her head but there was no choice for now. Her eyes flicked back to him. He was watching her carefully. His eyes twitched to where she'd been looking but were back on her in a fraction of a second – so quickly she might even have imagined it.

'Maybe,' she was cautious.

'And in the meantime, you could go home, and start to put this behind you.'

'OK,' she agreed. For the moment.

'Good,' he grinned at her and his eyes crinkled at the corners. Despite herself she liked that. His smile looked real even if it wasn't. He flipped her folder shut and stood up, holding his hand out to her, leaning forward so she could take it without standing – an old trick that; keep you at a lower level. It was dominance, and Jay had taught her all about dominance. 'Same time tomorrow, but in my consulting rooms? More relaxing. And we can talk for longer then – and about other things.' His smile deepened and his eyes flicked from her face down to her chest, then back to her face. The smile shrank and then widened encouragingly as he realised she'd caught him looking. Ah. The first inklings of understanding reached her. She nodded and took his hand. OK, she'd play whilst they assessed each other. The grip was firm and warm, holding onto her slim, numb icicles just long enough to thaw them at the fingertips. He let go and she was disappointed, but only for a moment. He was to be Jay's plaything, not hers.

'By the way, Erin – if I should call you that?' She nodded again. 'Thank you,' he paused. 'There is something that's puzzling me. When you first came round in the hospital, you kept talking about someone. A woman.' A trickle of electricity slid down her spine. So that was it? Not merely lust then – the medical staff had told him about that damn hallucination. Of course, he'd be curious. OK, at least now she knew. 'Is she the person your partner left you for?'

She almost laughed at the incongruity of likening Roseanne to the skinny, hard-faced bitch Jay had swanned off with in the little history she'd just recounted. And Beringer's gall at asking. She shook her head, mutely. Play along.

'That was Corinne,' she lied, turning her mouth down at the corners.

'And Roseanne?' he prompted gently. Damn! He wasn't going to leave it. The name ran round her head and tied itself in a knot in her chest.

'I don't know a Roseanne.'

That too was a lie, and his eyes told her he knew it. Of course, she knew Roseanne. Ro. She was here right now.

'Then …'

'I don't know a Roseanne,' she repeated. They locked eyes. Clearly, he wasn't going to let it go. OK, in that case he'd have to become acquainted with Jay, since he so wanted to play games.

# Chapter 9: Beringer

He'd asked her about Roseanne initially to dispose of the issue. A connection between the two was so unlikely, it was laughable – but because she'd apparently called out the name on coming round, he had to check – just in case. Yet, there was. His pulse quickened as she side-stepped his question. The nursing staff could have simply got it wrong – misunderstood the garbled cry for help, but for her reaction now. Her eyes flicked away from his face to a point just beyond him – not avoiding his, but seeking someone else's. Then they were down, studying the floor and she'd clammed shut. He'd touched one hell of a nerve there and now the same nerve was twitching wildly inside him. Had they known each other then? And what did Erin know? With difficulty he'd refrained from turning to see who she'd been connecting with. Some strange tingling sense told him that there'd be nothing to see anyway, and that he probably already knew – the same sense that told him now that Roseanne had probably been playing with him all the time he'd been naively humouring her.

Roseanne. He tried to call up an image of her, but it was blurred – hazy. A form with features rather than a person. He should be able to picture her face in detail and recall her exact words, but all he remembered of her, in truth, was the uneasiness he'd felt and used as an excuse to allocate her as little of his time and attention as principles allowed. There'd been no inkling – no suggestion that she'd do such a thing: jump. And yet she had. Or had he missed it? What had happened? What had happened in those last few hours that had ended with a lethal jump from a window? The policeman had implied she could have been pushed. Or that she'd not listened well enough to what he'd told her, just as he'd not listened well enough to her. His own explanation bothered him more. Damn Clarice and her game-playing. If he hadn't been trying to keep one step ahead of her and her progress to the courts to claim what she said was her contribution to his home, he might have paid more attention to Roseanne. No, in fairness. He should have paid more attention anyway. Something inside him twisted and pulled at his gut. He'd failed – again. But this time it could be bad. It wasn't as if there hadn't been red flags of all sorts, just that he'd not bothered to see what they were warning him of. That last prescription. How much had she taken of it? How had she taken it? To find out he'd have to ask the policeman – tell him. No. The possibilities that could ensue were not attractive, not attractive at all! In the meantime, it *could* still mean nothing, but why was this woman avoiding his eyes and evading his questions about Roseanne; dead Roseanne, whose name she'd cried out twice, and gabbled about in her sleep. Whether he wanted to or not, he had to take her case. There was no question, under the circumstances, but now he also wanted to know what she thought she'd just seen and why.

'Maybe it will come to you later,' he smiled; the caring professional's smile overlaying the cold professional beneath, observing with clinical abstraction. She was lying – maybe not about all of it but definitely about some of it, and she must be thinking he could certify her if she spoke out of turn. He needed her trust. She wouldn't speak freely without that. He cleared his throat and smiled warmly at her. She looked up and smiled back, a small, edgy smile; keen to escape.

'*Now* can I go home, then?'

'Of course. Once I've got you discharged.' She looked relieved. 'And we'll continue tomorrow, when you've had some respite from here.'

'OK.' She nodded, or rather, she inclined her head – an almost regal acknowledgement. This time her smile was more calculated, less jittery. It sent a jarring note through him – a warning. Potentially unstable? Be careful. He wanted to make a note of it in her folder, but maybe not – not yet anyway. See what she says tomorrow. Or in private. The distant sound of trolley wheels squeaking on recently mopped floors, redolent of wet dog smell mixed with hospital cuisine, signified lunchtime. 'And the food,' he added. The smile edged up a notch in warmth.

'Oh yes, definitely the food,' she laughed; an amused, breathy laugh, but still waiting. Waiting to go. And still he held back. She looked like she hadn't eaten all the time she'd been there. Not just the hollow eyes but the thin wrists and too-lean body covered carefully in an outsized diaphanous kaftan-style top. Anorexic? he wondered – or prone to it, maybe? The nursing staff thought so – although she hadn't been when she'd been admitted. The records had recorded her BMI as being on the high side, in fact. Nor did she have that feel to her. Test it, his mind prompted. It might open a door – a way in.

'Have you anything to eat at home? And transport?' Of course she hadn't. She wouldn't qualify for hospital transport, she'd crashed her car and she'd been in for weeks now, with no visitors. How the hell would she have a stocked fridge and a ride home?

'No, but I'll get a taxi and pop out again later, thanks.'

She looked as if she would fade away before then.

'That's not very good service,' he replied lightly. 'I'm sure we can do better than that. I've finished for the morning now and my next patient isn't till two. You know what? I'd like some respite from here too. Let me drop you home and we'll stop off at a supermarket for you to collect some basics on the way.'

'Oh, no, really …' she sounded edgy again. 'That's hardly my therapist's job – unless you're checking up on me?'

'I'm not checking up on you, Erin. I'm merely being a Good Samaritan. Take advantage of it – I may not offer again. I'm usually a mean so and so.'

She smiled – more relieved this time. She looked so different when she smiled like that – almost feminine in a boyish, angular way. Gamine. He hadn't noticed it before, but she was attractive when she smiled. Alluring. Interesting, definitely.

'Oh, well,' she hesitated. 'It would be nice to not have to go out again … and I could do with some milk and eggs and bread … I can't wait to eat something decent, actually.' She grimaced wryly and her features came to life. 'Yes,' she continued, as if suddenly making up her mind. Her demeanour changed completely. The intelligent but wary eyes gleamed with amusement and her mouth seemed fuller, redder. Not anorexic at all. Definitely not the right feel – but still unnaturally thin. For the way it made her look, maybe? Stylish; predatory in a passive way.

'Good,' he stood up. Too late to change his mind now. 'I'll go and sign off your discharge papers then and we'll go.' He strode away before she could protest. From the nurse's station he could just see her, still sitting as he'd left her – motionless – staring at the spot just beyond his chair. No, not entirely motionless. Her lips were moving, as if murmuring to herself. He strained to make out what she might be saying but he'd never been good at lip-reading. Talking to herself? This woman wasn't mentally ill in the perceived sense of it, though. She was shrewd. Planning. Something in that set another alarm bell ringing in him – that and the reference to Roseanne. He made another pact there and then with himself. He was going to find out what she was planning, and why.

'Erin Matthews?' the little dark nurse with the beautiful eyes prompted as he approached.

'Yes, to discharge to my care. She's agreed to follow-ups.'

'Oh good, I hoped she would. Tell her good luck from me.'

He scribbled his signature on the papers she gave him. He was going out on such a limb, taking this woman home – away from the proprietary protection of the hospital and his professional role. It hadn't ever ended well in the past, his conscience pricked him – and now you're doing it again? This was different, he reasoned. He hadn't understood the nature of the beast then – hadn't even recognised it, in fact. He had now, and this time there would be no jumping from a second-storey window.

He lounged against the nurse's station desk, pushing the piled folders on its top to the very edge. They smelt of regulation cardboard and medication. The whole place smelt of regulation cardboard and medication. He hadn't been lying about relishing escape. He'd always known that was the only reason she'd agreed to talk to him. Erin wasn't looking his way. She was still staring fixedly at the point about three feet beyond where he'd been sitting, as if mesmerised. His eyes narrowed. He stared at the same point, but could still see nothing. What was it she could see that was so intriguing, so all-consuming that her attention was so entirely focused on that one spot? His curiosity was distracted by a noise. *Busch-busch.* There was a fly somewhere in the ward or the rest room. He could hear it buzzing – *busch-busch* – as if it was colliding with objects and brushing its wings against them as it did so. Repulsed yet intensely aware of it, he could almost feel the vibration that the fly's wings created in his head – the buzzing. He shivered. He hated flies – all flying insects actually, except butterflies. Butterflies could just marginally claim a place in the world because they were beautiful and beauty had its merits, whereas flies ... but they were all God's creatures. His mother had made a point of reminding him of that, even as she'd clipped him round the ear and told him to swat it. Yes, we were all God's creatures – just some were uglier than others – in the body or the mind, and that, he supposed, was what made them more fascinating.

While the nurse filled in the rest of the forms, he took the opportunity to study his adversary more carefully as she stared into space. Gamine was a perfect description of her, actually. Soft dark hair, close-cropped but untidy, waif-like face, delicate features, dark brooding eyes, thin – almost malnourished figure, no breasts to speak of and small pointed feet with chipped nail varnish on the toes, tucked into high dressy heels. Hadn't anyone even got her some winter shoes to wear home? She'd be blue with cold by the time she got there – and no coat either. The dark-eyed nurse handed him a sheaf of papers.

'She should take them to her GP and … well you know the drill. And she needs to sort out her eating. Sorry if I'm speaking out of turn.'

'Thanks, Oji.' He winked at her. She blushed. Good to know he still had it, even if …

'Oh, and by the way, sister told us to watch out for that policeman who was here about one of your other patients a little while ago. He wanted to know who Miss Matthews was. She thought he might be a bit of a nuisance to her. If you're taking her case on, I thought you should probably know too.'

The policeman – the one who'd given him a hard time about Roseanne Grey?

'Thanks,' he frowned. What connection had the policeman made? He couldn't know anything, surely? He rejected the idea, taking the papers from Oji and tucking them into his own buff-brown folder before returning quietly to where Erin was sitting, walking heel to toe to stifle the little yelp that sole to floor contact usually made in the ward. He paused behind her before speaking, trying to focus exactly where she was focusing. There was nothing, just the annoying fly swooping past him with a dull drone – *busch*. He dodged it and the sole of his shoe lost contact with the floor. It screeched a complaint.

Erin jumped and seemed to reel herself back in at the sound.

'So, here we are,' he said aloud to cover his annoyance at the fly and losing the element of surprise. She stood up and a small, trickling shock started in his heart and ended in his toes. He hadn't expected her to be that tall – barely an inch or two shorter than he. Like Roseanne, but not tall and shambling. Tall and elegant. Maybe it was the heels. Seated, her thin frame gave the impression of slightness, when in fact she was an Amazon with no flesh on her bones. His view of her dipped and altered itself to a different angle. Not a waif, not anorexic, just naturally thin. And dangerously determined. He studied her. Something else too, some familiarity, but he couldn't quite pin it down. She smiled politely at him but it seemed more like she'd bestowed an honour on him than expressed her thanks. She picked up the red carrier bag from the hospital shop that had been by her feet whilst they talked. Under her other arm was a smart clutch bag which matched the toeless shoes. 'Have you got everything?

Your coat?'

She shook her head. 'I wasn't wearing one when I was brought in.'

'Did no one get you one?' She shook her head again. The kaftan thing was flimsy – almost see-through. If he tried, he could make out the outline of her underwear underneath. He corrected himself. No underwear, actually, just tight, high nipples touching the thin stuff of the blouse and budding at the contact. He felt himself harden inadvertently. Christ, this was wrong. He'd never reacted like this to a patient before – and maybe that told him he didn't know this beast after all, or the unexpected effect she was having on him. Model-girl skinny wasn't his type, but this woman with her reticence and air of enigma combined with an almost animal-sensual presence, she did things to his body through his mind. Be careful, he cautioned himself again. What she's hiding may not be worth your own madness – or your reputation. 'You'd better have my jacket then or you'll get pneumonia.' He pulled it off and had slipped it round her shoulders before she could protest. Her eyes met his full-on this time and he could see himself reflected back in them. The pupils were so wide they almost covered the iris. That was what made them so dark and unfathomable. He felt his own expanding to mirror them. The electricity between them could have burnt the whole building to a crisp in that moment.

'Thank you,' she murmured, still staring into his eyes. 'No one's been that kind to me in a long time.' His stomach turned molten and spilled down into his groin. He caught his breath until the moment passed. She pulled his jacket round her and her face looked less white, more substantial.

'We should always be kind to each other. It can be an unkind world and a long journey through it.'

'We begin and end in dust, and dust is what we have to be to start.'

He reeled backwards, sick to his stomach, all desire now wiped out. She raised an eyebrow, curious.

'I've heard that before … from …' he couldn't finish. Had she said it? Or was he just imagining it now?

'Really,' she sounded amused. 'But so true. And I like you being kind.' He could feel himself being pulled inexorably towards her. God, in a moment he might even kiss her. Her eyes were opaque, unreadable. 'Shall we go now?' and with that, the moment was dead – might never have happened. But it had. He took the red carrier bag from her and smiled courteously at her.

'Of course. This way.'

They walked almost the length of the corridor from Ward 16 to the main entrance in silence, feet slithering and squeaking on the wet-dog floor. They were approaching a capacious lunch trolley lumbering towards one of the wards, laminated menu swinging jauntily from the side when Erin spoke. One intern was labouring to push the trolley from the back whilst the other – the luckier of the pair – was opening doors and looking altruistic as their beleaguered comrade puffed through them, red-faced and exhausted. Erin paused, holding Beringer back with her.

'What an unfair division of labour,' she commented as the trolley and its operatives passed through the open door to ward seven. 'Someone should step in and do something about it. Share it out so one of them doesn't have all the hard work whilst the other is allowed to be lazy.'

'Maybe it's the way they've agreed it to be?'

'No one would agree something so unfair.'

'People agree to unfair things all the time. We make choices – maybe not always wise ones. Sometimes they're influenced by others or situations we're in.'

'Then they're not fair choices.'

'A choice doesn't have to be fair to be made. Have all your choices always been fair, or made of free will?' He watched her mouth turn down at the corners. 'It wasn't your choice for your partner to leave you,' he continued more gently. 'But it was your choice to drive the car that night – only subsequently to crash it.'

'That's not the same at all,' she turned on him angrily. 'And I thought this was just a lift home?'

'It is, but as a private individual giving you a lift home I'm as much at liberty to comment as you are.'

'Not on me personally.'

'But you were being personal about them. You were calling one of them lazy and, by implication, the other one stupid for agreeing to the arrangement. What if the one opening the doors has a heart condition?'

'Oh,' she looked surprised. 'Is that the case?'

'I don't know. I'm speculating. It's better to speculate than to judge. It's better to know than to speculate. That's why I asked you to tell me about how you came to be driving straight at the other driver. I'd rather know the truth than speculate about you. *That*,' he paused, 'is what I call fair.'

She was looking straight into his eyes again. This time he was ready for the reaction in his body. Her lips tilted at the corners, but her eyes remained deep inchoate pools of dark matter, with only his reflection peering back at him. He drowned in them, drifting deeper and deeper into their vacuum.

'Then I'd better come clean, I suppose,' she said.

He waited.

'About Jay,' she added eventually.

'Jay?' he asked, the sense of being drugged taking away all feeling from his body. He redoubled his concentration on her eyes, on himself in her eyes.

'The reason I drove headlong at the other driver. I thought for a moment it was Jay. Am I still allowed home?'

He pulled away sharply. 'Intentionally?'

'For a fraction of a second and then it was too late. But that wasn't just my fault. The other guy was on his phone. His reactions were too slow, my reactions were too slow. We crashed. Joint liability, isn't that?'

She looked troubled. He wondered if it was because this might mean he would take her back to the ward, or whether she was feeling a pang of conscience.

'Was that a fair choice?'

'No,' she said. 'But he was also on his phone when he shouldn't have been and that wasn't fair either. I was his nemesis. I'll bet he'll never phone and drive again. Clouds and silver linings?'

Suddenly they were both laughing hysterically in the middle of the corridor, the door to Ward 7 still swinging slowly shut behind the loaded trolley and the footsteps of the two interns squealing and screeching on the sticky floor.

'Will you tell me the rest?' he asked impetuously as their laughter slowly died down.

'Have I a choice?'

He shook his head. 'I don't think either of us have a choice in this. You are now officially my patient.'

'But you are bound to secrecy because of it?'

'For anything you tell me as my patient.'

'All right. Then I'll tell you the rest.'

And now there was no turning back. This choice was made; good or bad, and regardless of how she made him feel – God help him.

\*\*\*

He took her to the local supermarket. She bought milk and eggs and bread and cheese and olives and chocolate and wine.

'A healthy diet,' he commented, watching her load the trolley.

'No, it's not, but it's what I want to eat after all the crap in hospital. I want to eat my kind of crap now, then I'll go back to being healthy again.'

He shrugged, laughing. He was starting to get her measure now. Maybe. Determined, but intrinsically unsure. Confident, but essentially needy. Attractive, undoubtedly.

'Do you have time to share any of it with me before your next client?' she continued.

'Client? That makes me sound like I'm a broker or a pimp.'

'Aren't you? Of a sort? You sidle up to us and tell us you can help and before we know it we're paying you all our hard-earned cash just to be OK.'

'That's what you think?' He was shocked – not so much at what she said, but at the piercing accuracy of it. He was a parasite of a kind. He just preyed on sick minds, not sick morals.

'Not really. I'm a cynic – I see the cynic's view of things. You're much nicer than that, I'm sure.' She smiled at him with sudden and unexpected warmth – like her whole body had become irradiated from within. He couldn't help but be heated by it.

'I hope so,' he replied, unsure how to deal with her – or himself. This wasn't what he'd intended. No, he didn't know this particular kind of beast after all, or where it might lead him. She was watching him as carefully as he'd been watching her. She hadn't had that vacant stare since they'd left the hospital. She'd been engaged, lively, challenging. Was one of them an act, or were they both her? *Bipolar* threaded its way through his head. No, stop making snap judgements. She was complex – and she was lying. Stop being charmed by her, start analysing her. The problem was, the desire to discover her secrets had lessened as desire had grown. She grinned mischievously at him and the gamine was fully in play. She knew what she was doing.

'Come back and have lunch with me?' she pleaded.

He shook his head. 'If I have lunch with you I would be crossing boundaries. This is just being a Good Samaritan.' That one was too obvious. She must know he wouldn't get caught by that.

'The Good Samaritan took their charge home. Don't you dare?'

'I *am* taking you home.'

'You know what I mean.'

'I know what you mean.' He took the trolley from her and steered it towards the check- out. 'But I have a client at two – whether I'm a broker or a pimp.'

'And I'm the lazy one,' she teased.

'Or the one with heart trouble,' he replied.

'Oh, you're good, aren't you?'

'You told me yourself, Erin. You don't aim your car and yourself at someone who looks like your ex-partner without having some serious issues about them and yourself.'

'Then come home with me and I'll tell you what they are.'

He stopped in front of the check-out. The cashier was changing her till roll and the conveyor belt had the debris from the previous customer's broken flour bag spread across it. It looked like snow. Outside it had started to snow for real. Or sleet – that was probably closer to the mark. Freezing sleet.

'Why do you want to tell me about it now when you wouldn't in the hospital?'

She rubbed her fingers across her mouth. He could see the internal debate raging. Her eyes slipped beyond him and then back again. This time he couldn't stop himself. He turned round to look at the empty space himself.

'Ah! Do you see her too?' she asked when he turned back to her. Her face had the same pinched look as in the hospital.

'Do I see who?' he asked slowly.

'Roseanne.'

His gasp made a popping sound as he stared back at her.

# Chapter 10: Erin

She knew he would take the bait. She could see it in his eyes. Despite his agitation, he showed no inclination to leave after decanting the bag of shopping and the red hospital shop carrier bag from the boot of his car onto her doorstep. The snow wasn't lying. It sprinkled their shoulders and then melted, dead, into the wet pavement. Her toes looked small and shiny from the tiny droplets the melting flakes formed on them. Come in. Not a good idea, considering, he told her, although they both knew it made no difference. He needed to understand, and she needed to use that. It would happen anyway. Why not, she asked? Jay? he suggested. She laughed. Jay. She shook her head. There is no Jay now, she replied and waited on the doorstep, clutching his jacket round her. OK, he weakened, but he seemed important? He was. Once. That had been enough. It worked every time – tell a man he's made another man unimportant and he'll need to know more – even if there isn't any more. Male ego – the need for self-importance. Maybe not just male ego – any ego? Whatever. The ruse worked, so she told him a bit about Jay over bread and olives and wine – more wine than bread and olives, on her part anyway. The slow seduction, the even slower slide into confession, and then the sudden collapse into manipulation and control; it always all started and ended with control.

'Control?' he queried, wandering the room, taking in the swagged curtains, the proliferation of Impressionist and Fauvist prints covering the wall facing the long Regency window. He stopped by the reporduction harpsichord and touched its keyboard with tentative fingers, barely brushing a note from it. B flat, she thought. She left him to browse without answering him, searching the kitchen for plates, knives, the breadboard and two glasses. He was examining some of the pots from the last exhibition when she returned with them. Eclectic, he'd say. She scattered everything on the occasional table with the turned legs and glass top in the centre of the room.

'Yes, control,' she said, drawing his attention from the wall of prints. 'You must meet lots of control freaks in your line of work.' She sat down and smoothed an imaginary crease from the seat of the chaise longue she'd chosen, enjoying the soft burr of the velvet under her skin. He settled by the window, the place farthest away from her, a dark moth in a butterfly's habitat. He looked incongruous against the plush pink scatter cushions of the outsize tub chair that formed the centrepiece of the lounge. Incongruous, and yet complementary. The image appealed to her sense of the absurd – the juxtaposition of cool professional with luxuriating dilettante.

'I do, but usually their victims don't see they're being controlled. Clearly you did – and yet you let it continue?' The scepticism was clear in his voice. She shrugged. Let him think what he wanted to. He waited but she didn't reply. 'And now you're offended that I don't believe you?'

'You can believe what you want. I know what is true.'

'Then tell me, so I know too.'

'Control isn't about telling someone what to do and them doing it. It's about manipulating them. Making them *want* to do what you want them to do. Making it worse for them not to do it even though it's not what they want. Haven't you ever loved anyone so desperately that you can't bear to be without them – and yet when you're with them it's miserable too because you know they don't want you as much?'

'That sounds more like obsession than love,' he replied quietly. His eyes searched her face but she kept it closed. A mask. A façade in dedication to Roseanne. He hadn't asked about Roseanne again yet, but he would. Then she would have to decide how much she told him – how much she admitted.

'Isn't love a version of obsession?' she countered. He didn't reply to that, just chewed on another hunk of bread. She watched his teeth grinding rhythmically. Methodical. Was he methodical? He was certainly aloof. A cool customer. The cool would have to go.

'No,' he said eventually after he'd swallowed the cud. 'It's a version of need.'

'Seems like we both have odd ideas about love,' she laughed.

'Indeed. Interesting place this. Eclectic.'

There, she'd been right.

'Erin Matthews is an artist.' She flung her arms dramatically wide, encompassing the room and its diverse attractions. 'Sometimes she experiments on others, sometimes on herself. Do you ever experiment?'

He laughed, a shout of laughter, echoing around the room and making the glasses on the table ring.

'I'm not sure I could cope with the results. This you can swap for something else if you don't like it,' he swept his arm around the room. 'Yourself you're stuck with,' he paused. 'Usually ...'

'You can change everything if you know how,' she smiled.

He threw her a jagged look. 'So are you still in love with Jay?' It was completely unexpected and it threw her momentarily. She hadn't really thought about that.

'In love? Does it matter?'

'Not to me. But to you, maybe?' *Cold bastard!* He leaned forward and picked up an olive and popped it in his mouth. She watched its green skin disappear between his lips into the cavern beyond them. Green skin, pink skin. Long fingers too; probing.

'Maybe.' Her eyes followed the movement of his lips as the olive was sucked through them. Subconsciously she copied with her own and then realised what she was doing. Now he was watching her. Imagining, perhaps? Slowly she licked her lips. 'I'll have to find out,' she added, the saliva slick and glistening on her mouth. He stopped chewing and swallowed hard. His Adam's apple bobbed up and down like the olive.

'I think I ought to go.'

'It's only just gone one and you've hardly eaten anything.'

'Traffic.' He hesitated though. 'Will you be all right until tomorrow?'

'All right? Why?'

'What you said in the supermarket. About being able to see ...'

'Roseanne?' Her voice caressed the name. He was holding his breath – almost imperceptibly, but she could tell, could feel his tension. Her calculated risk back then had paid off.

'Yes, Roseanne.' They watched each other with suppressed excitement, each willing the other to make the next move. She could see he'd been holding back, desperate to ask, but terrified the asking would make her clam up again. Had he cared – this calculating man who seemed intent only on himself? He broke first, cutting through the silence as the name hung between them. 'You denied you knew Roseanne when I asked you in the hospital, but you called out her name, twice, when you were coming round. You don't do that if you don't know someone.'

She took a deep breath and picked up her wine glass. 'I know. I'm a Judas. I didn't want you to think I was crazy in there or I'd have never got out.'

He sat up straighter, straining. 'Why would I think you're crazy?'

'Because of her.'

'Knowing someone doesn't make you crazy,' he replied carefully.

'Doesn't it? It does in my book if they're dead.' She drained the glass and put it back on the table next to his full one. He stared at her. She imagined him computing what her statement might imply and coming up with confusion.

'Sometimes it's a matter of ...' he hesitated, clearly casting around for the right word, '...belief. What you think you see, and there are more things in this world still to be explained than we can even think of. Lots of people see things. Ghosts maybe? I don't know. It doesn't make them crazy. Some of them are the sanest people I know.'

Oh, he was being so careful! She contained her smile and replaced it with a wry grimace.

'So you know someone else who sees people – ghosts – too?'

'Only you.'

'Ah, so Roseanne is *my* ghost then?' She paused. Timing was all, they said. 'But not yours?'

He laughed but she could see he was nervous. Sweating nervous.

'Why do you say that?' He picked up the wine glass and cradled it before swigging it back in one go. He set it down next to hers and she filled both of them up again. She didn't answer. A light sheen on his forehead glistened in the wintery sunshine filtering through the window next to him. 'So what do you see? Of Roseanne, I mean.'

'Am I in therapy right now, or is this just between you and me?'

'This is just between you and me.'

He studied her, hand rubbing across his chin. She imagined the texture; rough, with an underlying suppleness to the skin. She could feel the bone beneath it. Tense. She enjoyed that. He was trying to be the concerned psychiatrist. Underneath he was trying to suppress the apprehensive man.

'Her.'

'And who was she to you?'

'Who is she,' she corrected.

His eyes narrowed. 'All right. Who is she? I know who she was, but you seem to regard her differently.'

'As my ghost.'

He sighed. 'There are no ghosts, Erin. Only what we believe we see. You say you can see her, but what do you really see?'

'Myself. And my name is Roseanne.'

'You see yourself as her?'

'No, I, as myself, see her. And I know there is something I can do, something very unusual.' She leaned forward, lips curving into a teasing half-smile.

'What?' He edged forward too. She picked up the refilled glasses and offered one to him. He shook his head. 'I'm driving – and working, I'm afraid. What is it that you can do – as Roseanne?'

She drained hers. 'I think I'll save that for when you have more time. Or when you come back later.'

He snorted with laughter. 'You're very sure of yourself. I might not be able to come back later ...'

'And I may have heart problems.'

'But?'

She laughed, letting the notes trickle over her empty glass and refill it. 'Come back later and find out.'

He kept to his word and left in time to get back to the hospital for his two o'clock appointment. She watched him go, a tiny smile of satisfaction playing around the corners of her lips. That had gone well – even better than she'd hoped for. It wasn't as originally planned – but then what in life was? He might not come back later of his own volition, but he was hooked nevertheless. He would return at some point, and then ...

# Chapter 11: Grant

Grant climbed out of his beat-up Renault. Time to change it soon. The gears were grinding and a new gearbox would probably be worth more than the whole heap put together. Maybe he should get a swanky little sports job like the bastard Stacey had gone off with drove. A pussy-puller, but then he was hardly likely to know what to do with it once he'd pulled it. He dismissed the idea and made a note to self to get an estimate from the garage on the corner for a new gearbox – reconditioned – instead. Roseanne Grey's place was beat-up too: a rambling monstrosity spreading over ground and two other floors, ending in a steeply pitched roof that could probably have been converted to a fourth floor if she'd been so-minded. She obviously hadn't been because the inside was ramshackle too. Jesus – far too many similarities to his own place already! He twisted the key from the evidence pack in the keyhole and pushed at the door. At the end of the corridor, the kitchen door was wide open. The mess in the kitchen had been cleaned up now, after having been photographed by forensics – just in case. It now looked pristine and empty although there was still a vague whiff of the stinking fish that had been scattered around the place. Grant wrinkled his nose. He disliked fish – almost as much as he disliked insects. Stacey had wanted a cat if they couldn't have kids. He'd been forced to give in on that but when she'd upped and gone, she'd left the bloody thing behind, and its cat food had been a constant reminder of both her and the smell of sea life going off. Luckily, even the cat had buggered off now, proof that he was crap at looking after anything. The same smell was here – loneliness and decay. He puffed out his lips and prepared for a long, demoralising session.

Ignoring the kitchen for now, he made his way into the lounge and the small dining area off it. The place might stretch over three floors but all the rooms felt off-kilter – ceilings too high but walls not far enough apart. She'd been quite a tall woman, Roseanne Grey, according to the autopsy report. Maybe she liked the height but not the space. The curtains had been drawn in the lounge, probably to keep out the eyes of the curious. Apart from the appeal for relatives to claim her body, she hadn't quite made the news but the unsolved mystery of 'the flying woman', as the local rag had dubbed her, had briefly sparked some interest from the ghoulish and the cranks who suggested she'd been possessed or was a witch. *For fuck's sake!* he'd have liked to have said to the greasy-haired lout from the *Aldwych Chronicle* who, it was recorded, had asked what the police were doing to keep local residents safe from the local coven. *What local coven?* Bloody idiot! With the curtains pulled back, the room improved. It wasn't quite as small as he'd thought in the gloom. Unusual design features though – a bit of a mix – as if she'd been testing things out to see what style fit best; a hotch-potch, he would have called it. Stacey would have had a clever word to replace that with and would have looked down her nose at him as she berated him for being so unimaginative with his vocabulary.

'Hotch-potch,' he said aloud in defiance. The word rolled around the room and echoed in the silence. He felt better.

A methodical review of the room produced nothing of great interest. Old furniture, some roughed up as if she'd started to rub them down, a swatch of material, some *Country Life* magazines, a newspaper under a bowl – typical detritus of someone's daily life – but no clue why she'd wanted to abandon said life. The sofa was a Chesterfield, hard-buttoned and upholstered in dun-brown leather. The table and its chairs were modern high-backed, with heavy floral seats and lean lines. The curtains, by contrast, were heavy tapestry-effect drapes, whereas the prints on the walls were a mix of abstract and old masters, and the bowl he'd noticed alongside the *Country Life* magazines was entirely modern, glazed in a swirl of orange, red and brown, standing on the highly polished glass coffee table that spread almost the whole length of the chesterfield. The bowl was balanced on top of a folded newspaper, a piece torn off one edge. A mess – or maybe the stage before she'd set about some prettying up. She could certainly do with some colour co-ordinating. Even he, with his general lack of appreciation of all things artistic or design-orientated was having trouble with the melee of brown, orange and red combined with the pink, turquoise and purple of the other soft furnishings. He moved back into the hall to give his eyes a rest and continued upstairs. The kitchen, and its smell, could wait until last. The less time he had of that odour lingering up his nose, the better. A giant mahogany mirror hung in the place of honour at the bottom of the stairs. What an atrocity!

Who could like that kind of thing? He compared it to the minimalistic light wood furniture Stacey had flooded their three-bed semi with and then expected him to match the house and its run-down forties décor to. By contrast, that was soulless. What was it with women? Why couldn't they ever be happy with the middle road: comfortable and classic, or adopt the masculine view: functional and efficient?

He made his way up the first flight of stairs, jumping as the stair third from the bottom creaked loudly. It was accompanied by a scuffling upstairs. Grant froze. He wasn't easily spooked, but this place did give him the creeps. He made his way gingerly up the rest of the flight to the first-floor landing. The doors to the rooms were all standing open. Empty rooms, with doorways like mouths waiting to swallow him up. He hovered at the top of the stairs, chiding himself for being a wimp – like Stacey would have. He peered round the door nearest the top of the stairs and into the room beyond. Its walls were painted a light, icy blue. It felt cool in there, blue water cool, and it was completely empty. Not even carpeted. His footsteps echoed as he crossed the room to the window and drew the curtains. Wintery sunlight streamed past him and when he turned, the room was transformed into a lake in the summertime. He gasped, with the impact of the sunlight on the blue of the walls. He'd always liked the effect of deep cerulean blue of water in bright sunshine, like those photos the holiday brochures always showed of the Greek islands, and the Brits all yearned for whilst having to make do with the watered down version of summer England offered most of the time. Hah! He laughed – cricket on a village green on a hazy day in June, or a slow row down a rural river as ducks and swans sailed past, apparently doing nothing to propel themselves. He found himself imagining ducks paddling the expanse of the walls and a swan coming in to land in a flurry of feathers and spume. He used to feed the ducks on a river like this when he was a kid, crumbling the dry bread his mother kept from the previous week and scattering it by his feet for the squawking, honking horde. The swans always waited, queenly, out on the water. They didn't mix with the bird-life rabble. They knew he'd keep the last pieces especially for them. They knew everyone kept the best morsels of their bread for them, didn't they? Everyone keeps the best for the most beautiful, it was just that the beautiful didn't always confine themselves to the morsels. Stacey hadn't. She'd left this morsel for whoever wanted him. Suddenly he was so morose he wanted to cry. Tears pricked his eyes and he couldn't get out of the sun-filled blue room fast enough. A last glance out the window set the geography of the place in his head. This side faced out over the back garden, where the gate at the end was flapping open. He made a mental note to ball out whoever'd been on duty outside for not closing it.

By contrast the room next door was pink, in full bloom, like an unfurled rose. The curtains were again pulled shut, and the pink was a dusky rose madder, pooling to sulky purple in the corners. Moody, musky – he could smell musk, or some heavy perfume in here. Incense; he wondered if she'd burned incense in here? There were no incense holders or any of that funny stuff paraphernalia, but the room had the feel of a place of worship. The type of feel a girl he thought he'd long forgotten from his twenties had created in her bedroom – although that had been dedicated to freeing the demon of free love, not freeing the spiritual. He snorted, trying to clear the cloying aroma from his nostrils. The floorboards had been burnished to an intense rosewood-brown in this room, whereas the blue room's had been the colour of bleached bone. The effect was of a carpet of soft earth, deep and yielding, but they still beat out his footsteps like a warning as he crossed the room and threw open the curtains to peer down over the front of the house. The woman, Roseanne's, room must be directly above here. The chalk outline of her body and the dirty brown stain of her blood could still be seen on the paving below. Despite the atmosphere of stuffy warmth in the room, he shivered. She must have chosen her bedroom window to jump from so she landed on the hardest surface. The back garden was covered in soft, overgrown grass. Funny thing that the rooms were bare but they all had curtains at the windows, and all drawn. Thin material so the light leaked through, but the whole place seemed to wallow in half-light, like she'd been afraid of seeing too clearly.

He paused as the noise he'd heard earlier returned. A soft scuffle, with an after-sound. Despite the heady ardour of the pink room, his spine tingled cold. He knew it wasn't just the noise. It was the thought of entering the woman's room. He'd never felt this way about examining a scene of crime before – and this wasn't even confirmed as a scene of crime. He'd seen some sights in his time: awash with blood, bodies left in ways one wouldn't have thought it conceivable for anyone to treat a fellow human, yet this place had something more about it, like she was still here, watching him blundering about. Willing him to do something – and it was that something that made him shiver.

The noise came again, this time louder, and overhead. Shit! He was going to have to investigate now, whether he liked it or not. He tiptoed across to the door of the pink room, slating himself for being a coward whilst telling himself there was no point in announcing his arrival either. Back on the landing, he breathed out, relieved to be standing on carpet that masked the fact of his presence. The noise was persistent now. A rustling scuffle followed by a *busch-busch*. Grant squared his shoulders and sucked in his stomach. Holding his breath he edged up the stairs, keeping his back flat to the wall. He felt in his pocket for a weapon, but all he could find was the hanky that always lurked in there in case, a biro with the cap off and his mobile phone. Stupid bastard, why hadn't he thought about bringing something with him? But then why would he? He was only examining the scene.

He paused at the top of the stairs, willing his heart to stop pounding. That merely made it pound more, in disharmony with the rattle-scuffle-busch-busch. The door to Roseanne Grey's room was closed, the door handle hanging slackly from it at an odd angle. He pulled the hanky from his pocket and crept along the landing until he was standing directly in front of the door. The noise was definitely coming from the other side, irregular, but with a repeating rhythm of a sort. Wrapping the hanky round his hand he took hold of the wilting door handle. It fell apart as soon as he touched it. He stared at it, mouth open in a soundless half yelp. The globe of the knob fitted perfectly in the cup of his palm but the other end of it had been sheared off with immense force and ended in a jagged twist of torn brass. Jesus! What was he going to find on the other side of the door? Cold rivulets of fear ran the length of his body and the stomach he'd been holding in gave way in a gut-wrenching swell of terror. He didn't even care if he'd shit himself. All he cared about was surviving what was on the other side of that door because it was coming closer and the door was opening, swinging inwards. His skin crawled and his calves went into cramp and locked him in place, rigid. The scuffling sound reached the door and the door swung wide to let it through.

'Fucking hell!' he croaked, gasping as a small black cat shot through the space the opening door had created, and began winding its way round his trembling legs. He doubled up, clasping his aching gut and laughing wildly. It was her bloody cat! He hadn't even thought of that. Her cat — the one they said had gone missing. He reached for it but it slipped through his fingers, unwinding itself from his legs and going to sit in the doorway, tail curled neatly round its paws. It watched him with glass-green eyes. The rattle-busch-busch sound was still coming from inside the room, but the cat wasn't bothered. Cats had sixth sense, didn't they? If the cat wasn't bothered then he shouldn't be. Still holding the mangled doorknob he pushed the door wide and stepped inside the room, the cat following in a tangle around his legs. He tried not to kick it, but not doing so was probably more because of the cat's nimble undulations than his nifty footwork. The cat settled about three feet into the room, sitting bolt upright with its tail curled over its paws again. The window was open, and the curtain billowing out in a grey-green cloud.

'What the – ' Grant lost all his fears in exasperation. 'Who the hell left that open? Someone's head really is going to roll!'

He strode across the room and yanked the curtains apart, but the window wasn't open. It was tightly closed, an intricately woven silk wind charm swaying and lightly tapping at the window from the force of Grant's intervention. Along the top of the window, just below where the curtain met the pole, a fly crawled sleepily along the glass. Grant waved it away and it flew at the curtains and rebounded back against the window. *Busch-busch.* So that was all it had been – a buzzing fly, the cat trying to catch it maybe, and disturbing the wind charm in the process.

'Bloody hell! If only everything in life was that simple,' Grant patted the curtains flat. And yet where had the cat come from? And the draught to set the curtains billowing? There must be a cat flap in the kitchen door. He made a mental note to check when he gave the kitchen the once over on his way out. Other than that, the scene was exactly as set in Steve's report. The covers on the bed and their small bloom of dried blood, a few scattered clothes, a book by the side of the bed – a thriller – a glass of water, half drunk, and nothing else. The vanity unit boasted a brush with long brown hairs caught in it, a cake powder and a dark red lipstick. No jewellery, no pretty perfume bottles like Stacey had littered hers with, or pots of face cream claiming to make you young again. Not one for frills and fancies, Roseanne Grey. A plain girl and an ordinary bedroom. No sense of anything in here. Empty, unremarkable – apart from that broken door handle.

He left the window and went back to the door. It was made of panelled wood, painted white that had now yellowed with age. Nothing else on it was damaged or even marked, apart from a few paint chips that looked as if they'd been there forever. He touched the door knob on the side of the door facing into the room. It was still intact here, albeit twisted at an angle, and crushed as if someone had taken giant pliers to it and squeezed as they twisted. It appeared to be held in place purely by the spindle that joined the knob on one side to that on the other, but as soon as he touched it, the whole thing tumbled to the floor. The spindle was twisted and weakened too. Grant frowned. He was sure this hadn't been in the report. A photograph of a damaged door handle, yes, but routine as part of the documentation of any damage noticed in the house. This, though, was a sure-fire sign of forced entry, although he'd never seen any forced entry like this before – from the inside out. It shed a whole new light on a suspicious death with no other suspicion. He bundled both knobs and the spindle into his handkerchief and carried them carefully back downstairs in his two hands. The cat followed him, overtaking and running past him as they reached the first-floor landing. It darted down the remaining flight, leaping straight over the creaking stair. Grant wasn't so light-footed. He trod on the step fair and square and the noise cracked through the empty house like an ancient tree falling. The cat appeared at the lounge door at the sound and mewed plaintively.

'Sorry, cat,' Grant said, pulling a face. 'I don't know the place like you do,' he added under his breath, 'nor would I want to.' He reached the bottom of the stairs and the ugly mahogany mirror beckoned. He stopped, surveying himself grudgingly in it. The silvering was going in places and it greyed him out, too, as if parts of him were fading away. The two doorknobs and twisted spindle wrapped in his hanky were digging into his palms. A tiny speck of blood from the scratch they'd made on his hand had mushroomed into a blob in one corner of the hanky. He frowned. Now he needed something else to put them in or he might contaminate the evidence. An idea hovered at the back of his mind but he couldn't place it. The cat miaowed at him again and disappeared back into the lounge. And he needed to do something about the bloody cat. The fly from upstairs brushed his ear, *busch-busch*, making him shiver with disgust. He'd have to swat the bastard or it would be laying its eggs everywhere and the place would be swarming with the things next time he or Forensics visited, because they were going to have to take another look at that door, for certain. He followed the cat into the lounge and the idea unfolded into the newspaper that the bowl had been left on top of on the coffee table. 'Ah, two birds with one stone,' he said to the cat as it watched him indifferently from the corner of the room. He laid the hanky and its twisted contents on the coffee table, containing them with one hand to stop the knobs rolling away, and pulled at the newspaper. The bowl that it was standing on was heavier than he'd anticipated. He pulled again, trying to slide it out from under the bowl without letting go of the door knobs or pushing the bowl to the edge of the coffee table. His arms started to prickle with sweat. It was no good he would have to ... he lost the thought as the fly buzzed him again and the cat took a leap at it – or him. Whether it was the cat or the fly that touched him first, his over-tensed nerves vibrated like elastic strummed too hard and snapping against skin. As the cat landed on the table top, Grant let go of the doorknobs in favour of the newspaper and swung it around overhead with all the additional force its sudden relinquishment by the bowl lent to it. In turn the bowl rolled on its base, like a slowing spinning coin and toppled off the edge of the table. He dropped the newspaper to catch the bowl and the newspaper landed in a soft thwack.

It shouldn't have broken – after all, it was landing on carpet, albeit thin and worn. But it did – into neatly sectioned pieces. Grant counted the seconds till it landed in swear-beats. Two. One to think, shit! The other to think about what the Chief would have to say about him damaging evidence. And that amounted to 'shit!' as well, really. He let out a long, exhausted sigh that emptied his body of breath. The door knobs followed the broken bowl, their jagged edges pointing towards each other like magnets to their opposite poles. The twisted spindle joined them, coming to rest at right angles to the orbs of the knobs, one smooth and round, one crushed and wounded, pointing to the jagged pieces of the broken bowl. He stared in abject horror. The fly settled on the edge of the coffee table and crawled along it until it reached the section the bowl had rolled off. It settled there, rubbing its front legs together as if in glee. This time he ignored it. The paper had fallen as it had been folded, but under-side up instead of the way it had been left on the coffee table. Staring back at him was the name of someone he knew that he knew – but not how, or who.

The article containing the name had been torn through the middle in the fall, but the name in the headline appeared intact, as did most of the photograph. They announced a new exhibition by some Erin, with a bold flourish to the sign-off of the name, as if everyone would know who 'Erin' was. The pointed hunk of broken bowl next to it boldly asserted it to be the work of 'Erin' too. It was the type of thing Stacey would have gone for, but not him. He brushed the folded paper edge straight. The paper was just over three months old. Grant got down on his hands and knees and pieced the two torn sections together to read what he could of the article. His hands stuck to the grime of the carpet and his knees tingled at the imprint of the miniscule shards of pottery sticking into them from within the carpet's thin pile, but he was oblivious to both as he tried to place the name. It was unusual. Not many Erins around but he'd come across one only a short while ago. Erin, Erin – damn! His brain didn't seem to work anymore. And now he'd have to kow-tow to Forensics for damaging a crime scene because surely the door handle must now make it one. Or could he blame the cat? He brushed the slivers of broken bowl from his hands and piled the rest of it onto the outspread newspaper, together with the door knobs and spindle, wrapped once more in the handkerchief. He flipped the top edge of the newspaper over like a parcel and on the corner of the outlying back page was a series of numbers ending in ones. He counted the digits up. It was a phone number. It had to be.

The fly was still perched on the edge of the coffee table and the cat had curled up on the settee, apparently no longer interested in him or the fly.

'If it wasn't for the fact that I'm using the paper for the fuck-up you helped create, I'd flatten you with it,' Grant told the fly. 'Although, I wonder who this phone number belongs to?' He pulled out his mobile and tapped in his PIN. 'Here goes fuck all.' He dialled the number. He could hear it buzzing the other end. *Busch-busch.* Bloody flies. *Busch-busch.*

'Hello?' it was a woman's voice, cultured, confident, controlled.

'Erin?' Grant asked, on impulse.

'Yes. Who's calling please?'

Grant's head spun and he held the phone away from his mouth so he didn't sound like a heavy breather. For fuck's sake – what had possessed him to say that name – and yet … He was going to ring off then he decided to try something even riskier. After all, what else could go wrong today?

'Roseanne gave me your number.'

'Roseanne?' She sounded brittle, afraid. There was a fraction of a second's hesitation, and then the voice came back clearly and forcefully. 'I don't know a Roseanne. You must have a wrong number.' The connection cut. Grant flicked his phone off. Lucky he'd set 'privacy' on his phone. So this was Erin's number, whoever she was. Erin the pot-maker, maybe? Erin who didn't know Roseanne – yet had been rattled. Interesting. He'd put Josie on tracing the number. It would be even more interesting to talk to Erin the pot-maker who'd made a pot that Roseanne the dead woman had bought or acquired, as well as Erin's mobile phone number. Who gave their mobile phone number to someone they didn't know without good reason? He pocketed his mobile and decided to leave the kitchen for another day. In the meantime, he'd simply let the cat through the cat flap, since that must be how it came in, and get this stuff back to Forensics. He stuffed the newspaper parcel under his arm and shooed the cat out the kitchen. The last thing he needed was to have to rehome a cat having just conveniently lost his own. He was going to spend long enough trying to explain away this little parcel of crap. The cat shot ahead of him, glowering over its shoulder, and sat by the back door.

'Shit!' Grant announced to the aroma of rotting fish and stale air. 'Where's the cat flap?' The cat looked at him as if he was sublimely stupid. 'So how did you get in?' The cat wound itself round his legs and purred. 'Bugger!' There was no way he was taking another one on! On the other hand, he couldn't just leave it. RSPCA, Cats Protection League and a host of time-wasting paperwork floated before him – all for a cat. On an impulse he pulled his phone out of his pocket again and speed-dialled.

'Alice Richards, Forensics.' The voice was as warm and efficient as always. Idly he wondered if she was warm and efficient with everything, not just work.

'Alice, its Grant – Darwin Grant. Look, I don't know what Mr Richards would make of this, but …'

'There is no Mr Richards,' she cut across him coolly. 'He died three years ago.'

'Sorry, that was clumsy of me. Stacey didn't say.'

'Why would she? Go on.' The voice was less efficient now.

'This is probably not the thing to ask you either, but I'm not sure who else to ask. Are you an animal lover? I sort of thought you might be.'

He listened to her surprised laughter at the other end. 'Really? That's interesting. Yes, I am actually – why?'

'Cats, by any chance?'

'Cats, dogs, horses – I even had two rats and a rabbit as a kid.' The smile was in her voice again.

'Oh.' He hadn't quite expected the childhood menagerie. He found himself adding another layer to this warm-voiced woman. 'Do you fancy being owned by a cat?'

Her laughter was spontaneous and appreciative. 'I'd rather not be owned by anything but as far as cats go, that's probably a fair statement. You've got a cat to rehome? Why?'

The stink of rotting fish seemed to have abated since he'd been on the phone to Alice. Maybe he was getting used to it. He leaned against the worktop and scanned the rest of the room as he talked.

'It's a long story but I need to do something with it. The RSPCA or something ultimately. But for the moment I've also got some evidence I need to get in fast – to you actually – with some explaining. I haven't got time to tour the local shelters with a cat so ...'

Maybe the bin in the corner hadn't been emptied? That might be why it still stank in here. He moved across the room and stepped on the pedal to ping the lid up. He was right. A layer of slimy fish skin in the bottom – bagged at least – and the halves of some gelatin-type capsules, the sort that usually contained proprietary medicines like paracetamol. Stacey had always done that – de-skinned them because she complained they were too big to swallow whole as they were.

'Oh,' there was a moment's silence then. 'OK. Drop the evidence into the lab and then bring the cat round. We all need a bit of TLC sometime in our lives. Maybe this is my time to provide it for a cat.'

He let the lid ping back into place. The smell abated somewhat. Other people's shit – that was what he was always dealing with; and his own now. Maybe it was time for a change. Maybe the Super's threats were a blessing in disguise. Not uniform, but something else. Something that wasn't always dealing with other people's shit.

'You're a life-saver, Alice. Remind me I owe you one. See you shortly.'

'Hold on, don't you want to know where to bring it?'

'Oh, shit – yes!'

She reeled off an address and added, 'I'll text you it too. See you later. I'll be home about six, and yes, you will owe me one. You bring the wine – that'll do for starters. And you can tell me all about your more current project than Robert Pakington.'

For starters. He was left listening to the rush of air the other end as the implication of what he'd just initiated slowly dawned on him. The rush of blood into parts of his anatomy that hadn't had use in a while followed rapidly thereafter.

# Chapter 12: Erin

She arrived five minutes early so she could establish herself. His waiting room was bland, formal – the usual kind of waiting room. His receptionist was polite but cool – the usual sort of receptionist. Erin sat quietly in the seat that gave the best view of both the door to the waiting room and the door to the consulting room, assessing. The receptionist was in her direct line of sight too, trying not to look at her as she pretended to be busy typing or something on the PC. It was obvious she was pretending because her eyes didn't follow the line of type across the screen. They flicked up from time to time, snatching another section of Erin and mentally storing it. It was obvious what she was doing: she was trying to place her. Reverse psychology worked best in this kind of situation. Be obvious, don't try to hide. Erin turned whilst the receptionist was pretending to type and deliberately positioned herself so that she was looking directly at the woman, a half-smile tacked into position on her lips – an, 'I know your sort' smile. The woman repeated her surreptitious glance routine and found herself looking straight into the cool, hard stare of Beringer's newest patient. A little 'oh' of embarrassment slipped through her parted lips, and she looked hurriedly back down at her keyboard. Erin's smile deepened. The receptionist wouldn't be looking at her too often from now on.

Behind the receptionist, the consulting room door opened and a nervous-looking fair-haired woman in early middle-age rushed out. Beringer appeared in the doorway behind her, firm-bodied and sleek in dark suit and pink shirt, straightening his crimson tie. Just the right mix of the professional and the charmer – clearly his patient thought so too.

'Same time next week?' he asked. He smiled warmly at the patient and she blushed deeply.

'Of course,' she thrust her appointment card at the receptionist, eyes still fixed on Beringer. 'And thank you so much again, Mr Beringer,' she simpered.

Erin watched with amusement. Both the receptionist and the departing patient were red-faced, but for different reasons.

'Miss Matthews is here – early,' the receptionist informed him, eyes sliding past the little nondescript blonde woman to Erin, and twisting away quickly without making eye contact. One in, one out.

'Ah, Miss Matthews,' Beringer smiled expansively, holding his hand out to her. She rose slowly, allowing her long limbs to unfold and her body to extend sensuously to its full height. She was wearing her highest heels today. The effect was gratifying. His eyes swept her from face to foot, resting on her thighs and breasts long enough for her to know he'd done so. That was good ... very good. Not as cool as he made out, then. And not just curious.

'Mr Beringer,' she replied, dropping her voice so it caressed him, low and husky as she swept past the receptionist. 'I said I'd be here, and here I am.' She reached him and took his hand, as she transferred all her weight onto her right hip and let her body bounce gently into position, right hip thrust towards him. He was a psychiatrist. He'd get it. And now I'm going to be in charge.

'Come on in and let's get started,' he said, eyes flicking from her thrusting hip back to her face. Today they were actually of a height, her heels making up the difference between them in natural stature. She held his eyes for a moment longer than necessary and she could feel the response in the disturbance in the atmosphere between them. She bet herself if she'd reached across right then and cupped his crotch, he'd have gone hard as iron in a second. Of course, she didn't, but the idea made her feel good. She deliberately brushed against him as she passed and the effect was electric. She took a seat across the room from him inside the consulting room, legs crossed and ankle gently swinging. Her flimsy outsize chemise had ridden up as she sat down, exposing a length of thigh. She didn't adjust it. If he looked carefully he might even see she was naked underneath.

He picked up a pad from his desk and came to sit opposite, carefully avoiding looking at her thighs, eyes fixed on her face. The receptionist followed him and plonked a folder on his desk. He nodded his thanks to her, balancing the pad on the arm of the chair, waiting for her to go. The polite professional, sweating. The fingers holding the pen trembled.

'Is it OK if I make a few notes as we talk? They're for my benefit only – to remind me of things I'd like us to go back to later.'

She shrugged, conscious that the movement caused her chemise to rub against her nipples. She felt them tingle, harden. She smiled, transferring the thought to him. Almost immediately his eyes dropped to her breasts then flipped back up to her face, lingering on her mouth. She licked her lips for his benefit.

'I never knew I was so ... interesting.' She raised her eyebrows and waited.

He snorted, and shook his head, resumed his smiling, unruffled exterior. 'We're all interesting, Miss Matthews ...' he lingered on her name and she took the point.

'Erin, please – I thought we'd got past the Miss-Mister yesterday.'

The door shut behind the receptionist with a click.

'Erin,' he agreed. 'So how are you today? Did you get some peace and quiet yesterday?'

'Yes, thank you. It was good to be home. In my own space.'

'Yes,' his eyes seemed to be assessing her. Deciding how to play it, no doubt. 'Good. I'm glad you feel rested. I hope we can talk a little more in depth today – pick up where we left off yesterday?'

'Pick up where we left off yesterday?' she laughed. It was throaty, amused, teasing. 'Now where would that be? There are quite a few things we could pick up on from yesterday, but here?'

'Er,' he tapped his pen on the notepad, laughing genially. 'I meant what we were talking about.' She knew he wanted to ask more about Roseanne, but thought it would be too precipitate to start with her.

'Love, life, control ...' she smiled sweetly.

'Maybe tell me about Jay – if you can?'

Jay? She hadn't expected that. Jay – dammit! 'More about Jay. Is he that important to you?'

'I thought he might be important to you since he seems to be the reason you find yourself here, ultimately.'

'Is he?' Momentarily that surprised her too – his perspicacity.

'He left you, the accident – you said yesterday. It might be a good place to start – officially?'

She thought about that. It was all a game but maybe he was right. Jay might be a good way to start, officially. Jay; her reason for being here ...

'All right,' she said, uncoiling one leg and crossing it over the other so a different area of her thigh was on view. 'You want to hear about Jay – for what good it does. This was the kind of thing Jay did – a favourite. Imagine having to stand in the corner of the room, like a childish dunce. You hate standing in the corner of the room. Of all the ways you could be punished, it's the worst because anything could be going on behind you but if you're not allowed to look, it's like being all alone in the vortex of a storm. You can smell and you can hear – you can even touch the walls, but you can't look round. Ever – not even when it gets dark, and you hate the dark too. If you let your imagination run riot, spiny fingers of fear crawl up your back and dig deep inside you, plucking at your gut, but you can't turn round because if you do, that will be the very moment that Jay will be there to see. And if Jay sees you turn round, you'll get the whip, across the back of your knees so it stings like vinegar in a cut, or on your back so it echoes like its hollow; an empty, hollow ache. And then it gets worse. Imagine needing to pee – really needing to pee. But you can't because then you'd have to move from the corner and Jay might see you then as well. You try to distract yourself, listening to the sounds of the house, or tracing the crease in the wallpaper from the ceiling to the floor. The clock on the far wall ticks in rhythm to your heart, but you wish it would stop because it sets your teeth on edge and that makes your gut tense up worse. There's a cobweb hanging from the corner of the room and its wafting to and fro. There must be a breeze from somewhere. Is it Jay? Coming back? It's moving now, like a fluttering moth. It must be Jay. Your stomach clenches and the pain is exquisite, but it's not Jay. You breathe out and go back to distracting yourself, following the shape of the flower in the pattern and where it repeats. You smell dinner being cooked somewhere – some normal household. You hear dogs bark, doors opening and closing, voices – asking, being answered. And your bladder fills until it's a straining balloon, like one of the water bombs the kids used to throw around in the playground. Sometime soon, it will burst, like they did on impact – a noise like guts splitting and slopping over the tarmac, oozing and pooling around exploded skin. But for moment, the clock's still ticking and it hurts now. Really hurts. How much longer? Oh God, how much longer … and just when you think you can't stand it anymore, palms prickling with heat and then cold, gut stabbing with pain, your legs buckle under you and Jay is there, shouting at you to stand up. And the clock's still ticking. Tick, tick, drip, drip. Muscle control fails. Slowly and painfully a thin stream of urine seeps, then trickles out of you. It dribbles down your leg, soaking into stockings, then shoes, until it's a warm sweet flood of relief and you don't care anymore, because you know it will happen anyway – the sting of the whip on your flesh, the crack of bone on bone. And when you're on your knees, begging for it to stop, that's when the recriminations, the abject apologies, the sorrow, the promise that it will never happen again come. Until the next time.'

'Jay did that to you?'

'It was a favourite.' She watched him, his eyes rounded, mouth taut; the shock, the revulsion. He was probably a good man behind the self-serving exterior. Shame to disabuse him of those who weren't. 'There were others, of course – all kinds of humiliations, but that was the worst because what is worse than feeling like a frightened, soiled child?'

'I didn't realise … I'm so sorry…'

'I don't need sorry.' The harsh edge to her voice cut even her. Consciously she softened it. 'It's over. Past. It's in the past now and I don't need to talk about it.'

'But did no one try to stop it?'

'I acquiesced, don't you understand? I could have walked away, I suppose. I could have walked out into the street, run away even. I didn't. I acquiesced because that is the nature of control. It's an agreement between the two of you – the one who controls and the one who is controlled. For all the fluffy pink psycho-babble you give the likes of Mrs Desperate who just left, this is what it's really all about.'

'I don't give anyone fluffy pink psycho-babble,' he protested.

'Don't you? Not even Roseanne?'

For a moment, he was silent – stunned. 'No! And I know what is meant by control …'

'So you understand what it means to *be* controlled, *really* controlled? Have you ever been controlled?'

'No, but I – '

'But you know the mechanics of it,' she finished for him. 'Knowing the mechanics is not the same as experiencing what it is to control someone, absolutely, utterly, completely. You take over their soul, their body, their will, their ability to do anything – even breathe. If they want to do something they know they have to ask you first. If they want to ask anything, they know they need permission from you first. And if they need permission from you, they know they need to grovel first. It's a cycle, one sordid need begets the next, and it's all fuelled by control. It's an obsession.'

'Of the person controlling?'

'Of both – it's a joint obsession; to control and be controlled, once the person being controlled is subjugated sufficiently.'

'You don't seem obsessed now.'

'I'm not. And I'm not subjugated, but I understand how it works.'

His eyes were cloudy, intense. She knew that look. It feigned sympathy to mask confusion.

'And that was Jay's forte – to subjugate? To control?'

'Yes,' she shrugged. 'But I don't need to talk about it. It's done. Finished. OK?'

He couldn't leave it. She knew he wouldn't be able to.

'I didn't realise about that. And that's why you drove straight at the man you thought was Jay? To end the control?'

'To re-establish control,' she corrected. 'My control.' She tightened her lips into a thin line. 'And for this,' she waved her hand languidly at him. He misunderstood.

'Us? Talking like this? For you to explain?' he nodded slowly. 'You needed to talk after all? I understand entirely.' She knew he didn't but it served well enough for him to think he did.

'Do you want to meet him?' she asked suddenly. Attack to defend, they said.

'Meet Jay? Well, I wouldn't normally meet a third party unless it was relevant to relationship counselling.'

'Then shall we leave him for now?' And retreat when able. Now she wanted him off the tricky subject of Jay. Too much elaboration could test her, trip her up.

'But you needed to talk and sometimes talking about experiences debunks them – makes it unnecessary to repeat them,' he said, smiling encouragingly. Oh God, he was irritating!

'Like driving into someone because they remind me of someone else?' she winked at him.

His eyes lost their kindness, sharpened. 'Whatever the provocation, it *is* a serious issue, Erin – and one that I might have to report on if there's a possibility of it happening again, whatever you may have been put through. It's my duty. In fact, all our conversations could have the potential to be the subject of police attention if they felt it necessary.'

She pulled a face. 'I'm sorry, that was flippant of me and I didn't mean it that way. I won't do it again. I'm a strong woman,' she paused. 'I wouldn't have survived this far if I wasn't. And you know, it's funny, you know my Christian name yet I still don't know yours.'

He softened a shade. 'Michael.'

'OK, I'm a strong woman, Michael. I know what the matter is with me. I know what my issues are but I don't need psychoanalysing to deal with them. I don't need help in that way. I'm here, cooperating with you as you wanted me to so I can get on with my life. That's how I need help. I need you to let me. There is only one thing left to deal with in my life now. Why I see Roseanne. But I can't deal with that in analysis – or as the subject of police interest.'

He sat forward and the notepad fell off the arm of the chair. He didn't even notice. 'But psychosis is something to deal with in analysis – I mean, the belief that you can see something that's not there. I could help you there – really help. Not fluffy pink psycho-babble, as you put it. Proper help. Why don't we talk about Roseanne? Tell me first what you see. I think we need to – certainly before I could sign you off from my care, anyway.'

The threat wasn't even implicit between them now. It was right out in the open. He was serious. This wasn't the way it was supposed to go.

'Why?'

'Why what?'

'Why do you want to help me?'

He sat back, surprised. 'Because I can. It's what I was trained to do. OK, fluffy pink psycho-babble *is* what I do a lot of the time, with my patients, but that's not all I am. I'm much more than that. I could help you – with all of this. With Jay, your past, what you see, the future. I can do far more than just pretend to make a difference. I really could make a difference. I could cure you.'

'Cure me?'

'Yes.'

'I thought I wasn't crazy.'

'Not crazy, you have issues – like you said. Issues that have led to here. I could help you get past those issues. Be healed of them. Be Erin with a future, not Erin with a past.'

She considered his earnest face, his tensed body. He believed, oh yes, he believed so badly, she almost felt sorry for him.

'And what do you want in return for that?'

He looked offended – a good pretence of it anyway.

'Nothing. It's my job.'

'Just your job? But fluffy pink psycho-babble is your job.'

'All right, it's my calling.' He hesitated. 'And your case could be fascinating – maybe even my breakthrough into more serious work.'

'Ah. You want to document me. Use me as a lab rat?'

'No, no – absolutely not!' Now he looked horrified, but she'd seen that look before – on Jay's face. *"Just try it – once, so we can see if it works ... "* Beringer had lowered his voice so it was gentle and appealing, like warm oil flowing over her. 'It would simply be good for me to be doing what I should be doing for once.' The note of entreaty hid in the undertones of his voice. 'And your reference to Roseanne has intrigued me.'

Ah. Now he'd finally got there. She studied him, taking her time. 'Because?'

'Because you knew her before she died?'

'Did I say so? I said I see her, not that I knew her.'

'OK,' he acknowledged. 'Because it's strange, then. Maybe some form of common memory. Fascinating to explore, anyway.'

'So you think I might also know what she knew as a result? Share her memories? Can do what she could do?'

His eyes narrowed. 'Do? What she could do?' The note of anxiety made his voice jagged and his eyes were guarded, watching her minutely. He had plans too, whether he admitted it to himself or her. She didn't like plans that involved her, but unless she let his plans unravel she wouldn't know what they were.

'You know what she could do,' she said quietly, the irony of it all twisting her lips at the corners. His own parted in a silent expression of surprise and admission. 'All right. On one condition,' she said eventually.

'What's that?' It rushed out like a bullet from a gun. She wondered if he'd been holding his breath all the time she'd been going through the motions of considering.

She wriggled in her chair and her chemise rode up higher. He must be able to see her pubic mound by now. Christ any higher and the bloody shirt would be round her waist.

'We give each other what we both want from each other.'

'Oh, I can't ... not here ... it wouldn't be appropriate.' His face was frozen, the moment before Munch's screamer screamed, but different to the scream the man in the car had screamed. God, he was predictable!

'Not that,' she laughed. 'I don't need to beg for sex, like the poor old dear who was in here before me. You want to take yourself seriously and think that curing me – as you put it – will do that for you. I'm only prepared to talk to someone who's my confidant. Not a therapist but a friend. Someone I could share *everything* with. Can you be my friend? My confidant?'

'Oh,' now he looked surprised. Hah! Yes, you didn't expect that, did you? But I know the little voice in your head is saying be her friend and you'll end up in her bed as well. 'I can't be your friend and your therapist. To be your friend I'd have to sign you off my register.'

'So sign me off.'

'But I don't know if you're ready for that yet. This is only our first proper session. And, anyway ...'

'Do I seem crazy?'

'I never call anyone crazy.'

'Unbalanced?'

'I never call anyone unbalanced.' He looked uncomfortable.

'Disturbed, neurotic, paranoid?'

'Erin,' he paused, considering the name. 'I haven't said you are any of those things, but you've barely told me anything to explain yourself yet – not really explained.' His expression was meaningful. 'About your worries, your psychoses.'

She leaned back in her seat. '*Really?* Wasn't what I just told you enough? That's not telling you anything? OK, so let's talk so you feel like I've explained enough for you to sign me off.'

'About Roseanne?'

'Since you're so obsessed with her.'

His jaw dropped. 'Me obsessed with her?'

She nodded. 'That's at least the fourth time you've asked if we could talk about her in twenty-four hours.'

'Only because you said you could see her and ...'

'But you believe me?'

'Well ...'

'So who's the crazy one – me who says she sees her, or you who believes me?'

'Neither of us,' he hesitated. 'All right, but we still need to talk about her.'

'So what was she to you?'

'Just a patient.'

'That's all?'

'That's all.'

'Then why are you obsessed with her?'

'I'm not – it's you who says I am, and how did we get on to me and not you, by the way?' He laughed, but it was an uneasy laugh.

'We got onto you because you wanted to talk about Roseanne. I don't need to, but you do.'

'I'm not the one ...'

'But you are the one asking about her, over and over again. There's something you really need to know about her, isn't there? Do you want me to tell you it – everything I know about her?' He didn't need to answer. He had that entreating look again. He felt guilty – oh God, did he feel guilty! 'Then sign me off and I'll tell you about her; *all* about her – as my ... *friend*.' She wriggled again and this time she knew he saw what else waited as the prize at the end of her long, long legs.

'And it's not quite ethical,' he protested.

'Neither is life,' she said as she got slowly to her feet, slid her hands along her breasts and down to her thighs, flattening the thin material of her shirt against her skin. 'Or any of this.'

'And what about the police?'

'What about the police?'

'You wouldn't be protected from charges for dangerous driving if I did. Whilst you're in therapy – '

'I don't need to be. He was on his phone. He won't press charges and the police can't unless he does. There's no proof other than what he gives as a witness – and he won't risk giving any.'

'But if they could insisted on seeing my notes on you ...'

'You don't have any notes on me so there's nothing to tell them. Unless you write some. How about, I drove into him because momentarily he reminded me of Jay, but it was temporary confusion that resulted in lack of concentration – and anyway, he was on the phone so deliberately not paying attention to the road. Compared to my temporary loss of concentration, which you're convinced wouldn't be repeated ...' She smiled at his weakening expression. 'Write that.' She walked calmly across the room towards him until she was standing in front of him, her pubis almost on the level with his face. 'And of course, you'd defend me, wouldn't you? You're my *friend* now.' He rose to greet her and they stood with barely an inch between them. 'And I'm yours, ready to tell you anything you want to know. About Roseanne ...' She could feel his heart pounding in the still of the room, the blood surging through his veins, the synapses in his head crackling as they connected the impulses and forced the decision on him.

'Ethically ...' he began again.

'Who decides what ethics are?' she breathed into his mouth, and the deal was done.

# Chapter 13: Beringer

He'd felt sorry for her. What she'd described had been terrible – typical of a sado-masochistic relationship, but terrible nevertheless. Yet she seemed so in control, he couldn't in all fairness say she needed help with what was the only psychological issue he could officially say she presented him with – the aftermath of an abusive relationship resulting in potentially suicidal tendencies, rigorously denied. There were no apparent suicidal tendencies present now, so what could he say she needed help with if she didn't actually want it? On every scoring system he could employ she would rate as sane, sorted and in control. Very much in control, he qualified, remembering the way she'd taken over his senses and his body in the end. The memory brought a rush of blood to his head and his crotch. His palms prickled and his face felt hot at the thought of what he'd wanted to do to her right there and then. Thank God Jenny had been on the intercom, reminding him that his next patient was due in five minutes. Five minutes to regain equilibrium and self-control. Five minutes to become the professional again, although maybe that was never going to be possible now.

He looked down at the bottom two parts of the discharge form that he'd retained. Erin had the top copy. There was no getting that back. One of the two parts he'd kept should go to her GP but that section remained blank. He had no idea who her GP was – or anything about her, in fact, and the hospital notes were less than useless. Both parts would remain with him, therefore – proof of the correctness of his decision, or of his complicity. That at least allowed him some chance of deniability. He fiddled with the corner of his part of the form. He'd done it because there was nothing else he could do, he told himself. If she'd insisted on a second opinion, on the strength of today's performance she would have been discharged anyway, and then he wouldn't ever have the chance to sort out the Roseanne business. No, he'd done the only thing possible under the circumstances. Now he had to quantify, record and prove that in her records. Create them, in fact. He pushed the two parts of the discharge form to one side and pulled his notebook towards him. The uppermost page contained only four words. Jay, humiliation, control … Roseanne. He'd underlined control three times, but he hardly needed that to remind himself of the abuse she'd described. Yet, anyone less representative of the abused, it was hard to imagine. Yes, outwardly, she had the frailty of a victim, but there remained a core that was determined, persistent, and authoritative. He wished now he'd found out exactly who Jay was. It would be interesting to know more about the person who'd managed to subdue this assertive woman.

In the meantime, there was little he could do but write up her account of the reasons for her driving recklessly at another road user, and add her claim that she'd lost control of the car. He would conclude that she'd acted under extreme provocation at the time, now sincerely regretted, but not with intent to harm, and that she seemed entirely rational and remorseful as of today's consultation. Also, hadn't the other driver been far more negligent, driving whilst on the phone? Note that specifically. Yes. He scribbled it under "control" on the notepad. Accordingly, he did not consider her to be a risk to herself or anyone else in the community.

'Except me,' he added aloud, ruefully. But it was a risk he had to take, both because of Roseanne and what she'd done, and Erin, and what she might know. And that policeman – what if he followed up on any of it. He pressed the intercom. 'Jenny?'

'Yes, Mr Beringer?'

'Have you made up a file for Miss Matthews?'

'That patient this morning?' he could hear the curl in her voice.

'Yes, that patient this morning,' he replied trying to sound as neutral as possible. There had been three patients this morning, but they both knew there had only been one patient of significance this morning. He pressed the button on the intercom and leaned back in his chair. Put it to bed, he told himself, but that immediately raised too many inappropriate associations and his imagination began to race. Christ, what was wrong with him? She was only a woman – and a scrawny one at that. Scrawny and obvious – as obvious as Jean Young, the patient he'd seen before Erin was obvious in a pathetic, undemanding way – yet the difference was indescribable.

There was a discreet knock on the consulting room door, and it opened immediately afterwards. Jenny walked through it, bearing a file aloft. 'Walk' maybe wasn't quite the right way to describe it. Stomp, march, tramp – that was Jenny. His indomitable barricade against the demands of his needier patients. She did that now – stomp. She stomped across to his desk and plonked the two files down unceremoniously. He didn't need to say anything. Clearly Erin had created an indelible impression on her. That made him want to laugh. God she was a clever woman – how had she got away with it?

'The Matthews file – what there is of it. Do you want to check it? There's nothing in it apart from her name and contact details.'

'Thank you,' he said mildly, taking the file from her and making a pretence of checking it before pushing it to one side. 'I'll write up her notes now and then it can go into the dormant range. Oh, and the Roseanne Grey file can go there too.'

'Both of them?' her left eyebrow was raised.

'Both of them,' he agreed. 'Since they're no longer my patients for different reasons.' He composed his face into a suitably regretful look.

'Well, I didn't think there was much wrong with *her* anyway – other than arrogance.'

'Her?'

'The Matthews woman.'

'Sometimes people put on a façade for protection, Jenny. We mustn't judge. Anyway, she won't be coming in again since I've discharged her now.'

'Completely discharged?' She was looking at the two bottom pages of the discharge form that was still lying on the desk and trying to read them upside down. 'Good,' her face lit up. 'I'll see to it when you give me the file back, then.' She turned on her heel and stomped back to the door, but hesitated on the threshold. After a while he looked up. She was watching him, her face had twisted back into a grimace.

'Yes?' he asked patiently.

'This is going to sound silly…'

'Nothing you say sounds silly, Jenny.'

'All right. That Erin Matthews. She reminded me of someone. I couldn't think who it was to begin with – thought it was probably some snooty-faced top model with her legs and stick body, but when you asked me to put Roseanne Grey's file in dormant it came to me. It was her.'

The idea brought a tiny electric impulse through his head and into his temples. He resisted the instinctive inclination to hold his breath. Consciously he told his body to relax. Remain immune, calm.

'Roseanne Grey? Why on earth would you think that? They're not at all alike.' He shook his head, to imply he couldn't see how Jenny could make any connection between them.

She paused, reflectively. 'Well, as much as I ever saw of her, no, they're not. Roseanne Grey was more of a fat rat, whereas the Matthews woman is a thin weasel, but she always gave me the creeps too.'

He laughed out loud. 'Do you always give my patients animal personas? Maybe I should be treating you too?'

Jenny smiled somewhat reluctantly. 'Well, Mrs Young is a dormouse and Mrs North is a big cat – maybe a panther ...' she admitted. 'It's what they remind me of – an impression.'

'Hmm, well I might agree with you about both of them but with the Grey-Matthews thing it's probably just an impression you've got because they're a similar height. Small things can do that for us – associations. Put it out of your head and enjoy some time away from people and their personas. Good job when the weekend's here, I think,' Beringer smiled. 'Clear the head and the spirits.'

'Yeah,' she smiled back. 'Maybe. Going to get a different kind of creeps with the kids, though. They want to see that horror film everyone's on about. Maybe that will desensitise me. That's what you call it, isn't it? When you have an allergy to something.'

Beringer laughed aloud. 'I'm afraid there's no desensitisation method for people, Jenny – but a change is as good as a rest.'

'Right,' she said, stepping into the doorway. 'Oh, mind you, she might still have to come in again – that Erin Matthews. She left her coat behind.'

'Her coat? I'm surprised she's not been back for it already then. It's freezing outside.' He glanced across at the window. The skies were obediently re-filling with swathes of threatening grey cloud, just as the weather forecast this morning had promised. Real snow was on the way, but its precursor, a biting wind nipping at any piece of unwisely exposed skin and chafing it red raw, was already hard at work.

'Well, she hasn't. No sense, no feeling maybe. It's still on the coat stand by the door.'

'OK.' He crossed to the window. Erin had left almost two hours ago. He'd seen his last patient of the morning and tried to decide how to write up Erin's notes in the meantime. 'Did she say where she was going next?'

'To me? The queen of condescension tell me what she was doing next?' Jenny's face was a picture.

'OK, point taken, although – '

'I know. Sorry. No, she didn't say where she was going.'

'I'd better drop it off on my way to lunch then.'

The thought of having a reason to see Erin again so soon was both exhilarating and disquieting. She'd made it clear he should leave it for her to make contact with him after a decent interval. The reasons were obvious, but so was what he could do if she didn't. How would she react to him seeking her out this soon? But it was to return her coat, for Christ's sake. That would be all right, wouldn't it? It occurred to him then that – as with her seemingly complete and spontaneous recovery from the abusive Jay, so he had gone from being her analyst to being her subject. The man in him was appalled. The psychiatrist in him was fascinated. The obsessive in him wanted to know how she did it so he could do it too. And about Roseanne, of course.

# Chapter 14: Grant

He had a bottle of Pinot Grigio and a bottle of Merlot. He wasn't sure which Alice's taste would run to, but he suspected the white would probably hit the spot better than the red. Red was a man's drink. Or beer.

It was dark by the time he arrived, but it was dark by four-thirty these days so dark meant nothing really. The wind was arctic. They said snow was on the way in time for Christmas, but then they said that every year, and every year it arrived late or not at all. 'Like luck,' he commented aloud. He'd put the cat in a cardboard box he'd found in the boot of his car, left over from when Stacey had moved out. He'd stabbed air holes in the top with his keys and the box was now perched on the passenger seat next to him, rolling and mewing gently. The cat didn't sound upset, just disgruntled. He supposed he would when they finally shoved him in a box too – except it wouldn't have air holes.

It hadn't rained, but the road felt slippery under the tyres as if sheet ice was already forming merely from the frost in the air. His fingers felt stiff and unwieldy as he fed the steering wheel between them, cornering the main road and turning into Alice's neat, well-presented close. He should have ignored the cat and put the heater on. On the other hand, the combination of heat and being confined in the box might have been too much for it. If he was delivering a cat and trespassing on Alice's good will in doing so, it ought to be a live cat.

He pulled up in front of Alice's tidy front garden – straight borders, no weeds, low, well-appointed brick wall bordering the pavement. That was more like it. Grant compared it to his shambling wreck of a semi. He was going to have to do something with it now. Knock it down, maybe, the way he felt about it. Alice had got the right idea – easy maintenance. The good life. Then he felt guilty. She'd probably had to. She'd said she was a widow, hadn't she? For God's sake don't ask how he died, he cautioned himself. Drop off the cat, have a glass of wine, tell her what you found and then go before you make an idiot of yourself.

He slid out of the driver's seat, scowling into the wind, and made his way round the back of the car to the passenger door. He yanked it open and the wind grabbed it before he could stop it.

'For fuck's sake,' he rasped under his breath as he battled the door and the wind. Somehow he had to get the box, the bottles and himself to the front door. He braced himself against the door, stopping it flying wide again and shoved the bottles one into each pocket either side of his coat. They bobbed just above the line of the pocket, messages in a bottle. Probably spelt danger if he'd been able to read them. More balanced, he eased the box off the seat. It hissed and howled at him. So much for it not being upset. It bloody was now. He wondered what Alice would say when he presented her with a hissing, spitting ball of fury instead of a cat. 'Too late now,' he said aloud, balancing the box against the front offside and kicking the passenger door shut. For what, he wasn't sure. Rolling like a seaman recently disembarked, he swayed up the path, bottles bobbing and cat heckling what he was planning to say; eloquent thanks for looking after it and putting up with him intruding on her peaceful evening. What came out when she opened the door was a cross between an apology and an oath.

'Bloody hell, sorry!' he exclaimed as the box leapt from his grasp and the Pinot Grigio followed it. Luckily only the Pinot Grigio made it to the ground as Alice deftly caught the vaulting box whilst the bottle splintered and distributed its contents onto her front door step. Grant stepped onto the wine puddle as he tried to steady himself and lost his balance completely, landing heavily on the grass the other side of the neat border embracing the path. 'Oh shit,' he announced as he rolled onto his left side to avoid smashing the other bottle still wedged in his pocket, and slammed his frozen fingers straight down on the jagged Pinot Grigio bottle. He flexed his hand and winced. It felt wet and slippery – either blood or wine. For a moment he was too stunned to decide which was most likely and by the time he'd decided, Alice was already helping him up.

'Careful,' she warned as he put his weight on foot that had twisted under him and started to cave in again. 'You could have sprained your ankle. Lean on me.'

'Where's the cat?' he asked looking around for the box.

'Safely inside,' she laughed up into his dismayed face, 'like you should be. Come on.'

She was surprisingly strong for a woman. He managed to hop across the wine puddle this time and into the hall, bringing a sprinkling of red droplets with him. Blood? The Pinot was white. He swayed like a giant crane, top heavy in a storm. She leaned him against the wall and closed the door. The wind howled a protest but it and the wreckage of the white wine remained outside. It was warm in the hall – incredibly warm compared to the hoar frost of outside. He held his hand up and forced himself to study the piece of glass sticking out of the mound around his thumb. And the blood. Oh shit! His head swam and Alice's face faded away like a ghost being sucked back into the grave.

'Don't go,' he called to her, and that was the last thing he remembered until he came round, still propped against the wall in the hall, but now with his arse on the floor and his knees up by his ears. He grunted and tried to straighten his legs. They couldn't quite lie flat to the floor because his feet bumped up against the side of the stairs as they led off the hall. Alice was crouching in front of him, holding his hand – or rather holding his hand wrapped in a tea towel and calling his name over and over again. 'Uh,' he said to her concerned expression. 'What you doing there?'

She laughed, but there was more relief than humour in it. 'Waiting for you to come round and ask me what I'm doing here. Do you think you can stand? You'd be better off sitting on the settee than on the floor. Or maybe the kitchen. I'd rather like to have a proper look at your hand.'

He looked at the tea towel cocoon. 'Ouch,' he said to the sodden red mass blossoming on one side of it, pulled his knees back up to his chin and put his forehead on them.

'Do you feel dizzy, or sick?' Alice's voice filtered through his knees.

'Both – and foolish,' he replied. He lifted his head, steeling himself to look at the bloody mass that appeared to be his hand. 'And a bit squeamish. My Achilles heel. I can't stand the sight of blood.'

'Oh,' she seemed genuinely taken aback. 'But you have to deal with that all the time in your job.'

'Yes,' he half-laughed. 'Bloody hilarious, isn't it?'

'Strong-minded,' she replied. 'It's not as bad as it looks,' she added, taking his other arm and pulling gently on it. 'Come on. Come into the kitchen and I'll have a look at it. You don't have to.' He allowed her to coax him to his feet and he stumbled after her into a wide, bright kitchen, with gleaming white surfaces and a cool grey stone floor. She gestured to an intense sap green bar stool and he perched precariously on it, holding the tea-towelled hand well away from the counter top to avoid spoiling it.

Alice brought a bowl of water and some cotton wool over and placed it next to him. Next to that she placed tweezers and some dressing pads. She took his hand and rested it gently on the counter top.

'So the cat's name is?' She began unravelling the tea towel. He looked away.

'Sammy, I think. Beringer – the shrink – referred to it. It must be Roseanne Grey's cat but, as no one could find it at the time we assumed it had taken itself off like cats do. Found another home.' Cats and women, he though sourly. 'Where is it now, by the way?' He could feel her teasing the threads of the tea towel away from his skin but he couldn't bring himself to look. Bodies and blood – they were different. Nauseating, but different. Over the years he'd learnt to detach the body from the person, and the blood from the reality of what it meant. The body had become THE body, and the person who'd inhabited the body, THE victim. This, however was him – his body, his blood. A wave of revulsion swept over him again. He focused on Alice's face as she tended to him. Not even the slightest indication of repugnance. How did she do this all day long – disassembling and reassembling body parts like they were parts of a jigsaw puzzle, and yet be so nice?

'She's in the lounge, already curled up in front of the fire. I suppose she thinks she's found her new home.' She glanced up at him and smiled encouragingly. 'OK?' she added. He nodded, threatening his stomach with a variety of abominations if it rebelled completely and actually threw up in Alice's surgically pristine kitchen. 'It's not so bad, actually. Just need to get the glass out and then we'll patch you up, but you should probably get a tetanus shot tomorrow.' He nodded again, then closed his eyes. 'I didn't notice any mention of a cat in the evidence summary I saw,' she continued.

'No, probably not.' He swallowed and opened his eyes again. He concentrated on her eyes to take his mind off what she was concentrating on as he registered the gentle pulling sensation in the fleshy part of his palm encircling his thumb. They were grey with flecks of amber – unusual. Nice. Warm. Kind. Not the kind of eyes you associated with someone who chopped up bodies – or befriended your cheating wife. Stop it, he rebuked himself. That's not fair. 'I thought it was a he, by the way – Sammy …'

'Could be short for Samantha too,' she said, flicking a glance at him before focusing on what she was doing again. 'We have this inclination to jump to conclusions, don't we? Even when we're trained not to.

Stereotyping. I suppose it's because it's easier to deal with a type than a complexity.'

'Who's the shrink, you or Beringer?' he laughed.

She looked up at him, serious-faced and he wondered if he'd offended her. He was relieved when she grinned back. 'We're all shrinks at times, Darwin. Living does it to you. So why didn't I find any reference to a cat in the report?'

'I guess because it wasn't there. They did look for it though. Josie's soft on cats. Got them on her screensaver and the pin board behind her desk.'

'Oh,' she barely changed expression, but he realised as soon as he'd said it that she might be wondering the same thing as him. Why hadn't he asked Josie to look after the cat until tomorrow?

'Anyway,' he continued hurriedly, 'there's more. I wanted to have another good look at the report myself tomorrow anyway, because I left some new evidence in the lab with your assistant.'

'Yes, I gathered you were going to do that from what you said on the phone. What new evidence?'

'A door handle and a broken pot. A newspaper too.'

'Sounds curious.' She cocked an eyebrow at him as his cue to elaborate.

'Yeah, curious is the word – although I think the door handle speaks louder than words. It's the bedroom door handle and it was forced – well, mangled really, but it implies there was a forced entry to the bedroom, I think.'

'That wasn't in the report either, although I think there was some reference to the door handle being damaged – but on the inside, not the outside – so wouldn't that mean someone forcing their way out, not in?'

'Ah.' He thought about that. 'But why would someone try to force their way out? Unless she was trying to escape him, of course.'

'Him?'

'Beringer,' he explained triumphantly.

'Beringer? Her therapist? Why?'

'He's the only bloke she seems to have had involved in her life – and he was cagey when I spoke to him. He's a strong bloke, could easily rip a door knob off I reckon – or push a woman out of a window.'

'Aren't you rather jumping to conclusions there? I thought she was merely a suspicious death that we were going through the motions for?'

'Maybe originally, but not now.' He surprised himself with the glee in his voice. He tempered it with gravity. 'There are too many oddities to this suspicious death. The blood on the sheet ...'

'Which might not be hers, 'Alice reminded him.

'Or might be but there's another explanation for the mismatch,' he countered. 'Then there's the missing cat, suddenly found stuck in the house when I go back for a routine check – but nowhere to be found when we were crawling over the place straight after the body was found.'

'Cat flap?' Alice suggested.

'No cat flap, no open windows, doors or other entrance points. What does that say to you?'

'I suppose someone must have let the cat back in,' she said slowly, stopping to examine his expression.

'Exactly – and if someone let the cat in, they had access yet we don't know about it, and they haven't come forward to say so. That alone is dodgy in my book. Add to that the forced door handle, the state of the place when she was found – like there'd been some kind of ruckus going on, the tricky shrink and the fact that only a short while after the road accident she was in, she upped and abandoned everything she'd previously had – job, social life, home. She wasn't just neurotic; she was hiding,' he finished with a flourish.

'Curiouser and curiouser,' she said, smiling archly at him. 'What was small has become big. My namesake,' she explained. 'Alice – through the looking glass?' She tapped him gently on the arm. 'And you're done,' she added as she whisked away the trappings of her ministrations before he could see them. He looked down at his neatly bandaged hand. No blood, no glass, no mess. He breathed out. He felt better already. Not quite intact, but on the way there – and he hadn't even noticed the transition. He realised with a bolt of self-directed wry humour that Alice had been deliberately distracting him with her questions while she'd been patching him up. The rush of gratitude almost spilled out. Restraint born out of months of shutting down and switching off since Stacey had left held him back.

'Thanks,' he mumbled instead, under cover of examining the neat swathe of bandage.

'Welcome,' she replied. It echoed round the spacious kitchen. 'Shall we toast what was small becoming big? Or what is closed becoming open?' He stared at her, but her smile was wide and open – no double meaning there, only in his head. 'You still have one bottle intact,' she laughed, gesturing to his sagging coat pocket.

'Oh, fuck, yes! Sorry,' he added to her raised eyebrows. 'And about my language – it's par for the course with the lads on the team.'

'And the girls?' she asked, eyebrow still arched at him. She took the bottle of Merlot from him. He looked blankly at her. 'Josie?' she added. 'The cat lover?'

'Oh, right. You know, I hadn't even thought of her as a girl. That's odd isn't it? She's just part of the team.'

'Well it's good that she's so integrated,' Alice replied, twisting the cap on the bottle and filling two wine glasses. 'But don't forget she's an individual too. Too much team work – or too much work – does rather slew your view of the world.' It was a direct attack. It must come from what Stacey had told her. He grimaced. 'I was very guilty of that after John died. It was easier to bury myself in work than in grief, but you have to dig yourself out eventually. Move on. Living requires that of you, no matter how strong the lure of the past, or of not facing it.' She put the two glasses down on the counter top in front of him. 'Would you like to slip into something more comfortable?' His jaw dropped again and this time her laughter sang out and echoed round the room like the high, joyous top notes of a symphony. 'Take off your coat and relax on the settee?' she explained between bouts of mirth.

For the briefest moment he felt as foolish as he had when he realised he'd passed out. The high tight knot in his gut twisted and the twisting continued up into his throat, then something released in him – some hidden catch to some forgotten trapdoor. The feelings of oppression, constraint and reproach that had steadily accumulated as he'd tried to head off Stacey's leaving in those last few weeks before she'd carried through her threat and actually left, emptied into it. He laughed aloud and it was as light-hearted as Alice's laughter. He laughed louder, harder, longer until he became aware that her amusement had dwindled to a contented chuckle. He matched it, but the light feeling inside his head and ribs remained.

They sat a foot apart on the settee. She curled her feet up under her and cradled her glass of wine, body turned towards him, knees pointing at his upper thigh. He adjusted his position so his crotch was turned towards her, without thrusting. Too soon for that. She surprised him with, 'So what is it about Beringer you dislike so much?'

'Do I?'

'You were rather jumping to conclusions earlier. I take on board what you said about no one else specifically in her life, but if that's the case, he's surely smart enough not to have done anything that could immediately be linked to him? And what would be his motive, anyway?'

'Malpractice? Or maybe he's just a sick bastard who likes to control women?'

'Is there any independent evidence to suggest either?'

'No,' he admitted reluctantly.

'Then are you maybe just biased? Stereotyping again?' she suggested, nudging his thigh gently with her right knee. He shrugged, but said nothing. What could he say? If he was being truthful, she'd hit it spot on. He glanced sideways at her. Those deep grey eyes were watching him intently, the amber flecks like little dots of gold in them. They made his head spin.

'No,' he said, 'I'm not that bad. I'm a policeman. I'm trained to work on evidence, not assumption.'

'So tell me your evidence that Beringer caused Roseanne Grey's death?'

'Well, that's still to be established, but I know his type, and my gut tells me ...' he paused, and looked down at his glass of wine, his legs, her knee, close to his thigh – so close it was almost touching. He looked back up into her eyes. 'OK, you got me bang to rights.' He snorted. 'Stereotyping. He's just like the bloke Stacey went off with.' It came out in a rush, a torrent he wished he'd stemmed seconds later. This wasn't fair either. The woman didn't want to be his counsellor. Maybe he even needed to go to see Beringer himself? The thought made him choke. 'If he hadn't come along we'd have been fine. Beringer is that sort too.'

'No, Darwin. Beringer has something about him that reminds you of this man, but we know nothing really of Beringer as an individual or his motivations. The same is probably true of the man Stacey left you for. And it is a fact that no one leaves a situation they're happy in.'

'Did she talk to you?' he asked suspiciously.

'No,' Alice shook her head. 'And it's none of my business either, but every truth is self-evident – or so someone once said.' She winked at him. 'Your job is to look for and find the truth. It's easier to do that when it's not a truth related to yourself, but nevertheless, you have to do that too from time to time, unpalatable though it may be. Mine certainly was.'

'What was your truth?' he asked, incredulous that there could be anything unpalatable associated with this warm, steady woman with the glorious eyes.

'That I was a coward. That it was easier to hide than live. That it was easier to deny than face things. I was in denial for years with John. He was slowly dying from MS but I convinced myself he would be with me forever, regardless. I immersed myself in work – wanted to reach the top because he couldn't work so I had to be the breadwinner. Or that was what I told myself. It was really just easier to work long hours and bury myself in my work than be near him and watch him gradually fade away. And then when he'd faded away, I immersed myself in work again to avoid the guilt.'

'You can't help it that someone dies.'

'No, but you can do something about what you do with them whilst they're alive. Living is paramount – living, loving, being. But living is painful because pain makes us appreciate joy all the more. I didn't understand that then. I do now, and I've forgiven myself. John had already.'

Grant shifted uncomfortably. This was too personal. He hoped she didn't expect him to recount the failings of his marriage too – the lack of children, the almost-denied pet cat, the countless evenings working late when Stacey was left home alone, bored and frustrated, the lack of empathy between them ... OK, so they hadn't been all right. Maybe it had been his fault. Maybe he had to forgive her and himself too.

'If it wasn't Beringer, then who?' he asked, shifting away from Alice so he kept his head clear. 'She knew no one. No, actually she did know someone. She knew someone who gave her a phone number. It was written on the side of the newspaper I brought back. There was an article in it about some pot-maker called Erin somebody and when I rang the number, the woman answered to the same name, then hung up. The pot was made by this Erin, so they had to know each other – or at least met.'

'There you are, then. Another dimension to consider.'

Alice hadn't moved and yet her knee was still almost touching his thigh even though he thought he'd moved away from it. He considered other dimensions, including whether he would go and wind Beringer up a bit anyway, despite the uncomfortable truths Alice had suggested. The expanse of red moquette cushion between them had dwindled again.

'I'll set Josie on it tomorrow,' he said. 'Maybe she'll respond to another woman.' There, he was recognising Josie as a woman. Two birds with one stone. He smiled at Alice, feeling vaguely like a dog awaiting approbation from their mistress – hoping for scraps, which reminded him when he bawled whoever was responsible out for missing the cat, he'd have a go at them about not examining the contents of the bin too. Might take a bit of the heat off him for breaking the pot, and Alice had mentioned the Grey woman had a high level of drugs in her bloodstream. The ones that had been in the discarded capsules in the bin, or were they something else? They could be something to do with Beringer too – happy pills and all that. He was about to mention that to Alice when she took him completely off-course.

'Why did your parents choose the name Darwin for you?'

He did a double take. 'I dunno.' He laughed. 'He discovered the origin of the species, didn't he? Maybe my mother hoped I'd discover the reason the species exists. Damned if I know though. Damned if I know anything.'

'You know plenty,' she tapped him gently on the thigh. 'You just need to implement it.'

He edged closer to her and leaned across the remaining red moquette. Her eyes funnelled into one, central in her forehead as he went in for the kiss. It was wet, awkward and barely reciprocated.

'I've just fucked up,' he said as he moved away afterwards, 'haven't I?'

'Not totally,' she replied, eyes still intense, but soothing. 'You don't discover the reason the species exists in one hit. It takes a bit of time and research.'

Time and research. 'Sometimes I think I'm really stupid – wonder how I even got to DS.'

'You got to DS through hard work and dedication.'

'Not the same as genius,' he said, suddenly feeling morose. How come when he'd felt so happy just now? Must be the wine. Alice had cradled her one glass and it was still half full. His, however seemed to have refilled itself several times over. He could feel its effects in his legs and the disinclination to move – or maybe Alice had something to do with that.

'Who wants to be a genius?' she replied lightly. 'Far too tiring. Tell me about your current project then – the one replacing Robert Pakington.'

'OK,' he settled more comfortably against the sofa back. 'Sarah Brakespeare. Approaching the three-year anniversary of her death. Found beaten to death in the kitchen. No obvious perp, but the murder weapon was found a short distance away a short while later. A form of club – baseball, rounders bat – that sort of thing, but proper – properly made. The patio doors to the house weren't fully secured. Shut but not locked, so seems like she could have let them in – gone out the kitchen to make coffee or something and wham! No witnesses, no arguments, no back histories of feuds. Entirely random. But I don't think it was.'

'And what are you researching primarily?'

'The murder weapon, I reckon. It belonged to someone because it didn't come from the house. And not everyone has a proper rounders bat – or a baseball bat, do they?'

'Which? Rounders or baseball?'

'I've got to get to the case file to find that out. It's a cold case now so I'd have to have a reason to access the evidence file – or the opportunity.'

'Ah. Darwin, that might be a bit dodgy?'

'I know. That's why I haven't done it yet.' They exchanged glances.

'But you're going to?' She smiled. 'I guess we all need a way to escape until we're ready to cope. My rabbit hole was work. This sounds like yours, but remember it's still only a rabbit hole. And let me know what you find out. When you know which kind of bat it is, I'll see what our database says about it – unofficially, of course.' She looked at her watch. 'Do you realise it's past midnight?'

'Oh,' he started guiltily and his head swam. He slumped back against the sofa again.

She smiled. 'Look, it sounds like hell on earth out there and you've drunk too much to drive.' The icy wind that had attacked him on the way obligingly rattled at some loose metal fixing outside. 'Do you want to stay?' Christ, she must have read his mind! Excitement brought the blood pounding into his ears and a central point midway between heart, soul and crotch only for it to settle and solidify there. 'It'd only be the settee, I'm afraid. I'm in the middle of decorating the guest room and the spare room is still full of stuff I haven't unpacked from the move.'

'Uh,' he'd been planning on saying no thanks, but his mouth had other ideas. A case of open his mouth and talk without thinking – what he did too often and it was rarely a good idea, but maybe this time …

He expected sleep to come with difficulty, despite the wine, but it slipped over him like a blanket pulling him into its depths, dropping him in and out of rabbit holes the shape of baseball bats until he wasn't quite sure whether he was above or below ground, real or inanimate. He woke just as the early morning light began filtering through the weave of the curtains, grey and miserable. His head felt like someone had been stuffing cotton wool in it all night and his mouth had been processing it as a waste product when the surplus overflowed out of his brain. Something was bearing down on him, soft and stifling on his chest. It was the cat, curled up in a round. He wriggled to try and shift it, but only succeeded in disturbing it so that it opened its eyes and stared unwinkingly straight into his. They were disturbingly like Stacey's – green and glassy.

'Sorry,' he whispered to the cat. It seemed to accept the apology and closed its eyes again. He could have moved – evicted the cat and sat upright; he could have done with a pee and his hand was aching now the anaesthesia of the wine had dissipated, but he couldn't be bothered. Restrictive though it was, the cat and the blanket were comforting, keeping him in place where normally he'd be tossing and turning like a demon if he'd been in his bed at home, listening to the tiles on the roof shift in the wind and the doors rattle. The only sounds here were from outside. Inside was – peace. He lay in the half-light for a while, mind drifting between the evidence he and Alice had been discussing and his insistence that Beringer was involved some way. Stereotyped. Yeah, OK. He had stereotyped Beringer, although he probably deserved it. He felt in his pocket for his phone, and as carefully as possible to avoid waking the green-eyed demon again, he withdrew it. He liberated his arm and the phone from the blanket cocoon and flicked on the phone, typing in the PIN one-handed. Bloody good job it had been his left hand he'd injured – again. The screen shone like a beacon in the dawn light. He selected messages and 'Stacey'. The last one was the worst: *Darwin, please just let this go. Let's part on good terms, not with me telling you never to darken my door* ...

Never darken her door. Fuck, why would he? But he knew why. And yes, he had to let it go – somehow. He switched the phone off and returned to the Grey case and the evidence he'd found yesterday. Erin – but Erin who? And who was she to Roseanne Grey?

He closed his eyes and slid his arm with the phone still clutched in it back under the covers. A number and a woman who didn't want to reveal her identity, a death that looked like suicide, blood samples from the same person that weren't the same, a mangled door handle – mangled from the inside, a shrink who wouldn't talk, and drugs in the bin. Oh yes. This was murder all right. *What was small has become big* ... And Alice's dark grey eyes and rich, contralto voice were starting to bug him as much as the case.

# Chapter 15: Erin

She was shivering by the time she got home, teeth chattering and flesh frozen almost to numbness. She hoped the tight-faced receptionist wouldn't hide her coat away so Beringer had no cause to contact her. It was a knife edge, this game – getting to him, establishing rules of engagement. Should she have given him more then or was what she'd said enough? She grabbed the thickest jumper she could find, and slipped it on over the flimsy chemise, pulling on jogging pants and boot socks to complement it. Then she settled in front of the wood burner, stoked it full and waited for the ice to melt from her bones.

The Jay story she'd treated him to – she'd liked that. Probably one of her best. The power of returning to childhood again; the vulnerability, the irrational fears. Everyone reacted to those. And she'd skirted more questions well. Steered him without him even realising where he'd been going. She stretched out her long legs and allowed satisfaction to flow through her. He was hooked. She knew that. He knew that. Her carefully placed remarks and he *needed* to know now. OK, maybe the coat might not work on its own, but the anticipation, the curiosity, the needing to know, would do it. And her doppelganger seemed to have gone now – gone wherever you went when you were no longer here. That made her feel relieved. Freed. She wriggled her toes. They used to do that as children – stretch out their legs, side by side, wriggle their toes and compare. Her legs were always longer and she was also always taller even though she was the younger. She smiled to herself and wriggled her toes again. And now she was both – both older and taller and there was only one of them – OK, two if you still counted Jay. A log split and crumbled into two pieces inside the wood burner. A shower of sparks sprayed against the glass panel, making her jump. *Busch-busch.* She laughed and waited for the log pieces to settle, still wriggling her toes luxuriantly. The noise repeated. *Busch-busch.* She stared into the fire. The log glowed red hot but it was static. Where was the noise coming from then? Never mind. She lay back on the rug and stared up at the ceiling. Her right side was glowing like the log – red hot. She imagined her body flickering with flames, as if she was a living fire. Now that would be impressive, but impossible, unfortunately. She would have to make do with weathering extreme cold to impress – and what else?

Her mind wandered, examining other ideas, other ways to impress, reviewing where they were at now she was freed; discharged – but still trapped. Beringer wasn't going to leave Roseanne alone. He wanted to know about Roseanne, talk about Roseanne, question about Roseanne. How much might Beringer figure out? How much had he noticed without paying attention? Now she not only needed to get him off her back, she needed to find out too. Research – research was key. She hadn't researched enough first – that had been the problem. She'd rushed in before she'd really figured out the situation. Beringer was too curious, too interested – and he felt guilty. Maybe he was also too keen to feather his own nest. He had to be kept in check, and ultimately escaped from. Maybe Jay would help with that? Jay had always been careful, a planner – precise and particular, despite the wildness other times. She'd always been precipitous one, too ready to jump. Jay would have an idea, for sure.

'What do you think, Jay?' she asked aloud. 'You plan, I execute. He's yours in exchange for leaving me be.' The response felt positive. They could come to an agreement – an accommodation. 'Then I need ideas,' she said. 'The kind of ideas Erin can execute.'

She sat up. The rosy glow on her right side had become intolerable. She swung herself round on the spot and stretched out in the opposite direction so her left side now sweltered to the log-burner's output. She dragged a cushion from the nearest chair and tucked it under her head. The position gave her a perfect view of the sweeping bay window, with its arrangement of pulleys and cords to draw the curtains. The view gave her an idea – a Jay-type of idea. Don't just tempt him, enlist him, conquer him, control him. He's never been controlled before. Give him a new experience.

'How?' she said to the ceiling.

Emulate Ro. Something simple but effective. Astound him. Who crosses a magus? In fact who wouldn't want to be a magus given the chance to – and Beringer was definitely that sort. But use trickery – not for real. That would be too risky at the moment. How then? She studied the curtain pulley. It might be possible. She sat up abruptly and crossed the room to a small desk tucked into the corner. It almost blended into the wallpaper, but for the Mac on the top of it, apple icon gleaming softly at her from its silver surround. She settled at the desk, tucking her legs underneath but kicking off the boot socks. They lay, baggy and redundant, like deflated balloons on the polished wood floor. She wriggled her toes against the cold of the wood instead, relishing the contrast – hot to cold, real to unreal. She laughed quietly to herself as she found a website with exactly what she wanted on it. She couldn't be Ro but she could be as clever. And it was so simple – a child could do it! She closed the Mac and rummaged in the desk for pen and paper, then started a list. If Beringer didn't call with her coat by this evening, she'd ring him and tell him about Ro and the accident, and why she'd really driven at the other guy. Copying … because ... that would seal it. Then it would be show time.

The same *busch-busch* noise as earlier distracted her from completing the list. A fly was beating itself against the bay window. She exclaimed with annoyance. Flies, at this time of the year? She pushed the chair away from the desk and swung her legs out from under it. The chair scraped the wooden floor. It sounded like the thrashing fly and she winced. To fly. That's what she'd always wanted as a child – one day, to simply fly away, but she couldn't, no matter how much she'd tried. It had never worked. And there was no turning back if you tried to fly and didn't – and she'd been right. There hadn't been for Jay, even though Jay had returned.

She should never have gone back there afterwards, when Beringer had left after dropping her home. It had brought it all back. Erin squeezed her hands into fists and forced the memories back down. The cat winding away from her, hiding so she'd had to abandon it – hope it would find a way out. The red and white figure on the hard, grey slabs. The smell of death … No! Not now. She'd release the fly for Ro's sake – and hers. Something should fly free, even if it wasn't either of them. She pushed the curtain away from the window and the fly crawled across the pane until it was so close to her face she could have licked it up like a lizard eating its prey. She examined it, up close – the hard-cased body, the nervously twitching limbs, the delicate blue-sheened wings. She felt Jay in her head, taunting her. The fly was almost worthless, and completely in her power whether it lived or died right now. She'd be better than Jay. She'd be magnanimous. This time. The fly rubbed its legs together as if in mock applause. She opened the window and it crawled to the edge of the pane. *Busch-busch*, like it was a salute, and then it was gone. And now for Beringer.

# Chapter 16: Beringer

Beringer shut the door thankfully on his patient. Nice woman, but exhausting – so much worry in such a small package. He was surprised she hadn't worried herself away by now – what was that saying? Frazzled to death? He flicked the intercom switch on his desk.

'Jenny, can you grab me a roll or something when you go out. I think I'd better skip lunch and get these notes written up instead.'

Her voice was tinny and sympathetic. 'Oh dear, what a pain. Of course I'll bring you something back. The usual?'

'That would be great. Just buzz me when you're back and I'll pop out rather than you disturb me – there's quite a lot to write up here and I don't want to be distracted.'

'Absolutely,' the tinny voice cut off, then resumed somewhat hesitantly. 'Oh, and I forgot to tell you earlier, there was someone from the local police on the phone just before Mrs Allen arrived, asking when you would be free later on today.'

'Who?' he tried belatedly to soften the sharpness in his voice.

'A woman PC; I think it was Atkins?'

'Oh,' he relaxed. Not the belligerent policeman from the hospital. 'Why did she want to see me?'

'Oh, it wasn't her, she was asking on behalf of her superior – something he thought you could help with. She said he'd make contact again later, so I don't suppose it's that urgent. Do you want me to ring around and find out? I'm sorry I didn't get the details, Mrs Allen arrived then and you know what she's like ...'

'Yes, I know what she's like,' he said heavily. He put the phone onto voicemail to ensure he was left alone, weighing up the likelihood whether the enquiry originated from the pushy policeman or was simply some spurious enquiry from another unconnected official. Whichever it was, it made him more convinced than ever about what he had decided to do.

He waited for the click of the outer door, indicating Jenny had left. He

102

knew she would go as soon as he mentioned missing lunch – predictable soul. Now he could sort out the Roseanne Grey file without her knowing. He counted to ten in case she'd forgotten anything and then slipped out into the main reception area and twisted his master key into the filing cabinet. Roseanne's file was still in 'current' despite his instruction. It was a paltry buff folder, filled with desultory notes, the occasional theoretical observations and no questions – until that last time. A lot of nothing to justify ongoing payment for the sessions on the NHS, more to help maintain his expensive offices than for what good he was doing the woman. Until that last session. His unease grew – how much more than he already suspected he'd overlooked had he missed? Those other red flags. Initially he'd observed a variety of issues in her – none particularly important, but the one thing he hadn't observed was fear. Anger, yes. Agitation, yes. A little paranoia even – yes. Much like everyone, ill or otherwise, walking the earth. But not fear. He'd noted and ignored it originally, but later when he'd been forced to think about it, it was odd. Paranoia and fear usually went hand in hand at some stage, and yet they hadn't seemed to with Roseanne. It had been like she had no fear. Or maybe that was what she'd wanted him to think until it was too late?

Most people would have been afraid to get back in a car after the type of crash she'd survived – and yet she'd actually been keen to get back behind the wheel as soon as she got the all-clear to drive again. Bravado? He frowned. Or sublimely indifferent to whether she lived or died? He hadn't thought about it enough at the time. Maybe he'd done what he said you should never do – assume. If you switched off fear, you switched off a number of other responses too – responses that modified behaviour. Limited it. But she was NHS, not private, even though he'd allowed her to come to his private consulting rooms. Laziness on his part, rather than have to fit in a visit to the hospital. Her consultations were of necessity limited to the basics and you didn't do much with the basics except keep notes – and switch off; switch off merely because you couldn't do much else unless the problem was dire. And it hadn't been. It hadn't been a problem at all, really. Introverted, was his main diagnosis – the kind of person that faded into nonentity, apart from the height, as Jenny had noticed. Where Erin Matthews appeared fleet of foot and as supple as a willow, Roseanne Grey had been outsized and shambling. A fat rat, as Jenny had observed, and there was pretty much where his observation of her as a woman had ended. She was large framed and long-haired. If there had been things about her he should have noticed, he'd chosen not to –

better not to, actually. Until that last time. It was that which bothered him now – as much as the possibility of what she'd done with the newly prescribed drugs.

He turned the pages of the folder. She'd first been referred to him after her accident. She still couldn't sleep and it was causing physical problems. She felt jittery. She needed to get a handle on her life now it had all changed.

'I'm different – different to everyone else. I always have been.'

Only in that you're too tall and therefore trying to hide from everyone, he'd wanted to say. Instead he'd smiled encouragingly and said what he always said.

'Of course, you're different. You're unique; we all are. Tell me what you feel is different about you, though and we'll find a way for you to reconcile yourself with it.'

'I can do things other people can't.'

'Such as?'

'Oh, you know, sometimes I think I ...'

Mentally he'd groaned, but they weren't ridiculous things she'd cited. Just vaguely narcissistic – slightly at odds with her introversion, but nothing to make her that unusual. He'd labelled her neurotic, but in much the same way as most people were neurotic about something – I can't stand spiders, I have low self-esteem, poor body image, and so on. No doubt the accident had contributed to it and she just needed to feel like someone was listening to her. The notes from that first meeting made that quite clear, and so he'd switched off and let what Erin had called the pink and fluffy psycho-babble run on auto-pilot whilst he reviewed the state of his own neuroses – the too-high mortgage, the increasing demands of his trophy girlfriend, since passed on to a competitor with more kudos than him but still wanting her pound of flesh – and the general lack of progress with everything in his life. He'd checked in periodically on where she was in her ramblings and just fielded it in time – that first time.

'... and leap tall buildings ...' He'd jerked back to concentration at that, and laughed as he assumed he was meant to.

'Superwoman,' he'd added, smiling, and paid attention for a while until her self-evaluation droned him mentally off to sleep again. She really only needed to talk to someone – like they all did who came over his threshold; the lost, the lonely and the confused, so let her talk. He was helping by simply listening, wasn't he? And after all, it was her choice to keep coming. It wasn't that often, and it wasn't as if she was paying. NHS retainers helped to maintain the façade of success, of elitism that brought the Mrs Norths and Jean Youngs of this world through the door, arriving, regular as clockwork almost every day for their fix of sycophantic sympathy. They were his baseline, but if someone more genuinely in need of his time had come along then of course he would have politely and kindly told her she was cured and the system could stop paying for her so they could replace her with a worthier recipient of his pink fluffy psycho-babble.

He sighed. And yet, he was kidding himself. One of the reasons he hadn't wanted to take note of what she said was that – like Jenny – she'd unnerved him too, when he *had* listened properly. And then there were the times he'd noticed little things that he dismissed because it was easier to; a small rearrangement of items on his desk that neither he nor she had made. A change in what he thought she was wearing even though there had been no time – or indeed, place – for her to get changed. So imperceptible that they could have just been tiny time-slips in his memory. He must have put that pencil in the drawer earlier. The cushion on the consulting couch had fallen on the floor and rolled – even though it was square – not been tossed into the corner of the room. His cufflinks – he must have forgotten to fasten them properly because he was in a rush. Or maybe he was remembering what she'd worn last time she'd been there, not seeing different clothes altogether. After all, how could he say – hand on heart – that he really remembered what she'd been wearing when even now her face was merely an indistinct mass of unruly brown hair and pasty skin. He pushed the folder away from him, like he'd pushed the niggling questions away from him then – apart from that last time. Then he hadn't been able to ignore it. Then he'd had to get involved – and got himself in the predicament he was in now. But he'd never have expected her to jump. Not her. She wasn't weak at all. She was strong.

He'd tried to dismiss the suicide as an unfortunate accident. But maybe it wasn't – like the policeman, Grant, had implied. Maybe it had even been his fault? He cupped his chin in his hand. Delusion. It had to be – on her part, or his. But he wasn't on opioids – and maybe he shouldn't ever have prescribed them for her. And then definitely not stronger ones. Damn! But nearly all near-death survivors had strange dreams and it was normal to prescribe tranquillisers for disturbed sleep. Temporary psychosis was a common feature after a spell in ITU – they even put it in the literature they sent patients home with. It was par for the course – the result of facing mortality. He sighed and toyed with the pages of the file.

In this case, though, maybe there had been something more to it after all? And now there was Erin, saying strange things about her when surely she couldn't even have known her? Or maybe what Roseanne had claimed when she first came round, and then again that last time she'd turned up for her routine appointment hadn't just been attention-seeking nonsense after all.

'Have I ever told you what I could do as a child?'

'As a child?' He'd smiled. Indulged her, as usual. There was half an hour to fill and there wasn't anything to talk about otherwise. 'What could you do as a child?'

'Fly – almost. I almost did it.'

'Fly? Like the birds? Or a butterfly,' he'd laughed as he made wing movements with his conjoined hands. 'I think we'd all like to be able to do that, wouldn't we, Roseanne? And as kids we believe we can do anything.'

She'd given him a strange look – pitying – and changed the subject. 'I like your tie. It's my favourite colour. Blue.'

He'd laughed and looked down, only to freeze with surprise. It *was* blue. But he'd put on the red one this morning. He always put on the red tie with the pink shirt. He'd never put blue and pink together – too like sugar candy for girls and battle blue for boys. It was hackneyed – clichéd. She'd smiled at his open mouth. Showing off. He'd laughed again to cover his confusion, but she knew what effect she'd had on him. He'd frowned. She'd got up to leave.

'But we've another half an hour left,' he'd said as she wafted towards the door.

'And you don't believe anything I'm saying.'

'I only said all children think they can fly. We dream about it too – it's our subconscious mind seeking expansion – to do the impossible. It's a positive sign. It means your outlook is positive.'

She laughed aloud then. 'If you knew all the positive things my mind could do, you'd be shocked.'

His attention was all hers suddenly. This wasn't mildly neurotic Roseanne; the Roseanne who sometimes surprised him but mainly because he wasn't paying enough attention to her – as he hadn't been just now. He'd felt bad. He'd not been doing his job properly, whether she appeared to need him to or not. He'd followed her to the door and put his hand on it to stop her opening it. She'd looked at him and then at his hand and he'd felt the pressure of hand against door easing, as if someone had puffed air between the two.

'There's no point me telling you anything if you don't believe me.'

'What do you want me to believe?'

'I don't know. The same things I believe, I suppose.'

'And what are they?' Every fibre of his being was straining to keep his palm flat against the door now, and the door shut – and failing.

'What I tell you.'

'Let's go and sit back down and you tell me what they are, then.' The sweat was pooling under his armpits now, beading on his forehead at his hairline. He felt giddy, sick.

'Are you all right?' she asked suddenly, smiling.

'I'm fine, fine,' he'd said, trying to sound calm and relaxed. He'd peered at her through the sweat beads dribbling down his forehead and threading their way through his eyebrows. 'Let's talk about this.'

'OK, let's sit down.' And there they were sitting again. No sweat, no tension, no blue tie.

'Have I ever told you what I could do as a child?' she was saying.

'As a child?' He'd smiled. Indulge her. There was half an hour to fill and there wasn't anything to talk about otherwise. 'What could you do as a child?'

'Fly – almost. I almost did it.' His mouth had dropped open. He'd shivered, knowing that something was wrong but not what it was.

'Why didn't you? You said "almost"?' the words had flown out of his mouth unbidden.

'I hadn't mastered it properly then. It's hard, flying,' then she'd burst out laughing. 'Oh my God, and I think you did believe me then!'

'I, I ...' he stammered. 'I don't think I'm with you.'

'No, sorry. It's a game I shouldn't play. When I was a child I was convinced I could fly because I could do so many other things, but the one thing I could never do was fly. Since the accident, it's begun to play on my mind though.'

'You've never said you've been worried about anything before?'

'Not worried, exactly, but it's something that's come back to haunt me, I suppose – that possibility.'

'Roseanne,' he'd said gently, carefully, 'You don't mean that really, do you?' He'd put on his most sympathetic, yet most quizzical expression – the one he'd spent years honing in front of the mirror so it hit just the right note for his more difficult patients; the sympathetic yet logical therapist.

She'd studied him for a while. 'I'm not crazy.'

'I didn't say for one moment you are. We just all get crazy ideas from time to time and need to talk them out. That's where I come in. Shall we talk this one through? What would you like to tell me?'

'Nothing,' she said, equally carefully. 'There's nothing to tell really – like you said, just a crazy notion.'

'One you've been having since the accident? Why didn't you say before? Let's talk it through now, shall we?'

'No, no,' she'd laughed. 'I'm fine, really I'm fine. Honestly, just tired – too much DIY probably, and dust flying around, filling my head up with nonsense. We begin and end in dust, and dust is what we have to be to start. I refuse to let her be the one that reduces me to it.'

'Her? Who is her?'

'Did I say her? I meant me. I'm fine – really, and my half hour is almost up now too. I probably need some more medication. The other stuff doesn't seem to work anymore. Is there anything stronger?'

He knew he must have looked worried. He couldn't straighten the creases from his face even though he tried. She'd never asked for more medication. She'd never rushed away before either.

'I'm not sure that …'

'I should have it? But it keeps me sane, Mr Beringer. Stops me thinking I can fly. Unless you think I can too?'

That glint to her – he'd never seen it before. Maybe she did need something stronger? Maybe he needed to be more careful with her – listen more. Who was she? Really, who was she? He didn't know – even the stories of her as a child; he hadn't recorded more than a few lines on them. He cursed himself for his complacency now.

'All right. I'll come round later – bring a new prescription. Jenny isn't here to print it off at the moment.'

'It's not necessary. I can wait until she's back.'

'I'd rather. Just to make sure.' It was out before he could stop it.

She'd opened her mouth but the protest had died in it. 'All right,' she'd said instead. 'Filled? Save me going out to find a chemist later. And maybe you'll help me hang that enormous mirror I've been meaning to get up on the wall at the bottom of the stairs too.'

'Of course.' He'd been relieved – would probably have agreed to anything right then. And he'd been as good as his word. He'd dropped by that evening. They'd hung the mirror. She'd made him a mug of coffee and chatted aimlessly whilst she waited for him to drink it. No more comments about flying or dust, or anything else out of the unusual. He'd remarked on the unusual bowl on her coffee table in the lounge for something to say. Picked it up and examined it whilst she hovered anxiously.

'It's worth a lot of money,' she'd said to explain her nervousness.

'Oh, I'm sorry.' He'd felt like an oaf, turned it back over from the EM marking on the base and set it carefully on the table next to the newspaper with the numbers scribbled along one edge. 111 they'd ended in – like a row of exclamation marks. She'd put the pot firmly on top of the newspaper and ushered him politely away from it. His unease had matched hers, yet there was nothing to pin it on. Nothing unbalanced. She just didn't want him there – and he deserved that, but just to salve his conscience, he said again, 'And you're sure you're all right? Nothing else you want to talk about?'

She'd studied him, close-faced, cool. He deserved that too. It made him feel clumsier still. This awkward woman with the grip of iron and quiet detachment suddenly had him completely off-balance. Even her rounded cheeks and smooth face had looked more angular tonight. He coloured up, just thinking about it – ridiculous though it was. The shrink and the young woman in her home; anyone who wanted to destroy his reputation could make mountains of that, but he hadn't been attracted to her. Not at all. There'd been something about her – like she might invade him, suffocate him– and that had made him keep his distance too, not look her in the eye, not allow there to be any real personal contact. And now her face was a blur, as if someone had smudged the image.

'No. I'm fine – especially now I have my new pills.' They'd reached the front door by now. The hall was gloomier than the lounge, the bare light reflecting harshly in the monstrous mirror he'd helped her manhandle onto the wall. She'd cut her hair. He'd only noticed that literally as he was about to leave.

'The pills – yes, remember they must be taken exactly as prescribed, though? They do have side effects if taken wrongly, and you're out here on your own.' He'd repeated the instructions of earlier.

'I understand. It'll be fine. I'll be fine.' She started to close the front door on him and so he'd left, virtually ejected. He'd done all he could. All she'd asked him to do. All he should have done. He closed the file.

Except stop her flying.

The file was slimmer still by the time he slipped out to reception and slid it back into the filing cabinet. He rolled the removed pages into a tube and stuffed them in his pocket. They banged against his hip. He should shred them – yes, that would be the best thing to do with them. No evidence at all then. He'd use the shredder in his own room – the one he used for the confidential reports even Jenny wasn't allowed to see. As he locked the cabinet, he noticed the coat on the coat rack. Erin's. He'd better ring her too, and arrange to return it. That, however, was better done from Jenny's extension. More formal that way. He returned to his office and collected the file he was collating for Erin Matthews. The first page inside contained her personal details, address, email address, phone number, mobile phone number. He grabbed a piece of paper from Jenny's workstation and began to jot the number down. He faltered when he got to the last three digits. They signalled at him like exclamation marks. 111. Outside in the hallway, footsteps indicated Jenny had returned. Damn! The tube of pages he'd extracted from the Grey file still banged against his hip. No time to shred them now. He stuffed them in the back of the file for Erin Matthews. No-one would be looking at that for the moment and the only place it was going now was into the dormant range. He'd come back to it later and shred the hidden pages when Jenny wasn't around. In the meantime, there was something else he needed to do now. He pushed the file back into the filing range and relocked the cabinet without making the call. He'd only just arranged the file and the sheaf of notes he'd made on Mrs North's free-association when Jenny called.

'Lunch is served,' she announced gaily through the intercom.

'Thanks, I'll be out shortly,' he replied, then switched the unit to dormant. He pulled his mobile phone from his jacket pocket and dialled.

'I have your coat here, and a question. How did Roseanne Grey have your phone number?'

The reply came back as smoothly as he'd expected – but not containing what he'd expected.

'Because we're the same – she and me. I told you that, but you didn't listen – obviously. We can do the same things – ever since I died.'

'But you're not the same, and it's Roseanne who is dead. You're very much alive.'

Her throaty laugh wound down the phone at him. 'Oh, yes, but I'm a Lady Lazarus, aren't I? Defeated death. Come over when you can and I'll show you what I can do.'

She made no sense, no sense at all, but the sweat was pooling under his armpits and beading on his forehead at his hairline as he watched 'Erin Matthews' fade from the phone's screen, exactly as it had when Roseanne Grey had held the door shut without touching it.

# Chapter 17: Grant

Josie had got a trace on the phone number. It belonged to a woman. Erin Matthews. She'd also enquired when Beringer would be around for him to go and talk to again, but hadn't had much luck with the receptionist. Grant would have to follow that up for himself. Her voice was sing-song and he half-listened as he went over the evening with Alice and then drifted onto the baseball bat death. He'd had another idea about that since last night – but he needed to look in the evidence bundle to check it out. He'd managed to place one or two artful phone calls, including to one of the victim's neighbours first thing this morning before Josie had appeared, but the best information was always obtained when you were eye to eye, toe to toe. That would require a visit to the area, including maybe having to go so far as pretending he was actually there on official enquiries, not private zeal.

'Potter extraordinaire, design guru, very private, lives locally now but only moved here about four months ago, just before a debut exhibition someone arranged for her at local gallery. No known close family, no suspect friends, one relationship – ended, rumoured by someone in the local press to have broken up a short while ago with no comment on either side. Probably the person who arranged the show for her though.' Josie was still sing-songing. It reminded him of children chanting their times tables. What did they get out of that? Two times two makes four, three times three makes nine – he should be able to make ten or more out of this but the thing that he felt should add up in his head just wouldn't. What was it? Damn! 'She was in an accident recently too. Possible dangerous driving. Traffic are still considering whether to prosecute or simply put points on her licence. It will depend on the medical report, I guess – and what they turn up about the other guy.'

'The other guy?'

Grant had visions of a woman partying with two men in a small car as it careered across the highway.

'The one she bounced off. He was on his phone at the time. Name of Hubert Ffynes.'

Grant gave a shout of laughter. 'Ffynes? He'll be more than that if they can prove it. What kind of name is that anyway? Rich bastard I suppose, and that's why it's on hold?'

'Umm, that and the fact that it was recommended we have a psych's report since Erin Matthews was treated for head injuries. Can't prosecute a crazy, Guv.'

'Really? So we potentially have an "in" on her?' Grant asked, perking up. 'You talk, we don't prosecute. Interesting.'

'Well, probably wouldn't put it quite that strong, Guv. I mean professional ethics and all that.'

'Who was talking about professional ethics? I was talking about leverage.'

'Men.' Carly had come in at the tail end of Josie's report. 'You think every woman can be manipulated. I suppose you think she would sleep with someone for a clean bill, too?' She looked at Grant as if he was the scum of the earth. 'We aren't all like that, you know.'

Grant sighed. Women's lib at its finest. 'That wasn't quite what I meant,' he replied. 'Do you need me for something?'

'No,' she said, 'just being sociable.' She flounced out, slamming the door behind her.

He and Josie exchanged glances. 'Do you get on with her?' he asked impetuously.

'Er, OK, but then I'm a woman.'

Grant stared at her. And what the hell did that mean? He gave up. Easier to interview a slimy shrink than work out office politics at this rate. Alice would understand, but he couldn't keep asking her about everything. She might get the wrong idea.

'I need to go and see Beringer again – see if I can prise Roseanne Grey's file out of him, and then I'd better interview this Erin Matthews to see how she knew Roseanne Grey. Can you change the status of the case to active/ suspicious, Josie?

'Is it, Guv?'

'Well, someone had access – or escape. With the door handle evidence and the cat finding its way back in, it's not simply a straight suicide any more, is it?'

'No-o,' she looked uncertain. 'Whose authority do I cite for the change?'

'Mine,' he retorted, chin jutting pugnaciously.

'OK,' she said and slid behind her PC screen. 'I'm on it. And the other cases?'

'What other cases?' She gestured to the pile of buff folders still sitting precariously on the edge of his desk from yesterday. 'Oh, those. I'll have a look at them later.' He dragged his coat from the rickety coat stand by the door. It rocked but remained upright – just. Much like him and his team at the moment, Grant reflected. 'I'll be back in a couple of hours,' he added as he slipped his injured hand cautiously into the sleeve of his coat. 'I'll tell Fat Fa- ... I'll tell Carly to pass my calls to you for the moment.'

He could see Josie's head bobbing up and down behind the PC screen. Whether she was nodding or laughing at the name slip, he didn't bother to find out. Carly gave him a sour look as he delivered his instructions on his way out.

'Careful with that hand,' she called after him. 'Don't want to be investigating yourself for dangerous driving too.'

'Sod off,' he said under his breath as he tramped down the stairs and into reception where a man and a woman were arguing the toss with the desk sergeant as referee. Another woman in a dark grey coat and fur hat was waiting quietly for them to finish. The desk sergeant looked fed up and exasperated too, despite the festive tinsel looped above his head and around the reception desk frontage. It fluttered cheerfully as Grant opened the door and let in the morning's dose of the icy winds left over from last night.

'Shut the b- door,' someone called after him. If he could have, he would have given them the finger, but it made his injured hand hurt to flex it and he was carrying the Grey folder in his other hand. He made do with a mental image of it. Season of goodwill? Pah! The only goodwill he'd experienced recently had been Alice's.

Beringer's offices were as expected – minimalistic yet luxurious. Seats covered in leather – imitation, but *expensive* imitation leather. Perfectly groomed, bored secretary, nose in the air. Greeting the privileged amongst the patients with a snooty smile and viewing the likes of Grant with distaste. She gestured to a plush cream seat directly under her nose whilst she buzzed Beringer.

'There's a gentleman here to see you,' she said, emphasising gentle as if he wasn't. Beringer obviously queried what kind of gentleman. 'An official gentleman,' she elaborated, still looking down her nose at him.

114

The woman sitting in the far corner, bag pulled in tightly to her camel coloured coat, eyed him suspiciously too.

Sod this for a game of soldiers, Grant thought. 'Detective Sergeant Grant, CID,' he announced loudly for the benefit of the camel-coat woman and the snooty receptionist. 'To see *Mister* Beringer about a suspicious death of one of his patients.'

The receptionist made a shushing gesture at him, and said, 'He can only see you for a few minutes, Mr Grant, but you'll have to wait. He has patients, you understand?'

'But I don't,' Grant quipped back. 'Have patience, that is. I have a suspicious death to look into, so maybe he could spare his few minutes now and get me off his back?'

The receptionist glared at him.

'I could come back another time,' camel-coat woman offered timidly.

'Not if you don't mind waiting ten minutes,' Grant suggested magnanimously. 'That's all I need. Thanks.' He stood up and moved towards the consulting room door. His mother had said if you don't ask, you don't get, but sometimes asking wasn't enough. He'd found that out later.

The receptionist buzzed frantically and then jumped up to follow him through the door. Beringer was sitting at an expansive desk that looked as if was made of polished granite. It was completely bare apart from the combined phone and intercom device he and the receptionist had been playing footsie with, a pad and a pen. The pad was open, with some scrawled words on the top page.

'I'm so sorry, Mr Beringer, he just barged past me.'

Grant held out his warrant card and then shoved it in his pocket to replace it with his hand, outstretched, to shake.

'Good of you to spare me these few minutes, Mr Beringer,' he out-descanted the receptionist. 'And nice to see you again. This seems to be becoming a habit, doesn't it? I won't take too much of your valuable time but there is the little matter of the suspicious death of one of your patients I'm looking into, so your help would be much appreciated.'

Full marks to Beringer, he swung into action as if he'd been planning this all morning. 'Detective Sergeant Grant, of course. Please come in and take a seat. Jenny can you square it with Mrs North for us to be a few minutes late starting? Tell her we'll make up the other end by over-running into lunch.'

'Of course,' she said, throwing Grant another look of disgust. Grant gave her the thumbs up and she swept out, shutting the door behind her with a sharp click.

'So Detective Sergeant Grant, you've made it to the inner sanctum, and now how can I help. A suspicious death, you say?'

'Roseanne Grey, suspicious death just under four weeks ago. You remember?'

'Uh, I remember – of course. But I thought she was a suicide?'

'I did say at the time, if you remember, *sir,* that there were other things to consider. What more can you tell me about her?'

'Not a great deal, I'm afraid, Detective Sergeant. Patient confidentiality, you understand.' Beringer shrugged, his face bland and charming. 'Like I said then.'

'Ah, yes; the old patient confidentiality issue again. But that doesn't cover everything. You can at least tell me why Roseanne was seeing you, even if you can't tell me precisely what you talked about together?'

'Well, that's where it's difficult too. I mean, to tell you why she was seeing me, I'd have to refer to what we talked about. Catch 22.'

'But you can at least confirm that she was suffering from some form of mental disorder?'

'I'm afraid not or I would be telling you she was ill, and then we're back to square one. All I can confirm is that she came to see me.'

Grant leant back in his chair, frowning. This guy was good, but why was he being so good? If the woman had been referred to a shrink, there was obviously something wrong with her mentally. So why not admit that? Beringer leaned back in his seat, mirroring Grant. Stand-off.

'OK, so what if I told you this is no longer simply a case of suicide. There is evidence to suggest something more sinister. Can you elaborate more on her state of mind now?'

Beringer shook his head. 'I'm sorry, Detective Sergeant, 'but it makes no difference to my professional commitment to patient confidentiality. Out of interest though, can you tell me why her death is no longer thought to be suicide? If I can, I will add anything I know to assist with that.'

Oho! So he did know something. Grant sat forward involuntarily, trying not to narrow his eyes or let his body language show his interest – but of course he'd already failed in that by sitting forward. Shit! However, Beringer had edged forward a fraction too.

'The bedroom door handle was forced.'

'Forced?' Beringer sat up straight and Grant had the distinct impression that was involuntarily as well.

'Yes, but from the inside. The inner handle was crushed so that the whole thing fell apart.'

'From the inside?' Beringer frowned. 'I don't understand. How does that make it a suspicious death? Surely it would need to be forced from the outside for someone to be breaking in to threaten her – which is what I assume you must be implying?'

'Or she was trying to get away from someone – break out not in. The window was the only escape in the end.'

Beringer sat back again. He looked surprised. Behind him the expanse of glass that looked out over the spreading landscape gave the impression of an ice sheet, even though it was warm in the consulting room. The moody skies, still threatening the long-awaited Christmas snow, had gathered momentum since last night, clouds swelling from powder-puff white to succulent purple, even though the wind had finally calmed. The calm was more intimidating than the storm, to Grant's mind. What was to come? It hadn't been good so far.

'I don't know what to say,' Beringer said at last. 'You're saying that she was trying to escape someone, and that was what caused her to jump?' Now he looked worried, despite his urbane cool. Grant sucked in his breath. The guy knew something. He'd been surprised – shocked even, but now he thought he knew something.

'Maybe? That's why I'm here – asking for your help.'

The clouds outside rolled across the sun and Beringer's face darkened with the gloom of the day. 'I'm afraid I still can't help,' he said at length. There's nothing I can add to that.'

Grant leaned back into his chair. 'And the cat must have been let back in by someone after we'd checked the whole place over, but no one had a key – unless you did?'

'Me?' Beringer laughed dismissively. It sounded false. 'Why would I have a key? I was her therapist, not her lover.'

'An odd comparison to make,' Grant said lightly.

'Extremes, that's all. I wasn't her lover, Detective Sergeant Grant. I can assure you of that. I used the analogy simply to emphasise the unlikelihood of my having a key to her home.' From the look on his face, Grant believed him – but even that was an extreme reaction.

'But you had been there?' he pressed. Beringer's hesitation was barely disguised.

'Only once. Delivering medication – and I shouldn't even have told you that.'

'Oh, yes. The happy pills. So she *was* being treated for something then? Depression? Schizophrenia? Paranoia?' A tiny tic twitched at the corner of Beringer's mouth. '*Paranoia*,' Grant repeated. He cocked his head at Beringer in thanks.

'I didn't say that.'

'No need. So she was paranoid about something – in your opinion? Or someone?'

'That's really as far as I can go, Detective Sergeant Grant.' There was something in his eyes – something Grant couldn't read. Was it fear?

'Or afraid?'

Beringer got up. 'My next patient ...' he began. Grant remained where he was. No, it wasn't just fear.

'Is calling, I know. But so is the truth. Aren't you going to answer its call, with your professional responsibilities?'

'The truth is your calling, Detective Sergeant. Mine is to see my patients on time.'

'I would like to see her notes. What she was afraid of.'

'That's impossible. They're confidential.' That look again. Anxiety would be a better description for it, but he was more than worried – he was afraid too. There must be something in those notes, but he was buggered if he was going to get them – damn! He'd have to get it re-categorised to murder to get a warrant for them, and without a motive, or proof that Roseanne Grey was pushed rather than jumped, that wasn't going to happen. It had been risky telling Josie to write it up as a suspicious death. He used the phrase anyway.

'This is a suspicious death, and she was your patient. Don't you want to serve the cause of justice?'

'Get a warrant. We'll both be serving the cause of justice with that.' Beringer walked to the door and opened it. 'Goodbye, Detective Sergeant.' He waited, handsome face rigid and unsmiling. Reluctantly, Grant stood up; bloody, but not bowed. Beringer knew he couldn't get a warrant on what he had, but he could rattle him a little more. He walked to the door and stood face to face with Beringer, nodding gently as if he knew something Beringer didn't.

'Interesting,' he said. 'Thank you. Food for thought – what you've told me.'

'What have I told you?' Beringer looked confused. Grant smiled smugly and pushed past him, leaving the psychiatrist staring after him. He hadn't got fuck-all on the bloke or anyone else, but it was all about belief, wasn't it?

By the time he got downstairs, the brief satisfaction that winding Beringer up had given him had dissipated. He'd avoided the lift – as plush as the offices – and taken the stairs. Thinking time. And now he was frustrated. Everything was bloody frustrating; this death, Stacey, Carly presiding over the office as if she owned it – and him, Alice and her dark grey eyes flecked with gold like someone had sprinkled star dust in them … He stopped mid-step. Where the fuck was he heading with any of it – and more to the point, with the route he was currently taking? He'd left his car round the corner from Beringer's offices and here he was walking in the opposite direction, collar turned up against the chill and his own eyes firmly fixed on his trudging feet and the leaden pavement. He looked along the length of the road and realised exactly where he was heading – to Alice's.

'Damn!' he swore gently under his breath. It puffed out in front of him; an icy cloud of desire dampened by dissatisfaction. He needed to get himself back in hand, focused, but maybe a walk would be good anyway – time to clear his head before the joys of Carly and the secretly amused Josie. And Steve – if he ever returned from his everlasting nappy-buying quest. It was rumoured he had been in – but only by Josie, and then in a vague, non-specific way so that 'in' could have been in relation to 'some time' but not when precisely. That was what kids did to you. That was why he'd said no to them to Stacey – that and the fact that he didn't feel sufficiently in control of his own life to be responsible for a kid's too. As for Archie – he'd forgotten what his wingman looked like since the bloody case he was giving evidence for was dragging on so long. Or maybe Archie was dragging it out so long to avoid the pile of crap the Super had been generous enough to land on them. He trudged past the entrance to Alice's neat close, on towards the part of the city that Stacey had moved to – the arty-farty end. How could anyone do that to a door handle? He'd told Alice that Beringer could have forced it, but he couldn't. Not even Superman – or some fantasy creation out of one of the plays Stacey's arty-farty replacement wrote – could do that to a door handle; a brass door handle at that – solid, almost. And even if there was someone who could do it, what was it about Roseanne Grey that would make them want to? Or want to push her out of a window. What did she know? What threat had she been to them? Or herself?

The little voice niggled at him. He stopped to consider what it was saying. He was in the middle of the railway bridge, looking down the tracks. Unexpectedly, the sun had come out – edging past the line of storm clouds to throw a feeble late winter glow along the tracks so they glistened like silver. They meandered into the distance, abandoned, disused – until rush hour. Then the trains would rumble through with the monotony of a Sunday evening, disembowelling themselves in the station as their passengers spilled from their guts and continued on home to their neat little lives full of wives and kids and evening TV – the kind of life he'd spurned. Maybe if he hadn't, Stacey would still be there now, polishing the already polished furniture, planning tea, looking up what was on the TV later, waiting for him. He scowled and imagined instead what it must have been like for Roseanne Grey, perched on the window ledge, waiting to throw herself – or be thrown – out towards the hard, unwelcoming ground. He leaned as far over the edge of the railway bridge as he dared, relishing the sense of vertigo staring straight down gave him, putting all of himself in Roseanne's head and –

'Are you really going to do it?'

He pulled himself back upright and swung round. There was no-one behind him.

'What the fuck?'

'Because you can't fly, you know.' The woman was the other side of the bridge, the sun behind her. A long thing shadow against the sun. 'You don't know how,' she added. 'You don't know how because you haven't been dust yet. We begin and end as dust, but you can't be dust until you're ready.' Then she was gone.

He stood on the bridge and stared at the empty space where she'd been standing. He hadn't imagined it – had he? Was he going mad now? Paranoid like Roseanne? That gave him an idea. He pulled his phone out of his pocket. There was a new text showing on it.

'Tetanus,' it said. Alice. He grinned. No, not mad – not that sort of mad anyway. He speed-dialled.

'Josie?'

'Yes, Guv?'

'Can you do something for me?'

'Now? I'm right in the middle of all those stats you wanted me to enter and then I'm going to get my hair done because Mac's taking me to his Christmas do and – '

'No, no – when you have a moment.' He remembered Alice's admonition to remember that Josie was a woman as well as his junior. 'Get your hair done – get Steve's done as well if he shows up, but by tomorrow could you get hold of Roseanne Grey's phone records and see when she rang that Erin number and the duration of the calls.'

'Oh, I can tell you that already, Guv. Never. But ask me the question the other way round – how many times did the Matthews number call Roseanne Grey?'

'Go on,' he smiled. She might secretly laugh at him but she was a smart girl – had got there way before him this time.

'Off the page. So what the hell is that about?'

'What the hell, indeed. I need to speak to this Erin Matthews. She's got some explaining to do, I reckon.' He rang off and tucked his phone back in his pocket. Tetanus and an idea – that was what was next – via a detour past the arty-farty area, just in case. It couldn't do any harm to see if Stacey was enjoying tea and TV in her new pad, or whether that was palling yet, even if it did feel a bit like an addict needing a fix. A little of what was bad for you sometimes did you good.

# Chapter 18: Roseanne

Of course, I never intended it to turn out like this. Not originally. It was expediency. How else could I escape – because in the end that was all I wanted to do? Be free. When I was a child, I always imagined life would be one long game. And it has been, just not the kind I anticipated then. There was always Erin, holding me back – and Jay, urging me on. Oh, to be free of both of them – and one day I would be. That was always a vow to myself.

# Chapter 19: Erin

She turned off the TV. The appeal on the local news was the same as the one they'd run on the radio. Only a small appeal but, nevertheless, it was annoying. Anyone who'd known the deceased, that sort of thing. Well no one had known her recently and there was nothing to connect them, other than the opening night at the exhibition and the little that Beringer knew, but he didn't know that. Anyway – what could he say? They'd either laugh at him or charge him if he told them what he knew. The only problem with him was if he felt the weight of pressure from the appeal or his conscience, but what she had planned should deal with both possibilities.

She reviewed the things she'd collected up ready for his arrival. She'd do Ro proud with them. They'd even give Ro's real life performance a run for its money – but not for real of course. That had been the one thing Jay had taunted them with that was fair – that Ro always had over Erin. Ro could do it all for real. Erin had to cheat. She had to be true to life. The risk was too great that she'd do more than she should otherwise. Erin touched the polystyrene cup lightly with her fingertips. Static. It would cling to them and move if you'd already rubbed it hard enough beforehand – psychic trickery! Or magic, however you wanted to describe it. It depended on the onlooker. If you wanted to believe you did. Ro could do it without even touching the cup though. No static, no magic, no trickery. She could make the cup move. It had been her first party trick as a kid. She'd progressed a long way from there.

Erin flicked the cup over with her forefinger.

But Ro had almost always held back on the real deal. And eventually it had been too risky to try anything extreme after that fiasco when she was fourteen, especially with the old witch next door watching like a hawk. Her ankles were always a problem after that anyway. She paused, the dark grey concrete ground and the flailing arms as she fell helplessly towards it confusing her for a moment. She shook her head to clear it.

But now was about to be show time. Beringer had known about the phone number – although how, she couldn't even begin to imagine. How the hell had he known about the phone number? Could he even have been the one who'd rung her? That disembodied voice that had informed her he'd got her number from Roseanne – crap! How would that have happened? She searched her memory for clues. No, it couldn't have happened. And yet someone had the phone number, and apparently via Roseanne? The only logical suspect was Beringer. Even more reason for today's little sideshow.

Erin got up and paced the room, straightening a cushion here, twitching the corner of the curtain into place, despite it not being disarranged. She lingered by the window, peering down into the street. No cars. She bit her fingernail, then consciously laced her fingers together to stop herself. These long elegant talons had taken all of the time since the accident to grow. He'd said he'd be here in half an hour. That was an hour ago. She hated tardiness. Ro had always been late but it was a bad habit. Erin had different habits. At the exhibition, it hadn't mattered. People were coming and going all evening – and Ro hadn't been expected to make an appearance there. Safety in numbers – out in the open. She'd been barely recognisable too – a bloated version of her former self under the shapeless clothes, blue veined shadows under sleepless eyes, hastily covered with make-up, hair lank and lifeless, hanging like Medusa's snakes, not Ro's usual bouncing curls.

'What have you done to yourself?' she'd asked, sickened and yet exultant too.

'I had an accident,' Ro said.

'Intentional?'

'No, of course not!'

'Oh. Why not? It's the kind of thing you could do to test it out.'

'Oh, my God! Why did I come?' Ro shoved her hands deep into her pockets and hunched her shoulders. 'I thought you might be different after all these years, but you're just the same.'

'And so are you. The question is, what are you doing about it?' Ro had turned to go. 'No, don't please – let's talk.' She grabbed Ro's hand and held it between hers. They'd stayed like that; one pair smooth and unlined, the other criss-crossed with a network of signs and portents until she'd been sure Jay wasn't listening.

'For God's sake. Can't you leave it for once?' Ro was rebellious – challenging. She couldn't remember Ro ever really challenging before. 'I came to see you because it had been too long. Or maybe not long enough.' She'd started to pull away – to melt back into the crowd, be lost again.

'Oh no, you don't do that to me twice. There's no escape now you've shown yourself again.' She'd held on, her grip harder than the other's struggle to escape. 'We need to talk.'

'No, we don't. This was a mistake. I shouldn't have come. It was only because of the article in the paper and you looked so different – fulfilled. I thought *we* could be different too.'

'We can be. Don't go. Have a look round my exhibition and we'll talk when everyone's gone.' She'd started to pull Ro towards the series of stands at the entrance to the gallery. 'Which pot do you like best? Tell me. It matters a lot to me – your opinion.'

She'd weakened. It had been written all over her face. 'All right,' Ro paused. 'That one – the big oval one.' She'd pointed to the centrepiece of the exhibition – the most expensive one; small price for keeping her there. It didn't matter that she knew it had been picked purely because it was the centrepiece and without it there would be no exhibition.

'It's yours then – it's my show piece. It could sell for thousands but it's yours. That's how important it is we talk. Can we? I'm worried about you – especially the way you look at the moment.'

'I'm fine. Don't interfere.'

'I have to, Ro. I have to. Please?'

It had been grudging, but they had talked – long enough to find out her new name and get her phone number from the guest book.

She slammed her fist against the glass and it shivered. She shouldn't have told her about the accident, or what it had enabled her to do. But they had the same genetics. Why hadn't it worked? Why hadn't she flown instead of fallen? And why hadn't the falling got rid of Jay?

'Because you didn't want it to,' he whispered at the back of her mind. 'Because I'm strong where you're weak. I am control, and you need me.'

# Chapter 20: Grant

Grant crossed the railway bridge and stood in the spot the woman had stood in – or so he thought. It was muddy, but the mud was crisp and rigid. *Earth stood hard as iron.* He grunted, the carol creating ridges of childhood memories in his head. Below him the railway tracks streamed off into the distance like two frozen rivers – *water like a stone.* Yes, it was the bloody bleak midwinter today, even with the brief boost the sun appearing through the clouds had given the day. He hated the winter – bare trees, bare skies, bare life. He preferred bare legs and bright sunshine. Give him summer any day. He examined the ground nevertheless, in case the hard ridges of mud had been trampled, their crests crumbled by careless feet. They hadn't. He scratched his head. No one had been there. Maybe he *was* going mad? Or maybe the whole world was going mad? He kicked the pleat of mud nearest him, still bearing the imprint of a bicycle tread in its valley.

The route back to the car took him right past Stacey's new place – that's what he told himself, anyway. Of course, he could have followed a different complex of streets and pathways but why not go the most direct route? Or almost the most direct route. He passed the front door slowly; dead slowly, glancing surreptitiously at the name plate under the bell. The front door opened straight onto the street, straight into his life. The name plate said Roger Jones, MA Cantab. Pretentious asshole. No Stacey Grant there yet then – not given the full seal of approval? His lip curled appreciatively at that – the idea of Stacey having to qualify and maybe failing, coming back to him, sorry-eyed and submissive. Forget it, his more pragmatic self said. It's a pipe dream and you don't smoke. Ha! And you're becoming obsessive about her.

Obsessive? Sod that for a game of soldiers. No way was he obsessive. How did you become obsessive, anyway? And why was this Erin person so obsessed with Roseanne Grey that she rung her 'off the page' as Josie had put it? How did anyone become that obsessed with anyone else? He found, with surprise, that instead of continuing to the end of the road, he'd crossed over and was on the opposite side of the road to the glossy black front door with its Roger Jones, MA Cantab name plate. Bloody good job too because the glossy black door was swinging inwards and a long leg in a high-heeled stiletto boot was emerging from it, followed by the rest of Stacey. Christ! Since when had she dressed like that? She'd always said those boots looked like tart boots. Roger Jones clearly didn't think so, and neither did Stacey now. He was right behind her, hand strategically placed over her left arse cheek and squeezing it. She turned and smiled up at him, coy, before letting her gaze swing outwards along the road, encompassing it in one wide sweep that spotted Grant, pinned him to the spot like a moth pinned to a display board, and then stopped there. Her mouth opened in an 'ooh' and she froze.

'Fuck!' Grant said under his breath, swiftly turning his back on them. He could still see their reflection in the shop window he pretended to be intently interested in though. Jones was looking across at him too now. Stacey must have pointed him out. Grant's stomach gurgled and pushed the meagre contents of breakfast – a stale cheese roll he'd found half-eaten in the dash on the passenger side of his car – towards his throat. Combined with the excess of red wine from the previous night the pH balance of his gut was way over the upper acid range already, burning a hole into his chest so his heart could be seared too. He stared at the reflection in the shop window, breath held like a child with hiccups, willing himself not to throw up or do anything else equally embarrassing. Jones and Stacey consulted as they stood on the pavement outside the burnished front – the entry to the pleasure palace – then Jones linked arms with her and swung her away with him. They marched, almost matching leg for leg, step for step as they devoured the road, heading in the direction of the railway bridge. Grant let his breath out in a long, slow draught ending in a sour belch. Stacey must have gone bionic to keep the pace up in those heels. The semi-digested wine-cheese roll aftertaste stayed in his mouth alongside the bitter tang of Stacey and Jones walking away. He grunted and swallowed hard. Time to get back to work. He shoved his hands deep in his pockets, ignoring the dull ache contact with the rough seam of his pocket set up in his injured hand again, and made his way back to his car.

Josie was full of the joys of the season back at the station. The tinsel from downstairs had made its way upstairs as well now, winding round the stair rail and through the door to his team's office. She and fat Fanny

Adams Carly were making paper chains when Grant arrived, licking the ends of the brightly coloured strips of paper and giggling like schoolgirls. His PC monitor and desk had already been garlanded and a sprig of mistletoe was hanging on a long string directly above his chair.

'Oh,' Josie said guiltily as he stomped through the outer office and into the inner sanctum. Carly paused mid-lick, a red sliver of paper chain hanging from her tongue. She looked like an overweight spaniel panting at him with her carefully tousled hair style and too-long false lashes.

'We're brightening the place up,' she said, removing the red strip from her tongue and eyeing him belligerently. 'Everyone else has already recognised it's the season to be jolly except you, but it's not our fault if your wife has run off with another bloke.'

'Carly!' Josie cautioned, eyes wide and mouth pulled into a creditable version of the frog from the wide-mouthed frog joke Grant always used to tell in the old days – when he wasn't a morose, miserable bastard.

'Well, you said it,' she countered, before collecting up a handful of the paper strips and flouncing off into the outer office. 'I'll carry on at my desk,' she added, outstaring Grant. 'Then you can't say I'm not working.'

'Bloody hell!' was all he could muster, amazement robbing him of the rest of his known vocabulary. The paper chain ringing his PC monitor fell off in sympathy, landing in a trail of dead ends and curling edges.

'Oh God, Guv – I'm sorry. I didn't say it like that. I just said we could do with a bit of livening up since it was almost Christmas and you were so down in the mouth since Mrs Grant, well, you know. It was meant to cheer you up, not piss you off. They've even got them up in Forensics – well, not in the lab but in the offices, so – '

'Bloody hell,' he repeated, then burst out laughing. He pulled the limp festoon from the base of the monitor. 'You're going to have to do better than this, then. Never could abide paper chains. They look like shit. Haven't we got any money left in the kitty from last year to get some bling?'

Josie dropped her handful of paper strips in the bin, and grinned at him. 'Glad to have to you back, Guv,' she said. 'There's a tenner in the coffee tin, or thereabouts.'

'Then get something decent for God's sake.'

'Right on it!' she announced, hands on hips, 'Oh, but before I go, I've got something else that might make you smile. A link.'

'A link?'

'Yes, between someone who was also in a RTA recently and being treated by your Mr Beringer. Better still …' She looked smug.

'Better still?'

'Is the name. Our mystery caller, Erin Matthews. Admitted a few days after Roseanne Grey jumped.'

'Of course, she was!' Grant almost choked on his own hubris at not putting two and two together, fact-wise. His mind must be going. Too much booze. He could even picture the name as it was written up in the whiteboard above the nurse's station, and the trim little nurse writing it as he watched. 'He was treating both of them. I already knew that! Dammit! I knew that bastard was up to his neck in this!' Grant thumped the desk and the mistletoe landed in the middle of it. The drawing pin holding the string into the ceiling pinged down next to it, bouncing twice and ending, point down on the list of phone extensions Grant kept tucked under his phone because he was useless at remembering numbers, except one – or maybe two now Alice had told him hers. The point was touching the extension for Forensics right now. He smiled. That was why he'd known Beringer had something to do with it, whatever Alice said. A reminder to trust his copper's gut – and not to forget to pull even the most apparently insignificant facts together. 'Go get your bling,' he added to Josie, shoving a twenty pound note at her. 'I've got some links to forge –and they're not paper ones.'

Josie's laughter trailed behind her as she exited. Grant slammed the connecting door shut on Carly before she could say anything to object. Her desk was littered with slips of paper like a rainbow that had been chopped into pieces. He smiled grimly, thoughts of how he might chop her into little pieces at her next appraisal, spoiling the magnanimity of his gesture to Josie, but who cared? It might be the season of goodwill to all men that didn't have to include all women – two in particular.

He picked up the phone and dialled Alice's extension. It was engaged. Suddenly he felt as deflated as the collapsed paper chain. He pushed the mistletoe across the desk and stuck the drawing pin in the notice board on the desk behind him. The office was a lurid mix of monochrome furniture and multihued paper. It unsettled him. It unsettled him being unable to tell Alice about the development with Beringer too, even though he didn't *need* to tell her. He didn't need to tell Alice anything. But he wanted to. Dammit! He pushed his chair back and stood up decisively, pocketing the mistletoe. He'd take the spirit of goodwill to Forensics.

Alice was just putting the phone down when he barged in, grinning expansively. He plonked down in the seat next to her workstation and laid the sprig of mistletoe and the Roseanne Grey folder with Josie's new bit of information on its surface.

'Season of goodwill,' he said, 'and for catching out lying shrinks who –'

She interrupted him with, 'Stacey called me just now. She said you're stalking her.'

He hadn't noticed until then how quiet it was in the Forensics lab. Alice's accusation seemed to echo around it, bouncing off all four white-tiled walls at him.

'Stalking her? Christ – how am I stalking her? I'm here. Talking to you.'

'You weren't just over an hour ago.'

I was on my way here. I'd been walking and thinking.'

'Thinking, or thinking about interfering?' she asked. Her eyes didn't look warm today. They looked steely – the same colour as the slab she dissected bodies on.

'Observing, just observing. Not interfering. Not stalking – just observing.'

'In that case, you observe too much and live too little, Darwin. Live a little more.'

'How do I do that?' he fiddled disconsolately with the mistletoe. It seemed to have wilted since he'd picked it up off his desk. One of the milky-white berries had fallen off and lay forlorn and hopeless on the smooth grey worktop. Alice smiled suddenly – that enigmatic smile that said she knew a secret but wasn't sharing it. And he hadn't been stalking. Bloody Stacey and her tart boots. He had a good mind to ring her up right here and now and tear her off a strip for shopping him to Alice … His racing mind stopped, frozen in mid-thought. Shopping him? That would imply he *had* been guilty of something. 'Anyway – forget that for the moment. There's a double link to Beringer now.' He pushed the folder towards her. 'This woman, Erin Matthews, was in the same hospital as Roseanne, Roseanne had her number and her pot, and Erin kept calling Roseanne. Now we find out Beringer is treating her too.' It had come out too quickly. He sounded like a hyperactive child, not a bloody detective.

'She kept calling Roseanne?'

'Yes, hers is the number written on that newspaper I brought in.'

'And did Roseanne ring her back? What did they talk about?' Alice picked up the folder and opened it to the page Josie had just inserted.

'No, and I don't know.'

'So had they met in hospital?' Alice's eyes scanned the page. Better than scanning him at the moment.

'No, Matthews was admitted sometime after Grey was there, but –'

'Then they didn't necessarily know each other. Maybe it was a wrong number?'

'No, you don't keep ringing a wrong number over and over again. They knew each other. They must have done. Through the hospital or something. There's a connection.'

'Maybe, but the hospital connection is rather tenuous, isn't it? And the phone calls need verification. What else links them that isn't tenuous? And how does Beringer come into it? I don't see that link at all.'

'They both knew him. He was their shrink in both cases, even though Roseanne Grey died before the Matthews woman came round. I even heard the Matthews woman being referred to him. I just forgot about it.' He grimaced, a rueful moue that could hardly look attractive, but then he didn't feel particularly sharp for having forgotten.

'She died beforehand? Where does it say that on here?' Alice thrust Josie's scrawled note at him.

'It doesn't,' he said without looking. 'But I know that because I was there when the Matthews woman came round. I was interviewing Beringer so we could finalise a verdict of suicide. The ward sister turfed us out of her office because she needed to deal with the admin for an RTA who'd just come round after sustaining head injuries. She told Beringer the woman would almost certainly be referred to him because she was talking about seeing angels. He joked that they usually saw devils. There's your link!' He slammed his hand down on the worktop and winced. It was his injured hand. 'Jesus fucking Christ!'

'Darwin!' she looked genuinely horrified.

'Sorry – but that hurt. But that's the link to Beringer.'

'It's still tenuous. One woman was already dead, and Beringer is a professional. He wouldn't discuss one of his patients with another one – or anyone else. It would be more than his reputation's worth.'

'Don't I know it,' Grant commented, mouth crumpling into an expression of annoyance. 'Lips sealed as tight as a monkey's arse when I wanted to see Roseanne Grey's file. But here's something else,' he added, the memory of that conversation finding a clarity he wouldn't have thought possible mere minutes beforehand. 'When she came round, the ward sister said Erin Matthews had been calling out someone else's name. *Roseanne.*'

'Were they sure?' she shook her head at him, but her eyes were warming up, the little amber flecks starting to spark whilst her forehead creased into a series of little furrows. 'Maybe she was saying her own name and they misunderstood?'

'Even with an oxygen mask on your face, Roseanne isn't Erin.' He plastered his hand across his mouth and muttered the name. This time her head nodded instead of shook, lips twisting into a reluctant *maybe* as she stifled laughter. He ignored her amusement. 'So why should she have been saying the woman's name when she was coming round? And the ward sister told Beringer about her in front of me – actually told him he had another potential patient. Bloody hell! But he's got some system going there, hasn't he? That must be good enough for you?'

'OK,' she smiled. 'Maybe.'

'Good, he exclaimed, and on impulse picked up the wilting mistletoe and kissed her hard on the lips. She didn't resist, but nor did she respond, just shook her head indulgently when they drew apart.

'Bloody hell, what's wrong with me now?'

'Life, Darwin.'

'Life? Wasn't that living?'

'There's a difference between blundering through life and living it,' she replied. 'Stalking Stacey and then kissing me is blundering.'

He opened his mouth to reply but luckily he was saved by the bell – or the buzz – as his mobile phone agitated in his pocket. He answered it, cursing himself for being such an idiot.

'More info, Guv. Research has drawn a blank on Roseanne Grey before the age of about seventeen. She just appears out of nowhere then. Are we treating this as murder or suspicious death, by the way as the Super was in just now, admiring our new tinsel town, but also asking why I was still working on the Grey case. You said to change it to a suspicious but we should have escalated it to action or demoted it by now, shouldn't we? And, um, the stuff you told me to let the local rag know about? It's ended up on radio and TV too. The Super wasn't happy. He's looking for you now. Seems he might have had a bit of aggro from the shrink, Beringer.'

'Well, there's new evidence with Forensics now. That changes things. What else have you got?' The little shiver of silver uniform buttons slid down his spine.

'Oh? OK. Well, anyway, her real name quite possibly wasn't Roseanne Grey, but so far there's nothing to confirm that.'

'That's the next job, then, Josie,' he said, trying to emulate bonhomie and team enthusiasm.

'That's easier said than done, Guv. I need a link, or a date of birth or something that isn't manufactured. And what about the Super?'

'I'll get back to you on that,' he cleared his throat and ended the call, frowning. Alice didn't say anything but he was aware she was waiting for him to. He relayed what Josie had told him.

'I need someone who knew Roseanne Grey – in any capacity apart from work and hospital to come forward,' he added.

'Your Erin Matthews?' Alice suggested.

'Yes, but she hasn't.'

'Then obviously she needs asking?' she paused. 'Carefully … I do agree with you on one thing though. This is a suspicious death. Forensics on the door handle suggest massive force was used to cause it to buckle in that way. Someone exerted it, but from the inside, not the outside. Maybe there *was* something going on there? Or someone was afraid of something there?'

'Roseanne?'

'No, Erin. Maybe Erin Matthews is – or was – afraid, or confused. People tend to keep what they know to themselves, whether that's a good idea or not when that's the case, don't they?'

'Yes,' Grant agreed. 'That's worth pursuing too. Frightened or confused.' He compared himself to the latter category and his mouth twitched. Totally buggered, really. 'I'll question her next.'

'No, just talk to her, Darwin. Softly, softly, catchee monkee – subtlety is much more effective than force with someone who is afraid – or confused.' Her mouth copied Grant's and he wanted to kiss it again, but this time he knew – positively knew – that would be the wrong thing to do. He had to not feel confused – or afraid – to do that again, and this woman made him feel both at times.

'How do you suggest I catchee monkee then?'

'Come round later and I'll explain.'

The confused feeling lessened whilst the afraid one grew. 'With wine?' he asked.

'That's up to you,' she said picking up the fallen mistletoe berry and putting it close to the mistletoe sprig so it looked as if the berry had reattached. 'They represent kisses, you know,' she added.

# Chapter 21: Beringer

'I think she could do things. Strange things. Roseanne, I mean.'

Erin smiled. 'I know,' she replied.

He stared at her. The room was hot – far too hot. He could feel the sweat building under his collar. He perched on the edge of an overstuffed tub chair.

'So now I've admitted it. What next?'

'Tell me why you said that first.'

'Because she could.' He could feel his face burning, but what was so embarrassing about telling her what he'd observed but not mentioned until now? 'She could make things move without touching them. Or change things – the position of objects, the clothes she was wearing – or I was.' He sighed and shook his head. 'It sounds crazy when I say it aloud.'

'Are you crazy?'

'No!' he exclaimed.

'Then it doesn't sound crazy either. Did she do it all the time?'

'I'm not sure. Maybe. I didn't pay attention to begin with. She was just another neurotic patient who didn't really have anything wrong with her except loneliness and confusion. That's often why my patients come to me. They're lonely – or they're lonely with the person they're with. I'm the someone who listens.' He shrugged. 'Not what I signed up for originally, but after a while you accept it – and it pays. The only problem is, after a while you tend to switch off when there's nothing to listen to. Then you miss things or you don't notice things and it's only when you do notice something you realise how much you might have not been noticing.' She was looking at him intently, waiting. 'It was like that with Roseanne.' Suddenly he felt irritable. 'But you know already know about this, don't you?' She must know all of this. She must have known Roseanne. That would explain the phone number and calling out her name – although why, for God's sake, he had no idea. She did though. He was the one who didn't know anything. 'So can we dispense with this and just talk about what really matters? What you know?'

'What really matters? How do you know what that is yet? I want you to tell me what you know first. Tell me how you'd tell someone else asking you about it all. Let's start with the crash. Did they contact her family after the crash? Did you meet them?'

She was watching him carefully. It made him feel uncomfortable – or was that because of what he was telling her? Yet it felt incumbent on him to reply. After all, he'd opened the whole can of worms with her in the first place. It was his fault that now they were wriggling all over him.

'No, no. In fact, they didn't get very far with that at all at the hospital, but all the while she was stable, it wasn't a great concern. Then she came round and amazingly she seemed fine – no ill-effects at all, apart from a bit of double vision for a while, and the bad dreams. She called it "seeing things." It stopped her driving but, when it settled, she was discharged and went home. She was sent to me because she couldn't sleep and that was – apparently – making her confused. Imagining things. It was mainly sleep deprivation in my opinion. I recommended some medication. She slept better but she carried on coming to see me anyway. I simply did my job but I didn't take enough notice of what she said. I should have. I realise that now.'

Erin had sat on the floor by the tub chair, resting her arms on his lap so her breasts rubbed against his legs. He could feel her nipples hardening through the thin stuff of the top.

'Go on,' she urged, resting her chin on the backs of her hands and tilting her face up to stare into his. There was suppressed energy about her, like a spring about to uncoil. 'When did you first notice you hadn't been noticing?'

'Some way in, I guess, but by then I hadn't noticed so I wasn't sure whether I simply hadn't noticed or something was different.' He broke off. 'I feel like I shouldn't be telling you this. It's breaking all the rules of patient confidentiality.'

She laughed. 'But you want to,' she prompted. 'In fact you need to. And the rules are already broken, aren't they?'

He gazed at her, his lips a thin, bloodless line. 'I still feel like I shouldn't.'

'Then why are you here?' She leaned away from him, eyes cool and assessing. He felt rejected. He leant forward to lessen the gap between them.

'Because you asked me to come,' he reminded her gently.

'No, I didn't. You offered to return my coat.'

'I did?' he frowned. 'Yes, all right, I did. But – '

'And because you wanted to. You wanted to talk to me about Roseanne. You needed to talk to me about Roseanne.'

He leant back and she moved with him, pressing her breasts against his knees again. The spring and its tension encompassed him too.

'I need to talk to someone about her, certainly.' Her eyes narrowed and he wished he hadn't said it in that tone.

'So talk.' She pressed closer, resting her arms on his lap and her chin on them.

He sighed again. He'd gone too far already. What difference did it make now? 'She talked about nothing much for about half her session and then she told me that when she said she could see things, she meant she could *really* see things – things that weren't there. Or people. I told her it was just a by-product of the drugs and the concussion, most likely. She told me she had always been able to do it, but since the accident it was greatly enhanced. I told her – again – it was a by-product of the drugs and so on, and when I asked her what it was she could see, she said flies, butterflies – that sort of stuff. One minute they were there and the next gone – like people. That's when she first said that thing you said the day I brought you home.'

'Thing?'

'We begin and end in dust, and dust is what we have to be to start.'

'Ah, that.'

'It was typical of a depressive – the ephemeral state of life, and so on – and of post-traumatic stress following a near-fatal accident, but she didn't seem perturbed or even depressed so I put it down to that and we moved on. Or we moved back to how she had been – her talking, me listening without really listening but thinking of her as now mildly depressed and following the usual post-trauma rules. Easy to deal with – just do what I was doing. The day before she died, though, she told me she thought she could fly.'

Erin sat up straighter. 'And what did you think of that?'

'Well,' he laughed. 'Impossible, of course. I know. I should have been more alert – seen that coming. Depression sometimes causes an inability to deal with reality – escapism to escape the depression. But I still didn't think she was serious so I did the usual psych-talk and made a joke about all little girls wanting to be butterflies – which was crass of me – '

'Yes, it was,' Erin interrupted. She took her arms off his lap and shuffled away from him so she was sitting in front of him, hugging her knees to her, long elegant feet with bold red toenails pointing at him like tiny daggers. From where he was sitting he realised with a start that she was wearing no panties. Her pubic mound rose in a soft swell between her thighs, covered with a downy shadow, reminiscent of the curves she no longer had. Immediately he felt himself becoming aroused.

'I didn't mean to be crass,' he continued swiftly, trying to recover himself. 'I was trying to make light of what I thought were fanciful notions that the medication and the stress of the accident had left her with. It's often better than taking something too seriously and therefore potentially give it credence.'

'But it made you think? Why?' She'd begun to rock herself to and fro, displaying glimpses of her naked thighs and crotch. He could imagine himself inside her, rocking to and fro with her. His attention wandered from what he'd been saying. What had he been saying? Oh, yes. Jesus! This was going badly!

'Because of what she did,' he gasped, desperately wishing he could tear off his collar and allow the cool air to get to his body – but the air wouldn't be cool here. It would be hot, sticky hot – stifling hot, enflamed hot. Erin stopped the rocking motion and let her knees drop sideways to the floor, cross-legged, the soft blue top now in folds around her thighs and displaying the whole silken expanse of them, hair curling in neat ringlets like it had been carefully arranged around her pubis.

'And what did she do?' she whispered.

'She rewound time.'

'Ah,' Erin burst out laughing, throwing her head back and letting her jaw hang slack.

'You're laughing at me,' he objected, desire subsiding.

'No, no, I'm not. I'm not laughing at you, I'm laughing about what she did to you.' She stopped laughing and studied him under her eyelashes. 'It must have been the accident.' She nodded to herself. 'Yes, it must have been the accident.' She looked up at him and smiled brightly. 'Thank you for telling me.'

'So, you were going to talk to me about her too?'

'Yes, I was, wasn't I?'

'Could she really do those things?' As an afterthought he added, 'and can you?'

'If you believe she could, then she could,' Erin answered, nodding again. She pulled her knees up again, like a drawbridge, and rocked her weight forward until her feet were flat on the ground, then rose to standing in one fluid movement. He found himself face to face with her pelvis. She reached down and cupped his chin in her hands so his face was tilted towards her body. 'And what do you believe about me?'

'I don't know. You say you can do what she could do as well. I don't know. Can you?'

'Would you like me to show you?' Her hand constricted his vocal chords but he didn't want her to let go. She pulled gently and he rose to a standing position, body hard against hers. 'Shall I show you what I can do?' she asked again, softly.

'Yes,' he breathed. His eyes were glazed. Yes, he was ready – desperately ready.

'Then watch,' she wiped her hand across her mouth like a conjuror donning a false face and then put her lips to his, parting them with her tongue. It was hot and sweet on his, slipping back out to leave his mouth tingling like acid drops had burst in it on their way to the top of his skull. His head spun. She slid her lips across his cheeks and forehead and then back to his mouth. The skin on his face tingled like fireflies were bombarding it and he could feel her hands on his waist, on his hips, on his crotch. He moaned and it resonated throughout his body. She was pulling him, hands still on his crotch, tongue still in his mouth and he moved with her as if they were attached. He fell, helpless onto something soft and only then realised she was straddling him on the chaise longue that was in the corner of the room. His collar was loose, his tie gone, his legs bare and his head pounding. He tried to move but she pushed him backwards. His head thumped against the arm roll of the chaise longue. It was pink. Pink brocade, paisley swirls going round and round in endless loops. He tried to tell her that – and that he wanted her. Looking down the length of his body, he could see his erection, pointing heavenward – a homage to the god of desire. It didn't even look like part of him. It must be a false phallus like the Greeks had used – an object for pleasure, a device for gratification – and yet it was him because he could feel every sensation, every feather-light touch as she worked him to a frenzy. She was tying his right hand to the leg of the chaise longue now. My God, she was even using his tie. He tried to protest but his words garbled to grunts. His left arm flailed and fell, thrashing the back of the chaise longue in a wild sweep. 'This is what I can do,' she said as she lowered herself onto him and the last thing he remembered was the thundering in his head and his prayer that this never end.

He woke to find her curled into him like a child. They were in bed – her bed, the soft floral bedlinen a pastiche of the countryside. The late afternoon light had gone, replaced by something cooler and sharper. For a moment he couldn't figure out how he'd got here, or where he was, then the sticky heat of the lounge came back to him, and her long limbs.

'Christ,' he muttered under his breath. How had he got himself in this deep? He'd broken every rule there was already and he'd only known this woman forty-eight hours. He was still too hot, but it was an exhausted hot, like he was dead and his body lifeless, but on life-support, blood still pumping, senses still active, merely unable to respond. The sunlight filtering in through the half-closed curtains was of a new day.

'When is it?' he asked, trying to sit upright. The bed covers tangled round his legs like weed in a river, pulling him back down into its murky depths.

'Monday,' Erin mumbled drowsily into his chest. 'When do you want it to be?' She raised her head and smiled archly at him.

'Monday?' he flopped back against the pillows. 'But it was Tuesday. I came here on Tuesday.'

'Clever, isn't it, this time trick?' Erin lifted herself on one elbow. He stared up into her face. Now it was impish, not gamine, the angular planes curving into mischief. By contrast, he could feel the rigidity in his own. 'Only joking. Maybe.' Her laughter was rich and teasing. 'It's Wednesday, and you'd earned your rest. Now of course, is a different matter ...' Her laughter deepened; become throaty and suggestive, He started to protest. Exhaustion still made his limbs leaden.

'I don't think...' Her hand crept down his chest towards his stomach and the familiar molten lead of desire flowed into the pit of his gut. The rest of the reaction was immediate. 'How do you do that?' he gasped. 'I'm still dead in the water.'

'I'm your Lady Lazarus,' she whispered into his ear, her breath piquant on his cheek. 'And I can make *you* rise from the dead too. Do you want that? Do you want me?'

The dead. Yes. Now he remembered. Roseanne. Only a suicide – even though the policeman had implied otherwise. Even as only a suicide it was arguably at least partly his fault she'd jumped. Desire was replaced by despondency. He'd got it all wrong then and now he was doing the same – but maybe worse. He'd wanted to be a good psychiatrist – reputable, respected, principled, but he'd failed. Roseanne's voice of dissent might remain silent, but Erin's would be voluble and strident if he didn't get things back under control. She wasn't even his patient any more now. She could say anything – do anything. He needed to understand precisely what was going on now, and what it was she knew about Roseanne. He took her wandering hand and pinned it to his stomach before it travelled further.

'We need to talk,' he said. 'I told you everything you wanted to know about Roseanne. You were going to reciprocate. Tell me what you know about her. And you – I need to know about you too. Not about your time with Jay, but about now. Who are you? What are you going to do next? Are you planning on staying here or moving on?'

'You want to know a lot, don't you? Even more than when you were my shrink.'

He could sense her withdrawing. That wasn't good. Use what you know, you idiot. Manipulate the situation. Find something related but non-threatening.

'Well, we are rather intimately involved here, but I know virtually nothing about the real you – the woman who's behind Erin Matthews. For instance, have you ever been married? Had children?'

She frowned down at him, still balanced on one elbow, hovering over him like a hawk marking its prey. 'Children – none. Married? Once.'

'What happened?'

'He asked too many questions.' Her hand escaped his grasp and continued on its journey south. He gasped. 'Anything else?' But it was no good. Concentration left him and travelled the same journey as her hand. He shook his head and gave in to the renewed current of molten lead. He was her slave, he was her nothing.

'You are dust now,' she said. 'My dust to discard or re-form.'

# Chapter 22: Erin

She padded out to the kitchen. Beringer was still asleep. Beringer. She couldn't bring herself to call him by his Christian name. That would personalise him too much. She was still naked, the slick of sweat from their exertions drying slowly on her skin. She ran her fingertips over her belly and then licked them. Salt. She liked it. She put all three fingers in her mouth and sucked. Now she was thirsty. She turned the kettle on. Afternoon tea, and then a different kind of show time to last night and this morning. Beringer wouldn't wake for a while. It was only the drug that had kept him going in the end. She smiled to herself. He probably hadn't even known if he'd been alive or dead by then. Personally she'd become immune, but then she'd had time to get used to it and its tendency to distort the world if not taken as intended. She dropped a teabag into a mug and poured boiling water on it. The teabag floated to the top of the mug, bloated – satiated – like Beringer. She left it brewing whilst she collected the sheet of paper from the drawer of the desk in the lounge.

The curtains were still drawn from the night before. Tucking the paper under her arm, she pulled them back and light spilled over her and into the room, tracing her body with cool, steely sunlight and casting her shadow long across the floor. She turned and admired the shape it made, crawling across the bare boards and onto the brightly patterned rug. She liked that too – dark overlaying light. Returning to the kitchen she put the paper on the counter top next to the mug, and taking a long handled spoon from the cutlery drawer, ducked the teabag; squashing it flat to the bottom of the mug.

'Beringer,' she said, eyes narrowing to a squint. The teabag deflated and gave up its guts as the water in the mug darkened to a dirty brown. From the bedroom she heard a stifled grunt. She smiled. Should she? Or should she play another game with him? Test herself first, perhaps? She had been abstemious a long time.

She fished the teabag out and tossed it in the bin, splashing milk in before padding off to the bathroom with the mug in one hand and the paper in the other. She ran a bath almost to the brim, and climbed in, having first positioned the mug of tea on one corner away from the side, and the paper underneath it. She left the door open so she could listen for movement from the bedroom – not that she anticipated any for some while. She stifled a giggle. And he thought he was a good therapist – a seasoned observer? He hadn't even observed he was suffering from precisely the symptoms he warned about with the medication he so easily dished out. The instructions that had come with the bottle had warned that symptoms of exhaustion would follow taking the drug, and those with raised blood pressure should seek medical advice before ingesting it. *Do not remove from gelatin shell* it warned in capital letters. *This medication works on time release and too much in concentrate could cause disorientation or even hallucination.* Hallucination – well, he responded well to those! She hoped Beringer was as fit as he looked. Too late now if he wasn't.

She submerged herself in the water, counted to ten and then opened her eyes. It stung but she didn't move. Get to thirty to begin with; lungs aching, head pounding, eyes smarting. She burst back up through the meniscus of water on thirty-one and gasped for breath as her skin reddened with the heat of the water.

'Ah.' She closed her eyes and let her head sink back against the back of the bath, chin and mouth still submerged but nose clear of the surface. She blew bubbles, exactly as they'd done as children – except Ro had always got to forty or fifty then – or even sixty as she got older and developed more control. Maybe she should practise longer? Try for forty this time? She thought about it for a moment, then dismissed the idea. She was out of shape. It wasn't worth the effort if she didn't need to for the moment. This scrawny-bodied Erin wasn't made for such extremes. Beringer didn't know that though. Ironic that he should have noticed without understanding. The time-slip. Only someone as sensitive to it as a time-slipper themselves would be able to detect it. The burning match trick was how they'd established that. Ro could turn it back to the point just before it flared but Erin hadn't even known it had happened until she was told. No big deal – other than to Erin, of course.

'You must use that, practise. Master it!'

'Why? So I can fiddle with time. A few seconds. What good is that to anyone?'

'Things happen in just a few seconds – awful things, incredible things. They could be changed. You could change them.'

'Only if she's told to,' Jay had reminded them, pinching Ro to remind her who was boss.

'I know, I'm sorry.' But there was a look in Roseanne's eyes that hadn't been there before.

'And I'm telling her not to. You know what will happen if you don't do as I tell you, don't you?'

'I know, I know,' she'd said, hastily.

Ro had been fourteen then and Jay's old tricks had still worked – for a while longer, anyway. That was when they'd turned their attention to flying – at Jay's behest. Jay had always had a thing about flying. More tangible, more controllable. She pictured them as they'd been then. Erin, the graceful willow. Ro, the outsize baby bird – learning to fly. Jay hadn't liked the idea of Ro being able to do something that couldn't be detected. Ro had. It was the way she'd left. Going back in time to the moment before the key was turned in the bedroom door, and slipping out. They'd been nineteen and almost seventeen when that happened. Nine years ago. Nine years of hiding and waiting, and eventually giving in to the slow slip of time that had pushed her into needing another escape. Then incredibly, the Erin who'd been left behind had found Ro, walking right back to her, willingly. And now she was gone, and there was only Erin, playing Ro-type tricks on Beringer. And still he had no idea, no idea at all – but that alone made him dangerous; that and his zeal to understand – to observe, treat and cure her. He thought knowledge was power, but power could be turned on itself.

She pulled the paper out from under the mug and checked through its contents. She had all of that. She drained the mug of tea, put mug and paper back in position and set about soaping herself, systematically covering her whole body, section by section, washing him off. Then she slid out of the bath and wrapped herself in a towel. Her skin looked scrubbed, raw, a frail cocoon covering a stick-limbed pupa waiting to become a butterfly. She was so thin these days; too thin, but that could change too – slowly, imperceptibly, until she was back to what she had been. Like she'd said to Beringer the first time he'd come here, everything can be changed – even oneself. She tore the sheet of paper into shreds and flushed it away down the toilet, then she let the towel drop to the floor and examined herself. The harsh red the scalding water had made of her skin had now softened to a healthy rose. Better. More appealing. She removed the patchy make-up now streaking her face and the hard-faced Erin faded to a softer version without the painted hollows and angles. Her feet left footprints on the tiled floor as the steam condensed and formed water droplets. The invisible woman and her trail – leading nowhere – if she was clever. She smiled. She was more than that. Especially with Jay to help her.

She dressed silently in the ante-room to the bedroom. It had been turned into a walk-in wardrobe and the rails of clothes hung like empty puppets waiting to be brought to life. She chose an appropriate puppet – a long dark negligee affair with a gold tasselled belt. The magus. Then she remade her face, carefully pencilling in thin brows, adding shadows to her cheeks and around her temples. Her hair was still damp, beginning to kink into the first signs of a curl. She brushed it flat, plastered to her head and settled into the close cap that was now Erin's trademark. Good. And now the scene was set; all she had to do was wait. Whether she played tricks or actually performed, the end result should be the same. She padded back into the bedroom and sat on the edge of the bed, watching him sleeping. Asleep he had the face of a boy, not a man. The laughter lines around the eyes drained away, together with the naso-labial folds that delineated youth from adulthood. His skin was still clear, soft – not pock-marked and stubbled like most men of his age would be. Soft brown hair sprung away from his forehead in indulgent curls and the flush of sleep and exertion dusted his cheeks with a healthy glow. He was quite beautiful, actually – and fragile. There was something about him that was vulnerable, like she had been once. Maybe it was the potential that could so easily be either nurtured or crushed. The life force that could be protected or cast aside. She leaned across and blew on his face. He stirred, wrinkled his nose like a child would, and settled back into slumber. She looked across at the window. The sunlight still had a steely tinge to it, but it was beginning to diminish in strength. It was already past two according to Beringer's watch, lying abandoned on the bedside cupboard. By four it would be getting dark. She wanted this done in the bright of day so that reality was fixed for him, not obscured by the onset of twilight so he could later say it was all a trick. She blew again and this time his eyes opened.

'Hel-lo-slee-pee-head,' she whispered by his ear before withdrawing far enough for him to see her whole face.

He blinked hard, trying to focus on her. 'Hello,' he said thickly. The drug was still lingering in his system them.

'Are you hungry? I thought I'd make lunch – even though it's way past lunchtime already.'

'Past lunchtime?' This time when he struggled to sit up she allowed him to. He rolled on his side and grabbed his watch from the bedside cupboard. He groaned. 'I've missed all my morning appointments.'

'No you haven't. I rang your snooty secretary and told her you weren't well – ate something that disagreed with you. She didn't raise a murmur in protest. Sounded quite guilty actually.' She laughed, allowing the memory of the moment to mature – the pretence she was his neighbour and the embarrassment of the bitch-faced receptionist. 'Why would that be?'

He stared at her, as if he hadn't understood. 'You rang Jenny? What did you say?'

'What I just told you.'

'Oh,' he collapsed back against the pillows. 'She probably thinks she's responsible. She brought me back a roll for lunch yesterday.'

'Use it then. It's her fault you're ill.'

'But I'm not.'

'She doesn't know that. I've just done you a favour.'

He frowned. 'Poor Jenny, she'll feel awful.'

Erin slid off the bed. 'Forget about her' she said crisply. 'She'll get over it. Everyone gets over their conscience eventually, whereas I'm going to show you something you won't ever get over. You wanted to know about Roseanne?'

'Yes,' he leant forward. Now she had his attention. Poor unguilty Jenny was well and truly forgotten – like she'd said. Hypocrite.

'I'm going to show you what she could do – what I can do.'

'I don't understand.' He looked wary.

'All those things you were telling me about last night and you said you weren't sure if she was really doing them? You've been going a little crazy about that, haven't you? Well, I'm going to heal *you* by showing you that you aren't crazy. I can do them too – since the accident. Get dressed. I'll be in the kitchen, cooking.'

She left him to it and went back to the kitchen, making sure she'd split and emptied another capsule onto the worktop just in case. It looked like flour. Innocuous as hell. She grinned. When he joined her she was setting the breakfast table there. He hadn't showered, just dressed. His shirt was crumpled and his tie askew, but his hair was brushed and he seemed more alert.

'Sorry it's a bit makeshift. I'm still getting organised. I was going to make pancakes but I ran out of flour, so it's eggs only instead.' She gestured to the floury worktop and the saucepan.

He looked at the laid table and nodded absentmindedly. 'Shall I sit?' he asked. He was getting the idea already. Ask and you're granted permission. Jay would approve of him if Jay was allowed back again. He picked up one of the polystyrene cups and looked at her quizzically.

'Oh, I ran out of coffee too so I had to get some from Costa before you woke. I have decanted it, of course. Here – give me the empties. I'll get rid of them.' He handed her the two cups and she threw one into the swing top bin in the corner, keeping hold of the other, careful to keep the bin and the two cups shielded from him by her body. She turned, still holding the discarded cup that hadn't made it into the bin. She held it out in front of her and it floated, mid-air.

'What the …' he stared at the cup and then her.

She laughed disparagingly. 'Sorry it's a bit theatrical, but you said Roseanne could move things without touching them. Like this?'

'Bloody hell! Yes – just like that. Is that for real?' He pushed his chair back, stumbling over himself in his haste to get to her. The smell of burning from the frying pan behind her was right on cue.

'Damn,' she said, turning and swiftly replacing the cup she'd been holding with the one she'd supposedly thrown away. She pulled the smoking pan from the hob and swept the cup into the bin just as he reached her. It was still hot form the transferred energy. 'That wasn't planned,' she added ruefully, handing him the other cup as she nudged the swing bin with her foot and its lid settled shut.

He examined the polystyrene cup. 'I don't understand. How could you make it hover like that? Static?' He rubbed it against his shirt and held it out in front of him. It fell with a gentle popping sound on to the slab-tiled floor. 'Not static,' he added. 'You really did that just with your mind?'

She nodded. 'By concentrating – hard. And that,' she gestured to the burnt pancake, 'by not concentrating at all.'

He turned the cup round and round, then stared at her.

'I don't believe you. It was trick.'

'Really?' she smiled politely at him. He frowned back. She delved into his head and turned his thoughts spinning so he frowned even more. She shouldn't have done it, but it was too easy – too boring this. ''You really think so?'

'Uh – oh.' He winced and rubbed his temples. 'No, maybe. I don't know. Last night, yesterday – and this morning. I've never felt like that before – like I was so completely out of control my body wasn't even mine.'

'Did you like it?'

'I don't know. Why did I feel like that?'

'Because of me.'

'Because of you,' he repeated slowly. 'But how? Did you drug me?' he added, suspicious again.

'Oh, my God, Michael, and how did I do that? Did you see me slipping you something in your drink? You didn't even have a drink. Or maybe I forced something down your throat? And what would I drug you with?'

He went back to spiralling the polystyrene cup again.

'I don't know, but I'm a scientist. I need rational explanations – or I seek them, anyway – in order to believe.'

She took advantage of his intent examination of the cup. Licking her finger, she dabbed it in the powder sprinkled on the worktop and deposited it on her tongue. She crossed the kitchen and cupped his face in her hands, kissing him long and deep. When she pulled away, his pupils were deep black holes. Just enough to blur the edges – blur logic.

'Is that rational enough for you.' She took a step back from him and waited. His eyes remained fixed, pupils still dilating. Maybe she'd overdone it? After all he already had one dose still in his system from last night. He breathed out but his jaw remained slack, mouth an open cave. She breathed out too and smiled as he focused on her.

'There's nothing rational about that at all,' he said, blinking. 'OK, I give in.' His voice was stumbling, but not quite slurred yet. He nodded absently, hands still clutching the polystyrene cup like it was a life line. 'It's you.' Then he smiled, slowly, greedily. A kid in a sweetshop. 'So what else can you do then?'

'What else?' she rubbed her lips with her finger tips, as if thinking, removing the powder residue with them. 'You're sure you believe me?' She returned to the hob and leaned against the worktop, withholding, tempting, teasing. 'Sure I'm not drugging you?' She laughed, rich and mocking.

'Maybe,' he nodded, head bouncing the same way his pupils were now. 'But show me more. Convince me!'

'All right,' she pointed to the bottle of sparkling water and the straw, still in its paper casing on the table. 'I got those at Costa too. I really need to go shopping again! Empty the water into that jug over there. Water is too dense to deal with.' She pointed to a glass jug standing empty on the countertop at the far end of the kitchen. 'Let's see if I can move something else. It's tiring so I'll do it with the straw. That's light. It's like lifting heavy loads with your mind you see? It wears you out, the bigger the load.' Obediently, he took the bottle whilst she skinned the straw of its paper covering, rubbing it to and fro before pulling the paper completely away from the end. 'Now put the bottle on the table.'

'So the water in the bottle makes a difference to the weight of the straw?' he asked. His eyes had the narrowed look of the sceptic.

'No, I want to drink it later,' she laughed, positioning the straw on top of the bottle so it balanced; a tightrope walker's pole without the walker. She spread her hands with palms face in to either end of the straw and began to move them. The straw followed, swinging reluctantly in orbit around the top of the bottle.' She frowned and strained as the straw moved, swinging north, and then back to south. 'Uh!' she gasped, letting her hands fall onto the table with a smack. 'Whew, that's me done, I think.' The straw wobbled and fell off the bottle top, bouncing on the table and then rolling off the edge.

'And not static,' she said, looking at him under her eyelashes.

He touched the straw and it rolled across the table. 'No, OK, not static. For real.' He frowned. 'You really can do this stuff? Like Roseanne.'

'I really can,' she agreed. 'And now I'm starving.' She left him examining the polystyrene cup, bottle and straw whilst she found another pan, cracked eggs into it, stuffed bread into the toaster and put two plates of scrambled eggs, smoked salmon and toast on the table. 'Done yet?' she asked, collecting up two side plates, empty glasses and the jug of water and adding them to the table. She removed the empty bottle, straw and polystyrene cup to the worktop by the sink. She went back to the table and sat down. 'Eat,' she urged. 'Before I eat yours too. It always makes me ravenous.'

'Pyschokinesis?' he asked.

'No, sex.'

Beringer looked shocked, then joined in her laughter. 'OK, too serious, but Roseanne changed things too,' he continued. 'My tie, her scarf, her shoes, my belt.' He looked expectantly at her. So now he wanted tricks to order? Oh no. He could have the grand finale and after that … She picked up the jug of water and calmly poured some onto one of the side plates. She could feel his eyes on her, hot, hungry for satisfaction, excitement. She ignored them. Picking up the pepper pot she dusted the water on the plate with it.

'Change,' she instructed and dipped her finger into the centre of the water-pepper mix. It dutifully changed, the pepper grains shooting off to the edge of the plate leaving the water in the middle clear. He clapped his hands together.

'Oh my God, that's amazing!' he announced, eyes bright with incredulity. Red-rimmed too now. Wearing off, but he had seen everything he needed to whilst it was active. The little mind-bombs had worked perfectly when they'd needed to, even on the supposedly so pragmatic scientist. How ironic. If only he knew. She smothered her smile. Now quit while you're ahead.

'And now,' she said, 'enough of the magic tricks if you're convinced.'

'I'm convinced,' he agreed, pushing his half-finished plate of pancakes to one side. 'Almost. What I want to know is are you saying this is a physical change in you – in your brain function or chemicals, or an ability you've always had but only recently been able to access?'

'Because of my accident, you mean?'

'Yes.' he leaned forward excitedly. 'Exactly! Could the brain trauma resulting from the accident cause an alteration in your psychic powers, or merely an unlocking of them?'

'And how would you find out?'

'By studying you,' he grinned engagingly.

'Studying me? Back to that. The lab rat.'

'Well, you are rather special.' His eyes were focusing again now – harder, calculating.

'Special? I've always disliked that word. People use it to mean abnormal and as far as I'm concerned, I'm not.'

'In that case, what are you then, Erin?'

Carefully now ...

'Lonely,' she said. 'And afraid. Imagine what a side show I'd be if anyone else found out.' She paused and added carefully, 'and imagine what they'd do if they found out about Roseanne too? What would you say? That you knew but did nothing about it? That you ignored her claims that she could fly and then she jumped to her death?'

'I hadn't thought of that.' His eyes lost their sparkle but none of their intensity. 'But what she did wasn't my fault. I went round to check on her

– even gave her new medication to try.'

'But …' she left it hanging between them.

'All right. But no one knows that.'

'No one knows *yet*,' she interrupted. 'About either of us. But only as long as we make sure it stays that way. I had a phone call the other day – from someone who said Roseanne had given them my number. Roseanne wouldn't have done that.'

'Who was it?'

'I don't know. The line just went dead, but someone is too curious for my liking. This all has to stay between you and me, you understand? I don't want to become a spectacle and you don't want trouble.'

'Agreed,' he said over-enthusiastically. 'I'm on your side – completely.'

'Whatever happens?'

'Absolutely.'

She could almost see the schoolboy in him crossing his fingers behind his back as he swore fealty. But then he didn't know what he was really swearing fealty to.

# Chapter 23: Grant

It was time to cement the link, whatever Alice said about softly, softly. He'd left it almost a whole day now but if the Super was going to get difficult about what he was doing with the Grey case then he was going to have to get moving on it now. The Super's heavy-jowled face loomed up in his mind – the way it had loomed at him round the bend in the corridor earlier when he'd been off guard.

'Grant?' the clipped tones had told him he was in for a thrashing before the moody frown had fully materialised on the Super's face. 'You've been digging around again where it says keep of the grass.'

'Sir?' his best blank expression.

'You paid a visit to a certain Michael Beringer? About a case that needs only to be closed, not investigated? Roseanne Grey?'

The question marks in the Super's inquisition curled round Grant's ankles and tripped him up.

'Well, that's not entirely the case, sir. I mean there are some aspects that bear further –'

'Nothing bears further anything if I've told you to get it closed down, Grant. And I certainly don't want to have to deal with complaints from the punters because you're like a dog with a bone that should have stayed buried. A word to the wise … don't let me have to talk to you about this again, or the conversation won't be as pleasant as this one.' He squared his shoulders as if heaving the weight of Grant off of them and stomped away. Grant let out a heavy sigh. And now he was standing on Erin Matthew's front door step, defying orders again, and not entirely sure how he was going to preface his request for information either. *You kept ringing a woman who then jumped out of a window. What did you have to do with her death?* Maybe not. He stamped his feet on the step to get some feeling back in them. It was a red step – polished tile red that you didn't often see these days. The hot spot, even though it was freezing. He hadn't thought it could get any colder than it had been, but it had –

freezing him out like the Super would if he ballsed up with this one. Britain was like bloody Russia – must be this global warming crap reversed. He made a mental note to himself to stop using spray deodorant and use roll on instead. That was what was destroying the ozone layer, wasn't it? Ignorance.

A tall, thin woman opened the door to him – model-girl thin, and easily the same height as him, in a theatrical type of long black gown, complete with a waist tie made of some sparkly kind of rope. He shuffled mid-stomp and almost lost his footing.

'Yes?' Her voice had a lilt to it. Almost an accent but not. She was young and quite attractive but not his type. Far too made-up, almost plastic. She'd look good in Stacey's tart boots but he liked some meat with his potatoes.

'Erin Matthews?'

'Yes,' her head tipped to one side like a bird did when it was surveying the area for hidden dangers.

'Detective Sergeant Grant, Thames Valley Police. Could I have word with you?' he held out his warrant card and she took it from him with long slim fingers tipped with fiery red talons. She turned it over to examine front and back before handing it back to him. There was a greasy smudge where she'd been holding it and he rubbed it on his coat before tucking it back into his inner pocket.

'What about?'

'A lady called Roseanne Grey.'

'Roseanne Grey?' she shook her head, pursing her lips as if she was blowing him a kiss. Kiss-off, more likely. 'Sorry. I don't know anyone by that name.' Her voice was crystalline, on the point of shattering. It irritated something in his central nervous system – his ability to detect bullshit. She bloody did – why lie?

'Maybe you don't know her well, or even by name, but I think you have had contact with her. May I come inside and tell you why?' She hesitated and her discomfort was palpable. Grant knew instinctively she had someone with her. The someone appeared behind her before she could wave them away. 'Mr Beringer!' Grant exclaimed, the bubble of delight inside him threatening to explode before he got his foot on the threshold, let alone past the door. 'Two birds with one stone – wonderful! I was going to have to ask you about Miss Matthews anyway.'

'Detective Sergeant, an unexpected surprise. I didn't expect to be seeing you so soon.'

'Likewise, Mr Beringer,' Grant said, suppressing the desire to laugh. Then he remembered Beringer had already complained about him and the laughter bubble popped. Beringer hovered at the end of the hall looking like he'd just done a bank job and been caught pulling off the mask. 'May I come in? Since you and Mr Beringer are both in the same place at the same time, makes my job doubly easy – and I barely need to ask, do I?'

For a moment the woman's face tightened then courtesy replaced animosity. She stood to one side to let him in.

'Ask?' Beringer interrupted, moving to block Grant's passage into the hall. 'I would have thought you'd already asked more than enough. What is it this time?'

Grant ignored the thinly veiled warning.

'Knowing each other, as well as Roseanne Grey.' Grant smiled politely. You don't wind me up that easily, Sonny Jim, he thought. You shouldn't even be here …

'Entirely circumstantial, Detective Sergeant. Nothing in it at all.'

'Like making house calls on your patients? Very dedicated, I must say.' Grant moved past the Matthews woman and into the hall, standing toe to toe with Beringer.

'Miss Matthews isn't a patient.' Beringer looked irritated.

'Oh,' Grant swung round to look with exaggerated surprise at the woman and then back to Beringer. 'I thought she was.'

The woman's silent acquiescence mutated into quiet aggression. 'I was discharged yesterday, Detective Sergeant. What is this about please?'

'Perhaps we could go somewhere easier to talk? I feel like I'm playing ping pong here, with you behind me and Mr Beringer in front of me. It'll play hell with my sciatica if we keep it up for much longer.'

Her lips twisted from cupid's pout to old woman's purse. 'In here,' she said curtly, pushing past him and leading the way into a room off the hall, halfway between where she and Beringer had been standing. Grant followed her and had to stifle another bout of laughter as he entered. Bloody hell, the woman had a boudoir. Or that was what Stacey would have called it. Not a lounge, but a bloody boudoir, the walls chocka with overblown Impressionist prints, floral flocked wallpaper, heavy skirtings and dado rails, ballooning curtains with swags and tails and every other bugger included. The effect was stifling – and it was hot too. Grant ran his finger under his collar. Beringer had followed them in and was standing defensively by the chaise longue – a great red raspberry of a thing. His feet were bare. Don't blame you, Grant thought. I'd strip off too if I had half the chance, although probably not for the reason you've been in the buff, Mr B, he reflected grimly.

He didn't wait for her to ask what he was there about again. He launched straight in. Keep them off-balance. 'You'd been in touch with Miss Grey – Roseanne – shortly before she died. May I ask what about?'

'In touch? I don't think so.'

'Really?' Grant fished the printout Josie had provided him with from his pocket. The off-the-page printout. 'But Miss Grey's phone records show you had,' he paused as if counting up. He already knew how many. 'Fifty-three separate phone calls to her from a number which apparently belongs to you, in fact.' He waved the printout at her.

'Rubbish!' She replied coolly, but it was brittle denial. Beringer moved away from the chaise longue and closer to her.

'No, really. Not rubbish at all.' Grant smiled charmingly at her.

'Let me see.'

Grant walked over to where she was standing in the bay window. It framed her like she was the heroine of a Victorian melodrama, earnestly declaiming her innocence. Even her elegantly arranged posture echoed its blowsy drapes with the long robe, tied sorceress-style by the knotted cord at her waist. He handed her the sheet. She scanned it and shrugged. Beringer tried to look over her shoulder at it but she flapped it away from him. Her hand trembled the merest fraction – or was he imagining that?

'Must be some kind of glitch in the system. Or maybe my phone malfunctioned. They do that from time to time.'

'Fifty-three times?' he enquired politely, scanning her eyes, her mouth, her hands for more signs of stress.

'If Miss Matthews says she didn't make those calls, then she didn't,' Beringer interrupted him. 'And why would she know Roseanne Grey anyway? Miss Matthews is a renowned ceramicist. Roseanne Grey was out of work and unknown.'

'The great and the good don't mix with the low and the lowly, huh? So why are you here?'

'That's extremely offensive, Detective Sergeant!' Beringer's jaw jutted. With difficulty, Grant refrained from smiling his satisfaction. He'd seen it so many times before – the self-righteous villain trying to assert the moral high ground as he sank further into the mire.

'I merely asked why you were here,' Grant looked pointedly at Beringer's feet as he stood on the moss green scatter rug in the bay area. 'Barefoot in the park, so to speak.'

'I ...'

The Erin woman and Beringer exchanged glances. There was a warning in them, but from whom to whom?

'Mr Beringer was simply returning my coat. I left it at the consulting rooms yesterday by mistake.'

'By mistake? Wow. Some mistake. Cold enough to freeze the balls off brass monkeys yesterday.'

She raised her eyebrows at him. 'I don't tend to feel the cold, actually.'

Grant allowed his mouth to drop open. Not feel the cold?

'In that case,' he asked courteously, 'do you mind if we open a window or maybe I should strip down like Mr Beringer here because I'm baking?'

'I don't think either will be necessary unless you have anything else you need to ask?' The woman replied calmly, handing him back the printout. The jagged crystal edge was back in her voice.

'When you came round after your accident, you said Miss Grey's name.'

'Did I? I'm not aware of that. You seem to have come up with a lot of things I have no recollection or knowledge of, Detective Sergeant. I think you must be in the wrong job. You'd do well in fiction.'

She smiled sweetly and Grant ground his teeth together. Fiction. What did she know about Stacey and Jones? No. Get a grip – she knows nothing. She's simply being facetious – smug bitch!

'I deal in fact, not fiction,' he replied tersely. 'Facts like fifty-three phone calls, and witnesses to what you said. There's also this.' He fished the central chunk of the broken bowl out of his pocket, still in its evidence bag. The EM stamp was clear even through the opaque plastic. 'Yours I believe, too?'

She took it from him and turned it over. He noticed her fingers trembled as she pressed the plastic to the jagged contents. 'Where did you get this?'

'Roseanne Grey's lounge actually.'

'Broken like this?'

'Sadly,' Grant agreed, clearing his throat. 'It is one of yours, isn't it?'

'Yes.'

'And?' he waited, eyebrow cocked.

'And what? She must have bought it. It was the centrepiece of the opening night display.'

'Bought it? The centrepiece, huh? Must have been pricey?' Grant made a face at her, implying – implying what? Dirty mind!

'It was. I don't make cheap rubbish,' she looked at him as if she assumed that would be what he would buy.

'An expensive purchase for an out of work woman – and surely the artist would have met and personally thanked her customer for such a sale. Good customer service.'

'I'm not a saleswoman and I leave the gallery to do that kind of thing.'

'Really? In that case I'll just go back to the gallery and ask them to confirm the purchase and when it was made.'

Her breath whistled as she dragged it in and then released it in a heavy sigh. 'All right, we'll stop playing games. It was a PR job – give away the central piece of the collection for press coverage.'

'Oh, and that worked? I must have a look at the article.'

'It was more internal press coverage – for if you are in the business.'

Grant grimaced at her. 'Really? I clearly don't know much about how PR and good business works in the art field then because I always thought grand gestures required grand coverage to be effective.'

'Maybe the art world thinks differently to you then, Sergeant. We work because of creativity and passion, not pounds and pence.'

'Pounds and pence surely pays for all this though, doesn't it?' he swept his arm round in a theatrical gesture and ended with his palm facing upwards in front of her. 'But of course, I acknowledge we are all different, and have different motivations for our actions.' She handed the pottery in its evidence bag back to him. 'Thank you,' he said as he accepted and re-pocketed it. 'Take the interesting association you have with Mr Beringer here – also Roseanne Grey's therapist,' he paused. 'I presume he has told you that, given your interest in her? I wonder what the motivation is there?'

'It would be irrelevant to me even if he had, Detective Sergeant. Roseanne Grey was, and is, nothing to me. And Mr Beringer is not my therapist. He is my good friend.'

'Indeed? So we have a woman who is gifted your prize work of art, without publicity, and who you ring fifty-three times and call out her name as you come round after your accident, but you say you don't know. And she's just died under suspicious circumstances. Then we have a therapist, who isn't a therapist, in his bare feet on a non-official visit, who also knew the woman you don't know, but he is now your *good* friend when you only met him a few days ago.'

'Your point being?' Her eyes had narrowed. They reminded him of a cat's.

'My point being I would like you to explain it all, please.'

'And I've already said there is nothing to explain. It's all circumstantial. Life is, isn't it? So I think we're done, now, aren't we? Or do I need to speak to someone more superior at the police station?'

Grant bit his bottom lip. Damn! Nothing to do in the face of outright denial but to find evidence to disprove what she said. He'd have to set Josie on trying to disprove the faulty phone suggestion and following up with the gallery about the pot. And he'd have to have another look at what Miss Erin Mathews might know about him – and Stacey. He sucked his bottom lip against his teeth and tied to fight off the feeling of despondency the idea of Stacey invariably engendered in him now.

A fly flew in through the other door that connected with the boudoir. It dive-bombed Grant and he flapped at it irritably.

'Bloody flies,' he added. 'Always buzzing round the shit.'

'Detective Sergeant!' Beringer looked outraged. 'That's enough!'

'I beg your pardon?'

'You're implying I'm a fly buzzing around shit.' The woman shushed him but Beringer was clearly in testosterone overdrive. 'That's offensive to both of us – and unacceptable.'

Grant's mood changed. He'd forgotten Beringer. He still had some explaining to do.

'Not at all. It's just a turn of phrase.' Grant considered Beringer more closely. He was sweating, but unlike Grant, apart from the bare feet he only had on a thin cotton shirt on, not a wool overcoat. The Matthews woman looked as if she wanted to gag him. He was on hot bricks, but so was she.

'Maybe, but I think we can do without crass comments from boorish officials who think they know something but in fact know nothing at all, Detective Sergeant ...' Beringer lingered on Grant's rank. Grant felt his fists clenching, despite the ache in his injured hand. That's what they always bloody thought when he said Detective Sergeant not Detective Inspector. Must be thick as shit not to have made Inspector by his age.

'Really? You discharged Miss Matthews yesterday, she says? Then you're an admin man, doing his final paperwork. I could have said nothing soaks up shit so well as toilet paper, but that wouldn't have meant anything either. I'm a policeman. I'm crude. That's the stereotype, isn't it?'

'I think we should all calm down, actually, and you should leave.' The woman's voice was lilting again, soothing. She looked softer too; persuasive. The fly buzzed Grant again and he flapped at it angrily. It dodged him and ringed Beringer who shrunk away from it.

'Got a newspaper?' Grant asked.

'Why?' the woman stared at him.

'To splat it,' he said venomously.

'Is that what you do to everything that irritates you? Aren't we all God's creatures?' Beringer replied coldly. 'In case that never occurred to you when you're harassing them.'

'They spread disease – flies. And lay their eggs in the dead,' Beringer stared at him, as if weighing up whether he was associating him with disease or with the dead. 'They feed off the dead,' Grant added. 'Parasites.'

Turning to the woman Beringer said, 'So shall I open a window? Let it out? Or splat it, like the policeman suggests?'

She hesitated, eying the circling fly with a distaste almost equal to Grant's. It swooped past her and away toward the window, where it perched, waiting. Beringer waited too, and the tension in the room was palpable – in her, in him; but mostly in her. Odd. And she looked suddenly anxious as she watched the fly crawling slowly up the curtain.

'Let it out,' she said eventually, throwing Grant a strange look – almost of acknowledgement. 'Let it fly away.'

She watched nervously as Beringer obeyed, struggling with the window and parting the billowing drapes. The fly bounced against the window pane and Erin winced at each *busch*. Grant watched on, fascinated by both the fly and the woman, a strange sense of déjà vu enveloping him. Without even realising he'd done it, he'd edged to what must be the kitchen door. It lured him like a mermaid siren to the rocks. He paused on the threshold as the sense of déjà vu faded and the policeman in him took over again. Beringer and the woman were still wrestling with the drapes, flapping the recalcitrant fly towards the open window, but to no avail. Well, he'd blown it now anyway, hadn't he? Might as well get as much gen on what they'd been up to before he got thrown out. If she complained to the Super, it would be him wallowing in shit, not Beringer, unless he had something to act as barrier cream.

He peered through the door leading to the other room, to the domestic debris still on the table and counter top. So, they'd been cosying up in the kitchen? Brunch? Or something more? That strange sense of déjà vu returned, drawing him into the room. His eyes scoured what he could see of it without actually passing over the threshold. He hesitated, then, what the hell – he was on his way out any moment, anyway... He stepped over the threshold and took it all in with just one hit – the table, the burnt saucepan, the bottle and straw, the polystyrene Costa cup. Yeah, brunch – and late. Just as he thought, the dynamic doc had become the lying lover – maybe had with Roseanne too. Pah! He was about to turn away when it struck him that two things didn't make sense. The polystyrene Costa cup – why? If you're making a lover's brunch, why go out to get coffee in? And why only one cup for two people? Glancing over his shoulder he could see Beringer still flapping at the fly, coaxing it towards the now wide-open window whilst the Matthews woman stood well back, a look of revulsion on her face. He crossed quickly to the abandoned breakfast debris. The swing bin lid had wedged ajar. Inside another red C for Costa beckoned to him and two little red and white gelatin half-shells. Other people's shit again!

He pushed the top aside and fished the other polystyrene cup out. It had lipstick on the top. Had to be hers. Might be useful for DNA – not that they had any reason for the need at the moment, but hell – who knows? Never look a gift horse and all that. Skin cell samples too, his well-indoctrinated mind reminded him. Never knew. He pulled an empty evidence bag out of his pocket and stuffed the cup inside it. He'd got used to being a magpie over the years. He stuffed the whole lot into his pocket as another oddity caught his eye – a plate with water and some kind of dark powder on it, blasted into a ridge around the edge. He crossed back to the table. Suspicious, he bent to sniff at the plate. Smelt like pepper. He straightened and his head reeled as if he was spinning through thin air, flying ... What the fuck! He staggered backwards before he could regain his balance, then bent forward to peer at the plate again. He picked it up and held it carefully at a distance, still struggling with light-headedness. A murky ring, like scum, had settled on the surface of the water in the very centre. He tried to push away the sensation of spinning and stumbled his way back to the bin to collect the discarded shells before he realised he had company.

'Detective Sergeant?' It was the woman, watching him from the doorway, eyes narrowed and lips thin like a cut. She was holding her hand out to usher him out of the kitchen, icy cool now regained. He bumbled towards her, still with the scummy-ringed plate in his hand, head as blasted as the plate. She took it from him and the sensation of spinning finally left him. 'I think we said you were finished?' She managed to make it sound like *he* was finished, as in washed up, crapped out, done.

He had no choice. He stepped back over the threshold into the lounge and his head cleared immediately. Dammit! Those gelatin shells? Had they been drugs? He'd seen something like them before. In Roseanne's bin. His heart lifted, even though he hadn't managed to retrieve them. Drugs would shut the Super up – and maybe tie in with Roseanne Grey being high as a kite on medication. He needed to find out what kind, though. They made all kinds of stuff in domestic kitchens now. What were these two up to? He made a mental note to ask Alice about it all when he next saw her. No, dammit, he'd go and see her right now.

He nodded. 'For now. But I'm sure I'll speak to you again – and you, Mr Beringer,' he called over her shoulder. 'Especially as you're no longer Miss Matthew's therapist, but her *friend*. No conflict of interest or patient confidentiality at all to wrestle with now, is there?'

He could feel the tension he left behind him even as he walked away down the road. Yep, they were up to no good. The question was, sex-scandal no good, or serious up to no good. Either way, he'd have to hope against hope Beringer was sufficiently wary of comeback himself not to go to the Super and make another complaint – until he'd figured it out.

Alice was hunched over her workstation filling in forms when he slipped into Forensics. The lab was as pristine as ever. Now he remembered what it reminded him of – Alice's kitchen. He grimaced, better not say that to her! See? He was learning. She looked up as he approached, bright-eyed and pleased to see him.

'Hey,' he said, slumping into the guest's chair she always had positioned next to the workstation, as if she was hoping for an interruption.

'Hey,' she replied. 'Tetanus?'

'Oh, shit! I forgot. Bit late now, isn't it?' He looked at his watch. It was four-forty-five. The doctor's receptionist would have already got her coat and bag ready to make a dash for it and A & E would be gearing up for another evening of Christmas drunks.

'A bit. Don't make that the story of your life. Lockjaw is serious. What would you do if you turned up dead? Who would ask the questions, do the observing?'

'I would have got it by now, wouldn't I?' he asked, suddenly unsure whether she was teasing him.

'Probably,' she agreed, chuckling, 'but even so.'

'OK,' he smiled. She was teasing him. That was good.

'You're lucky you caught me,' she added. 'I was planning on leaving early tonight – Christmas shopping and all that.' She glanced at the time display on her PC screen. It read five-twenty. He pulled the evidence bag out of his pocket. She smiled. 'But for you ... What's that?'

'Booty,' he laughed. 'Illegal at that, too. It's a polystyrene cup I liberated from Erin Matthew's swing bin.'

'Why?' Alice picked it up and turned it over.

'For DNA, and just because.'

'Just because?'

'Just because why go out and get coffee when you're cooking a cosy post-coital brunch for two? I mean, you'd either go out for the cosy brunch for two, or you'd make the coffee at home, wouldn't you?'

'It's got a hole in it,' she said.

'Has it? I thought it was intact when I bagged it.' Grant picked up the bagged cup and examined it, trying to picture how it had looked when he'd purloined it from the bin. He shook his head in irritation. 'Damned if I know how that happened. Why would it have a hole in it?'

'I don't know.'

Alice put it down. 'What do you want me to do with it?'

Grant shrugged. 'Not sure yet, but they'd been playing footsie – and Beringer is no longer her shrink. He discharged her yesterday. That makes him fair game.'

'Be careful. You've no charges to follow up. In fact, I'm surprised you've been allowed to carry on toying with the case for as long as you have.'

'I know, and that might not last much longer – unless I can get something on one or both of them. I think Beringer is up to something – or was – and this Matthews woman; why keep ringing the Grey woman if there's no connection, as so she says? Here,' he remembered the plate and its strange outer ring of grey particles. 'How about this – could they be doing some kind of drug together?' He described the plate with its powdery ring.

'Some kind of reagent and its reactant? Pepper and – ' Alice paused, frowning. Grant gazed at her, enjoying the way her nose wrinkled when she was puzzling over something.

'I thought it was some new way of taking crack or something to begin with, but you could be right. In fact, I'm pretty sure now it was just pepper. Made my nose tingle and my head spin, but what the hell is that all about?'

'Ah.' Alice pushed her chair away from the workstation and crossed the lab, returning with a plate, filled with water, a small pepper shaker and a bottle of detergent.

'Jesus! You eat down here?'

'Why not? When we're busy ...'

'But all these dead bodies ...'

'They don't mind,' she grinned. 'They usually skip lunch.' She put the plate down on the workstation and pushed the forms to one side. 'OK, something like this?' she asked, sprinkling pepper over the plate, dribbling detergent onto her fingertip and then dabbing it onto the peppered water surface. The pepper shot off to the sides of the plate, creating a grey ring round the edge, and leaving the water in the centre of the plate clear, apart from a small oily patch in the middle.

'Fuck! How did you do that?'

'A magic trick,' she laughed. 'My father used to love them – wanted to run away with the circus and be a magician but my grandfather wouldn't let him.'

'What did he do instead?'

'Married my mother.'

'Oh, is that all?'

'No, he invented things too, but he always said his biggest achievement was marrying my mother and convincing her to put up with him for the rest of his life.'

'Oh,' Grant thought about that. 'Why?'

'Because it's harder to keep someone's love than it is to be a magician.'

He thought about that too. She was probably right. 'How did he do it?' he asked as an afterthought.

'Forget yourself,' she replied, 'but remember them.'

'Oh.' That, he didn't understand at all but he decided he'd better not ask again or Alice would think he was stupid. 'So, one of them was merely showing the other a magic trick?' He felt disappointed.

'No, magic *tricks*. Look,' she rummaged in one of the desk drawers and pulled a polystyrene cup out. It contained a selection of paper clips and elastic bands. 'Close your eyes,' she urged. He closed his eyes hoping she wouldn't magically disappear on him. 'Now open them.' He opened them. The polystyrene cup was hovering in front of her, her hands either side of it but not touching it. 'And it's not static electricity doing it either,' she added.

'How?' he was open-mouthed.

'Look again,' she invited. She held her hands out and the cup moved towards him. He made to back away and she laughed delightedly. 'No, look; look inside,' she repeated. He looked. Inside the cup her thumb wriggled through the hole punched in the side. 'Optical illusion if you get the angle right.' She pulled her thumb out of the hole and put the cup down on the workstation next to the one in the evidence bag. 'Magic tricks, plural. I could do loads more with straws balanced on bottles – that *is* static – unwound paperclips, elastic bands; all kinds. It's very easy to make people think you can do magic. You just need some basic knowledge, the right props and a willing victim.'

'Is that what they were doing, then?'

'Maybe.'

'Why?'

'For fun?'

'No way. They were edgy.'

'Edgy, or irritated?'

'I know the difference,' he said, then cursed himself for sounding sulky.

'OK, my mistake.'

'No, sorry – I didn't mean it to sound like that. I just meant they weren't merely pissed off with me turning up. They were nervous. And the woman didn't like me going into the kitchen at all.'

'In that case,' Alice said slowly, 'you need to ask yourself why you're seeing things in the kitchen would make her edgy?'

'And, who was the willing victim, and why?'

'Now you're getting somewhere. Ask the question behind the question.'

OK,' he said, waiting for her to elaborate. She didn't. 'By the way, I've had an idea

about that other case – Sarah Brakespeare. The murder weapon – we rather assumed it was what it was, didn't we?'

'Did we? Well, I think we must have because the bat was covered in so much blood.'

'But you're wondering if it was?'

'Well, you did say ask the question behind the question? And there was something that was vaguely out of place in the lounge, I think.' She looked more closely at him, eyes narrowing so her lashes looked thicker and longer and her eyes darker and more intense. Beautiful eyes, in fact... He gave his head a little shake. That weird feeling was coming back again. 'Just a feeling,' he added awkwardly. 'But if I get hold of the scene of crime photos could you tell me if you spot it too?'

'OK, if you'd like my input.'

'I would like your input – I'd like your input very much indeed,' then he realised what he'd said and flushed a deep ugly red. 'How's the cat?' he asked to cover his embarrassment.

She smiled. 'Settling in. Why don't you come and see for yourself later?'

# Chapter 24: Erin

She sat in the half-light after Beringer had gone, allowing the evening to fall around her. Once the policeman had left there had been an awkward atmosphere between her and Beringer, and he'd been jittery. She'd assumed he was feeling guilty again – well, let him. A little discomfort wouldn't do him any harm. He'd known what Roseanne could do and yet disbelieved her, treated her as a neurotic fool. How dare he? Roseanne had been many things, but never neurotic. She'd known what she could do – what her potential was. He should think himself lucky Roseanne hadn't used it on him. Instead she'd cried out for help and he'd ignored it. She stuffed her fist into her mouth and bit on the knuckles to hold back the tears of frustration and misery. A cry for help that should have been heard if he'd been worth anything. But it hadn't been. Now it was time for him to listen – and listen hard. She bit her knuckles again and tasted the bitter iron tang of blood. She withdrew her fist and examined the puncture wounds in the fleshy part of her fingers above the knuckles where her front teeth had penetrated her skin. She ran the fingertips of her other hand over them, marvelling at the way the wounds didn't hurt unless you let them. She could trick Beringer but she couldn't trick herself.

She pictured Roseanne as she'd been, pinch-faced despite the round cheeks.

'I'm going – don't follow me. This was a bad idea.'

'Please, let's talk,' the voice hollow with unhappiness, chasing after the fleeing figure. 'It can be different this time. I'll help.'

'There's nothing to talk about. The answer is still no. It was always no, you just didn't listen. I should never have come here.'

'But you did. Please. You can't just run away again. There's too much between us.'

She'd faltered then; half-turned, and faced her, pinch-face sad. 'Yes, there. Far too much. I should have realised that. I can't be what you want

165

me to be.'

'But you don't know what I want you to be.' There had been desperation in her voice. 'Ro, please.'

'You go your way, Erin, and I'll go mine. You've found success. That is what you are now. You are a success. You don't need me.'

'No,' she'd drawn back – surprised and hurt. 'No! It means nothing without you.'

'You've got all this,' she'd swung her arm round the exhibition, ending on the centrepiece. 'All this.' She stopped to stare at it and the price tag. 'You don't need me. I'll go my own way to damnation.'

'No, you're as much the heart of me as that's the heart of my exhibition. It's worth thousands, maybe, but it's worth nothing without you here to be part of it.'

'I've seen it. I've seen you. We're still intrinsically the same, so nothing's changed.'

'No, it has. I've missed you. I'm nothing. I've been nothing all these years since you've been gone. I've just filled in the gap.'

Ro hung her head. Erin would know she was wavering. It was what Ro always did when she wavered.

'No, Erin, it's impossible,' she said at last, but she hadn't turned to go.

'No, it's not.' The gap between them was closing, slowly, stealthily. Don't frighten the beast ... They were within feet of each other now. 'That bowl is like the bond between you and me – a precious one, a priceless one.'

'Our bond broke years ago,' Ro put her hands up to her face and rubbed at it wearily. 'I broke it before you broke me.'

'Our bond will never break, Ro. And I didn't want to break you either. You know that. Never. Always, wherever we are – even when we're dust – there will be a bond between us. If we were sunlight we'd be twin beams. If we were insects we'd fly together. There is no escaping us – you and me.' Ro dropped her hands and gazed into the distance with those gazelle eyes she'd always had. 'Jay would say so too.'

'Jay.' It was no more than a whisper.

Seize the moment, seize her! She'd grabbed up the bowl and thrust it at Ro. 'Here, take it. It's yours – a reminder of what is precious. Then we'll talk. And I'll help you.'

Ro shook her head vehemently. 'No. I can't. It's your centrepiece. Not having it on display would ruin your exhibition.'

'Then let me bring it round to you after the exhibition is over, and we'll talk then.'

Ro hesitated, then, 'No. I said we should go our separate ways and I meant it. Keep the bowl. It's beautiful and I'll remember it that way – and you in the centre of success – but I can't and won't go back to how it was. I shouldn't have come, but I'm glad you're doing something with your own talents, like I should do something with mine.'

'Ro, don't – don't do anything silly ...'

She'd turned on her heel and disappeared into the evening, stumbling – half-running – away as if she was fleeing a monster, a bad dream. But she'd left her number in the guest book. She'd left it because she'd wanted to be found. They both knew that. So the bowl had been delivered and they'd talked. And Ro had demonstrated what she could now do. She'd broken and remade the bowl as if it had never been broken, but now the policeman had it – a piece of it – exactly how it had been when broken. And he was asking questions. Damn those phone calls! If only they hadn't been made, there would have been no link. Even the people at the gallery had only seen Erin Matthews talking to an unknown woman that evening. She hadn't been in there in case. To subject herself to too close a scrutiny would be a bad idea, but now she'd have to tell them about the fabricated PR stunt to explain away the entry in the guest book in case the policeman actually went round there asking more questions. And they'd look at her hard, questioning. Damn it! Why hadn't she thought of that at the time? She should have said she had Roseanne Grey's number in order to arrange the delivery of the bowl and *then* her phone had malfunctioned. Too late now. She had to live with what was. Grant would need to be shut down, but carefully so what he had to say didn't have any credence to it. Discredited, in fact.

As for Beringer ... She'd been glad when he'd gone but he'd also been unexpectedly silent leading up to his departure where he'd previously been volubly effusive and impressed. She'd expected a barrage of questions from him, but he'd gone back out to the kitchen and silently studied the plate with its ring of blasted pepper. She'd followed him, waiting, preparing herself for more persuasion.

'What he said – the policeman ...'

'What about it?' she'd snapped back. The policeman – damn the policeman and his prying!

'I just wondered why ... never mind. Maybe I should go now. I should check on what's been going on at the consulting rooms,' he'd added as she'd swept the other Costa cup into the bin.

'OK,' she'd feigned indifference, irritated with him. He was running away. 'As you wish.'

'Don't be like that. We'll talk later?' he'd suggested. 'After I've checked in on the office. We'll talk about what to do next.'

She'd shrugged. 'As you wish,' she'd repeated.

He gave her a questioning look, still lingering, but nevertheless he went soon afterwards. Yes, running out. They always did that. She'd wanted to say something cutting or hurtful to him, but all the words she'd previously used on Ro wouldn't have worked on him. He marched to a different kind of drum. Not Erin and Ro's. Even when Ro had begun to rebel, she'd still allowed her small mutinies to be overthrown by the routine of subjugation. Of Jay. She pictured the soft brown head and bowed shoulders as Ro had stood in the corner of the room. The muffled, 'Do I have to, Jay? Please? I'm sorry. I'll do what I'm told next time. Just not this again.'

'You know you have to. It's what we agreed. Jay wants you to.'

It had worked every time.

And then it hadn't.

'Why does Jay want me to?' The soft brown-headed child had become almost a woman, taking her and Jay completely by surprise. 'He's never said so to me. In fact, I don't think he even exists. You're just saying it, because there's no-one to dispute it ...' Ro had been fourteen, and Erin sixteen – almost seventeen. There was silence – all of them speechless for a moment, shocked. Then Erin had recovered her balance.

'If Jay knew you'd said that, what do you think would happen to you?'

'Nothing. He doesn't exist,' but Ro's voice wavered.

'Doesn't exist? So who do you think allows you to do what you can do? Shall I tell him what you've said? Would you like your fingers pulled out of their sockets so you can't move them?' Erin had taken hold of Ro's little fingers and pulled. They were the easiest to pop out.

'That hurts!' Ro had whined.

'Or your eyes pushed into your skull?' Erin let go of Ro's fingers and grabbed her face, placing her thumbs over her eyes. Ro wriggled and cried. 'He might even remove your knee caps so your legs can't stay rigid.'

'Stop it! No, stop it. Tell Jay to stop it. I'll stand in the corner. I agree. I agreed.' She twisted away and huddled into the corner of the room, shoulders heaving. 'Tell him not to hurt me. Erin, please tell Jay not to hurt me.' She didn't turn, merely braced her hands against the wall and sobbed.

'I'll tell him,' Erin had replied, assessing – as always – when Ro's panic was enough. It could be enough. It could indeed be enough. 'He wants you to prove you're really sorry though.'

'Anything, just please don't hurt me.'

'He wants you to fly.'

'To fly?' the shivering stopped. Ro's body was still, like she was a corpse propped against the wall like the Victorians used to do when they photographed their dead relatives. 'I can't.' Ro's voice was hushed.

'Jay says you can. You're just pretending you can't. It's time to stop pretending.'

'Oh no, oh no – I can't do that. I can't. Anything else, but not that. If I try and it doesn't work …'

'Jay says you can. It's what he wants you to do.' Erin flattened her voice in direct contrast to the bubble of excitement that was growing inside her. 'I'm just telling you what he wants, Ro. You know that.'

Jay hadn't apologised later. Jay didn't apologise. Jay told. Erin apologised – for having to tell Ro what Jay wanted her to do, later when the ugly plaster set in clumps round Ro's ankles and her thin face was mottled with bruises.

'I wish Jay had never come back to us,' Ro had whispered to Erin as she slipped into sleep. 'Will he ever go away?'

'Don't say that. He might hear you. And he'll never go away then. He'll always be here.'

'Then maybe I'll have to go away,' Ro whispered back, but Erin hadn't believed her. Not for another three years.

'You can't escape Jay, Ro,' she said aloud. 'Jay is inside you and inside me. He is us. It's our genetics. You can't escape Jay, not matter how far you run or where to. Not even by dying. We are Jay. And Jay will get what he wants. Even if you die, Jay will get what he wants. He'll simply find a new toy to replace you.' She smiled suddenly. She'd found Jay a new toy already. His name was Michael. And it was time to play, but first she needed to take stock.

She went back into the kitchen. It was full of lumpen shadows in the rapidly falling twilight. She flicked on the overhead light and it flooded the room with harsh artificial brightness. The lid on the swing bin was still firmly shut but she could envisage the two polystyrene cups nestling against the other debris inside it. She swung the lid open. Grant had taken a cup out of the bin. It didn't really matter that he'd taken it, but what might matter more was that he could have seen the empty drug capsules. And Beringer had been too thoughtful when he'd left. If Beringer weakened and decided to talk to Grant... She needed to make some adjustments. She stared at the oversized kitchen clock with its Lao Tzu quote about time. It read five-sixteen. Yes, adjustments.

She concentrated on the clock hands, nudging them gently backwards to the time Beringer had finally made it into the kitchen earlier, crumpled but curious. She repositioned the polystyrene cups on the counter top, this time poking a hole in the one she later discarded. Next, she added a droplet of detergent to the pepper-rimmed plate. Magic tricks – conjuror's tricks. All tricks – that's what she would claim later if Beringer tried anything. Shame she couldn't reconstitute the capsules but the mind-bomb effect was still a necessary part of the charade with Beringer. Without it he would have been too alert, too sceptical, too hard to convince without still performing for him – and then she'd be back to square one if he decided to talk. Never mind. She could get round that in other ways.

The overhead light looked weak and inconsequential in the bright of the afternoon. Time to get on with the game. She spun the clock hands back to five-sixteen and the world outside darkened again whilst the kitchen burst into fluorescent brilliance. Now to discredit Grant. She found her phone and dialled. Harassment should do it nicely. On all counts.

# Chapter 25: Beringer

He left shortly after the policeman, Grant, did. Grant's last words bothered him. *No conflict of interest or patient confidentiality at all to wrestle with now, is there?* No, indeed, and that made him – and Erin – fair game. In fact, more than fair game – the targeted prey, quite possibly. But he could hardly complain now – that would produce more questions, and not just from Grant, since he'd protested he'd had no involvement with the Roseanne Grey death, yet Erin was quite clearly involved in it somehow. It wasn't just that though. He needed time to think, now he knew what Erin could do. And he needed time to decide what to do about it for himself too. He was tempted to go straight back home but the vestiges of professionalism made him detour via his consulting rooms. It was past five and Jenny had obviously decided there was no point staying on past basic working hours if he wasn't there to work for. He was relieved, and ashamed. How was he going to face her tomorrow, and lie? The way you lied to the policeman, the irritatingly blunt voice in his head reminded him. Why had he done that? Why hadn't he simply told him everything? Especially now he'd seen what Erin could do too. None of it was his fault and he was guilty of nothing yet – other than complacency and a weak will. He hadn't caused a death, he hadn't even covered it up. He'd simply not told anyone else what he knew about it. She'd clearly thought she could fly, but couldn't – whatever else she might have been able to do. Was it his fault she couldn't – that she'd been deluded, by herself or someone else?

On the other hand, you could ring him now, tell him you do want to talk to him after all. Explain, deny responsibility – even show him the damn file so he could see it wasn't your fault. And then what? Then there'd be an enquiry into why he'd prescribed potentially psychotic drugs to a woman who was probably unstable, claiming she could do things obviously no one could, really – whether that was true or not. And Erin would be involved too – through him – apart from through that odd series of phone calls Grant had been grilling her about. Whereas if he stayed silent and waited to see what happened next – what interesting and possibly reputation-building discoveries might flow from it? The Psychology of the Paranormal. Yes – he could see it now. A paper by Michael Beringer, BMBCh (Oxon), based on direct subject observation. It could be sensational. If Erin would co-operate.

He let himself into the office, locking the outer door after him. It was cold and dark in the outer reception area. The heating was off – must have been off for a while. Maybe Jenny had left earlier than five? The plump-plush chairs in their discrete rows loomed up like brutish beasts readying to rebel against him, the beast master. He flicked the lights on hurriedly and they sank back into inanimate objects, sterile and static. Jenny's desk was pristine-clear. He felt the PC monitor. Not even warm. He felt a rush of irritation. While the cat's away, huh? He wondered what she would have recorded as her working hours. He pulled the reception desk drawer open and pulled out the folder that read 'HOURS' on it in laboriously precise capitals. Wednesday 21$^{st}$ December recorded 'in: 7.45, lunch 12.45 to 13.15, out 15.45. A text-book day in terms of working hours, and Jenny was text book. He felt even more ashamed now. She'd been there, ready to work, whilst he'd been sprawling in Erin's bed, lying to the police and forgetting all the principles he'd promised to uphold when he'd first joined the profession. He put the folder carefully back into the desk, trying to mimic the position it had been left in before he'd picked it up, and pushed the drawer gently shut.

He opened the door to his consulting room and stood in the doorway. He didn't need the light on in here to see the proliferation of notes spread across his desk. Outside the lights from the passing traffic flickered across the window like warnings – dot-dot, dash-dash. He crossed the room and sat at the desk, hands cupping his chin as he surveyed the notes. The arrangements Jenny had made for his cancelled appointments. Listlessly, he picked up the nearest one and strained to read it. He couldn't. There was enough light filtering in from the window and the brief spotlight beams of the cars as they drove past to make out the chaos he'd caused, but not enough to see how he was going to get out of it. He flicked on the desk lamp and the problem came into sharp focus.

'Mrs North: got rather upset that you weren't here. Had to fit her in first thing Friday – assuming you're back by then. Quite volatile. Just letting you know. Miss Clark: can't fit anything in when you have free so is going to make appointment with someone else. Sorry, couldn't persuade her to wait. Mr Aarhuus: threatened to book his flight to Switzerland. Think you should ring him first thing if you are in! Other appointments successfully rebooked for next week as follows.'

She'd listed the remaining three appointments and added that she would be leaving early as there wasn't anything else to do after that. He pushed the note away from him glumly. What have you become, he asked himself. You doubt her principles whilst abandoning your own. He almost missed the last note because it had slipped under the list of rearranged appointments.

'That Detective Sergeant Grant called by to see you again, but I told him you weren't available. He said he would come back later. I told him to leave it a day or two as you are unwell.' The note was annotated eleven-thirty-five.

'Shit!' he exclaimed. Clearly his earlier complaint had cut no ice anyway. No wonder Grant had been so sarcastic – and threatening. His credibility was completely blown now. 'Damn!' he added under his breath. Despite Grant's abrasive attitude and the openly aggressive comment when he'd left, the possibility of coming clean with Grant was still not without advantages. Yet the temptation to see if the Erin-Roseanne manifestations could be used to bring professional kudos to him further down the line was stronger. He grimaced. But Grant could have been an advantageous ally. Firstly, it would have got the police off his back if they knew that Roseanne had been unstable, even if it did provoke an enquiry. It would make the suicide verdict almost a dead cert under the circumstances. OK, there might be doubt about the validity of his handling of the Roseanne situation but there was enough in the notes to also show he had *tried* after that last, strange conversation, and she'd been fine after he left her. What had occurred after he'd left had been out of his hands. Simply because he was her therapist, it didn't mean he was responsible for her choices. No one was responsible for someone else's choices. And he could have applied for it to be a closed court case because of the need to release confidential information from her medical file. Maybe he wouldn't get as many referrals from the hospital if anyone there picked up on it but that would be unlikely, and most of his business was private anyway. He could simply carry on as before – with the fluffy pink psycho-babble, as Erin put it. And anyway – with a ground-breaking paper under his belt, what would that matter? He would be news – *real news*!

It might have worked for Erin too. Erin could continue to develop whatever her unlikely skills might turn into privately, under his watchful eye. He could name her 'patient A' in the paper and only reveal her identity to the most trusted of colleagues so the methodology of his research could be validated. And after all, who better to shield an innocent member of the community than the police force of the community? He didn't like the policeman, Grant, but he didn't doubt that Grant was basically solid, just obsessively persistent. He sighed and toyed with the note about Grant's phone call.

And yet, what *had* been the truth about those phone calls Grant had kept on about? And the exhibition bowl? Erin hadn't really explained either. Was that how she and Roseanne had known each other? Then why not simply own up to it straight away? It could be innocent enough – although the phone calls were odd. And from what he could see on the glimpse of the printout he'd managed to get, they went right up to the night before Roseanne's death.

Right up to the night before Roseanne's death.

*And Erin had unusual abilities too.*

Could that threatening stance the policeman had taken with Erin over Roseanne's death been warranted?

He leaned back into the soft leather of his chair and laid his head against the back rest. His head still throbbed a little. He encircled his left wrist with his right forefinger and thumb and counted the beats of his pulse. High, and he was usually well within the healthy range. Was that down to Erin too? He'd never known anyone so resistant to answering his questions and yet so able to manipulate him. The memory of how his body had disobeyed all attempts at control last night and this morning whilst yielding completely to Erin suffused him with renewed desire. Erin and her angular curves but soft skin, her feather-light finger tips and probing tongue. His head pounded and his stomach bubbled like smelted ore just as it had then. He swallowed hard. He needed to think straight. He needed to decide what to do. He didn't know anywhere near enough about this woman, yet hazardous though it might be to become further entangled with her, he wanted to. God, he wanted to! He wanted her body hard against his again, her tongue taking the words from his mouth, her soft flesh enveloping him – but more than that, he wanted to know how she did it; all of it. There was only one way he was going to be able to do that, and that was play along with her. But that mean he had to carry on lying to Grant.

# Chapter 26: Grant

Grant left the car in the pound with a scribbled DO NOT MOVE note wedged up against the windscreen. It was an old trick but a good one – free parking almost on site. It nestled comfortably amongst the assortment of other wrecked and seized vehicles – part way between abandoned and relinquished – much like he felt at the moment. He needed to clear his head. What Alice had said about her father had stuck in his head – why he had no idea. So how did you keep someone's love? And how did you lose it in the first place? Forget yourself, Alice had said. How could you forget yourself – and how would that make someone stay in love with you? He'd done everything Stacey had always wanted him to – apart from kids and the cat and the working late too often, but that had been to get her the house she'd been so keen on renovating – the rambling wreck she'd left him with. Actually, the cat maybe wouldn't have been so bad. The one he'd left with Alice had been quite appealing once he was no longer worried about what to do about it; those big eyes and the way it kept winding itself round his legs last night, like it wanted him to stay.

He decided to pop into the office first since it was almost lunchtime. He could offer to get Josie a sandwich when he got his. Teamwork. That was what Alice had applauded. Treat Josie as properly part of the team – for God's sake! For the time being, it was really only her and him, anyway! He'd clear his head on the way to the sandwich bar. But there all thought of head clearing was blasted by the overwhelming head-banging of the Super, on the prowl to see how 'things were coming along' as he put it. Josie ducked her head down behind her PC screen and that left only him – the intended target anyhow – to reply.

'Er, as intended, sir.'

'Intended? So what's that, Grant? Closed down now?'

'Not as yet, but moving towards it.'

Carter-Rowles plucked at one of the files still decorating his desk. 'And this one?' Grant made a pretence of grabbing it up as if its contents were about to spill onto the floor.

'Shortly, sir.'

'Hmm,' he felt the Super's eyes boring into him as he shuffled the Grey case file to the bottom of the others just in case Carter-Rowles picked it up and looked inside. 'And the November monthlies? Are they done yet? Friday, remember – I want them for Friday.'

'Almost sir. They'll be ready for then, certainly.'

'On my desk on Friday, then. Modern policing is all about showing the paying public they're getting what they're paying for. Meeting targets, getting results. Get those cases I gave you closed down.' He tapped the cascading pile of files. 'They're not your little pets. They're my targets.'

And he was gone, leaving the stench of brimstone hanging in the air.

'Whew!' he heard from behind Josie's PC.

'Whew, indeed,' Grant agreed. No comeback from his little visit to Erin Matthews yet, at least. 'How are you getting on with the Blues?'

'OK,' she replied warily. 'Almost done.'

'In that case,' he picked up another folder that had been buried under the cascading buff ones. 'Can you enter as many of the stats from here on the monthlies spreadsheet while I get you lunch?'

'Double decker from the good place? And I can go early if I get finished?'

He grinned. She would go far.

He headed for the sandwich bar at the end of Orchard Street. It wasn't the nearest but it was the best – and he owed Josie a decent lunch given how foul-tempered he'd been – and for the monthlies entries. It was now Thursday, twelve noon – high noon – and he still hadn't got anywhere with this bloody case. The Super would want the week's round-up by this evening ready to dismantle – it and him – tomorrow morning. What could he say? He'd shelved everything else for the last week because he was convinced a suicide wasn't, but he had no motive, no evidence and no-one fitting nicely in the frame either. And he'd spent the rest of his time on a pet project the Super would probably string him up for dabbling in. He rounded the corner, diving his hands deep in his pockets and bracing himself against the blast of icy air as he emerged onto the main road. He'd walked this way the day before. The railway bridge was off to the left. He wondered if the disappearing woman was still lying in wait in the clearing at the near end of the bridge. Rubbish. He gave himself a little shake. There was no such thing as a disappearing woman, just like there was no such thing as heaven or hell, ghosts or fairies. There was only life

– and that sucked most of the time. He crossed the road at an angle and passed the antique shop he'd stared in the window of the day before, noticing absentmindedly that the window display had changed. He paused, about to pass on by completely when the reason he remembered the window display occurred to him. He stopped, turned, and stared with revulsion at the shiny black front door in the centre of the warehouse-style conversion opposite. Shit! What the hell had brought him this way again? If Stacey was home, or worse, came out, she'd accuse him of stalking her – being a nuisance – and then she'd tell Alice. What would Alice call him? Obsessed most likely. What should he do? Continue on to Orchard Street, or backtrack to the café at the end of the road the nick was in and make the best of it.

He dithered, turning his back on the shiny front door and staring into the antique shop window like he'd done yesterday. The reflection of across the street was clear, almost mirrored in the plate glass. It hung, like a backdrop on a stage set, setting the scene for the shop window wares – out of place new against old, and yet oddly appropriate – the inexorable passing of time, of change forcing its way new on old, of times past that should only be remembered, not lingered within. A porcelain doll stared glassily back at him, accusing. Grant studied her as he ruminated on obsession and how to avoid the charge of it from Alice. Her yellow hair hung in perfect ringlets around a pink-cheeked face, perfect pout lips and piercing grey-blue eyes – not like Alice's at all. Not like eyes that came alive with compassion and warmth, amusement and sympathy. More like Stacey's – they'd always had that blankness to them too, and dark brown – or hazel? He thought about that, trying to picture Stacey's eyes. He couldn't remember actually. Wow! How could he forget that?

The doll watched him, ice-cool. There was a hairline crack down her cheek. It looked as if it had been expertly mended, but if you looked really hard, you could still see it. Her brittle fragility reminded him of the Matthews woman – cool and assessing but vulnerable. She hadn't liked him seeing what was going on in her kitchen – hadn't liked it at all. The hairline crack – that was what he needed to attack before she got it fixed. And that was what he needed to fix too – the hairline crack he was teetering on the edge of before it turned into a bloody great precipice and he fell into it should Stacey see him here again. He hunched his shoulders, dropped his head down into the collar and returned the way he'd come, thinking about obsession, Erin Matthew's phone calls to Roseanne Grey, magic tricks, twisted door handles, fear, and tricky psychiatrists. What was the real connection; the explanation? He pulled his phone from his pocket and rang Josie.

'Chicken mayo and prawn, Guv,' she prompted as soon as she picked up.

'I know. I don't forget everything,' he batted back. 'I'm not senile yet.'

'I'd never dare, Guv. And you're an elephant most of the time – just not about the domestic stuff.'

'Cheers! I'll test you then – what is Beringer's specialism?'

'Psychiatry,' she said, the laughter barely contained in her voice.

'Yeah, I know,' he said exaggeratedly patient. 'But all trick cyclists have a pet trick, don't they? What's his? Look him up too. Where'd he study? What's his career progression? All that kind of stuff. You could ask the hospital too but I expect they'll close ranks.'

'What are you looking for, Guv?' Now she sounded interested, the mischief gone from her voice.

'Anything that links him and Erin Matthews and Roseanne Grey that's not simply due to his job.'

'Why? That *is* how they're linked, isn't it?'

'Yeah, but he was on hot bricks when I asked to see Roseanne's medical records, and the Matthews woman is saying nothing – not even when presented with that printout. By the way, can phones malfunction? Continuously and spontaneously redial one number?'

'Only if you already have it on your phone – say on speed dial or something. Then you could accidently set it to redial and it might keep trying until it got through.'

'Right.' He considered that. 'Then she'd still have had to have put the number on her phone – or been rung first and set it up as a speed dial?'

'Yeah, exactly. Did I mention the Super has been by again?' She dropped it in almost casually.

'No,' he stifled the makings of a groan. '*Again?*'

'Muttering about why we were still looking into the Grey suicide and why it had been changed to a potential suspicious. Did the Matthews woman play up? I sort of wondered if she'd ...'

'Made a complaint?' he grimaced. 'And?' Grant prompted.

'And he wants those other cases sorted and closed as a priority too. The Downston and Amberside burglaries. The insurers want confirmation they're kosher.'

'What did you tell him?'

'About the burglaries? That you were on them as we speak. About the Grey case, that there was some new evidence we needed to tie up, but not what.'

'And he said to that?'

'Nothing, just nodded and said you knew what you had to do. He would talk to you again on your return.'

'Nothing else?' Grant asked, surprised the admonition had been so mild.

'No.' She sounded wary, 'Only that he'd had another phone call about it. And, by the way, Forensics said that door handle could also have been damaged years ago and it simply fell apart to order when you touched it.'

'Damn!' He wondered who the phone call was from. 'Alice in Forensics?'

'No, that guy with the little glasses.'

'John Lennon?'

'Really? No!'

He couldn't tell whether she was teasing or not. Bloody same old problem – could never tell what women really meant. Probably didn't matter too much with Josie though. She no doubt already guessed he was a hopeless case – or fat Fanny Adams Carly would have delighted in telling her so anyway. 'No,' he agreed. 'His brother, Fred.'

Josie giggled. 'The Super said he'd come back later when you're in,' she reminded him. 'When will that be?'

He was tempted to say never, but that would have been too soon.

'With lunch,' he said heavily. Might as well get the rocket on a full stomach – more padding when he landed. 'In the meantime, dig up what you can on Beringer, and how the Matthews woman could have got Roseanne Grey's number. And get the address of the gallery her exhibition is on at. I ought to check that out I suppose. I want to see the medical records Beringer kept on her too, but we can't get a warrant without a murder, and we can't prove a murder without a motive. I want a motive.' And this time I'm bloody well going to get one, he added under his breath.

He carried on down the road, stopping only to check the text Josie sent him. The gallery's address and phone number.

'Checked exhib still on – yes, just. Have to make an appt to meet the artist tho. She's gone AWOL. Want me to ring that number we have for her? Check it's still current?'

'Thanks and NO!' he texted back. He could do without suggestions of police harassment charges after his run-in with Beringer and the Matthews woman. He rounded the corner and ran straight into her; the woman he'd seen on the bridge – maybe.

'Why are you asking questions – about my mother and about Martin?'

No, not the woman on the bridge. She'd been tall and intense. This one was shorter and looking for an argument. For a moment he was nonplussed, stunned, then he placed her. She was wearing a high-collared dark grey wool coat and a fur hat, exactly like in the photos of her at the funeral.

'Sarah Brakespeare?' The baseball bat victim.

'My mother; and you – or someone – has been ringing round her neighbours, asking questions. I assume it's you. The person said they were Detective Sergeant Grant and that's you apparently. The man on the desk at the police station pointed you out to me the other day. You haven't spoken to me though. Why?'

'Ah.'

'What are you up to?'

'Nothing.' He could feel himself colouring up at the lie. She clearly didn't believe him. The tip of her nose was red from cold. His probably was too; his Pinocchio nose. 'I wanted to find out,' he faltered. 'To solve the case.'

'You're re-opening it?' Her eyes lit up.

'No, oh no – not officially. It's my ...' He could feel his cheeks flaming now, despite the cold. '... hobby,' he ended. He couldn't meet her eyes – see the hope turn into disbelief, then disgust.

'Your hobby?' she spat at him. A fleck of spittle landed on his cheek and felt like it was freezing there, an ice needle piercing his conscience. He managed to drag his eyes from his boots and face her.

'Not like that – not weird or ...' Stacey's description came to mind, 'ghoulish. I really want to see it solved. I've got twenty or so of them on the go – all murder cases that have never been solved and just left to go cold. I may never get anywhere with any of them, but whatever extra I find out is better than nothing, isn't it?'

He stared down at his feet again, seeing himself for a split second how Stacey must see him – or the Super; the failed fart of a policeman who had to resort to pet projects and hopeless cases to make himself feel like he was doing something worthwhile. A hopeless case himself, in fact. He looked up apologetically. And this woman's mother was one of them too. How the hell could he have been so crass as to tell her cracking her mother's murder was *a hobby*. Yet her eyes were alight with hope again.

'So you could find out who did it – really? After all this time? You could find them – bring them to justice?'

'I … er, it's not my job though. I'm doing it unofficially.'

'I could pay you – we could pay you, my brother and I.'

'Oh, no. I couldn't. It's against the rules.'

'Don't detectives ever go freelance? Aren't rules made to be broken?'

'Not police rules,' Grant said ruefully. The Super's heavy-jowled fury bearing down loudly on him made his stomach turn, closely followed by his dismissal with no pension and the house being repossessed, not refurbished.

'So you won't help – even though that's what you claim to want to do?'

'I'll do whatever I can unofficially, but …' he shrugged, Gallic-fashion, hands flaring out to emphasise the gesture and then she was grabbing the uninjured one and pressing something into it.

'We would pay you – a private job, and probably so would others in the same situation. Oh, I know we can't bring her back but we could make the person responsible pay – if we knew who they were. Think about it. What's more important, following rules or finding out the truth?'

She was staring at him, and now her eyes were red-rimmed too, and he felt cold and weak and useless. He pocketed the card, nodding stupidly, not knowing what else to say.

'I-I'll think about it.'

She nodded back, turned on her heel and walked away, shoulders hunched against the wind. It blew straight through him and beyond. The rules or the truth. Pah! He couldn't figure either out at the moment.

# Chapter 27: Roseanne

Once upon a time there was a girl who flew away …

'We begin and end as dust, and if you don't do what I say, that's what you'll be. I'll make sure of that,' Erin twisted her hair until Ro's eyes smarted. When Erin let go she looked distressed. 'Oh Ro, I'm so sorry. Are you all right? Does it hurt?' She gently smoothed the strands that she'd been twisting.

'Why does Jay always have to hurt me?'

'Pain makes you stronger and Jay wants you to be strong.'

'I don't want to be strong. I don't want to do any of the things he wants me to either.'

'Shush, he'll hear you.' Erin put her finger to her lips as she wound a long thin arm round Ro's shoulders.

'I wish he couldn't. Can't you shut him off?'

'No, he's just there all the time, listening in, but as long as you do what he wants you to, he won't hurt you or me.'

'He just did hurt me.'

'I know, but only because if you're strong, you can do more, and pain makes you stronger.' She'd sighed. It was true, to a certain extent. When she smarted from some ache or pain inflicted by Jay – through Erin – she did feel stronger. More determined to one day get away from Jay. The only problem was that meant getting away from Erin too, and then Jay might hurt Erin. 'He wants you to try something now, actually, because you're strong now.'

'What?'

It didn't occur to her then – at eight – to disbelieve. Jay was Jay – powerful, demanding, cruel through Erin's strong fingers, but Erin had explained that to her when she was much smaller, Jay had found them. That made them very lucky. Mum had made it possible. Mum had sacrificed herself so Jay could find them, in fact, because Ro was special, clever – could do things other people couldn't do. Move things, change things, see things – but she couldn't see Jay. That was her test of faith. Mum had found Jay and that was what had sent her over the edge so she needed pills just to keep her calm and asleep most of the time. Ro didn't want that to happen to her, did she? No, she'd silently shaken her head to Erin's question, remembering Mum before the pills. Before Jay. But she couldn't disagree. Jay would have known, and then she'd have been punished.

'Fly.' It had been a repeating theme from about then onwards; one that had provoked arguments, tears, and eventually serious injury. When Mum had gone to Drumconn, someone had visited and asked what supervision there was over the two girls, but it hadn't been taken any further. She was fourteen and Erin was almost seventeen. Erin would have to act in loco parentis then since their mother was so incapable and their father long gone. Maybe Jay would go to Drumconn too? But no. Jay found Erin then. And Erin had promised solemnly that she would be in charge of Roseanne , and Jay had enforced it. But one day she had flown. Not really flown – that was still something for the insects and birds. She'd flown in her own way though; become dust, scattered to the winds so her trail couldn't be found, and landed in England. In her new life, there was no Jay, there was no Erin to do Jay's bidding and there were no unexplained occurrences – things she shouldn't be able to do. Not to begin with, anyway.

# Chapter 28: Beringer

His brain felt bigger than his head – struggling to get out. And he was still struggling with what he'd been struggling with ever since he'd left Erin's. Maybe Erin had slipped him something after all, although, when? He massaged his temples with his forefingers and thought about what she'd done. He frowned, even though it made the throbbing in his head worse. The whole of the last twenty-four hours or so felt vague and confusing now. The sex a muddled imagining of desire and frenzied action, and the morning after a mix of light-headedness and the same pounding, pummelling pain as now. And yet she had done things he couldn't explain by mere trickery. He needed to know more – yes, he definitely needed to know more.

And what about Erin's claims about Roseanne? Without being able to tell the policeman anything, he was going to have to figure out the connection between Erin and Roseanne for himself. He could ask Erin again – and whether she thought it was Grant or someone else who'd rung her. It seemed to him that it could have been Grant. Otherwise it was a stalker. Someone who already knew what both Roseanne and Erin could do, perhaps? But who might that be?

The mysterious Jay? If that was the case – and if Roseanne's death was suspicious – Erin could be at risk too. He'd had a devil of a job finding Roseanne to deliver the new medication the night before she died. The address she'd given had been vacated – suddenly. It had taken him hours to track her down to a new address; the one in the middle of nowhere, and then only because she'd made contact herself asking about the prescription. How long had she lived there? Oh, forever, she'd said, laughing. But that had been a lie. He'd known it and she'd known he knew it. He should have pressed *her* to explain that too, but he hadn't. It had been a long day and he'd wanted to get home, but he'd remembered that phrase nevertheless.

"We begin and end in dust, and dust is what we have to be to start.

But I refuse to let her be the one that reduces me to it."

That phrase. He frowned. Actually, he hadn't thought about that until now. "I refuse to let *her* be the one that reduces me to it." Not him – *her*. If she'd been talking about Jay, surely, she'd have referred to *him*? His mind dragged itself out of the sludge of dust and desire and began to whirr. *Her* could be Erin. And she was rich. Rich equalled power. Power and money. He should be ashamed but he wasn't. He'd been in the game long enough for disillusion to temper principle. The rich got what they wanted. The poor paid for it. Erin was sex and power on legs. And maybe danger – but that made it exciting too. Maybe there was more possible from this than that ground-breaking paper. Maybe there was money and power to be had too. Play this carefully. He picked up the phone.

'I've been thinking,' he said.

'A dangerous activity for a man,' she replied. Her voice sounded further away than it should have – even on the phone.

He laughed. 'Maybe, but I've been thinking on your behalf, so perhaps that will be my salvation?'

'Go on.'

'Well, you clearly knew Roseanne – from what that policeman said, and no!' he broke through her protests. 'I'm not prying or trying to make anything of it, but if I'm going to help you – protect you even – I need to know enough to be able to do so without walking into a trap by contradicting what you've said.'

'That makes it sound as if I have something to hide.'

'Don't we all have something to hide? It's not necessarily wrong to keep some things to yourself, but I can't help you if I don't know what they are.'

'Blackmail?'

'Gracious, where did that come into it?' his lip curled appreciatively. He'd known he wouldn't have to spell it out for her. 'Informed assistance, more like.'

'And why would I need informed assistance from you?'

'Because you've already told me someone has been on the phone to you, saying Roseanne gave them your number, and now Grant turns up with a printout of the number of times you rang Roseanne before she died, and an – albeit speculative – link between you through that piece of pottery. So what gives, Erin? You did know each other. In fact you must have known each other well, given what you knew about Roseanne.' He waited. He could sense her hesitancy, but this was one to wait out. Not prompt. The pink fluffy shrink had learnt that at least from hours of couch talk. Timing was everything. Now her hesitancy needed priming with anxiety. 'Grant will work it out sooner or later. He's that sort. So will I. If it's Jay you're hiding from, I can help, and if it's something else, I need to know about it.'

'Jay?' she said. Her voice sounded choked.

'Yes, Jay. Was he the one who phoned you? If it was, he knew Roseanne as well or how would she have given him your number? If it was Grant, there's something you're not telling me. He was almost threatening at one point. We can sort this out, but not if we're keeping secrets from each other. I've told you everything I know about Roseanne, now you need to come clean with me.' He paused. 'Or maybe I'll have to give in to Grant's pressure and release my files on both of you.'

She was silent. Considering. That proved he was right. There was something more to this – and maybe that would put her in his power. That ground-breaking research case that would set all the tongues wagging and his name in lights, and more, was within his grasp – so close he could almost see it and the storm of publicity and praise it would garner for him; the first serious examination of the phenomenon of paranormal abilities; reality or myth exposed! And in the meantime, the sex, well ... he licked his bottom lip and bit down on it to stop himself over-doing the persuasion whilst she decided.

'All right, I'll explain but not on the phone. Meet me in town. At the south side of the park near the lake. There's a clump of willow trees there.'

The phone clicked off. He was left with the sound of silence and a sense of ominous calm. Too easy. Be careful – she could manipulate you too, remember. You haven't totally played it by the book, and yet her choice of meeting place was in full view of anyone who chose to walk through the park. Safe enough. He thought about removing the Grey and Matthews files from the filing cabinet, but that might cause more problems if he had to explain the reason for their absence. Leaving them in situ spoke of innocence, but he could maybe manipulate that situation a little more too. After all, they didn't need to be intact.

She hadn't said when to meet but he assumed the summons was immediate. Her methods in bed certainly had been. In spite of himself, desire surged through his veins and set them alight. He clenched his fists and forced himself to focus on what he needed to do before he left. God, why couldn't he help himself with this woman, even though he didn't trust her? But whatever her intent, she could only meet him when he arrived, couldn't she? In the meantime, he had some notes to remove and some to create, just in case.

# Chapter 29: Roseanne

It all went wrong with the accident. Or maybe before that. And she knew it was her fault. She'd been weak. How strange that in the deepest, darkest corner of our misfortune, we still hanker for what we escaped from. Trapped, we plot and scheme to regain freedom; freed, we regret what we fled. Did she believe in Jay? Did she dare not? But Jay understood – and so did Erin. Without Erin there was no Jay, but there had to be Erin, and without either there was no understanding. For years she'd denied it. Lived out an existence. And that was what it was – an existence, because when you can do something no one else can, to deny yourself it is like denying yourself breath. Gradually you suffocate. She suffocated in normality, in kindness, in tedium. Oh, to be extraordinary again – to suffer the pain that released her abnormality! She yearned for it, ached for it, thirsted for it. Perhaps it had been fate that had set that newspaper article in front of her. By then she was beginning to wonder if she'd escaped one prison merely to slam herself inside another, or whether there was another, better form of escape; one where no one could follow – not Erin, not Jay, not even herself. And then there was the newspaper article, and Erin, smiling out at her, minus Jay, holding up an exquisite piece of pottery that the article said Erin had made.

She'd devoured it and her, storing every tiny detail of Erin's face, how it had changed – matured, intensified – and that she looked happy. No shadow over her soul, merely happy. So Erin had found a way of channelling Jay into something physical after all – something beautiful. Or maybe Jay had even left after she had? With no Ro to command, there would be no need for an acolyte. Ironically, maybe she'd set Erin free even though she was still trapped herself? Suddenly she'd needed to know.

The caution of the previous nine years had dissolved like snow under rain, but she'd been wrong. Jay had merely been hiding – sly demon that he was. He'd been hiding behind Erin's happiness, and she – stupid girl –

had released the bottled genie again. No, on reflection, the accident had really started it. She'd released the genie from Erin, but the accident had released its counterpart from her. The recurring pain from the whiplash had been the culprit. It had primed her, honed her, developed her and no matter what she did, the inevitable demonstrations of what she could do slipped out in the quiet moments – the moments when she wasn't concentrating or was bored or frustrated. It had slipped out when she'd been talking to the counsellor – the psychiatrist the hospital had recommended to help her with her bad dreams. How could she tell him they weren't dreams, but memories? Memories of Jay, of fear, of subjugation, but Jay wasn't even real. He was a figment in her sister's head – an example of how the madness in their genes presented if it wasn't channelled into a more physical form. She'd managed to keep Jay to herself, but not the little slips – the little magic slips that the psychiatrist hadn't believed right up until the last. But Jay was cruel, and if he didn't hurt Erin, or her or their mother, he was wild and uncontrollable – wouldn't stay hidden. He could hurt someone outside of their close-knit tragedy. He could hurt someone out in the real world, and then they would all be trapped forever in the confines of an asylum like the one at Drumcomm.

She'd understood all this when she was older, and with understanding had come the acceptance that usually only comes with age. So she'd entertained, practised her clever tricks, suffered Jay's routine miseries, funnelled her own madness into the unexpected, the incredible, the unreal, until it was no longer unreal.

Until it was time to use it.

# Chapter 30: Grant

Grant detoured via the gallery where Erin Matthew's exhibition was still on display, still turning the woman's card over in his pocket. *Maria Brakespeare*, it said. *Financial Advisor*. Bereaved daughter, justice seeker, or dissatisfied customer, in the Super's parlance – that was what it didn't say. What it said to him was quite different. It accused him. Every letter printed on it accused him of weakness and cowardice. Of what he should do but hadn't. Of what he couldn't face just yet. Maybe if he was being pushed, like Roseanne Grey must have been. Maybe then. He sighed and tried to set aside Maria Brakespeare's pinched face and red-rimmed eyes. Erin Matthew's display was relegated to a smaller area of the gallery now, the rest given over to half-wall sized canvases of mottled reds and greens mixed with browns. 'Earth Mother', one of them was called – a great untidy splat of brown with pink blobs which he assumed were breasts and black blobs which he assumed were the earth mother's eyes. Damned if his mother had ever looked like that. He stood in front of it, half-closing his eyes and squinting through them. They said if you didn't look at things head on, sometimes they were clearer. The impression was anyway. It wasn't working here. The earth mother's eyes had collided with her breasts and the whole thing was one bloody great mess.

'One of Jackson's finest, don't you think?' The woman had too much make-up on and hennaed hair shaped into a bob, so red it was almost the colour of the scarlet in some of the other pieces Jackson – the artist, he assumed – was making innocent visitors to the gallery suffer.

'Um, maybe not my thing, really. I was more interested in the Erin Matthews pottery.'

'Oh, that's almost over now. We've been asking for more pieces to keep the exhibition going but the artist is on a break at the moment.' The woman looked put out. 'But we can hardly have an exhibition without anything to exhibit,' she added testily, before pulling her lips into a thin line as if she wished she hadn't commented.

'That's awkward for you. Especially after that big PR stunt giving the centrepiece away.'

The woman stared at him, eyebrows pulling into two arrows meeting over the bridge of her nose. With the bright red hair she looked somewhat like one of Jackson's monstrosities. 'Are you anything to do with Miss Matthews?' she asked cautiously.

'Police, investigating some break-ins,' Grant improvised. 'And that centrepiece which we've now found in bits. Can you tell me when it was sold?' He wafted his warrant card under her nose and she sniffed at it like a red setter.

'Oh, well – yes I can. She rang us only about an hour ago to tell us about that. I hadn't realised until then. I thought she was pulling a fast one on us. We take forty per cent commission on sales, you see, but now she says she gave it away so we've lost nearly a thousand on it. She promised the publicity would bring in more sales once it went live – but as we haven't got anything much left to sell, how does that work? To be honest, I still think she's pulling a fast one on us.'

'So you didn't know the centrepiece had been donated to someone?'

'I'm here all the time, Detective Superintendent. I should know!' Grant grinned impulsively. Detective Superintendent Grant – now there would be a thing.

'Do you know why she might have tried to make this sound like a PR stunt – apart from the commission? Presumably if she gave it away she also lost money on it?'

He pulled his lips back into a straight line and forced himself to listen attentively to the red woman's diatribe against Erin Matthews, describing the farce of an opening night leading to no sales and the artist more interested in running after a stranger than talking to her adoring public. It ended with, 'And believe you me, she *knew* that person.'

'She knew her?' Grant's attention wasn't forced now.

'They were arguing – or that's what it looked like. Then Miss Matthews tried to give the woman the pot. I was horrified but she said she'd square it with us. Luckily the woman insisted on it staying on display, and then left, but Miss Matthews took the pot away the next day, saying she'd square it with us. Now we're told it's a PR stunt. Well, really? Where were the cameras, then? Or the official presentation, or the press?'

'There were no press here that night? I thought she was a big shot in the pot world?'

'She is – of a sort. Her ex-husband set it all up for her but he's gone AWOL too now. Like her – she hasn't been back since the day after the opening night either.'

'Interesting,' Grant said, sticking out his bottom lip and studying her. 'So tell me about this argument.'

'Nothing much to tell, Superintendent.' Grant managed to quell the smile this time, but still revelled in the idea, nevertheless. 'It was over in a few minutes, the woman went and Miss Matthews told us at the end of the evening that she was taking the pot with her but she'd square it with us. Oh, she asked to see the visitors' book too. Everyone attending that evening had to sign into the visitors' book.'

'Really? May I see it?'

She shrugged, the red bob bobbing with her shoulders. 'It's on the desk.' She led Grant across to a small and contorted piece of furniture in the corner of the gallery near the entrance to it. 'Here,' she gestured to an elaborate vellum and leather book that took up most of it. Grant opened it and flicked back until he found the opening night of the Matthews exhibition in late October. Running his finger down the list of names it bumped up against R. Grey about half way down the third page for the date. There was a phone number clearly listed against the name too. So R. Grey had wanted Erin Matthews to be able to contact her. That was interesting too – and yet when Erin Matthews had rung her – all fifty-three times – she hadn't answered. Nor called back. Not on the number the calls had been made to, anyway. He tried to recall whether he'd noticed a mobile phone in Roseanne Grey's possessions. He couldn't. Something to check up on when he got back to the nick. He'd better see what these burglaries the Super was on about entailed too, since he'd just used them as cover to ask the gallery woman about something he hadn't really the authority to ask about without a crime yet. *Only* a suicide.

He left, giving his thanks to the woman for her help and to God for not being in a job where he had to look at Jackson's finest pieces all day. Maybe blood-soaked bodies and dingy grey offices weren't that bad after all. He returned to his own dingy grey office via the evidence room, and dumped the box on Josie's desk before she got in. The other, much older one he'd managed to raid whilst legitimately accessing the evidence store, was still in situ, minus the evidence list and accompanying photos. He might not be able to do much officially but he would do his best for Sarah Brakespeare and her daughter privately. The evidence box for Roseanne

Grey, though, that nestled slyly in amongst the tinsel and Christmas cards, an unexpected festive surprise for Josie. He went back to his own desk and pulled the monthlies stats up onto the PC screen. It was a toss-up between the stats and the two burglary cases but the Super would be on at him about the stats at the weekly round-up, and this time he wouldn't be able to wriggle out of the fact that they were still not complete. He could just hear it now, the Super's drawling cut-glass accent, asking him what he'd been doing for the last four weeks, knowing full well he'd been spending his time on things that were not only not sanctioned but also likely to get him bumped back down to uniform unless he was bloody careful. And he didn't yet know who that other phone call the Super had mentioned to Josie had been from – or about.

He frowned, and then grinned. Josie had done a grand job though. Almost all the monthlies were complete – just needed signing off. He'd got to week three when Josie bustled in, hair in bunches with silly string dangling from them like multi-coloured worms.

'Bloody hell,' he said. 'I hope you didn't pay anyone for that hairdo.'

'Hairdo?' she giggled. 'You sound like my mum.'

'I probably am your mum,' he replied. She giggled again and dumped her bag down on her desk.

'Oh,' she exclaimed. 'Did I miss something?'

'No, I think I did and I want you to find it for me. That's Roseanne Grey's effects. We still haven't found out who she was, have we?'

'No,' Josie agreed, pushing the Christmas cards out of the way and emptying the contents of the box onto her desk. 'Steve's missus went into labour this morning, by the way. Or that's what he thinks. He was a bit panicky from the text.'

Grant grunted. 'Did he get his shit-load of nappies?'

'Yes, I think so. Enough anyway. Ten packs.'

'Ten! Seems rather a lot. How many in a pack?'

'Forty-eight, I think – or there was in the pack I found for him down the road.'

'Forty-eight? Jesus! That's four hundred and eighty craps he's planning on the kid having over Christmas?'

'Babies do go quite a lot,' she grinned.

'No wonder I never wanted kids,' he replied.

'Oh, was that the reason? I thought it was because you were too busy.'

Grant glanced at her suspiciously but she was arranging the contents of the box in lines, apparently oblivious to the effect of her remark on him.

'What you got?' he replied gruffly.

Josie looked up and smiled gently at him. 'In the file, two addresses – one before and one after the RTA. The address of her employer before the RTA, unemployed afterwards. From her, the nightdress she was wearing – not very pretty now of course, and a locket. Not a lot in her possessions at the house either – purse, a bank card, some cash, no address book, nothing personal on her laptop, just some old work things. Browser cleared but nothing particularly inspiring or relevant when reconstituted, and all emails deleted, apart from a couple of bits of junk mail.'

'No mobile phone?'

'No, Guv, only what I said.'

'A real grey girl then?'

'Seems so, Guv. Nondescript.'

'Beringer doesn't think so though, or he wouldn't be so precious about releasing his file on her or talking about what's in it. And Miss Erin Matthews wouldn't be lying though her teeth about knowing her. They met at the gallery that her pots are on display at. What's in the locket?'

'A couple of photos and that's all. A couple of girls – one is probably her, and the other – I don't know; mother, sister, girlfriend?'

'Girlfriend?' he raised his eyebrows.

'It's a modern world, Guv,' Josie shrugged.

'Hmm,' he grunted, wondering where he stood in this modern world. 'No inscriptions?'

'No, although it looks quite old. Family heirloom, perhaps? It's got what could be a jeweller's name stamped on the back – somewhere in Cork.'

'Maybe they can tell us a bit more about our grey girl then – and why anyone would want her here any longer?'

'Is that so, then Guv? I didn't think we had anything to prove that really, now the door handle damage is in question? By the way, the Super was muttering about that burglary over in Downston again. I think he might know the victims. Francis and Luanne Winton-Jones.'

'The rich and get even richer quick brigade? They can survive a bit longer without their silver dinner service.'

Josie cast him a doubtful look. 'And the insurance scam someone reported on Tuesday. It's not big enough for fraud but they'd like us to gather some more gen before they pass on it completely.'

'Put Steve on it. He's good at figures – with all those nappies.'

'Steve's wife has just gone into labour,' she reminded him gently.

'OK, Fat Fa – Carly can ring up fraud for the files and I'll have a look at them on Monday. In the meantime, let's get this one cracked, shall we?'

She smiled weakly at him and he knew she was humouring him until the Super relieved her of the responsibility. Fuck it! He was right this time, he was damn sure he was!

'What would you like me to do?'

'Get on to that jewellers and see if they can trace who bought the locket and when. It's a long shot, but it's a start. And see if you can get any more background from the ex-employers. She was with them for nigh on eight years. Someone there must know something about her. I'll borrow this though,' he picked up the locket and pulled the Brakespeare file out of his lower drawer. If he was going to see Alice … He turned off his PC screen and was making for the door when he heard the dulcet tones of the Super in the outer office. 'Shit!' he exploded.

'Need a nappy?' Josie enquired cheekily.

'No, a whole bloody pack of them. Now I'm buggered.'

'Shall I get Carly to do her routine?'

'Her routine?'

'Yes,' she grinned. 'Her piss-you-off routine.'

'She does that all the time, doesn't she?'

'Oh God, no. You've seen nothing yet. She's got a soft spot for you. Listen and learn.' She picked up her desk phone and buzzed the outer office. 'Guv needs to escape,' she hissed into it. 'What can you do?' she waited, then, 'OK, great.' To Grant she said, 'Not entirely out of the woods, Guv, but she can cause a major distraction if you can hot foot it. Been to the gym recently? You'll need your running shoes.' She beckoned him over so they stood at an oblique angle to the inner door. Carly and Detective Superintendent Carter-Rowles were framed in outline in the upper glass quadrant. Carly was clearly holding forth, gradually advancing on the Detective Superintendent, clearing a path to the outer door. He, in turn was backing into the corner, the polite expression of a superior suffering an inferior's barrage of complaints, whilst trying to side-step it, spread all over his puffy face. 'OK, Guv, go – and good luck.' Josie gave him a gentle push and he exited the inner door into the outer office at speed.

'And another thing,' he heard Carly exclaim, nasal twang making the thing resonate like a guitar string snapping.

'Ah, Grant,' The Super said. 'I want a word with you. This Grey case – quite enough now. I did warn you … and I've had …'

'About these tea breaks,' Carly continued, edging closer and blocking the Super's access to Grant.

'Back later, sir,' Grant tooted and catapulted through the outer door.

'I don't like having to have a tea break to order, I mean I work hard and I need a tea break when it works for me …' floated down the corridor after him. God bless her. Maybe he'd have to revisit the fat Fanny Adams nickname and change it to sweet Fanny Adams. The rumble of the Super's conciliatory response accompanied him into the stairwell and he had escaped. The thought of spending the next half hour away from the nick was as sweet as the thought of having dodged the speeding bullet of the Super – for the time being. He made it over to Forensics in record time, probably way before the Super had made it away from Carly. As usual all was peace and calm in the lab adjacent to the morgue. He'd never have anticipated actively seeking out the company of the dead and their gatekeepers once upon a time, he thought ruefully. Then, he'd never have actively done a lot of things once – like ask advice and actually take it, or question why he was repeatedly doing the same thing over and over again, like he was doing now. There was certainly no likelihood of rapprochement with Stacey, only his stubbornness in wanting it – so why was he still obsessing over her? And like Josie said, there was no proof of murder in the Grey case, only his gut instinct. There was similarly no direct encouragement from Alice, only – and there he got stuck. That was too complicated to figure out just yet.

'Can we blow up these two pictures and then advance them in age to equivalent to about twenty-seven?'

'Oh! You made me jump,' she exclaimed as he dumped the locket on the worktop next to her. Her hair was pulled back into a bun today, sleek and shining; a lover's knot of silky strands, revealing milky-white skin feathered with stray curling hairs too short to be clicked into the complicated arrangement. He had the disconcerting urge to put his lips on the skin to see if it tasted of milk – semi-skimmed or full cream. The idea made his head spin.

'Sorry, I shouldn't have crept up on you.'

'No.' Her eyes had those iridescent gold stars in them again, sparkling at him. 'But I'll forgive you this time.' She made it sound as if she'd forgive him next time too. His head spun faster. 'Why do you want me to?'

'It was Roseanne Grey's. I'm trying to get to know her – see if I can find out who she really was.'

She sighed imperceptibly but he caught it. 'Darwin,' she began. 'The Super …'

'I know, I know, I guess he's been on to you too, but there's something odd with all of this and I'm going to get to the bottom of it. At the moment, it's as if her life didn't start until she was seventeen. Why? It makes no sense and the less sense it makes the more sense it makes – if you get my drift?'

'Not really, but I understand what you mean.' She sighed again, this time audibly. 'OK, as it's you …' She examined the locket more closely. 'By the way, I probably shouldn't encourage you but if it will help you to get to know our girl Roseanne and close her case sooner, we've got the tox report back on her blood. She had taken a combination of oxycodone and acetaminophen, which are usually related to pain management. Strong painkillers, really. However, they can be potentially addictive, and under certain circumstances can cause hallucinogenic effects, but generally not when only at the level in her bloods.'

'So she wasn't high as a kite?'

'She was medicated, and relaxed. And some suicides deliberately take drugs to get them past the fear of actually committing suicide if their plan is to jump. I could cite you a number of authorities and papers on that. On the other hand, the very act of taking a relaxant means that you're less likely to be so stressed you'd be jumping out of windows; but that's only my opinion. Don't quote me.'

'But she did – and smashed herself to smithereens.'

'Well, not quite to smithereens. She had lethal cranio-cerebral damage – head injuries in layman's terms – with multiple fractures of the skull, so her face was unrecognisable, but ironically the rest of her body was relatively unharmed. A couple of the cervical vertebrae were fractured, plus some ribs and her collar bone. No main limb fractures though, and no liver, spleen or lung damage.'

'Is that unusual?'

'No, not really. Our head is the heaviest part of us so generally it's not unusual for fall victims to sustain their worst injuries from the head down. Most falls from height suffer or die from cranial damage. About two-thirds, in fact. The remainder usually have side impact trauma – major limb damage and internal injuries. Your girl fell to form, really. Head wrecked, body relatively intact.'

'Here's an idea, then – had she any old injuries we could use to marry up when we have an idea who she might have been before she seemingly popped up as Roseanne Grey?'

'No, none at all. Obviously one of those lucky ones who never fell out of a tree like I did as a child and broke my wrist.' Alice held her right arm out in front of him and pulled the sleeve of her lab coat back. The kink in her arm was slight but obvious. 'Stopped me becoming a surgeon, unfortunately. I've had mild osteoarthritis in it since my early twenties.'

'Is that what you wanted to do?' Grant reached out and gently touched her sloping wrist. Their eyes met briefly before he withdrew, embarrassed.

'Once, but if you know something's not possible, you find something else that is, don't you?'

'Yes,' he snatched a glance at her gently smiling face. The pause hung between them. 'Yes, you do,' he said, squaring his shoulders, thinking of the Super and his own imminent lethal fall. No, he bloody well wouldn't be pushed! If he did anything, it would be to jump, when he was ready. 'I'm going to try the jewellers on the back of the locket, but this one,' Grant pointed to the younger of the two girls in the photographs, 'I'll bet is Roseanne, so who is the other one?'

'Why do you think it's Roseanne?' Alice asked. 'It's from a while ago. People's faces can change a lot as they grow. Or do you have a theory?'

'Why would I have a theory?' he asked innocently.

'Because I'm starting to know the way your mind works,' Alice replied. 'You've got a scent and now you're being a bloodhound. Nose to the ground. Not looking up.'

'Christ, I didn't think I looked that bad,' he replied ruefully. 'I know I haven't been sleeping well ...' he chuckled, enjoying himself – the kind of enjoying he used to do with Stacey. No, better than that.

'Oh, it's not the bags under the eyes or the floppy ears,' she teased, 'it's the fact that you don't notice what's right under your nose.'

'Huh!' he chuckled again although he suspected there was a sharp barb to the comment as well.

'Anyway, be careful with your bloodhound nose. A little bird tells me that you should have put this case to bed long ago as it's only classed as a suspicious death and if it doesn't happen soon, you might be joining it, professionally.'

'It might only be a suspicious death at the moment but it's the word suspicious that matters,' he replied, now anticipating a refusal to help. Bloody Super – he *had* got to her too!

'Like I said: bloodhound,' she countered, smiling mischievously. 'I'll see what I can do with your photos, but I'm not promising anything.' He relaxed. No, not Alice – the Super couldn't get to Alice. 'Nice tie, by the way. Different to yesterday's.'

'Thanks,' he pondered the milky-white neck as she bent over the locket again. He added, 'Oh, and I wondered – does this make any sense to you?' He showed her the evidence file from the Brakespeare case. He pointed to the description of the murder weapon. 'What I said...' he reminded her. She took the file from him and placed it open on her desk.

'Is there a photo too?' He rifled through the folder and found a grainy enlargement of the bloodied bat. 'So you want to know if it matches the injuries because you have another candidate in mind that throws a different complexion on things?'

'Great minds,' he laughed, surprised at how fast she caught on.

'Or fools,' she added, but smiling.

'Like you said, they just assumed – pretty obvious why, especially if the blood matched.'

'Can you leave it with me?'

'It's unofficial,' he lowered his voice even though here was no-one else around.

'I know,' she winked. 'I'll let you know, then you can slip all of this back – somehow. Undetected, Detective.' He grinned, suddenly happier than he'd felt in a while, despite the Super on his back.

His phone vibrated against his thigh. He pulled it out of his pocket and looked at the opening lines of the text message that ran across the screen. It was from Josie.

'Avoid office at all costs. Super is smoking and you're on the barbecue spit.' He sighed. But hopefully not fully roasted before he worked out how to get off of it – and the best way to do that was to nail this case. No way forward but further into the shit now!

Reluctantly, he left Alice to it, officially signing the locket over to her safe-keeping, and wondering what she meant about things under his nose. Her fresh floral scent went with him. Odd that she could smell so good in amongst the debris of the dead and dismantled. In fact, it took him all the way through the rest of the day without thinking about Stacey once, but wondering about new ties instead.

# Chapter 31: Roseanne

When the phone calls started, she'd known that was it. Jay was back, and Jay was back to stay. There were two ways to deal with it. Submit, or fly away. She didn't answer the calls. What would be the point? Just escalate how long it took for Jay to take up residence instead of merely attempting entry, but one day, there would be no alternative. She thought of telling the psychiatrist, Mr Beringer, but he wasn't really listening – never had been. That had irritated her to begin with but she'd got her own back by testing out how observant he was by occasionally throwing in one of her little tricks. Still he hadn't noticed. God, to be so ignored when you should be so observed! Ironic that now she wanted recognition when before she'd always attempted denial. But he had paid attention eventually – when it was too late, and that was a shame because he noticed what she hadn't expected him to notice, as if he was attuned to it. Could this madness extend to others outside of their family? They said the world was one big gene pool and on the other side of the world could be your identical gene reservoir. Who knows? Shame too. She could have taught him so much yet that in itself would have trapped her. He was the type that would have used it for his own benefit, forgetting hers.

He came round the night after – after he'd noticed. Or maybe it should be the night before – she'd jumped. He was feeling guilty, but she could tell he was feeling uneasy too. He followed her around like a puppy, asking repeatedly 'Are you sure you're OK? Are you sure? Do you have any family around – to be supportive?' Watching her. He must have felt guilty he hadn't noticed before. Well, that was his problem, but now he was watching her it wouldn't take long for him to figure things out – especially if he was attuned. Yes, she was sure. And then it all slipped into place. *Do you have any family around – to be supportive?* Yes, she did, and now she knew how to use their support – exactly how to do it. Tomorrow she would ask herself the same question one last time, but for now, she was sure. There were two ways to deal with this: submit, or fly away. Mr Beringer had given her the means – and the idea. Now all she had to do was use it – and fly away. She should probably thank him really, not torture him – but life was never that simple.

She returned the last phone call from the pay-as-you-go mobile phone she'd bought especially for that purpose. She tossed it in the undergrowth in the woods beyond her garden sometime later. It was probably still there if anyone went looking for it – frozen solid and defunct now, of course.

'All right, I give in. Come round. We'll talk.'

She came – later. Jay came with her, of course. And the next day, she'd used the idea and the clever little pills Mr Beringer had brought with him – the stronger versions of the ones she already had.

'In the capsule – never out of it. That will turn you into a zombie!' he'd joked.

'Well, I don't want to be that!' she responded, smiling as calmly as the pills would make her. But they didn't calm her down. They didn't calm Erin down either. They turned her into that unwanted zombie – Jay too – and then it had been easy.

'And you're sure you're all right?' Mr Beringer had insisted, petting Sammy gingerly as she wound herself round his legs whilst trying simultaneously to brush the cat hairs from his trouser legs. Sammy so loved the attention. Mr Beringer obviously didn't. She didn't like that about him either.

'I'm sure I'm all right now. In fact, everything's all right now,' she'd reassured him.

And now Mr Beringer, run away and play, or just run – run like hell is behind you, because if hell isn't, then Jay is.

# Chapter 32: Grant

'Has Josie turned anything else up yet?' Alice had seen him coming this time. She gave him the once over. 'And are you in court today?' she added.

'No?' he stood awkwardly in front of her, adjusting the new tie nervously as it sat stiffly on the new shirt. High noon was coming up fast over the horizon. He'd kept as far away from the office as possible since yesterday, with his phone off. He hadn't been able to maintain radio silence completely though and as soon as he'd turned it back on, what he'd been expecting had arrived. 'Up in front of the Super later though.' Forget the monthly Inspector meeting. The summons had come late evening. *Tomorrow, nine am sharp. With explanations.* This was official, and it hadn't sounded good – but then he knew what he shouldn't have been doing. 'Just on my way there now, but thought I'd see how the photos were coming on since I was passing.' He realised, suddenly, that why he thought he'd come here wasn't why he'd come here at all. What he'd said wasn't true – or not entirely. He'd come to see what she'd done with the photos, yes, but he could have rung and asked her about that. The visit had been more pleasure-driven than official. Or maybe comfort-driven would be a better description. She smiled, that enigmatic glint lighting up the gold dust in her eyes. Had she figured that out – like she implied she'd figured so much of him out, and too often for comfort these days? He hoped against all that was sacred that she hadn't figured that out. Then he really would be up shit creek.

'Interesting,' she said, eyes twinkling. 'And worrying? Do you know why he wants to see you?'

'I can probably guess but I'll find out soon enough.' He paused, looking down at his feet because he was tempted to tell her what he thought it was about and why that worried him, but that wouldn't be fair. 'So how are they coming on?' he prompted clumsily, cursing himself for not starting with a pleasantry or leading into the question more gently.

The lab felt cold and bleak and he, gauche and inept under her amused gaze. He wasn't a bloody research subject or a sample to be dissected. Her smile deepened and the temperature in the place improved dramatically.

She put her hand on his arm and drew him with her towards her office. 'Come in here and have a look – the photos are on my laptop, not the Forensics system.'

'Oh?' he followed her.

'Well, this isn't *quite* official, is it?'

He'd never been in her office before. She closed the door behind him and they were cocooned in a pastel blue hush. The walls were bare apart from a couple of cleverly placed seascapes. The effect was of calm, rolling waves, swooping gulls, birdcall and tidal drift. He felt his shoulders dropping and was surprised how tense they must have been.

'No,' he agreed. 'This is nice,' he added. 'Peaceful. Good place to think.'

'Yes,' she said simply. 'Don't you have a good place to think?'

'Not really,' he replied, reviewing where he could think. Not in the office with the ton of tinsel Josie had now spread liberally around the place and with Carly glowering at him from the outer office, Steve antagonising him with his entirely reasonable, yet irritating perpetual absence, and the ever-present threat of the Super bearing down on him for news of how the Grey case had been resolved and what about the burglary in Downston and the fraud case in Amberside – the Smythes or some other poshed-up version of Smith? Not at home either – if you could call it that? The kitchen reminded him of his parent's place before it had been demolished, the lounge of the public bar at the Crown, and the bathroom and the opaque plastic shower curtain of the shower scene from *Psycho*. Why Stacey had wanted them to buy the bloody place, only to walk out on him months later, he had no idea. Alice was looking at him sympathetically, as if she could read his mind.

'Then you should make a place,' she suggested.

'I don't know how to,' he said and it was true. How sad was that – and him.

'Trial and error,' she said, placing her hand on his arm again and drawing him to her, eyes intense and welcoming. He breathed in sharply, preparing for the kiss at last, heart pounding and knees suddenly losing their integrity, but it didn't come. She drew him close to her side and maximised the document on-screen. 'I'll help you if you'd like me to?'

She glanced sideways at him and he blushed again – dammit, he blushed like a schoolboy! She smiled. He opened his mouth to say 'yes, yes, please!' but was distracted by what flickered on the periphery of his vision. 'How about that then?'

The screen was filled with a picture of a childish Roseanne Grey – almost a mirror image of the ID photo, but younger. It altered to, 'Wow, she didn't change much, did she?'

Alice pulled the folder on Roseanne Grey towards them on the desk and flipped it open to the photos of the dead woman sprawling on the ground as she'd been found.

'No, seems not,' she agreed. 'Although, how about this, then? This might bolster one or more of your little theories.' She maximised another page and arranged it side by side next to the enhanced image of Roseanne Grey on the screen. Grant was silent apart from a muttered expletive, hastily stifled in case it offended Alice.

'You know who that is?'

'I can take a guess,' she replied, 'but enlighten me.'

He fished in the evidence folder and pulled out a photocopy of the article in the newspaper he'd brought the broken pot back in. Erin Matthews smiled back at them – with less make-up than when he'd visited and found Beringer there.

'So how come?' Alice picked up the locket, nestling in its evidence bag. 'Are they related?'

'I would say it's a distinct possibility, wouldn't you?'

'Is that what you suspected?'

'Not entirely, but ...' Grant turned the locket over and studied the jeweller's imprint on the back again. Cork – Southern Ireland. 'If she came over from Southern Ireland, she wouldn't have a national insurance number, would she? She'd be entitled to work because Southern Ireland is in the EU, but she'd have to apply for a national insurance number.'

'True,' Alice agreed.

He grinned at her. Thinking places obviously worked. In which case he really needed one for himself. 'Now I've got you, Roseanne Grey,' he said. 'Let's see what you said about yourself when you applied for that.'

He rang Josie and quickly filled her in.

'Is this official, Guv, because the Super's PA has been looking for you.'

'Yeah, yeah. Stall her, or tell her I'll fill him in when I'm back.'

'Back? I don't think ...'

'Yeah, well, neither do I most of the time,' his spirits soared. 'But we're motoring now.' He flicked the phone off and shoved it into his pocket. His shoulders still felt relaxed, not hunched. Turning to Alice he asked, 'So, they're sisters?'

She considered the two older photographs. 'They don't look that alike, so it's difficult to say, although the weight and hair style can make a dramatic difference to how we look. As girls, they're more similar. We'd need DNA testing to ascertain that really, but it's certainly an interesting idea to pursue, isn't it?'

He nodded thoughtfully and they stood companionably, side by side, studying the two girls on the screen. Grant's mind made more links, including the Super. 'Is it OK having it on there – for you, I mean? It won't cause you any hassle?'

'If it helps you, I can deal with it. Oh, and by the way,' she reached into a drawer in the desk and pulled out a large brown envelope. 'Brakespeare. You were right. It doesn't match. You'll see the test results in there – privately. You've more blood hounding to do but you're on the right track, I think – whatever it is.'

He opened his mouth to thank her but was cut off by Josie's call reporting back, sotto voce.

'That was a brainwave, Guv! Roseanne Grey – otherwise known as Roisin Liath – that's Irish for grey, Guv. Born County Cork 3rd July 1990. Came to the UK September 2007. Applied for a national insurance number and a name change the same month. According to her previous employers, they have her down as Roseanne Grey because she wanted to use the anglicised version of her name straightaway to avoid prejudice. Don't really get that – it's the Middle Eastern races get all the flak, isn't it?' She didn't wait for answer. 'Anyway, they apologised for forgetting that. She's down as Roseanne on all their records otherwise. Father deceased, mother no specific information but she and sister possibly still living, it seems. Last recorded address for them,' and she rattled off an address. 'But don't send me over there, Guv. My brother's in the army out in Northern Ireland and we've been told to avoid travel there unless necessary. Security measures. And please don't tell the Super that I'm still looking stuff up for the case, will you? He was very clear, this morning … Is that OK?'

'More than an OK,' Grant replied warmly. 'Well done! And your secret is safe with me.'

'More like well done you, Guv.'

Don't send me out there … He hadn't actually anticipated sending anyone anywhere, but then once he'd been in to see the Super, no-one would be going anywhere for certain – unless it was him down to get fitted for a blue serge uniform. So this was it – the moment of truth where he could prove Roseanne Grey was a woman with a past, with things to hide and a reason to be pushed, not jump – or jump himself, with the Super's hand firmly on his back, helping …

'Looks like I'm on a jolly,' he said to Alice after the call ended. He took the envelope from her and tucked it under his arm.

'On a jolly?' she looked bemused.

'To talk to Mrs Grey senior. Or rather, Mrs Liath – that's Irish for grey. Our girl has a new identity. Roisin Liath.'

'Does that change things?'

'Yep! Sure does! It means we're investigating a potentially suspicious death if we have a hidden past to factor into everything, plus what you said about the drugs in her system making her relaxed not anxious. Put that in your pipe and smoke it, Detective Superintendent Carter-Rowles!'

'Be careful,' Alice cautioned. 'You're still meant to be winding this up, not escalating it, even if your Roseanne has been leading a double life. Will you be able to get the trip sanctioned?'

'Don't need to,' he replied cockily. 'I think I'm owed a couple of days Christmas shopping since everyone else is doing it, don't you? I'm just going to do mine in Cork.' Smugly, he squared his shoulders. 'I'll put this back first though, I think. Enough shit readying to fly already!'

Alice nodded appreciatively. 'Suits you,' she smiled. 'Bold blue; is it new?' she added, gently touching his chest.

He looked down at his new shirt. Bold blue. 'Yes,' he said grinning, 'fresh on today …'

# Chapter 33: Beringer

He unlocked the filing cabinet and rummaged through the G to N range for the Grey and Matthews files. His body prickled hot and cold. They weren't there!

'What the—' He'd clapped his hand to his mouth, breathing hard. His fingers felt like frozen twigs, about to snap until the heat from his breath melted the ice in his fingers. Had Grant prevailed on Jenny to hand over the files without her telling him that? Or got a warrant and forced her to? Then Grant would have all the Roseanne Grey notes he'd hidden in Erin's file. 'No...' Logic had taken over then. Jenny was by the book. She would have tried to make contact first – even if Grant had produced a warrant. He pulled his phone from his pocket. No calls yesterday or today so far. And she would have said so in the note. 'No,' he'd said aloud again. Think! The dormant range; the dead range. He'd told Jenny to put both files in there once he'd completed the notes for Erin's file. Despite the chill in the office, sweat beaded his forehead and stuck his shirt to his back. He slammed the G to N drawer shut and stooped to yank open the dormant drawer. It was only half full and in the middle were their two files. He retrieved them with relief and returned to the consulting room.

Spreading them out side by side on the desk he turned to the medical reports. Trauma, swelling, possible short-term memory side effects. They both said the same, Erin's to a far lesser degree. Erin, also, had taken comparably longer than anticipated to come round given the more minor injuries, but had recovered rapidly when she had. Both had displayed surprisingly few ill-effects ultimately – other than temporary visual disturbances. Roseanne's were described as 'double vision' or 'ghosting', Erin's as visual anomalies. Visual anomalies. A catch-all term. He turned to their MRIs. The main similarity was a preponderance of activity in the limbic system area on the left-hand side of the thalamus, but that could be explained by a number of things, including the short-term memory loss and the efforts the nursing staff had made with both to stimulate self-identification as their patients rehabilitated. More interesting was the increased cross-talk between V4 and V5 in the visual cortex showing up on the PET scan – commonly linked to a diagnosis of synaesthesia. Simultaneous cross-multiple sensory experience where normally there was only one main association; sight or hearing alone, for instance. Well, Erin certainly made him feel like that! And it would explain some of their more unusual responses. He sat back, fingertips resting on the two files. A curious duplication – unlikely even. Without realising he was doing it, he drummed his fingers on the papers. The sound resonated as a hollow echo. He thought of raindrops, dripping persistently on a window sill, of windscreen wipers clicking rhythmically backwards and forwards, of Erin's tapping foot whilst she'd waited for him to agree she could go home that first time they'd talked, and the way her eyes had flicked beyond him into what for him was merely empty space. Roseanne had done that too at times. Seen beyond him. Seen more than him. After his initial remarking of it, he'd put it down to reduced attention span, but now he wondered again what else they'd both been seeing.

He put the two MRIs side by side, still puzzling, then on impulse, on top of each other.

'Jesus!' he exclaimed. He slipped them apart and then repositioned them. There was no doubt there was a very clear explanation for the strange similarities. He was tempted to ring Grant, but then what? In order to explain he'd have to admit he'd been negligent; entirely missed the signs of psychosis, of potential danger to others – of actual danger, in fact. Maybe even been accused of being an accessory after the fact – or an accomplice given his closeness to them both? Shit, he could be struck off! Or if he managed to worm his way out of that, he'd almost certainly be discredited. No, this couldn't become common knowledge. There had to be another way.

He'd leaned back in his chair and concentrated on calming his agitation with the methods he encouraged his patients to use. The irony was they worked, he laughed humourlessly to himself. And with calm there was the ability to think. Now he really had something on her, not the other way round. Now he could control *her*, not the other way round. The little voice he'd been trying to ignore whilst he'd been deciding what to do had finally slipped out into the open away from Erin and her insidious animalistic influence. He and Erin *would* now have to effectively become partners in crime – if crime was the right word. He would use her for research – to break new ground; be more than just the fluffy pink psycho-babble shrink for the fluffy pink psycho-babble neurotics who paid far more than his fluffy pink psycho-babble time was worth. Maybe he could even learn how to do what she did too? Then he needn't be any kind of shrink at all, nor slave over research and papers to publish. He could be anything he wanted. He laughed – a long, low rumble like thunder in the distance. Oh yes, now that *really* appealed! But he needed to protect himself too. He pulled a sheet of headed paper from his top drawer, and began to write.

By the time he left to meet Erin, the passenger compartment of the dashboard contained another file – an amalgamation of sections of the Matthews and Grey files – the essential parts. The parts that would prove what he suspected Erin was going to tell him about Roseanne when they met. His insurance – along with the letter. The rest of it, the drawn guts of the two original files, with the tell-tale serrated edges of the removed pages evident, just in case, he'd replaced in the dormant range where Jenny could produce them if needed. All bases covered, whether the outcome of this meeting was good or bad. The pit of his stomach had developed a new batch of molten lead, churning and agitating as he walked, but this time it wasn't desire that could be satisfied by physical stimulus; a hunger to dominate and possess softer flesh than his. This hunger was far more difficult to slake. It was for power, and that power came through knowledge. Yes, they still had negotiating to do. He'd promised Erin he'd help. And he would – up to a point. But he hadn't promised Roseanne that. For her to have his assistance, she would have to reciprocate.

He left the office and drove to the rendezvous spot, walking the last part. The frosty ground crunched underfoot. Did she really think he was so weak she could manipulate him that easily? He wasn't dumb. He was smart – smarter than her. His teeth clenched together at that. Damn her and the way she ordered him around. He wasn't her plaything or her servant. And he'd already thought it through far further than she had. He'd even parked the car where no one would find it in case she tried to coerce him with her magic to cashing in his insurance policy – after he'd got rid of the letter, of course. He was bomb-proof now, whatever she did. He smiled as he approached her. He felt good. Better than good. He felt alive. In control of his life at last. In control of her.

# Chapter 34: Erin

He met her exactly where she'd told him to. No quibble, no fuss, smile hanging casually from his face, but she could tell he was up to something. The charming therapist had given way to the enthusiastic lover, then the fascinated audience whilst she performed for him, and now the calculating crook revealed himself. But still he played. He was a charlatan. Of course, he had blackmail on his mind. Luckily, he clearly also had sex on it too. That at least had worked. He drank her mouth greedily and fumbled under her coat as they skirted the lake and stood under the willow trees in the freezing park, almost into the reed bank by the edge of the water.

'God, I want you!' he exclaimed, reaching into the depths of her clothing, icy hands touching bare skin. 'Oh Christ, and you're naked under there!'

She placed his hand on her crotch and gyrated against him. No one could see. The willow branches spread around them like a ragged fluttering curtain, but the place was empty anyway. That was why she'd chosen it. Even the birds had left the frozen lake and were huddling in the reeds, geese honking at the imposition of intruders in their private space. No one in their right mind would be strolling the meandering wintery paths today, or lingering on the scattering of frozen park benches. Too cold, too inhospitable today. Perfect for a lovers' tryst, or an extortionist's assignation though – passion to heat them up, and cool detachment to set them hard.

'I thought you'd like that.'

'I do.' He lunged at her and she allowed him to fasten lip onto lip, skin onto skin, fingers digging into the warm folds of her. At the height of his ardour, she pulled away, tongue having completed its work again. So what if he OD'd now. 'What's the matter?' he asked, leering towards her, eyes wide and lascivious.

'Do you think you were followed?'

'No, of course not. Why?' he paused, frowning, trying to concentrate. 'Have you had more phone calls?'

'No.'

'Good. In that case my theory was wrong.'

'What theory?'

'The same as the policeman, Grant, I expect.'

'Which is?' she moved against him, encouraging.

'That Roseanne might have been killed because of what she could do.'

'Oh my God, really? By who?' She forced the mockery down.

'I don't know,' he said slowly. 'But there was something going on with her. I'm sure of that now.' He watched her, eyes narrowed. Not completely mind-bombed yet then.

'What?' she asked. Was he playing her?

'Maybe she was worried about the same thing you are – being discovered.' She watched him. If he was playing her, he was good. 'Being made a side show of,' he added. 'Being controlled.'

'Ah.' They stood slightly apart, surveying each other.

'I said I'd help you,' he reminded her, words slurring gently.

'Yes,' she replied, waiting.

'But I need to know how.' He squinted, struggling to focus.

'I see. And you want me to tell you?'

'Well,' he looked diffident, but it was put on. God, he *was* playing her! Even now – like this, he was trying to play her. 'I mean,' he continued, 'after all, you're the expert, I'm the novice. I need to know how this all works, don't I? I mean why, how, what causes it. We should work that out – together, couldn't we?' he frowned. Confusion was rapidly ousting manipulation now.

'But I know all of that already.'

'You do?' he seemed genuinely surprised. 'What have you discovered since we last talked, then?'

'Actually, I'd worked it out before then. But you still want to help?'

'Of course, but how?' he lurched against her, steadying himself by pulling her into a rough embrace. Briefly she allowed the contact, before pulling away to peer into his face.

'Well, what if I told you I'd figured out a way not to be lonely *and* be protected – and enable you to understand how and why, and what causes me and Roseanne to be as we are.'

'Which is?' his expression was greedy, eager. 'Is it replicable?'

'So *you* want to be like me too? Do what I can do?'

His breath was coming fast and shallow. 'Maybe.' He hesitated. 'But how could that be?'

'Suppose I told you? Or better still, I showed you?'

'My God, yes!' His breath came out in a rush with the words. 'Now you're talking! Show me!'

'All right then,' she smiled slowly and lasciviously, enjoying what she imagined the anticipation was doing to him. Cold sweat gathering under his arms and a sharp electric thrill stabbing through his gut and into his genitals – oh yes. 'Let's get on with it.'

'Here? But …'

'No buts,' she said, placing her finger against his lips. 'You'll just have to trust me.' She leaned over, barely having to raise onto the balls of her feet to kiss him, keeping her eyes open as he closed his and desire overwhelmed him. He might be playing her, but he couldn't stop her playing him too – and she was far better at it. She drew slowly away from him.

'And if I do?' he grinned, moon-faced and stupid with lust and avarice. 'What are you expecting back from me?'

'Obedience,' she smiled.

He recoiled. 'Obedience?'

'Yes, complete obedience, and this is a one-time only offer. Unless you'd like me to ring up that policeman and repeat to him everything you've told me?'

'No!' His face was suddenly pinched and set. He swayed towards her. 'But as for obedience? We've got a little negotiating to do first.'

Ah, so now it began…

# Chapter 35: Roseanne

It felt like the culmination to one of those suspense films – everything focusing in on one point, Erin and the sibilant, whispering phone calls, Jay and his threats, and Mr Beringer and his now overly-careful observance. She went to bed that last night with them all in her head, going round and round.

*'I know where you live.'*

'Ro, there's no ignoring me. We must talk.'

'Are you sure you're all right?'

*'I can find you anytime I like.'*

'I can't help you if you don't talk to me. Talk to me, please.'

'You can make another appointment any time, you know that. I'm here to help.'

*'And I can make you do anything I want you to.'*

'Ro. This is ridiculous. Don't shut me out. He'll find you anyway.'

'We could talk about what you think you see.'

*'There is no escape. You know that don't you?'*

'All right, don't talk, but now he's coming for you. I can't stop him.'

'What makes you think you can fly? Is it something from your childhood?'

*'You are dust ... '*

The temptation had been immense – to ring Erin back. She'd even scribbled the number on the side of the newspaper that had contained the article about her. The very fact that she could do that – dial last number recall and listen to the emotionless voice recount the number that had just called her – meant she was halfway to not being crazy. And anyway, what was the point? Jay was coming to find her anyway. Was already in her head, if not controlling her body. That meant Erin was too, and still there was nothing to talk about.

In the morning, when she opened her eyes and remembered Erin was already there, she'd rolled on her side and pulled the duvet higher, all the way up over her head, like she used to as a child. That childish notion of *I can't see you so you can't see me* had for a brief moment felt possible. Maybe it would work now? She held her breath and waited. Under the covers it was dark and comforting, a butterfly's cocoon, but she was no butterfly. And then she'd accepted it couldn't. That there were only two ways – to submit or to fly away – and the decision had already been made the previous night.

Erin and Jay were waiting. She merely had to play her part now. She was dust, waiting to reform. A Lady Lazarus.

# Chapter 36: Grant

He stared up at the first-floor windows; peeling green paint over flaking bone-white wood. The place was deserted – like most of the places had been that he'd driven past to get here. Ireland – the emerald isle. The forgotten isle more like. He shivered. The place gave him the creeps, like Roseanne Grey's place had. It had more than a touch of the same sense of abandonment about it.

'Abandon hope all ye who enter here.' He even said it aloud. It seemed the residents certainly had, or simply abandoned the place to its fate. It echoed the fate Josie had texted to him. *Being reassigned, Guv. The Super is fuming, and there are rumours ...* He knew what they would be. His blue serge was already on the hanger, waiting for him – or worse, even that was no longer an option.

'Not quite as bad as that, but that *is* where she jumped from.'

Grant felt his stomach tense and relax with shock. It gurgled ominously and he hoped it hadn't followed through in an embarrassing way. He spun round, telling himself sprites and leprechauns were all a load of crap created for gullible tourists, but still ...

The woman was standing by the garden gate directly behind him, leaning on a stick, gnarled hands curling round it like twisted vines. Her face was lined with the marks of great age, weathered and battered by life, and yet still fresh and vibrant. It was the eyes that did it, he decided; still unexpectedly blue and intense when he would have expected them to be rheumy and bloodshot. She was dressed in an old-fashioned full-length dress with a shawl criss-crossed over her chest. The hem of her skirt was mud-spattered and skimmed her boots. He could feel his jaw hanging open but seemed unable to close it.

'Up there,' she added, waving at the peeling first-floor windows with her stick. Her voice had a soft burr to it so the 'there' lingered on the air and caressed him. He shut his mouth only to open it again. The old woman nodded at him. 'That's what you've come about, isn't it?' The lilt made the question rise and fall like a song.

'Uh, yes. About who lived there,' he stammered eventually. 'The Liath family?'

'That's right. For years. All gone now.' She shook her head sadly.

'What did you mean by that's where she jumped from?'

He went to join her at the gate. It swung forlornly on its hinges, whining at him. Roseanne's gate had been left swinging open too, as if someone had just escaped from the place and disappeared into the undergrowth preceding the fields that ran on down into the woods on their far side. The paint on the gate was green and peeling too, revealing rusting wrought iron underneath. They'd been gone a while, the Liath family.

'The younger one. She jumped out of there.' The burr caressed her words again. He'd heard that accent somewhere before. 'Lucky she didn't kill herself.'

'Roisin?'

The old woman looked up into his face, eyes shrewd and curious. 'And who be you, being wanting to know?'

'Ah.' He rummaged in his inside pocket and found his warrant card.

She took it from him and smoothed his photograph with her crooked thumbs. 'Darwin Grant.' She studied him. 'Yes, you're a Darwin all right. Always searching.' She handed the warrant card back to him and he glanced curiously at the photograph before putting the card away again. The face that looked back at him seemed so much younger and more carefree than now yet the card was only a year old.

'Searching?' he asked.

'Searching,' she repeated. 'Yes, Roisin. That was her name. But they're all gone now.'

'Do you know where? I'm trying to find out what happened to them. Roisin died recently, you see.'

The old woman studied him much as she'd studied his photograph. He could almost imagine her thumbs brushing over his cheeks in the same way. He blinked to bring himself back to full concentration as she started talking.

'Roisin dead? You surprise me. Not a one to die, that one.' Grant waited, consciously biting back the torrent of questions that were trying to flood out of his mouth. This one wasn't to be rushed. 'I can tell you some. Then you'll need to go searching again. Father drank himself to death, mother was worse than useless – always ill. Fanciful too.'

'Ill?'

'Ill. She went down the road to Drumcomm. The older one took over the younger one then.'

'What's Drumcomm?'

'The asylum – the madhouse. The two girls – well Roisin, she left. I don't know where she went – as far away from her sister as possible I'd be guessing. They said it was the mother's fault she jumped out that window, but I always thought it was the other one – the sister.' She waved her stick towards the first-floor windows again. 'I saw her, standing up there after Roisin had jumped, smiling. Then she ran outside and started up all the fuss, but I saw her.'

'What happened to the sister?'

'She got married and left a while after Roisin went. Some English fella with a man's name.'

Grant waited but she just nodded at him knowingly. He nodded back, disappointed. Did the old dear have all her marbles?

'Do you remember it – the English fella's name?' he asked automatically.

'No, I'm old, mister policeman. I forget.' She turned and started to plod away. He felt like he was standing on a fifties horror set just after one of the characters had forgotten their lines and ruined the take. His instincts told him he was on a hiding to nothing even if he had found Roseanne Grey's alter ego and a surprising coincidence in her past, but old habits died hard. Ask, even if you know you won't get an answer. It would be his epitaph.

'Please try to remember. This is important.'

'To whom?' she turned and stared at him.

'Me,' he said simply. There, he'd admitted it. This wasn't for justice or Roseanne Grey or because she wasn't 'just' a suicide. It was for him; proving the Super wrong, proving Stacey wrong – and proving Alice not wrong for believing in him.

'Erin,' she said. A bolt of surprise shot through him. He stared at the old woman with her bright blue eyes. They twinkled back at him like Alice's did.

'Erin?'

'The sister. Married some bloke with a man's name – Mark, Martin – that sort of thing.'

'Matthews by any chance?' he asked.

'Could be,' she said indifferently. 'Matthews. But it won't have lasted. She was only using him to get herself to England – to find the sister again. She owned her, you see? In here,' she tapped her head. 'Jacinta – Jay. That was the mother. Thought she was someone else in the end too. A man. Plain mad if you ask me. Keep searching, won't you? You'll find it.'

'What?' he demanded, frowning.

'Whatever you're searching for.' She clanged the gate shut behind her and stomped off into the cloddy field across the lane, leaving him staring after her.

'Well, that would be useful,' he said to her slowly diminishing back. 'Especially if I knew what it was.' He looked back up at the window and a blast of cold air rushed at him as if he was falling, falling. 'Fuck!' he added, groping for the rickety gate to support him. *Jacinta – Jay. That was the mother. Keep searching, won't you? You'll find it.* He resolutely shook away the feeling – the same feeling as on the railway bridge, and again when he'd been sniffing the pepper-blasted plate in Erin Matthew's kitchen. 'This has got to stop, whatever it is!'

Whatever it was, it was swiftly replaced by the need to find a way out of the storm that was now past gathering back in the UK, but had seemingly broken full force. The voicemail on his phone, that pinged its existence to him, elaborated.

'Detective Superintendent Carter-Rowles' PA here. As you missed your meeting with Detective Superintendent Carter-Rowles this morning, Detective Sergeant Grant, please report in at five o'clock this afternoon for your pre-disciplinary hearing. You are being charged with harassment of Ms Erin Matthews and outright insubordination. Bring the case files for Roseanne Grey, Henry Smythe, Francis Winton-Jones and Hubert Ffynes. You are being relieved of them, and of duty.'

Shit! And Henry Smythe and Francis Winton-Jones? Who the hell were they? Hubert Ffynes was the bloke Erin Matthews had driven into, but the others? And why was he being charged with harassing the Matthews woman? Beringer maybe ... or the Matthews woman herself? She was cold as hell frozen over and twice as determined. It wasn't within the bounds of possibility for her to have actually taken the fight to Grant by complaining to Carter-Rowles. She was just that sort. But how had he harassed her? What had she made up about his visit – and that Beringer would no doubt have backed up. Lying bastard! But insubordination? Vaguely something filtered back to him from the messy pile of case folders he'd left spread across his desk for Josie to clear away in order to tinsel his PC a few days ago. The burglary in Downston and the fraud case in Ambleside. Shit. He'd been meant to clear them too – and there were murmurings the Super was pally with the Winton-Jones bloke. If he was being relieved of them and relieved of duty, that meant full stop – suspended. Preliminary to being discharged without pension.

'Shit!' he said, this time aloud. 'And not other people's this time. Mine.'

He turned on his heel. Drumconn. He'd seen a sign for that on the way here. He might as well be hung for a sheep as a lamb. He made his way carefully to the gate, picking his way round the cracked and uneven cobblestones that made up what passed for a path. He was fucked, but he might as well avoid breaking an ankle before he actually *got* fucked. He stopped, bells clanging like it was a royal wedding in his head. Broken ankle – or two. Roseanne had, but the body on Alice's slab hadn't. And the blood samples; they hadn't quite matched ...

'Bloody hell – she's not even Roisin Liath either.'

# Chapter 37: Grant

Grant bypassed the luggage carousel, pitying the poor buggers who had to wait for their suitcases to appear whilst everyone else's baggage circled round and around. A never-ending stream of other people's crap. He laughed ruefully. Wasn't that what life was, though? Stuck on a conveyor leading nowhere, with a ton of inconsequential garbage that was important to everyone else but irrelevant to you?

Time to get off. Time to show the Super he still had what it took and his baggage was well and truly left behind. And the Super? Well, he was still stuck on the conveyor belt made up of cases to close down and be rid of regardless of the human story behind them. Sherlock bloody Holmes? He'd show him Sherlock bloody Holmes; the kind that used imagination as well as facts to get results. This *only a suicide* *was* the murder he'd suspected it was, and now he had enough to prove it warranted proper investigation. The Matthews woman was the deceased's sister and she was obviously targeting Beringer – that was why she'd been cosying up to him. That meant she probably suspected him of something too. Now all he needed was to establish Beringer's motive and then he'd have his murderer twirling all round his psycho-babble.

Grinning, he rubbed his hand across his chin to hide the self-satisfaction from the rest of the crowds hustling to get out of baggage reclaim and through customs. It rasped like an old man's wheeze. It was only then he realised he was already a good five hours past his rendezvous with the Super and suspension. His, then, reasonably tidy shirt was now as crumpled and unkempt as his face and his professional reputation. He ducked into the gents and glowered at himself in the mirror.

'Christ, you're a mess, boy,' he said to his reflection. 'You need to smarten up or no-one will take you seriously.' He pulled out the warrant card the old woman had stroked so tenderly. Was that really only a year ago? Had he changed so much? Lost so much stature and credibility? He placed his hands on the worktop surrounding the washbasins and leaned in closer until he was almost nose to nose with himself. A vision of the Matthews woman and Beringer laughing at him – taunting him – made him grind his teeth. His eyes funnelled into one so he became a cyclops staring into his single eye, seeing only one thing – a too close version of himself. It brought him up short with a start. He was seeing things alright – but with tunnel vision. He leaned away and looked at himself again, the too-long hair curling over his collar, the shadowed eyes from months of waking at three am and not being able to get back to sleep as he wondered again and again why Stacey had done it. The downturn to his mouth that seemed to reflect his mood most of the time – unless he was talking to Alice ... why on earth was Alice nice to him? He looked like shit and he behaved worse. He thought back over their conversations and the number of times she'd gently pushed him to reflect on what he was doing before he just blundered on and did it. 'Oh God!' he exclaimed. 'What an idiot I am!'

He let go of the worktop and pulled himself up to his full height, assessing what else he'd misconstrued. The Matthews woman, Beringer, the tricks ... He rubbed his chin again. Maybe he'd focused too narrowly on all of that too? There was something ... He could feel it, but he couldn't quite put his finger on it – like with the Riggs case. He'd felt that too – in his gut; but, of course, he couldn't say that to anyone. The strange spinning in his head came and went again, and with it, almost an answer; almost clarity ... For God's sake, he was already in the shit, but in the shit and spooky too – there'd be no coming back from that! And Stacey, he didn't own her, and she didn't own him. In fact, if anything maybe he *owed* her – all the late nights, all the refusals of what most married couples considered par for the course – kids, pets, even bloody DIY. Erin Matthews had felt she owned her sister though – that had been an odd statement to make. Yet she'd totally denied even knowing her. Why? Had she confided in Beringer, or was he as much in the dark about the relationship between his two patients as Grant had been until now? And if she was after revenge, why not simply take what she knew to the police? This stank – stank of deceit. Who was the body lying in the freezer at the morgue? Someone was certainly tricking someone – those little tricks Alice had demonstrated – magic tricks. And the mother; Jacinta – Jay, nutty as a fruitcake. Dead now after she jumped out of the window there and broke her neck. Thought she was a man who could fly – or was immortal, or both. The doctor at Drumconn hadn't plumped for one or the other, just a noncommittal, 'she was deranged and a danger to others', but there had been something else unspoken that had unnerved him too.

The free flow of Grant's mind snagged there and dammed solid. The answer niggled somewhere beneath the surface thoughts that he couldn't yet reach. He needed Alice's thinking space, but Alice would do as well as her space. In fact, Alice would do a darn sight better! He left the gents as the next wave of passengers flooded in and was hurried on through customs and out the other side with nothing to declare but personal revelation and a glimmer of an idea.

Outside it was already pitch black, and for once there were no rows of lights or tinsel garlands bedecking the halls. Gatwick airport had enough to light it up with its runways. Oddly he wished there had been. The festive season seemed more appealing all of a sudden. He found a quiet spot just outside south terminal and propped himself up against the wall. There'd be no reception in the car park and once he was en route, he'd have to fiddle around with Bluetooth or hands free and he hated all that tech stuff just to talk to someone.

'Hey,' he tried to sound casual. 'How's tricks there?'

'Darwin,' she sounded pleased to hear from him. 'Are you back?'

'Landed about half an hour ago.'

'Oh, and was it worth it? I hope so because someone's on the warpath and we've heard about it even in the depths of Forensics.'

'Ah,' he grimaced. 'Well, I hope so, but there are a couple of things I wanted to ask you first.'

'Ask away, but you'll have to make it quick, I'm afraid. I'm the only one available on the late shift at the moment and there's a call coming in on the other line.'

'OK, the first one is this – have we still got Erin Matthews' car in the pound?'

'Erin Matthews'? Not Roseanne Grey's?'

'No, definitely Erin Matthews'.'

The phone went silent. He watched a plane circle and come into land, skimming so low over the terminal he could see its undercarriage twinkling. A risk-taker. Or carefully planned. Alice's voice filled his ear like music. 'Yes, it's still in the pound since they haven't yet decided whether to pursue her or the other driver for dangerous driving. She drove into him, but he was on the phone at the time. The case has been marked as on hold.'

'So, was the wreckage examined for faults or possible reasons for the crash?'

'I think it had the usual checks done on it but, as she openly admitted to losing control, there was no real reason for anything too detailed.'

'She admitted she did it on purpose?

'Well yes, she said so.'

'I wasn't allocated the case. Why?' She was silent again. This time she wasn't checking anything. 'Oh, I get it. Grant will make a mountain out of a molehill. And the other guy? The other driver? What do we have on him? And why hasn't he pressed charges yet – or come to that, been charged himself with dangerous driving?'

'He's a local businessman. Name of Hubert Ffynes, lives in The Firs area.'

'Yes, the fine Mr Ffynes.'

'Yes,' she hesitated.

'And?'

'Someone said the Super knows him, but I don't know ...'

This time, Grant was silent, then he exploded down the phone, 'Is that why he hasn't been hassled over this, because I assume he hasn't? And why I wasn't allocated his case or that of Erin Matthews?'

'I don't know Darwin. It's nothing to do with me.'

'Sorry,' he bit his lip. He imagined her doing the same at the other end.

'She's got a high profile too – of a sort,' she reminded him. 'Artist and so on. You do need to be careful with this. All of this. Especially if she's complained ...'

'Yeah,' he disliked the bitterness in his voice but he couldn't mute it. High profile; *and who took the flak for that?* Yes, he knew why the other driver hadn't been pursued and Erin Matthews had been left to roam free after deliberately driving at him. There was no flak that way. 'I want to know what the report on that car says,' he added. 'Can you tell me?'

'I shouldn't as you're ...'

'Suspended?'

'Well, we heard ... never mind. Just a minute, I'll switch the other phone on to voicemail. That call is still waiting.' He heard a series of clicks and then echoey silence. He imagined Alice walking the length of the lab to the filing range at the far end, by the door, locating the report on the Matthews woman's car and walking slowly back, immersed in it. He counted the paces there in his head, and then all the way back. He knew how many there were. He'd counted them the same way almost every time he'd entered the lab in search of Alice over the last few days without even realising he was doing it. There were thirty in total from the door to her workstation, skirting the marble slab in the middle where she and her assistants diced and sliced whoever was unlucky enough to be resident on the slab. Two times thirty; sixty – sixty seconds. And sixty seconds were all it took to take a life. His head spun again. The merest glimpse of an idea flashed through his mind in those sixty seconds.

# Chapter 38: Erin

'Negotiating?'

'Yes. I know…' He looked meaningfully at her. 'And I have proof.'

'Really?' She stared at him then turned on her heel and walked out from under the tree and onto the ice-crisp grass. The geese honked a klaxon farewell, fading to a distant braying sound, rising and falling in urgency as she continued across the park.

'Wait,' he called after her. 'Where are you going?' he was clearly unsteady now, swaying in time with the willow curtain.

She swung about and pulled her coat around her. 'I'm leaving.'

'Why? You were going to tell me how you and Roseanne could do all that stuff. Show me how to do it too.'

'And you were trying to blackmail me. You really think that's a good idea when you know what I can do?'

'I'm sorry. Come back,' he sounded forlorn – even looked forlorn, rocking to and fro on his heels under the winter-iced willow. 'Please? I do want to know how you do it. And I'm not blackmailing you. Just being cautious. I'm … I'm confused. I never experienced this before – any of this.'

She walked back towards him, studying him. He was weak but weak men were more dangerous than strong ones. She pushed a handful of the willow branches aside and stepped back inside the fairy ring.

'So who has control here?' she asked quietly.

He paused, still rocking. His eyes were dark and hollowed. 'You,' he said, his voice fading to a whisper.

She laughed, and let the coat fall away from her body. She stood white and naked amongst the shards of icy fur round her feet. His eyes clamped to her body, consumed with desire.

'We need to trust each other. Do you trust me, Mr Beringer? Do you trust me to blow your mind?' She raised her eyebrows and looked up at him through her eyelashes. The result, she hoped, was licentious;

breaking one kind of tension by creating another – disarming him. It was. He laughed nervously.

'Oh, I trust you to do that all right.' He stepped closer to her, reeling gently. She caught him as he reached her. Tugged him gently so he followed her.

'Then we're going to try a little experiment.'

'Experiment?'

'You'll like it,' she added. 'Remember I said sometimes I experimented on myself and sometimes on other people? Well this time it's on you. But I'll join in. Now follow me.' Obediently he followed her instructions, his shuffling feet making the crisp ground crackle. 'Now close your eyes and stay right there, absolutely still.' She backed away from him, watching to make sure he hadn't opened his eyes, found the end of the rope where she'd left it twisted round the cleat she'd nailed into the far side of the tree trunk earlier, and released it, lowering the noose until it dangled behind him. His breath was making puffs of mist in the air as he breathed out, eyes still tightly closed. She unbuttoned his flies and pulled his trousers down to his knees.

'Hey!' he exclaimed, opening his eyes and clutching at her to steady himself as his trousers bound his ankles tight. 'What the hell are you doing? We're in public here.' Despite his protest he was already erect, excited.

'Are we?' she asked. 'Who can see us?'

He scanned the inner circle of the tree. The branches hung down like frozen streamers. An igloo of wood and willow, shielding them from the icy world outside.

'Well, no one,' he said surprised. His fingers dug into her shoulder and there was a fleck of spittle in the corner of his mouth.

'Then shut up and close your eyes again.' She took him in her hand and caressed him. He came alive to her touch, moaning softly. 'Shall I stop or continue?' she asked, lips soft and sibilant, as she ducked down to take him in her mouth. He moaned louder and thrust at her.

'Oh my God, go on. No, wait – how is this showing me how you can do it all?' He was plucking at her, forcing her to straighten up and look him in the face again. She sighed.

'Listen, it's all about control and letting go of it. Pleasure and pain help most. Pain causes trauma, pleasure causes euphoria. You feel both at the moment of most danger and that enables your senses to expand beyond what they were capable of before.'

'The accident?' he exclaimed. 'So it was that?'

'Not just that. I could do things before too, but it enhanced the ability.'

'OK. But I still don't see how this will help me.'

'Close your eyes and let me take control while you let go of it – let go of everything. You said you trust me.' She rubbed him rhythmically and his jaw slackened. His eyes rolled. The little mind-bombs helped, of course – increasing intensity, lowering inhibition, obscuring clear thought.

'But … Jesus, that's good!'

'Then close your eyes again and trust me.'

He closed his eyes. His face went slack, abandoned to the sensations starting to overwhelm his instinctive attempt to resist her. She smiled, slipped the noose round his neck and pulled on the end of the rope. His eyes opened wide – as round as they'd been when she played the saucer trick on him.

'Erin, stop it, for fuck's sake!' His face was jagged, split into fragments of fear and fury, calcifying into comprehension. 'You'll kill me.' He sounded harsh, croaking. He tried to peel her fingers away, scrabbling desperately to pull the rope from his neck. No chance, she thought. Roseanne would tell you that. So would Erin's potter's wheel. You need strong fingers to create remarkable art. He coughed and gagged.

'No, stupid,' she pulled harder on the rope and wound it back round the cleat in the tree. It held fast. She studied him as he danced on the cold earth. 'Don't you want to be a Lazarus too?' His face was reddening, eyes starting to bulge but he could still breathe. A rasping, hoarse wheeze, dragging in air and trying to hold it in his lungs. Perfect. 'Relax into it,' she advised. 'Pleasure and pain. Trauma and euphoria. Or for the scientist in you, if you rob your brain of oxygen, you experience a high – euphoria and dizziness whilst lowering inhibitions, before losing consciousness. The perfect combination for expansion and transformation. And far more exciting than a car crash.'

'Oh God, oh God, oh God …'

She knelt on all fours in front of him.

'Now tell me what you know about me, and where you're keeping it.'

'I …'

The fingers of her left hand dug into the crisp tufts of frozen grass, whilst her right hand pulled him back into her mouth as he choked and struggled.

'Tell me,' she whispered, mouth against flesh, teeth sharp and teasing'

'Letter ... a letter.'

'To the police?'

'No ... to no-one.'

'Ah.' She smiled to herself, and slowly, slowly, he relaxed until the release came as a thin, high wail that she realised must have been his climax, not a siren far in the distance. It resonated in her head like a tuning fork had been struck and engaged. It set the geese off too – squawking and complaining that their peace had been disturbed. His struggling stopped and he went slack, the air he'd managed to gulp in exuding from his mouth in a wispy white cloud of mist. Her first thought was, 'He's dead, and that's his spirit escaping.' Her second, 'I need to re-group and re-position in case it's not.' If the geese kept up their alarum it wouldn't be long before someone came to investigate, deserted though the place seemed. She scrambled to her feet, and released the rope a little. He tumbled onto his knees in a tangle of legs and dishevelled clothes, still half-dangling like a broken puppet, but with airflow once again enabled. The noose kept him balanced – as if on a high wire, moving neither forwards nor backwards. Static. She secured the end and left him there whilst she grabbed up her coat and wrapped it round herself, shivering with cold and excitement. Now who was in control? Now who should have listened carefully to everything Ro had told him? Now who would have to rely on her to help him simply stay alive? The shout in the distance was both useful and irritating. Step two of the plan had been initiated. And he'd told no-one. Yet.

# Chapter 39: Grant

'I've got it.' Alice's voice suffused the airwaves – and him – with warmth. 'Unremarkable – airbags went off, front end damage in line with a collision of above 25mph velocity. That ties in with the air bags firing, and ...'

'Could she have driven at the guy knowing that she wouldn't hurt herself?'

'Only if she'd been going much slower, and so had he, although,' she went silent again. 'Hang on. Let me do some calculations. No one's looked at velocity or force of impact because it was put on hold.' Grant waited, mentally counting steps again. She came back on the line as he was still counting. 'Actually, that's a bit odd. The car was set to cruise control at twenty-five miles per hour. Any slower and the air bag mechanism doesn't work on impact. The other driver estimated that he was travelling at about forty miles an hour but slammed their brakes on when he realised the other car was heading straight at him, so they were down to much less by the time they impacted. Airbags activate at combined impact speeds of twenty-five miles per hour or greater hence both hers and his inflated anyway. But that makes a mockery of her statement that she just lost control at speed – with cruise control on? There is one other thing that's odd.'

'What's that?'

'There was a neck collar handed in by a passer-by later on.'

'The kind you wear for whiplash injuries? Roseanne Grey would have been given one after her accident.'

'Did they find one at her place if you're trying to make connections between them?'

'Not as far as I know. But maybe she no longer had it by the time she jumped.' Grant's mind was already moving into Alice's thinking space without even being near it. What Alice did to him ...

'You could check with the hospital if it had been returned by then?'

she agreed. 'But who drives head on at someone at twenty-five miles an hour on cruise?'

'Someone who's playing games? Or mind-magic. What your father would have called sleight of hand or magic tricks. You trick someone to convince them about something else.'

'Such as?'

'Such as they had a near-fatal crash which was carefully planned not to be – for effect.'

'Or to put yourself in the position of officially making contact with someone you wouldn't otherwise be able to make contact with.'

'You're still after Beringer?'

'Well, Beringer is a shrink. He knows how minds work and therefore how to manipulate people. But Erin Matthews is a manipulator too, it seems. What if she deliberately set up that accident so she could mimic Roseanne and end up being legitimately introduced to Beringer?'

'Why? That doesn't make sense, Darwin.'

'None of it makes sense. Nobody thinks they can fly. Nobody deliberately causes an accident they don't want to get injured in. But who is manipulating who here? That old woman said Erin felt she owned her sister, but Beringer is a controlling personality too. People do strange things out of obsessiveness.'

'Yes,' Alice agreed. She sounded thoughtful. He could feel himself colouring up even though she couldn't see him. But he was past that now. 'But it smacks of prejudice – and untested leaps of faith,' she added before he could think of a reply. 'Yes, Beringer and Matthews are obviously involved. Erin Matthews obviously had contact with Roseanne Grey before she died – persistent but seemingly rejected attempts, anyway. And Beringer was Roseanne Grey's psychiatrist, but all you have at the moment is an odd form of eternal triangle and everyone lying about their part in it. No murder, no motive, only a pointless and sad suicide that should have been averted. If anything there's the guilt – that Beringer didn't avert it, and Matthews maybe precipitated it. Do you need to let this go now, though, Darwin?'

He ignored that and continued. 'And one other thing. Roseanne Grey – or Roisin Liath, as that's who she really was – broke both her ankles in a fall when she was fourteen. Your Roseanne Grey hadn't previously broken anything.'

'What?'

He smiled. He'd thought that would get her – his ace in the hole. He'd been going to save it for the Super, but he might as well make as much use of it as possible since he was likely to go down with his ship if he hadn't figured out a battle plan before the Super found out he was back in the UK.

'The old woman told me that too. Roisin Liath jumped out of a window at fourteen and broke both ankles.'

'Oh!' He imagined her expression as she put two and two together and got the same number he had. 'Our body's not Roseanne Grey – or Roisin Liath – then. So who is it?'

'I rather think Beringer knows who, that's why he won't let us see his file on Roseanne Grey and is keeping so close with Erin Matthews. I'd say Erin Matthews has a pretty good idea too – and that's why she wanted to make contact with Beringer.'

'You're saying Beringer is some kind of Svengali? And what about Erin Matthews? What is she after? Revenge? But it's not her sister who's dead if you're right. And if you go up against them without the Super's support you'll have the whole weight of the establishment against you. Beringer is respected, even if he is a rich-man's psychiatrist, and Erin Matthews is too – it seems. Apart from which I was told that ...'

'That?'

'The charge against you is harassment of Erin Matthews. Darwin, that's serious.'

'I know, so I'm going to have to leave no stone unturned in order to find the evidence because the evidence is there, even if I can't get hold of those medical records or force Matthews to admit what she's up to.'

'Which is?'

'I don't know, but I'm going to find out right now.'

'How?'

'Ah. By being a bloodhound.' he grinned, about to ring off. 'Sod the Super. If I'm being accused of harassment, I'm going to bloody well earn it!'

He was pulled up short by Alice's, 'Oh my God, Darwin! Wait!'

'What?' he said, anticipating a sharp admonition.

'Darwin, something terrible's happened. My assistant's just come on shift and left me a note. It was what that call I put to voicemail was about.'

'Tell me?' he asked, feeling like the colour was draining out of his body and leeching into the ground under his feet. A pool of dirty yellow marked its point of departure – the dirty yellow of a Gatwick streetlight and another failure. But he knew what already. It was just a case of who and why.

# Chapter 40: Erin

Beringer was still alive when she checked on him – alive but unconscious, and his head was at an awkward angle. The shouting was coming their way but was still distant and no doubt more would be following soon, given the racket the geese were now making. There was still time at the moment though. She collected the bag that she'd stashed behind the tree – the same red carrier bag she'd brought home from hospital with her. It had seemed appropriate. She threw off her coat and dragged on panties, dress and jumper from the bag, then pulled the coat back on and wrapped it round her tightly. She folded the bag into a square and shoved it in her coat pocket before leaving the protective dome of the willow curtain. Outside the geese were even more vociferous at her approach and likely to inhibit the rest of her plan. She sent them scattering like the pepper had scattered on the plate of water by throwing stones at them, then hunted amongst the rocks lining the water's edge for a bigger one that was fit for purpose. She found one on the first recce; a flint with a sharp edge. She threw the mobile phone she'd used to return Erin's calls into the lake and turned back towards the trees.

'Hey!' the distant shout was much closer now. Looked like a park keeper or a gardener, investigating the disturbance amongst the geese.

She ignored him and ran back to Beringer. His head had now lolled far over to one side and he was silent. 'And now for me,' she said aloud. She gritted her teeth round the cuff of her sleeve and slammed her head hard against the tree trunk. The stars were bright fireflies dancing in front of her eyes as she murmured to herself over and over again, 'don't pass out, don't pass out, don't pass out.' The words had become her mantra by the time the gardener arrived to investigate.

He was on his phone as he ran towards them, no doubt calling an ambulance. As he approached, she renewed her efforts, helplessly sawing with the sharp-edged flint at the rope holding Beringer semi-erect, trousers still round his ankles and penis shrivelled and wet like a popped party balloon. Beringer's face had a bluish tinge to it now, but amazingly his eyelids were fluttering – trying to open. As she stared into his face one eye opened and stared back at her, then the other. He appeared to be conscious but unfocused, both eyes glazed and bloodshot. Good! It had worked the way she'd hoped. Now for step three. She put her fingers to Beringer's face and touched his cheek gingerly. Her fingertips left white indentations where they prodded.

'Don't!' he rasped, unmoving.

She jumped. 'Can you see?' she asked.

'Feel – face but nothing else.' The words were guttural, slurring into each other. 'Why?' he moaned. Her head pounded where she'd cracked it against the tree trunk. 'Mad bitch! Why?' he gasped and a stream of blood-streaked spittle trickled from the corner of his mouth and over his chin. Damn! Not quite as she'd planned after all. She loosened the noose enough to allow him to drag in a gasp of cold air.

'Jay did it for you.'

'Jay,' he half-laughed and it ended in a choking cough and more blood-streaked spittle.

The gardener was within metres of them now. Approaching from Beringer's side. Time for damage limitation. She dabbled her fingers in the graze on her forehead and daubed it around her eyes and over her cheek bones. She wiped the rest of it on her coat then hissed at Beringer. 'Listen, you wanted to know what I could do? Well I'm showing you. This way you get to be able to do it for yourself. Say nothing other than that you were experimenting and it went too far. I'll tell them I tried to stop you. Follow my lead. It will be worth it, believe me. Jay will make it worth your while.' She put her hands to his face again and pressed, hard. This time he didn't speak but she felt him flinch. 'Remember,' she cautioned. 'Leave it to me and everything will be all right – no contravention of ethics or patient confidentiality, no negligence charges, no blame, just absolute power at the end of it for you and for me. Now shut up and say nothing.'

The gardener loomed through the willow curtain. 'Christ almighty! I wondered what was going on over here.' His eyes took in Beringer, the noose and his state of undress in one sweep. 'I've read about this kind of thing but never come across it until now. Is he still alive?'

'Oh, thank God you're here.' Beringer struggled against her. 'Just about, I think.'

Beringer choked out, 'Police. Graan.'

'What's he saying?' The gardener pushed closer.

'I don't know. He's hurt. Delirious too, maybe?' She allowed her breath to catch in her throat. It whistled around them, an eerie gasp.

'Sounded like police?' The gardener reached them and struggled with the knot on the noose.

Beringer gargled. 'Graaan.'

'Oh my God,' she sobbed. 'Not him again.' She allowed her legs to cave in and she dangled with Beringer, tightening her grip of his cheeks and applying tension to the noose as she did so. Beringer's attempts at speech stopped.

'Here, you let me take over now.' The gardener gently disentangled her and nudged her towards the tree, grunting as he took all of Beringer's weight.

'I tried to stop him but he was like a madman,' she sobbed. 'He threw me against the tree when I tried to stop him.' She sunk gracefully to the ground and the cold invaded her bare legs as she turned her bloodied face up to the gardener, beseechingly. 'Is an ambulance on the way? I don't want him to die.' She ended in a high-pitched wail.

'Jesus Christ!' The gardener sounded horrified. 'Neither do I! But what the hell was going on?' He shook his head, but his expression softened as he glanced at her. 'You're hurt too. Did he do that?'

'He pushed me into the tree when I tried to stop him.'

'Sick bastard!' he hissed.

'No, I think he's ill, mentally ill.' She shook her head despairingly. 'He's been acting strange for days – ever since that policeman started pestering him. Some woman who'd committed suicide. I think they both knew her, or both knew something about her they were hiding. I think the policeman was threatening him. The next thing I know, he's begging me to meet him here because it's the only way. He needs me to help him.'

'Policeman? Bloody hell!' The gardener threw her an appraising glance. Despite the bloodied forehead and cheeks her piquant face and heavy-lidded gaze still pronounced her as desirable. She screwed her face up into a plaintive expression.

'I know, and it's sick, whatever it is. Both of them are sick. The policeman tried to pester me too. I've had to file a harassment charge against him, and now this.' She paused, and added after a moment's silence, 'Please don't let him anywhere near me. Oh my God, please don't let him anywhere near me.' The gardener looked more shocked at that than the state of Beringer. She marvelled at the human capacity to suspend disbelief.

'Don't you worry, miss. I'll make sure they know not to let him anywhere near you – neither of them anywhere near you. What is this policeman's name?' The siren in the distance was getting closer.

'Grant,' she shivered, forcing the tears down her cheeks so they dripped wet and red onto her coat. 'Has he broken his neck?'

'Shit! I hope not. This is bloody sick!' the gardener announced disgustedly. A siren wailed in the distance. 'Are you going to be all right if I stay here with him? Someone will need to guide the ambulance here. I'm afraid that'll have to be you. Can you walk? Are you all right?'

'I think so. I'll try,' she gasped, pretending to hyperventilate as the siren's howl drew closer. 'I'll survive.' She scrambled to her feet and limped out from under the crisp canopy of the willow branches. 'I'm a Lady Lazarus,' she hissed as she passed Beringer's lolling body. Behind her she heard Beringer groan; a long low of groan of dismay.

# Chapter 41: Beringer

Sounds filtered through first. Or rather the lack of them. It was too quiet, too peaceful. A void. He hadn't felt this tranquil in years - not since he was a boy. Or maybe even before then, as a small child, lying on his stomach in the garden, grass tickling his nose as he wove his toy cars in and out of the blades. The world had been small then – microscopic. Or maybe it had been too immense for him to comprehend and so he hadn't even tried to. A child's focus is small, isn't it? Concentrated. Funnelled into that one moment and all it contained, not trying to encompass the world and all its complexities, rights and wrongs, principles and lies. Erin's lies. His eyes jerked open and he was intensely alert. The world rushed at him in a cacophony of noise and smells and light. He winced and screwed his eyes tight like he would have as a child. The light hurt. He preferred the dark – whatever might be lurking in it.

'So you're back with us?' her voice filtered through the disappointment that he wasn't a child again. That this was now, and now was far more complicated than he'd ever envisaged now could be.

He opened his eyes again and allowed the light to filter in little by little this time. She began as a shadow, quite near, gradually solidifying into a version of herself only marginally less perfect than the last time he'd seen her before the car. She sat on the edge of the bed, studying him.

'Jesus Christ!' he exclaimed, raw and jagged. 'You tried to kill me.'

'No I didn't – and only almost.'

Slowly it came back to him. The whole episode. The surprise, the shock, the pounding in his head as his body went out of his control again, the exquisite pleasure and the orgiastic pain.

'You strung me up. You strung me up to die.' He gasped and his lungs rattled as pain engulfed his chest like an invading army, bayonets fixed, stabbing and slashing as they beat through his defences. He couldn't move his head. It was in a neck brace. 'Why? Why did you do it? I'd done everything you asked me to. Why did you try to kill me?'

'I told you I didn't. It was Jay and he only almost tried to kill you. Listen to me!' she rebuked him. 'You never listened to me. Now you have no choice. You wanted to know what it was like to be me. Jay was showing you – and experimenting a little too. Keep your mouth shut or they'll want to know why.'

He stared at her, silent with shock. Now he was aware of the smaller noises in the room. The click-puff of the blood pressure cuff inflating and deflating round his arm. The gentle tap-tap of the chart on the end of his bed, swaying in a breeze that was coming from somewhere unseen. The *busch-busch* of a fly at the window, trying to escape. They spiralled into that one word.

'Experimenting?' His head was pounding again. The kind of pounding that warned him things weren't good. He put his hand to his temple and it came away wet. He looked at his fingers. Their tips were tinged blue. He was sweating profusely but he was freezing cold. The cold of fear.

'Yes,' she shrugged. 'I could have set up another road accident but there was pleasure in this too. Jay wondered if that would improve the result. But he never intended to kill you. What use would you be dead?'

'I don't understand?'

'It wouldn't have worked if you were dead. How can you have expanded abilities if you're dead?' She laughed, rippling water over stones.

He was silent for a moment, and then, 'And did it work, whatever it is?' Jesus, his throat hurt. Like his windpipe was still being crushed.

'I don't know yet. We'll have to wait and see.'

'Wait and see?'

'Yes, until we can test it out. See what you can do. Ro could do almost everything. Maybe you'll be able to as well. But then we were from the same genetic root. You might be from a lesser one.'

'Thanks. Inferior, you mean?' he croaked, watching her carefully, trying to compute the meaning behind her words even though his head felt like it was stuffed with cotton wool – or clay like his fingertips. It didn't help that his field of vision was so narrow. She kept bobbing in and out of it as she shifted on the bed.

'Not necessarily. Different, shall we say? But I'll help you. I'll tell you what to do. So will Jay.'

She cocked her head to one side and the shadows under her eyes became violet, mothy cobwebs. She looked too fragile and beautiful to be so cruel – so damaged. She reached down and rubbed her ankle.

'You're hurt? I hurt you?' It gave him a fleeting sense of satisfaction she hadn't escaped completely.

'No, not you. Old injuries.'

He was silent again for a while, pulling the strands of everything she'd told him and everything he already knew together. The calculations began to produce answers. What was there left to find out?

'How much could you do before?' he asked eventually, the words forcing themselves out through the constriction in his throat. She didn't answer, just remained, head on one side, watching him, body sinking into a round-shouldered shrug like Roseanne's used to.

'Roseanne? How much could you do?'

# Chapter 42: Grant

Grant parked where it said no parking and sprinted into the hospital. The floor was wet and slippery with yellow hazard cones dotted around the worst of the danger zones. He slalomed around them and skidded to an untidy halt at the reception desk, scattering ante-natal class leaflets and patient satisfaction surveys across it.

'Beringer?' he asked the receptionist. She stared at him, prim-mouthed and suspicious. 'Michael Beringer. Admitted last night.'

'Are you a relative?' she asked.

'I'm the bloody police,' he retorted, flashing his warrant card at her.

'Oh,' now she was flustered. 'Why are you looking for him?'

'He's won first prize in a beauty contest and I want to tell him.' He made an exasperated face at her and she flushed. His phone beeped. A text. From Josie – followed by another from Alice. Josie's looked official, Alice's personal. It started 'Your eyes only …'. He was tempted but he read Josie's, and left Alice's for later.

'Super on the warpath. Wanted to know why you'd been to Ireland when you should have been at his meeting. I'm reassigned from Monday. All files have been sealed down on Super's orders, and you're banned from going anywhere near B or M under threat of immediate arrest. Sorry, Guv.'

'Fuck,' he said under his breath. The receptionist stared at him in open-mouth disgust. 'Sorry, he said brusquely. 'Damn and blast.' Her lips straightened to a thin white line. 'Which ward?' he added more politely.

She tapped efficiently onto her keyboard. 'Ten,' she replied, equally brusque, voice as lethal as the wet patches on the floor. 'The name was? I'll tell the ward you're on your way up, and is there anything else I can do for you?'

'I'll know when I get there,' he replied grimly as he marched off.

The lift was engaged so he took the stairs two at a time. At the sixth floor he had to give in and slow down. The stitch in his side was like a jagged gash, splitting wider and exuding guts. He doubled over and breathed heavily into his knees until he felt less likely to pass out. Might as well read Alice's text whilst he was puffing and blowing.

'Your eyes only: Cork Co hosp records confirm RL broke both ankles jumping from window 2004. Body on slab had no old injuries … Seeking other ID now.'

This time he didn't bother to temper his language.

# Chapter 43: Grant

The little nurse had a pert behind. He enjoyed it as he followed her along the corridor, panting from taking the stairs too fast. She was a student – no more than about twenty, he estimated. He was enjoying the fact that he'd just made all the connections he hadn't made before too. Alice, you little darling! He almost relished that meeting with the Super now. He hummed as he kept pace with the nurse, jagged side stitch long forgotten. The ward was the same layout as the one he'd started out on this quest from. Pretty much the same Christmas decorations too. Maybe they were standard NHS issue as well as the uniforms. He hated uniforms, but some less than others: nurses' uniforms, for instance – and white lab coats like Alice wore. This nurse's uniform twitched as she walked, in time to the squeak of her rubber soled shoes on the clinically-clean polished floor. He was going to enjoy this too – the come-uppance, and proving the powers-that-be wrong. It had been murder, of a sort. The sort that it was difficult to prove usually, but this time, he'd have them by the short and curlies – especially if Beringer caved in as he suspected he would, and told all. It would be all he needed to verify what they'd pieced together and to exonerate him of the charge of harassment. Harassment? Damn it. It was just solid, persistent police work.

'He's only been round a short while so a few minutes only,' the nurse cautioned him as they approached the door. Here, the temperature had dropped appreciably.

'As long as he's not been cryogenically stored,' he quipped. 'I only need a few minutes anyway,' he replied. 'This is pretty much cut and dried. I think,' he added.

She frowned at him but her arms were covered in goose pimples – little pinpricks of white against plump pink.

'And I hope I'm not going to be told off for allowing another visitor in.'

'Another visitor?' Grant's pulse throbbed. 'Who?' he asked sharply.

She turned to stare at his tone.

'A woman. I'm not sure who. Everyone else is off dealing with an urgent admission and a re-sus. I'm the new girl, just minding the desk. And it is rather cold here, isn't it?' she agreed as she turned back to push the door open.

'Shit!' He rushed past her. The cold hit him like white wall of ice carried on a wintery wail as a gust from the open window snatched the door from her hands and slammed it shut behind them. The window was wide open. Gaping. The bed was empty, the room deserted. It looked bleak and forlorn, the tossed aside blanket dripping grey and dismal from the bed onto the frozen floor.

'I don't understand,' the nurse stammered. 'He was in a neck and body brace. He had a spinal fracture at C2. We'd immobilised him to give it a chance to heal without surgical intervention – he could barely move.' She pushed the red button by the door and an alarm echoed, loud and urgent along the corridor and around the room. Grant only vaguely heard her words through it. Behind him the patter of efficient close-shod feet announced the arrival of the emergency team. One he recognised well. The ward sister he'd encountered on his first visit following up Roseanne Grey's suicide.

'You?' she exploded. 'What are you doing here? There are instructions not to allow you anywhere near ... Call security!'

He ignored her and strode over to the open window. Looking down, he gritted his teeth to control the vertigo. Six floors below a little crowd was already gathering around the two bodies, one cradling the other, and the trickle of bright red against glum grey that was creating its own scene of crime outline around them. His head spun and he was flying again, just like he'd done in Erin's kitchen and looking up at Roisin's bedroom window in the little house in Ireland; flying out to meet them...

'Shit,' he said again, and ducked back in to puke.

# Chapter 44: Roseanne

The morning of the last day…

Or it had seemed it would be last night, but daylight made everything more real, more immediate. She rolled onto her side and pulled the bedcovers all the way over her head, like she used to as a child. Under the covers it was dark and comforting. She curled into a ball and imagined today wasn't today and she wasn't who she was. She was dust, waiting to re-form. She sighed. But dust didn't re-form on its own. And today would be the same as all the yesterdays, and the days before and the days after unless she made this the morning of the last day. She pushed the covers away from her head and heaved herself upright, thumping the pillows with her fists to plump them up before leaning back against them. She smoothed her hands across the cocooning covers. They came to rest and balled slowly into fists as she reviewed the arguments of last night. No. Reluctantly she conceded. It was the only way.

A droplet of blood had soaked into the sheet where her hand was nestling, still clenched tight. She watched it blossom and spread. It must be the cut from last night, when she'd tried using the knife, but couldn't go through with it. Clenching her fist must have reopened it. She sucked her fingertip and the blood left a sharp metallic aftertaste in her mouth. She made a face and put her hand back on the sheet and traced the blood petal that had grown there. She'd never liked the taste of blood, but the colour was pretty. She blotted the stain with her forefinger and the petal blurred, grew tiny filament stamens. She pulled the soft cotton into a bunch around the cut to blot it. The blood petal was joined by two more – almost a whole flower. Oh well, let it bleed. It would stop eventually. Everything stopped eventually, settled into nothing. Even dust.

She threw the covers back and swung her feet onto the floor. Her feet stuck clammily to the boards. They felt sticky, like she was melting into them. Soft. Feet of clay – soft sticky clay. Why was she so soft? So malleable? She straightened her shoulders, and thrust her chin forward.

244

Even those small adjustments changed her – began the transformation. She too would be dust one day, but not today. Today she would re-form. Her fingers prickled and a tiny shock ran through her at what she was about to do. She hesitated, but the thought of the alternative … No. She pushed her hair away from her face and sucked in her stomach. Standing in front of the mirror, she imagined altering, re-forming, transforming. She frowned at herself, surprised. Was it already happening? She shook her head and the quiver travelled down her spine. She was already quite unlike herself – and it felt surprisingly good. Downstairs in the kitchen, she turned the kettle on. Sammy was there, curling round her legs, like cats do when they want something. She resisted the temptation to scoop her up into her arms as she normally did. She had other things to do first because this was the last day and it had to be done perfectly. She spooned coffee into two mugs, slopped hot water into them and watched the stark white of the milk swirl into the black, gradually fading to muddy brown. She hesitated. Even now she could change her mind. Stay as she was, but then …

She rehearsed her reasoning again. It ran in long sentences around her head.

*'I'm not crazy. I know that now. But you? And Jay?'*

Not crazy, huh? But you're still talking to nothing, the little voice in her head taunted. And if nothing's there, why are you talking to nothing?

'I'm not,' she said aloud. 'I'm talking to myself about myself and my predicament. It's perfectly reasonable to talk to myself if I'm debating.' She paused and stirred the last traces of milk into the coffee. 'But this has to stop. Now. I am what I am and you are what you are and that will never change so one of us has to go, and I know that won't be you so this is the only way. I'm sorry, Erin. If you hadn't resurrected Jay when mum went it might have been different.'

A noise at the lounge door cut her short. No more debate. The bottle said *Take two with liquid*. Little magic pills if you took them the right way. Little mind-bombs if you didn't. That was the way they'd been described to her. She culled the white powder from two of the capsules and sprinkled it into the coffee. Drifting from the kitchen back into the hall, avoiding the lounge, she called out,

'I've made us coffee.'

She lingered there, in front of the mirror at the bottom of the stairs – a great elaborate monstrosity like the one in the hall from her childhood days. She imagined … and shivered. That was then. This was now. Here.

And she was now, here. About to … She realised then she was holding her breath. She let it go in a small perfunctory rasp and studied herself more closely in the mirror. She looked relaxed, but inside she was coiled tight. To distract herself she mimicked birdsong under her breath; Jenny Wren's melodic tune or a swallow's swooping call – but the birdsong mutated into an ugly caw so she stopped and counted to control her breathing instead. Nerves were getting to her. It had better be soon or she would need those little magic pills herself.

The lounge door opened behind her, and there she was; her alter ego. She was carrying both mugs of coffee and already sipping one of them, cool and commanding, like she'd been ever since Jay.

'So …' Her alter-ego came to a halt alongside her in front of the mirror.

Their two faces stared back at them, one defined and determined, the other diffuse, pensive. Waiting. The same. And that wouldn't ever change. Jay gave them no choice but to play out the same old routines, the same old miseries. Which mug had she chosen? Ah, the one with the little mind-bombs. Cup, sip, slip; slipping slowly with each sip. Fate had decided for them, then. This was meant to be. She took the other mug with a gesture of thanks.

'So,' she agreed, eyeing her counterpart with the poisoned chalice of coffee, mimicking the same tone.

'What now?'

'Can we not compromise?' She tried to make it sound the natural solution, obvious.

'Compromise? How?'

'Make this the last time like this.' She remained facing the mirror, watching the reflection in it. The reflection stared back suspiciously at her, still sipping coffee.

'The last time?' the reflection asked, eyes narrowing – no, squinting to focus. The little mind bombs had begun to burst.

'As we are now,' she explained. She sounded so calm – how could she? She cupped her hands tightly round her own mug to stop herself grabbing the poisoned one, throwing it to the floor, confessing her sins – like she'd always done. Until now. 'I'll show you how I do it. Everything. That's what you've always wanted, isn't it?'

'Really?' The reflection's eyes widened, then squinted again. 'After all this time? Why? What do you get from that?'

She began to marshal words, explanations, persuasion – but it wasn't necessary. The eyes were already glazing over, losing focus, body slumping – becoming as *she* had been all this time. Spineless. The little mind-bombs had completed their work. And so fast. No turning back now.

'Freedom,' she replied instead, so quietly she wasn't sure she was even heard. 'I want my freedom, so I have to give you it too.' Then louder, 'does it matter? If it's what you want?'

'What I want ... But ... You seem ... You're ...' A frown. Trying to quantify the change. 'Different. More like ... me...'

*Now* she took the mug – before it fell – cutting across the bewilderment; biting back her own sense of disorientation at how things were changing.

'Maybe I am. And you are like me. So, we shall be we. I'll show you how to fly too, if you want to?'

'Fly?' So slurred. 'But you said that was impossible. That was why Jay couldn't ... didn't ...' The usually strident voice was a shadow of itself. Unsure, confused.

'Not impossible,' she cut across the objection, pulse racing and heart hammering against her ribs. She clenched her hand into a fist and it shattered and re-formed. A good trick – one of the best – but just a trick by comparison to what she was about to do. *But careful – you won't be able to do any of it afterwards. Not for real.* That empty stare was starting to get to her. 'It was impossible *then* but I've learnt how to now. I can show you, if you want me to.'

'I ...' head swaying on her neck like a flower on a stalk. 'I feel odd – weightless.'

For a moment, her heart felt like it had stopped. She couldn't. No! She couldn't do this ... Hesitation trickled down her spine at the realisation of what it would mean. But, then, she'd always known what it would mean, right from when she'd first had the idea.

'Like you could fly?'

'Like I could fly. Yes ... Yes!'

But there was still Jay; always there, lurking behind those staring eyes, greedily gleeful that at last ... Her heart kicked back into rhythm. She shrugged doubt away.

'Then you will. Follow me.' There was scratching at the kitchen door. It must have slammed shut at the same time as the lounge door. 'Sammy.'

Automatically she started towards the door, then hesitated. Animals had heightened senses, didn't they? Maybe Sammy would know. She hadn't thought of that. Her plan mutated. Better test it. She led the way back to the kitchen and was greeted by Sammy, settling into a tight sphinx-like statuette at her feet and offering herself up for worship. She bent to wind her fingers into the cat's silky fur, laughing at how it preened and stretched to meet her trembling hand. Suddenly it froze, turning its head in a single swift movement to look up at her. The cat hissed and backed away, back arched and tail flicking indignantly. She grabbed at it with both hands, holding its scrabbling, protesting body to her chest until it quieted, eyes still wide and snout drawn back into a sneer. She laid her cheek against the top of its head, absorbing its fear. The cat tensed and spat. She sighed. Sammy would have to go as well. Sammy ... her throat closed over as she felt her life shift and splinter away from her irrevocably with that one small act of sacrifice.

The shutter on the back door clattered when she yanked on it. She teased it ajar. The crisp cold of early-morning winter invaded the kitchen, displacing the stale odour of last night's meal. She breathed in the cool air, relishing the ridge of the threshold bar on her bare soles as proof today was real. Stepping aside to make room beside her, she put the cat on the floor. It hurtled out of the door as the defiant breeze snatched the untidy brown hair away from her face and trembled the lace edge of her night gown. She glanced down at the long white nightdress.

'Should really put some clothes on. It's cold today.' The white-gowned figure shivered on the door step. She staring back, pupils huge and black. The borrowed night dress looked strange on her – not her style at all. 'Never mind for now, though,' she added, noting how her bare arms had goose-pimpled in the chill. It didn't matter though. It would be necessary for her to dress the part later anyway.

The cat had already been distracted into chasing a pair of tumbling spiny leaves, the last from the apple tree. The cat and the leaves played chase and she smiled indulgently at its exuberance, relishing the last moments she'd have with it. The perceived threat from earlier was now completely forgotten, left on the threshold of the house with her. Would Roseanne be forgotten so quickly too? They said cats only ever lend their company, never give it. Sammy would have to lend her company elsewhere now, sad though that was.

She was so near the gate, but Sammy wouldn't ever jump it. She hadn't yet realised she could, ridiculous though that was for a cat. How rarely do we see how close freedom is, albeit not the way we imagine it?

'I'll open the gate,' she said involuntarily. 'Show Sammy where freedom lies.' Not that it mattered. Nobody was paying attention other than her. The little mind-bombs had all exploded now. Her alter ego was passive – almost gone already. Reluctantly she opened the gate and left it swinging on its hinges. Back inside, the state of the kitchen surprised her. It was a mess from last night – the arguments. The debate. She should clear it up – but then why? Her transforming state militated against it. Actually why? She wouldn't be here to worry about it and neither would Sammy. In fact, the increasingly unruly streak in her urged – why not add to it? It might be fun, trashing the place.

'Are you watching?' That laborious, silent nod again, eyes far away. Film in slow motion. She pulled herself up to her full height. Odd to be so in control, but good. 'OK. This is how it works. Think, and it moves. It's all thought, really – everything we do. None of it's really real. It's only what we think we're doing. Some philosopher said that.' She removed some crockery from the cupboards and scattered it around the room to demonstrate. 'Now you try it.'

Her companion's blank eyes attempted focus, fixing uncertainly on some crockery on the other side of the room. She watched, enjoying the effort, and its failure. The trickle of anxiety in her spine was changing too – to excitement. Then impatience. Slow motion was too slow. She wanted more instant gratification. She tossed the cup to the other side of the counter. It spun on its base and settled, a hollow, rolling sound.

'I did that?'

'Who else?' she smirked, enjoying the prank element of the trick.

'You?'

She shook her head dismissively. 'You're learning fast. Time for another lesson. Upstairs this time,' but she lingered by the back door for a while longer. Sammy was still lazing in the grass, playing with something – one of the leaves? Maybe she thought they were mice. Silly thing! A vestige of her former self was frustrated with the lingering cat – and regretful too. Silly thing! Why didn't it go? Too like me, maybe; too timid – until now. She wanted to go and say goodbye, stroke the silky head and thank the cat for lending its company, but the morning of the last day was swinging on its hinges. It was time to go, like Sammy would too when she realised she could. She sucked in her cheeks, swallowed hard and let the icy trickle of resolve drain down her throat and into her heart.

'Come on,' she said, closing the back door and padding resolutely along the hall. She caught a glimpse of both of them in the mirror at the bottom of the stairs. There would need to be some adjustments – but if she could pull this off, she could certainly deal with those. Her feet pit-patted softly up the stairs. One flight, two flights. The third stair from the bottom on the first flight would creak like it always did. She stepped lightly over it, and the creak followed a few minutes later. She reached the top floor and strode into the bedroom. She closed the door firmly.

'This is a good one. Watch the handle.'

She caught a glimpse of herself in the vanity mirror. Cold and determined. Not herself at all any more. Her alter image obeyed, straining to watch with blank eyes. Staring intently at the door handle, she mimed willing it to turn. Nothing happened. Her head was full of crumbling metal, the taste as bitter as the blood that had been in her mouth earlier, but she held it there and waited.

'Is it meant to turn?' her mirror image complained. 'Because it's not.'

'You try then. It's all about what you think you're doing, remember?' She was holding her breath and the cold sweat was trickling down and soaking into her night gown as she held the handle in place until just the right moment. Then slowly, it moved; a celestial orb revolving in its sphere and suddenly she couldn't hold it back any longer. It flowed out of her in a stream of wild magic. Momentum gathered and the handle spun wildly until eventually it buckled and twisted, imploding on itself as the door bounced open. She stumbled backwards, steadying herself against the bed. The covers slipped off the end with a sigh and settled in a snow-blanket on the polished-board floor. 'Here endeth the second lesson,' she mocked. Her alter ego stared, open-mouthed. 'And now for the best one of all,' she added. 'The freedom trick.'

'Freedom?'

'What Sammy will do when she notices the open gate. Fly – simply fly away, like I said.'

'Fly?' She was looking at her, trying to focus again, focus on that word. Fly. 'But ...'

'No buts,' she took the limply hanging hands and positioned herself and her mirror image in front of the vanity mirror so they merged – almost one. 'This is it – the final trick.' Would flying away be freedom? Who could say? She thought about the psychiatrist's long considering look that had told her he might, unexpectedly, and belatedly, be able to see right into her mind and beyond so it was only a matter of time before she wouldn't be able to lie to him after all. Last night she'd been so tempted – to give in, to be understood. Tell him what it was like to want something so much and not be able to get it other than through someone else. To be controlled. To even want to be controlled. Poor Erin, poor Roseanne. She looked at the reflection in the mirror.

'The final trick,' she whispered in the ear of her alter image, 'is to become me. Here,' she added, turning the vacant stare towards her. 'Let's start with our face.'

She made what adjustments she could. It wasn't difficult at all. The little mind-bombs had blown a hole in all resistance. For a moment her heart clenched into a tight knot and she faltered. She could still tell someone – the psychiatrist, maybe? Then she remembered his expression when she'd told him the little she'd been prepared to share so far. No. She had no intention of being the subject of discussion or research – or pity. Trapped again, but in a different way. She added the finishing touch. 'We'll do,' she said sadly, gently touching the thin white cheek farewell.

The waiting window was open and coquettish. Should there be a note? But then what would it say? And it would take time to compose. No, they could all just assume. And it was time now – before the mind bombs dissipated. She led the way across the room, pushed the window wide and climbed up onto the sill, cramming herself into one half of the open space.

'Come on,' she called over her shoulder. 'Come and see how the world looks from here.'

'But ...'

'It's alright. You won't fall. You're going to fly.'

'OK,' the merest doubt hanging in the dulled voice.

Squeezed hard against the window frame and they rubbed shoulders in the cramped space. Together, they looked down over the emptiness below; the hard, grey slabs and cold winter morning. Her heart pounded.

'Ready to fly then?' she prompted.

'I don't know how ...'

'You do. Just think about what you want to do and you'll do it.'

'But I can't ... not like you ...'

She shaved the edge from her voice and forced encouragement into instead. 'Just try it. Think. Hard. Put the wish into your head and desire it.'

Blank eyes squinted into the distance and then back at her. 'I am, but ...' Vacant eyes, vacant mind. The little mind bombs had all exploded now. Time to self-destruct, but she couldn't. Her mind had already done so. She would have to push the button for her to start the countdown sequence.

'Shall I help you?' she asked. Kind. How they should have been to each other but for Jay.

'Yes.'

The gratefulness, the thanks in the inflection of that affirmative – oh God! She almost broke then, but no. This was just a shell of a body, she reminded herself as she peered sideways at the nodding, vacuous head. A Lady Lazarus in the making.

'I'll think it with you, then.' She put her arm around the hunched shoulders and filled her head with the idea. 'Now say it aloud with me too,' she prompted, squeezing the hunched shoulders. 'I want to fly!' she called aloud. 'Come on.'

'Alright. I want to fly,' the echo quavered like an undernote to her descant.

'Again! I want to fly.'

'I want to fly...'

'Now together, and think it too. I want to fly!'

'I want to fly,' they chorused, and their voices rang out even as far as the trees on the hill in the distance. 'I want to fly ...'

She paused just long enough after enunciating the words before pushing hard against knotted muscle and tense sinew. The drag of gravity would have taken them both but that she had hooked her other arm through the crack between window and frame. She steadied herself against it and pulled back, watching the falling body tumble after the echoing words. It twisted mid-air as the woman desperately attempted to grab at something – anything – to stop her fall, but the ground was already too close. Eyes not vacant now, but full of surprise, then fear. That tense knot of muscles in her back were only now registering the imprint of the hand that had pushed her, even as hope faded from her mind and her plummeting body met the harsh, grey ground.

# Chapter 45: Grant

Grant slumped over his desk. The next day would be Christmas Eve. The parties were already underway in some departments. His was over. The fat lady had sung, Beringer and Matthews had jumped, Josie been reassigned, Steve gone on paternity leave, he had a nonsense explanation for a crazy case and Alice had gone silent on him. The only one who wasn't silent was the Super. He had been very loud – and very definitive; exactly what was going to happen to Grant now the fat lady had sung and the flak had been flying again – worse than any that had flown in the war. What was the point? He hated uniforms but at best he would be back in one himself come the first of January. Pounding the beat again. He almost groaned aloud at the thought. He just hoped he didn't get allocated Stacey's area. At worst, he was out of a job altogether. At least the harassment charge couldn't be progressed for the moment without anyone to give evidence for it, but he was still public enemy number one where the Super was concerned – and based on the statement the gardener who'd found Beringer and Matthews in the park had given – possibly also at risk of being accused of being involved somehow himself. It all probably depended on how good a Christmas Detective Superintendent Carter-Rowles had.

He had tried. In fact, fate had tried too – tried to lend him a hand by delivering the circular about the cold case job right onto the Super's desk ready for Grant to read, upside down of course, as he was being bollicked. But that had merely made it worse.

'You?' The Super's face was almost apoplectic. 'And why would I recommend you for the job when all you do is disobey orders and cause me grief? It would be giving you a Christmas present, not a kick up the backside. No, I need bums off seats and feet on the beat. You may be a pain in the arse, but for the moment at least you know what you should be doing even if you don't actually do it. And they'd only replace you with some jumped-up budding socialist with their head full of their arts degree and ideas about set working hours. That blasted Carly is bad enough with her tea breaks. You get on with what you've got. They're bloody cold case enough for you already. Get them closed down and face your punishment like a man. I'll decide exactly what that is in the New Year. This ...' he screwed the cold case job circular into a tight ball, 'belongs in there – with you if you piss me about any more.' It had landed neatly in the bin. Little doubt of that's fate either, then.

But still, he had been right. It hadn't been suicide – and neither had the Beringer-Matthews jump. He knew that, with a certainty deep in his bones that he couldn't explain, but he had no way of accessing what could explain – or prove it, and without that he was for the high jump himself.

'I'm going in a minute. You need me for anything else?' Carly was peering at him round the door.

'No, thanks Carly,' he said, unable to control the misery in his voice.

'OK, don't stay here all holiday, will you?' she said. 'It won't solve anything.'

'Cheers!' he said. The sarcastic edge was unfair. She was right – it wouldn't. And he had deliberately got himself into this particular pile of shit, anyway. 'Thanks for fronting for me the other day. It was appreciated.'

'Oh.' She moved further round the door. 'No problem. You only have to ask.' She paused. 'And say thank you. I do most things for a thank you.'

He nodded glumly. 'I haven't said thank you enough, have I? Sorry.'

She smiled. She looked OK when she smiled. 'Accepted,' she shrugged. 'More stuff piled on your desk though. I'd get it shifted before you go. Might be something worthwhile in it. Cheerio.'

He watched the door glide closed behind her. He'd never noticed that either – that the door closed without banging. She was right about the pile of shit on his desk too. The Super had made it a pre-requisite for not getting immediately bumped altogether for direct insubordination. Clear the stuff on his desk and then clear the hell out of his office until January the 1st. He hadn't expected it to have been added to though. He sighed heavily and began making a pile of the files he'd been left with. The robbery case in Downston and the suspected insurance job from the neighbouring road were two of them. Winton-Jones and Smythe – the two files he'd been supposed to hand over to the Super with the Grey file at the non-attended rocket launch meeting. Listlessly he flicked through the two folders. Typical rich bastards – and with the insurance job – hoping to get richer since the insurance figure was considerably greater than the street value of the stolen goods but as no-one could locate the stolen goods, the victim's estimate was likely to be indisputable. Posh nob names too. Hubert and Francis. Hubert? He looked at the name of the insurance estimator in the Smythe case. Hubert Ffynes. He paused. He knew that name. It was the head-on that Erin Matthews had crashed into – the bloke on the phone. The Super's friend. Hang on, he'd also featured in the other burglary. Were they making an insurance claim too? Both were reported on the same day too – the day of Erin Matthew's accident.

He rang Forensics. Alice wasn't there – or wasn't speaking to him. He spoke to her technician instead, asking, without asking, where she was. He didn't manage to find out. The technician, Casey, had obviously been well-drilled. That served him right too. The Super had balled him out about dragging Forensics into his little obsession party by enhancing the photographs so no doubt Alice had been balled out too. He wouldn't be speaking to him if he was her either. He did find out what the report on Hubert Ffynes car said though. It said a lot of things, but mainly it said he'd got a lot of broken china in his boot. On the way to a jumble sale, he'd claimed. Grant was willing to bet that this jumble sale would have been rather high class.

'Can I come and have a look at it?' he asked.

'I suppose so,' the technician didn't sound very happy about it. Probably wondering if it fell within what she was allowed to give Grant access to – apart from Alice.

'Don't worry,' he said. 'A couple of photographs would do, actually. 'Then I'll be gone. I think I'll have a man to see about a bloodhound straight after.'

He bumped into Alice on his way in. He approached with caution, hangdog and submissive.

'Ah, you know then?' she greeted him, stern-faced.

'I'm sorry. I should never have asked you to get involved. It's my fault if he gave you a hard time and ...'

'What are you on about?' she laughed. 'I told Mim not to tell you anything in case I was wrong and it got your hopes up too soon, but as you're here, well, come on in.' He followed her into the lab, completely bemused, even forgetting to count the steps across the lab to her workstation. 'There,' she thrust a toxicology report at him. 'Roseanne Grey, drugged – but it's not Roseanne Grey, according to the blood results from when she broke her ankles as a child. It's someone else –

closely related, given the genetic markers, but not Roseanne Grey. Or should I say Roisin Liath.'

'My God, actual proof then. So, who is it?'

'I would venture to suggest …'

'Erin Matthews,' they said simultaneously.

'Her sister,' Grant added. 'But that means it wasn't Roseanne Grey who jumped out of that window. It was her sister.'

'And drugged. Or more likely, doped, so she was probably hallucinating since she wasn't used to the drug. More trickery. We're trying to get the bloods matched on Erin Matthews at the moment but that's a bit difficult since, of course, it wasn't Erin Matthews who was in the recent RTA. It was Roseanne – or Roisin – pretending to be Erin. I may not be able to help you out there if we don't find another way of accessing her bloods – and we can't apply for exhumation on what we've got, I'm afraid.'

Grant shrugged. 'Thanks for trying – and at least coming up with proof I'm not completely bonkers. Why the hell would she have done it, though? Why the elaborate charade? And where does Beringer come into it?'

'People do strange things because of obsession. Maybe if you could get hold of the records Beringer had on them, it would be explained?'

'Fat chance of that,' he replied sourly. 'But I might be able to make the Super squirm a bit about his golfing buddies. Looks like they might have been up to no good with insurance claims with no less than a certain Hubert Ffynes – also known as target practice for Erin Matthews – or Roseanne Grey; whoever she wanted to be known as.'

'How so?' Alice's eyes sparkled and he still wondered how she got to have gold dust in them.

He tapped the two folders under his arm. 'Let me show you what expensive jumble looks like when it's jumbled. You might need a coat. It's in the boot of Hubert's car in the pound.' He explained his theory as they tramped across the pound and stood, huddled into their coats, surveying the crumbling Spode, assorted brightly painted Chinese porcelain pottery that now resembled a child's mosaic kit and a whole Meissen dinner service. 'That little lot would have been worth about forty grand on the black market,' he said. 'If he hadn't been on the phone – probably setting it up – and our crazy lady hadn't been aiming herself at him like a cruise missile, he would have been quids in. No wonder he's been so silent and not taking a pop at her or making an insurance claim himself. It was nothing to do with being on the phone. It was this little lot. He might even have pulled in a favour with the Super to keep it that way, although that's possibly pushing it a bit – but that's probably why I got these cases with the instruction to shut them down asap. Give them to the prat who's on the precipice. He won't jump. Except I did.'

'Well, you know where you could land with them, if you're still prepared to be the prat on the precipice? The principled prat on the precipice, I may add,' she said smiling up at him. 'The Super won't take kindly to that kind of slur on his impeccable reputation. He's very hot on reputations.' The tip of her nose was pink with cold and he wanted to kiss it. Yeah, he really was the prat on the precipice.

'Where?'

'Into the judge's chambers to get a warrant for Beringer's files. With the evidence that Roseanne wasn't Roseanne and Beringer must have known, surely there's enough to suggest that a crime is likely to have taken place?'

Grant grinned, a slow, delighted grin of appreciation. 'I may be the prat on the precipice, but you are the inspiration to jump.'

'I'm not sure that's a good thing,' she laughed. 'But I got you a new shirt and tie to go and make your approaches in anyway – just in case. That's where I've been. Happy Christmas, by the way.'

'And to Mr Hubert Ffynes and the Super's other cronies.' He pulled her to him and hugged her. 'I'm sure he'll want to lend his voice to mine when I tell him all about them. Maybe even take some of the flak …'

This time she didn't not respond. She melted into him like a snowflake into a drift. They walked side by side back towards the lab, hands not quite touching, but not quite apart.

His shirt was bold blue, as was the tie. He didn't look half bad in them as he rapped on the Super's door, running over his speech whilst he waited for the peremptory 'Come!' Nor when he and the Super repeated most – but not all – of what he surmised to the judge.

*** 

Beringer's files were in the dormant range. Apt. But not for long. Grant bore them away triumphantly, to the disgust of the receptionist, high pussy-bow neckline so tight it should have choked her. Back in his own office – at least for one more day – he spread them across his desk, overlaying the pile of shit he was supposed to shift with the shit of other's making. Thinking space. He hadn't got it yet so he would have to make it fast. There were only so many times you could blackmail a superior and get away with it. Outside, Christmas Eve was well underway and it looked like it might be a white one before it ended from the sullenness of the clouds hovering on the skyline.

Roseanne Grey – aka Roisin Liath, was described as a quiet, somewhat enigmatic young woman. She'd been referred to Beringer because she'd had trouble sleeping after her accident. She had bad dreams. What about? Escaping – or not being able to. Not being able to escape what? Myself, my life, my demons. Your demons? We all have them, don't we? It was clear from the transcript of the initial consultations that Beringer hadn't taken her seriously. Grant pictured him, self-assuredly supercilious in his expensive leather chair, nodding sympathetically at the woman pouring her heart out to him, whilst to all intents and purposes ignoring her. She was different, she said. He could imagine Beringer's response to that. Beringer must have thought she was nuts after that, surely? Disturbed, at least. There were no signs he had, though – other than the first prescription of happy pills, and the doodles in the margins. *Red tie, blue tie. Pens on desk. Clothes?* Of course! Her tricks. Her mind-magic. When had she first noticed his ignorance? When had she played the first trick on him? She clearly had played tricks – like the mind-magic Alice had explained to him with the polystyrene cup. It must have cracked her up – to be tricking him with 'magic'. Some of the tricks even seemed quite sophisticated. He read the notes describing her encounter with herself and it was as clear as day in his mind's eye. He could even hear her laughing – Erin Matthew's laugh.

He turned the page. No record of Beringer visiting Roseanne at her home later the evening before her death, yet he knew he had. Beringer had actually told him. He supposed it was no surprise really. If Beringer had been worried about the pills he'd prescribed after everyone thought it was Roseanne who'd jumped, the file could well have been carefully edited. He sighed. No suggestion of a motive for getting her sister to jump though.

He turned to Erin Matthews' file. There was even less in there. The cover sheet with her distinctive phone number, and underneath, a skimpy record of a discussion, concluding that her accident had been the result of a moment of inattention resulting in her losing control, compounded by the other driver's negligence – and phone use. Yes, she'd driven at him, but without malice aforethought. Accordingly, she was discharged as being of no threat to others or herself. A lie. That was obvious now from Alice's assessment of the final velocity on impact, and the neck brace. The discharge papers were dated the same day. He sighed again. This woman was smart. Planned, executed and covered up, but still no explanation for why. So much for obtaining Beringer's records. He should have known Beringer would have been sly about it all but he couldn't prove that either. He was about to close the file and admit defeat for the day but right at the bottom of the folder there was a small shred of what looked like a transparent sheet sticking out of the fold. He spread the folder wide and peered at it. What the hell was it? No clue, but something *had* been removed though, which meant he *could* infer that Beringer had deliberately suppressed evidence. He returned to the Roseanne Grey file and spread that wide too. Almost undetectable in the central fold was a similar shred of paper. There had been something else there as well; something similar – but someone had removed that too. Torn it out and destroyed it, or torn it out and put it somewhere else? He picked up the phone.

'Done?' Alice asked brightly.

'Maybe done, but definitely not dusted.' He snorted and outlined what he'd found. 'Where else could he have put that stuff? Could he have shredded it? If so, we need to get hold of the office shredder as soon as and piece it all back together.'

'Whew, Darwin, that's a long job. Are you sure?'

'No, but somewhere, there's something I'm not seeing.'

'OK, well, if you get hold of it, we'll do our best, but have you searched every part of his office, and his home, assuming the warrant covered that?'

'Office, home office, house, even the waste bins outside. Great big empty garage too. We got everything – apart from the shredder.'

'Where are you up to now then?'

'A long walk,' he said ruefully. 'But hopefully not to the gallows just yet.'

'Oh, OK. Let me know when you're done then. Are you on your own over Christmas?'

'What? Oh, yeah. I guess.' He picked up the post-it that had been lurking in amongst the other shit he was supposed to have shifted and fiddled with it. It reported a telephone call from Stacey in fat Fanny Adam's sprawling hand, with the invitation to meet up for a reconciliatory drink.

'Would you like to join me?'

He dithered. 'I'm not sure I'd be good company – or good for your reputation at the moment. I'm bumped back to uniform at the very least – if not bumped altogether come the New Year. I failed.'

'No, you didn't. It's just your timing was out.'

'My timing's always bloody out,' he complained.

'I know,' she said, 'but I'm asking you anyway. You might as well be a bloodhound with a full stomach as a bloodhound on the tiles.'

He laughed aloud then – the first genuine bout of humour he'd experienced in days.

'Trouble is, I'm a bloodhound with all the clues but none of the answers. I mean who jumped and who was pushed this time? There's no way Beringer could have dragged the woman over to the window and then out of it, the state he was in. But surely nor was there any way she could have picked him up – with all that gear attached to him – and jumped, unless ...' he paused. The image in his head made him want to wince. He shook it away. Some things you didn't want to imagine, and yet... He breathed out slowly and deliberately, burying the idea until he had time and space to examine it better. 'Stacey called me earlier, by the way. Left a message. Wants to know if I'd like to meet for a reconciliatory drink.'

'Oh,' Alice said. 'And will you?'

'I don't know. After all these weeks, and even telling you I was stalking her, why want to meet me now?'

'Maybe for the same reason Roseanne Grey managed to get Michael Beringer to jump with her out of a sixth floor window.'

'What's that?' He was mystified.

'You'll get it sooner or later,' she said. He was sure if he could have seen her she would have been smiling.

# Chapter 46: Grant

Where were those bloody missing records? Alice and her team had painstakingly pieced together the slips of detritus in the office shredder under Beringer's receptionist's desk. Nothing. They'd meticulously examined every piece of paper that had exited his home or office in the form of waste. *Nada!* The bloody man was going to take Roseanne Grey's and Erin Matthews's secrets with him to the grave at this rate. Grant pushed away from his desk and stretched. And he was probably following not long behind since the Super was even more pissed with him for putting him on the spot for a warrant which had yielded nothing. The same with the one in Beringer's office. He left the stuffy little office with its tawdry glitter and crossed the courtyard to the Forensics building. He might as well eat humble pie with Alice before he bit the dust with the Super.

She wasn't there but the John Lennon lookalike was.

'Alice is off until after Christmas,' he said politely. 'Left us boys to get on with the boys' toys kind of stuff.'

Grant looked sideways at him. John Lennon hardly looked like an enthusiast of boys' toys. He'd always thought him a bit of a nerd.

'You're into that sort of thing?' he asked, lips unconsciously pursing in surprise.

'Too right!' John Lennon agreed. 'That's Michael Beringer's car over there, by the way.' He pointed to a dark blue Porsche. 'Isn't he the guy they say you made jump out of a window?'

'No, I bloody didn't! Although, at the moment, I wish I had. Might have got some satisfaction from him for all the hassle he's causing me!'

John Lennon sniggered. 'We're going to tackle it this afternoon. We couldn't find the keys and the factory is closed for Christmas so we're going to have to do some careful breaking and entering to see if there's anything of interest inside. They couldn't use the cutting gear until now because it was too cold. Freezes the equipment.'

'Open sesame in all ways, then?' Grant grinned, in spite of himself. At least this little nerd was getting some pleasure out of Beringer's possessions even if he wasn't. 'Or maybe not, since he's such a tight-lipped bastard.'

'There's always the possibility of treasure where you least expect it.' John Lennon's eyes sparkled at him. Disconcertingly, for a moment they reminded him of Alice's. 'By the way, Alice left you this in case you dropped by between now and the New Year.' He handed Grant a slip of paper. It said, in Alice's neat, dainty hand,

'Looked again at the Brakespeare case but I couldn't see anything that wasn't discounted because the bat was such a good candidate for the murder weapon. However, the bloods definitely don't tie in.'

'I don't know what she means. Do you? What's the Brakespeare case?'

He stared at John Lennon, squinting at himself, reflected back in the small bottle lenses. The Brakespeare room joined him as background and suddenly the murder weapon signalled boldly at him from it. He stared. John Lennon stared back. He was clearly waiting for a response. Grant nodded.

'Oh, a cold case. Nothing current. But there is something else – in the photos of the crime scene. Right side of the room. The rectangular barometer. You'd have to test it of course, but on the face of it, if it was used with force. It would be eminently possible as an alternative murder weapon.'

'Right.' John Lennon gave him a strange look. 'You sure? We would have scoured the place and examined everything – unless it was nailed down, including the barometer.' He laughed. 'In fact, it probably was – to the wall.'

'It was, but they unscrewed it, then put it back.' He could see the scene unfolding in his head, like a film reel rolling. The careful hands, the planning, the clean-up afterwards. Jesus! Where was this coming from? First the Matthews woman and the strange flying sensations, and now this – something he hadn't even really been working on, just idly fiddling with. He focussed back on John Lennon.

'Have you got the file for us to take another look?' Lennon's lenses were blanks now, with just Grant wriggling awkwardly in the centre of them. Grant shook his head slowly.

'It wasn't one of mine – just someone mentioned it recently and I got curious.' He didn't want John Lennon to know about his hobby. Alice knowing was fine, but others ... He touched Maria Brakespeare's small business card, still in his coat pocket. 'Food for thought, anyway' he suggested. 'Is Alice away until the New Year now?'

'Yes, but she said you'd know where to find her.'

Grant nodded. Yes, he knew where to find her. But would he? He wandered aimlessly back to his office and his littered desk, thoughts of Alice and cricket bats and her 'curiouser and curiouser' kind of comments littering his brain. He gave up trying to clear the fug they created around four o'clock and since no-one seemed to be around and checking on him, went home. By the time he'd arrived home he still hadn't figured out what Alice's comments meant. Temporarily, he gave up trying and let himself in, dumped his coat over the banister rail in the hall, then immediately put it back on again. He'd been getting too used to warmth and normality in Alice's place. About time he got the central heating going again here. He'd call a plumber in the morning. He laughed without amusement. Or maybe after Christmas since tomorrow was Christmas Day. He went out to the kitchen and flicked on the lights. One of the lights in the three-spotlight arrangement in the middle of the room popped off, its bulb blown. That left only one. In the dingy light of the remaining bulb, Grant navigated to the kettle. Coffee or – he counted the remaining wine bottles next to the kettle. They were far too convenient there. He should move them. Away from temptation, he'd have a better chance of keeping a clear head. Resolutely he picked up two of them and headed for the lounge. They could go in the eyesore of a retro sideboard Stacey had said would look perfect in the room when it had been redecorated. And they could stay there. If anything would put him off the booze it was having to get it out of that cupboard. He skirted the hall and into the lounge, a bottle in each hand, and one under each arm. Bugger! Should have turned the lights on first, but he could hardly miss the ugly brown arc of the retro sideboard.

He started unsteadily across the room towards it, scraping his leg on the edge of something hard and unforgiving standing in his way, and banging into something else similar barely a pace further on from it. He swore and stood still, waiting for his eyes to fully adjust to the dark. Shadows dotted the route to the sideboard. He squinted to focus better. Boxes? Carefully he put the bottles down and retraced his steps back to the door and the light switch. Patting the wall, he located both it and a trailing piece of wallpaper that seemed to have departed the wall since he was last in the room. He flicked the light on and took in the disarray. The flaking wallpaper strand flopped forlornly by his left hand, displaying something even more hideous underneath. More layers of other people's shit. Even worse. Grant grimaced whilst surveying the rest of the room. Someone had planted boxes haphazardly around it, as if creating an obstacle course. He went over to the nearest one and pulled its flaps open. It was full of books. Stacey's books. She'd obviously been round in his absence to pack up the rest of her things. Yet she wanted reconciliation? Those tart boots had turned her brain!

On the top of the pile in the first box was a book entitled *The Unbearable Lightness of Being*. Grant picked it up and read the back cover. It contained the usual blurb about the story and a summary of the philosophical principle its author was exploring.

*Friedrich Nietzsche claimed the universe was in a state of perpetual recurrence. What has already happened will merely happen again – over and over. In The Unbearable Lightness of Being, Milan Kundera challenges this. Each person has only one life to live and what occurs in it occurs only once and never again – thus the 'lightness of being' of the title.*

'Bollocks! So why am I in this bloody never-ending loop then? And stuck in this bloody death trap of a place?' Grant threw the book back onto the pile. He surprised himself with his anger. Was he in a loop? He'd never thought of it that way before. Maybe he was. He pushed the book back into place so the flap would reclose and dislodged a book with a plain cover apart from Stacey's ornately inscribed *Poems*, with flourishes and curlicues as embellishment. He hesitated. They must be her poems. Maybe he shouldn't read them? But then she'd left the box in the middle of the room for him to fall over. Why the hell shouldn't he see what was in it? And if she'd left it behind when she left it couldn't have been that personal if she was only packing it up to take now with the rest of her other books. He fished it out of the box and opened it. There were a number of scrawled verses, each with a date, some months earlier. He turned to the end – to the last poem she'd written. *Ode to Joy.* He cringed. It only said four words. *There is none here.* He put the book back in the box.

'Seconded,' he said aloud to the room and its contents, feeling embarrassed. She'd written that about him – as well as their marriage. He picked up the wine and pushed it to the very back of the sideboard cupboard. Then he returned to the kitchen – the death trap of a kitchen in a death trap of a house. He looked at the kettle and the remaining two bottles of wine. Coffee or alcohol. Back to the loop? No way. He made a mug of coffee and went back to the boxes in the lounge, depositing the last two bottles of wine in the cupboard en route and slamming the door shut. One by one, he stacked the boxes against the peeling wallpaper, ending with the box he'd opened. He didn't want to know what Stacey was collecting up and appropriating as her possessions. It didn't matter. There was no joy in them for him or her. He pulled out *The Unbearable Lightness of Being* and bore it off to the bedroom with his coffee and climbed into bed with both. May as well be warm and comfortable whilst he learnt about challenging the supposedly inevitable and succumbing to the apparently unavoidable.

# Chapter 47: Grant

Christmas had come and gone with its own unbearable lightness of being – a solitary state though for Grant as he weighed up his options and found most of them wanting. Despite a gentle reminder from Alice on Christmas morning, he'd politely declined her invitation on the basis that his company was almost as wanting as his options. How could he foist a failure on her? And he had some thinking to do anyway – about states of being. She accepted graciously, but with a comment not dissimilar to Carly's. Now it was December the thirty-first. D-Day was almost here. And he wouldn't be celebrating – not the arrival of a new year, nor lamenting the year past and where it had got him. As the Super had said, he had to now face his punishment like a man and it would happen only once and never again – no matter how bad it turned out to be. There'd been no P45 in the post this morning so at least he was still employed – although of that, of course, there was no guarantee after he'd faced the full force of the disciplinary hearing set for later on today, and the Super's jowly disapproval. What was worse was if Alice turned out to be only once and never again. There was a gentle tap on the door and Casey, Alice's lab technician, peered round the door.

'Umm, Dr Richards thought you might like to know that they found some paperwork in the dash of Beringer's car. It turned up a couple of days ago when someone reported the car abandoned in Tower Street, a couple of blocks away from the park where he had his little...' he coughed discreetly, '... accident, but it got delayed in the system over Christmas.' She passed him a neatly zipped evidence bag with a dark blue folder in it.

'Thanks.' He took it from her and she scurried away. Why hadn't Alice brought it to him? He sighed. Stupid. He knew why Alice hadn't brought it to him. The contents comprised a folder, seemingly containing sections of the Grey and Matthews files – sections he hadn't seen before. He felt his heart begin to skitter about in his chest as he spread the folder across his desk. He pulled the two originals from the evidence box and added them to the arrangement to form a patchwork with the three of them. The two MRI reports were annotated, *"Limbic system, V4 and V5"*, and ringed areas with similar notes relating to the ringed elements featured on both. Grant put the two MRI images side by side. Damned if he understood! He turned to the last reported consultation on Roseanne Grey's file. It was the day before her death.

8th December 2016.

*Patient RG; follow-up consultation. Still getting along well following RTA. Discussed persistent sleep problems. Hoping will resolve with new medication to help with pain relief. (Whiplash). Discussed a number of other issues patient raised, notably her claim she can fly. Made a joke – fly like a butterfly. No. Dust. We begin and end in dust, and dust is what we have to be to start; that's what she said.*

In the composite file, the note was quite different.

*She wanted to leave and when I tried to stop her, she took me over. Yes, I know that sounds crazy, but she did. She stopped me keeping the door closed and then she rewound time. I am not mad! There is something very strange about this woman – and now she worries me too. When I look back, she's done inexplicable things like this before. I've treated her as merely another neurotic money tree; happy to spend, spend, spend while I listened to her yack, yack, yack – with the NHS kindly paying. This is different. She is different. She can change things, move things, adjust things without me realising she's doing it. When she went at the end of the consultation, I knew instinctively she was trouble brewing so I decided to check out what kind. I went out to her place to deliver her new medication. Yes, I know I shouldn't have done that – professional distance and so on, but this was different.*

*Yet she was fine –seemed entirely normal – as normal as a recluse can be. In fact, she couldn't wait to get rid of me! I'm hoping the new medication will be sufficient to keep her away from the office for long enough to file a report that she appears to be settled and currently no longer in need of further sessions with me as long as she continues her medication. With luck that'll go through on the nod and she's someone else's problem. She gives me the creeps.*

Grant broke off reading and went to stand at the window. Either Beringer was mad himself or he really believed Roseanne Grey had some kind of supernatural power. And to be fair, Beringer didn't strike him as impressionable. There was a dispenser's slip for some medication stapled to it too. Percocet. He googled Percocet. Oxycodone and acetaminophen – a combination drug consisting of oxycodone (an opioid drug type – research revealed) and acetaminophen (an analgesic and antipyretic drug type – the same research) for moderate to severe pain management. Potentially addictive.

*Could cause symptoms that are dissociative or hallucinogenic if the tablets are not taken whole as the drug will be absorbed too quickly. It is designed to work on a slow release basis.*

He referred back to the toxicology report Alice had shown him. High concentrations of an opioid drug source combined with an analgesic. There we go. Percocet. Beringer had prescribed it and someone had administered it just before she jumped – and in such a way that she was already flying high with it *before* she jumped. He consulted the website describing the less desirable symptoms Percocet might encourage if taken inappropriately – taken whole in its capsule, in other words. And what had there been in Roseanne Grey's kitchen waste but some cute little discarded gelatin capsules! Jesus! And Beringer had supplied it – the previous evening. But had Beringer prescribed the medication and told Roseanne Grey about its side effects so she could avoid them or make use of them? He would have to have told her. He was duty bound to warn her of the side effects if she ignored the instructions for taking them. Had he a handle then on the type of psychosis he was prescribing the medication for? Or had he really prescribed them simply to keep Roseanne Grey away from him? Either way it was negligence, and the obvious conclusion was that the woman they now knew as Erin Matthews had probably fed the woman they'd assumed was Roseanne Grey sufficient Percocet to make her think she could jump – and fly – and then left her body for everyone to assume she was Roseanne Grey. Or at the very least drugged her to the eyeballs, crossed her fingers and hoped – and the Erin Matthews he knew wasn't the cross fingers and hope kind.

Had Beringer known who Erin Matthews was, and who had been purporting to be her since Roseanne Grey had apparently jumped to her death? It would certainly explain the dismantled files if he had. Seemed like he might have figured out what was going on with Roseanne Grey and had been meeting Erin Matthews to blackmail her when he had his little 'accident', as Casey had so politely described it. And there had been discarded gelatin capsules in Erin Matthews' kitchen bin too. Maybe, ironically, she'd played it all back at Beringer and used them on him too? That would explain the weird sexual aberration in the park that had seemed so out of character with the suave, smooth psych. Christ, no wonder Beringer had kept all this hidden. He'd been playing with more than fire. He'd been attempting to manipulate high explosives!

One of the MRIs had even lost a small sliver off the side of it, and Grant bet, if he married it up with the Matthews file, that he would find they fit together. Similarly, some of the handwritten sheets must have been pulled out of the Grey file.

He looked out over the city. It was still lit up with festive messages, glowing in the dull of a grey day. Somewhere out there was a mad woman and the man she'd controlled, who'd mistakenly tried to control her. He'd been right after all – just not about who'd murdered who. At least now he had enough to make a case that Roseanne Grey had drugged her sister, Erin Matthews, and pushed her, or allowed her to fall, to her death from a second storey window, but where was the motive? No murder or intent to murder charge would hold up in court without a motive, regardless of its likelihood. This had to mean that it had been Erin – or maybe he should call her Roseanne, or even Roisin – who had tipped both her and Beringer out of the window at the hospital too. Double intent to murder. To keep him quiet? Or because she really believed she had special powers too? Or both? Presumably, it made no difference either way. They were all dead, or as good as: bloody shrinks and their crazies. Erin Matthews had suggested he was good at fictionalising. This was crazier than any fantasy. Yet, the biggest question of all still remained: why?

Grant leaned back in his chair and reviewed all that had happened over the last few weeks. One word probably summed it all up: obsession. He wrote the word and doodled round it. Or maybe self-delusion. That was another way of putting it. And traps. Allowing an obsession to trap you. Alice was right. He had got it – but later rather than sooner. Roseanne Grey – or Roisin Liath – had been obsessive. So had her sister. Their mother had been mad. And to his way of thinking, they'd all been psycho or sociopaths – delusional. They said madness was catching. Maybe Beringer had caught it from them, or maybe he'd just made some bad judgement calls and got trapped because he'd been trying to cover his arse. Incredible Beringer had survived really. Grant hadn't quite believed the report from the hospital, but stranger things – hah! He laughed. Yeah, stranger things had happened already! He'd need a psych report himself soon – and so would Beringer before he could be charged. The technical jargon eluded him but he knew what he meant. Once he'd interviewed Beringer he'd let Beringer supply it in due course – if necessary. One way or another, they'd all got themselves trapped in obsessions. And here he was still trapped in his. Belatedly he felt sorry for Beringer. He might have been a smug bastard, but he hadn't deserved what he'd got. And yet …

No. Forget that… But how was he to write this up so the Super didn't summarily dismiss both him and the report? God help him! It would all have to go into evidence nevertheless – body-swaps, madwomen, mind-magic and tarnished reputations; the kind of flak the Super would implode over, and he dare not mention the strange sensations he'd experienced around her. He flicked through the folders, alighting listlessly on one item, then another, toying with it, then putting them all back without a word. Bloody hell – really, how was he supposed to write this up so the Super didn't think he'd flipped too and send him off to see a shrink instead of the uniform outfitter? Or should he try to leave the weirder parts of it out? He closed the files.

His phone buzzed at him. Grant picked it up on the second round.

'Darwin?' It was Alice. For a moment he couldn't move. Paralysis seemed to have overwhelmed him, then he grinned elatedly. He'd hoped she'd make another move, but without really believing it would happen – coward that he was after ducking out of Christmas dinner.

'Alice,' he tried to make his voice sound as welcoming as possible.

He heard her breathe out before continuing. She'd taken the tone of his voice and translated it. 'I'm glad you're in. Have you looked through it all?'

'Most of it. I'm guessing you've already seen it too?'

'Yes. So now the Roseanne Grey case can be closed? Does that make you feel happier about everything?' The phone still seemed to be buzzing. He pulled the receiver away from his ear a fraction. They said phones emitted radiation didn't they? The scaremongers. Or was that just mobile phones? Whatever, it wasn't the phone. He pulled it close again.

'Well, better,' he said warmly. 'And you? Did you have a good rest over Christmas?' The buzz continued, a kind of *busch-busch*. Word association made his eyes stray to the window and the stringy wisps of the buddleia bush that now waved forlornly at him, outside the window, the way Stacey had waved at him as he'd driven away from her last night. No – as he'd driven away from her *forever* last night. His attention returned to Alice, and with it the sense of being warm and comfortable; contented like he hadn't been in a long time. The *busch-busch* continued in the background nevertheless.

'Well, actually I kept working. I wanted to wind it all up and put it all behind us both as quickly as I could. All of it.'

'And have you, because –'

'I have, and yes, to whatever you are going to suggest, but there's one little detail I wanted you to know before my official report comes through to accompany yours.'

'Oh?' He wondered if he should worry about that. Something else? He couldn't think what – clever though that she-devil had been. 'More proof? It still sounds more like a story of the supernatural.'

'Well, Michael Beringer is showing signs of coming round, although the brain scans are indicating he may have some long-term memory loss, but we already knew it was going to be nigh on impossible to untangle it all satisfactorily, didn't we? Anyway, I thought you'd still want to know that I've finally got some bloodwork results for Erin Matthews too, so you don't just have to rely on Beringer's evidence to show the Super that you were right.'

'Wow. That's a coup.' He felt like his head was singing. Maybe his whole body?

'It wasn't easy. But we managed to find an old record from when she was first married. She miscarried and they typed her then in case she needed anti-D.'

'Anti-D? That sounds ominous.'

'No,' she laughed. 'It's an injection mothers have after their baby is born if they are rhesus negative. Stops any antibodies being created by the mother should she have a rhesus positive baby in the future. But you have to know if the mother is rhesus negative first – hence the bloodwork. And it's good news. It all fits, just as we thought. They were sisters. But remember that odd marker I said was in Roseanne blood results? It was in Erin's too. Or maybe that should be the other way around?' Grant sat back in his chair, mind tumbling the idea. 'Darwin?'

'I'm still here. The same one – in both of them? So, were they – I don't know, both weird after all?'

'The weird sisters?' She laughed again. 'I don't know, but you did say yourself, Beringer couldn't have dragged himself and Erin over to the window to throw them out, could he – the state he was in? And neither did we think she could. Except maybe she did.'

'Still doesn't explain why, though.' *Busch-busch.* 'Bloody hell!' Grant exclaimed.

'What?'

'Bloody flies – there are *two* bloody flies in here this time. Don't flies know this is winter and they're meant to be hibernating or whatever they do?' He waved wildly at the insect hurtling past him and it swerved off-course. 'Just a minute. These damn things are driving me mad!' He put the phone down and crossed to the window. One of the pair of flies had settled on the edge of the pane, near the window handle, as if it was waiting for him to open it. The other was flying aimlessly around the room. He stared at quiescent fly and his head filled with noise and then absolute silence. Erin Matthew's voice came back to him as she'd spoken the day he'd found the magic tricks in her kitchen.

*Let it go. Let it fly away.*

A cold finger ran down his spine. He hated bloody flies, but somehow, he couldn't bring himself to kill this one.

'Out you go,' he said to the motionless fly.' He opened the window and the insect hovered on the edge of it. A rush of cold air had him sucking in his cheeks and shivering. A frisson of revulsion followed the cold finger down his spine, lingering near his gut. The now, almost familiar feeling of head-spin sent him staggering away from the window. The other fly dive-bombed him and he ducked wildly. 'But you,' he batted its dive-bombing companion away, 'are for the world beyond unless you bugger off.' He picked up the newspaper Steve had left behind yesterday, announcing the arrival of the bouncing Amelia Jane, rolled it into a tube and swatted the fly. It bounced off the tube and lay belly up on the window sill, legs waving frantically. Grant was about to pound it flat for good measure but he remembered the remark Erin – or Roseanne, or whoever she was – or maybe Beringer, had made about all God's creatures. And he was an officer of justice. Where was the justice in blindly killing anything simply because it made you shiver? If she or he could be merciful, then he was a damn sight better than either of them.

*Let it go. Let it fly away.*

He breathed out shakily and instead flicked the prone fly out of the open window and watched it arc into the sky and then float into the depths of the buddleia stalks. 'There, let natural justice do its job out there. If you're meant to survive, you will.' He stepped away from the window, the odd spinning in his head turning his stomach over and over. 'We begin and end in dust, and dust is what we have to be to start.' The fly on the window pane crawled to the edge and flew out. 'Christ,' he slammed the window shut. 'And bloody good luck out there!' He went back to his desk, sweating, and picked up the phone.

'What on earth were you doing?' Alice's voice asked as soon as he put it to his ear. Sod the radiation, he didn't care anymore. This was Alice.

'Sending some of God's lesser creations on their way,' he replied, 'so I can concentrate on one of his more sublime ones.'

The chuckle from the other end of the phone was reward enough.

'And the marker?'

'What do you think it means?'

'I didn't know when I first found it and I don't know now. It's unusual though – extreme, really.'

'In what way?'

'Well, it's not documented anywhere and I've certainly never seen it before. It's uncharted territory to me. It could mean anything – maybe even something we can't quantify.' She laughed and her amusement trickled down the phone at him. 'Maybe even superpowers. Do you want me to research it? Be a bloodhound? You said no stone unturned, but I'd have to wait to see if our girl comes round to do so in any meaningful way.'

'If she was responsible in any way for her sister's death and dragging Beringer out the window, I don't want you anywhere near the evil bitch! No. Leave it. You know what? We've turned over all the stones and there was nothing to find under any of them – not even an explanation why. But sometimes there is no answer. Just the question.' He thought about Stacey's book, now lying creased and worn on his bedside cupboard, and Erin's words, ringing in his head. Yes, best left – especially what it might mean if he investigated further.

'OK,' she sounded uncertain. 'And Beringer?'

'What about him?'

'Well, Beringer's blood work show signs of the same marker.'

# Chapter 48: Beringer

His body was inert; static – but his mind was moving fast, faster than light, pulling everything together, going over and over it again, refining how he should have dealt with it. How he'd deal with it now, if now still existed.

She'd jerked upright when he'd called her Roseanne.

'I'm not Roseanne. I'm Erin.' She frowned and her eyes narrowed.

'Erin, then. How much could you do before?'

'Erin could do nothing actually,' she sighed. 'The same genetic root meant nothing at all there. It was only Roseanne who could do anything exceptional.'

He hesitated. 'So you admit you're Roseanne,' he ventured. He continued cautiously when she said nothing, just carried on looking at him like a bright-eyed baby bird. 'I thought you could move things with your mind and … in fact, I saw you. And I saw you do the same kind of things yesterday – the kind of things you used to do when I wasn't paying attention.'

'What things? I'm Erin. Erin can't do anything. Only Roseanne can do that kind of thing. Tricks,' she said. 'You saw tricks. Sleight of hand, conjuror's tricks. Erin was always good at that. Even tricked Ro to begin with. She thought Erin was amazing then. It was later, when she was older, that she saw through it. But Erin had found Jay by then.'

'Jay?'

The clouds in his brain were gradually clearing. 'Jay. I see … but he's not real.' Risky, he knew, but he needed to know the extent of the psychosis.

'Of course, he is – to Roseanne at least. God, was he real to her! Every arm twist, every pinch, slap, burn, indignity. Every moment she stood in the corner waiting for the whip. Of course, he was real – she allowed him to be.' She smiled smugly at him. 'Maybe she even wanted him to be – he was her punishment for failing. Have you forgotten our

274

little conversation about control?'

In his mind he reviewed the events since Sunday, when she'd been discharged into his care. Not true – she'd been in his care much longer, but he hadn't bothered to look beyond the façade – the ditch-water dull girl, too tall, too shambling and simply neurotic. He'd been blasé, then naïve. Stupid. He deserved most of what he'd got – but maybe not this.

'Erin, you do understand who and what you are, don't you?'

'Who and what I am? I'm Erin Matthews, your friend who cut you down and who you beat up when she tried to stop you. The nursing staff here have strict instructions that if I push the panic button they're to get in here fast. You and Grant – you're a threat, a sick threat, but I'm being magnanimous towards you because you're clearly unbalanced. Need therapy.' She laughed, a throaty gurgle. 'And I'm showing how forgiving I am after what you did in the park – and about trying to attack me. I'm not pressing charges.'

He took a deep breath in, for all that it made his head pound from the blows of the army still battling with sticks and swords inside it.

'You're Roseanne Grey. And you were my patient. There is no Jay, and Erin is dead – I suspect. I have proof.'

She stared at him, the opaque brown eyes pulling him too deeply into them.

'You're confused. Roseanne's dead. She jumped. I'm alive. I'm a Lady Lazarus.' She reached across and touched his cheek – pressed so hard the flesh inside was pinched against his teeth. He winced. 'And I don't like being ignored, so don't ignore me again now, will you, Michael? Jay wouldn't like you to ignore me either.'

'Jay isn't real – you've just agreed that.' He could feel the panic starting to rise in his chest as the full realisation of his vulnerability dawned on him.

'Of course, Jay isn't real. He's in my head – her head – our heads. He's always been there. Jacinta – Jay. But what he can do is real. Why do you think Roseanne jumped? She wanted to get away from him – forever. It was an experiment but now we know. He can't chase dust. He stays here.'

'So is this what you did with her? Experiment? Test what Jay could do?'

He held his breath this time and tried to relax. It was easier to concentrate without the pain.

She nodded. 'I had to. Everything has its price – and sometimes it's failure. I thought with the same genetic root it was possible, but it wasn't. I took the contents out of the pills you brought me and put them in her coffee. She couldn't taste the difference – she always had no taste buds to speak of, but she was very – amenable. She didn't fly, but Jay didn't follow her either, so at least I freed her from that. The only problem was, he stayed with me, so now I need to find someone other than me for him to take an interest in. That's you.'

He breathed in sharply and the sudden inrush of oxygen made his head spin whilst his chest raged as if a flame thrower had just been fed to full force with the air. 'So everything you told me?' She smiled again. He didn't need the answer. 'And what is it you *can* do, as Erin?'

'Succeed,' she said, surprised. 'I'm always a success – at everything I do. Successful, talented Erin Matthews. Hadn't you realised that by now? Which is why you'll keep your mouth shut. That way we'll both succeed.'

'How will I succeed? You almost killed me and you've certainly ruined me. Who's going to come to a shrink who's been caught indulging in erotic perversions?'

'Only almost killed you though, remember? And Jay will take care of you now. You don't need to do anything other than what he tells you to. Obedience, remember?'

He sank back against the pillows, wondering what would happen next. Whatever it was, it had a price too. What the hell? There was a time to hold back and there was a time to confront. He'd held back on his principles way too long already. And what was there left to lose now?

'And Grant? What if I tell him everything? I have proof. From your two files and ...'

'And a letter,' she finished for him. 'I know. You told me, before ...' she smiled coquettishly at him. 'But that would be a very bad idea. A very bad idea indeed. And anyway, he's not allowed anywhere near you – until you've done what you need to do.'

'And what is that?'

'Fly, of course.' She smiled. 'When Jay tells you to.'

He should have said nothing more. Let the hospital rounds sweep her away and let fate take its course but he hadn't. He'd had to prove himself; damn fool!

'I'm not doing anything more – for you or Jay. We begin and end as dust, and dust is what we have to be to start. That was what she said to me, but that she wouldn't be reduced to it by anyone. And she wasn't. She reduced someone else to it in her place. You reduced someone else to dust in your place. That is murder, Roseanne.'

She'd remained smiling at him, but the smile wasn't a smile any more. It was the cool, appraisal of a self-appointed master. The door behind her swished open. A student nurse in crisp blue and starched white peered round it.

'Ah, I wasn't sure if you were awake but I thought you might be when I heard voices from here.' She'd looked uncertainly at Erin. 'Everyone else is busy at the moment, so you've just got me. I'll come and do your checks in a minute if no-one else is around, but a Detective Sergeant Grant would like a quick word with you first, if you're up to it?'

He'd looked across at Erin, and her dark eyes were unreadable – like Roseanne's had been when she'd told him her story. Or Erin's story? Damn, it hardly seemed to matter now. Sometime, even if he played along now, she'd come back for him and play out the rest of her story for him. They were like that – socio-psychopaths. So he was an experiment? Well, there had been enough experiments. Whether what she said she could do was possible, or whether she was merely a psychopath far smarter than he in the psychological manipulation stakes, he didn't care. Whatever it was, it was going to stop right here. Forget papers on paranormal abilities and professional kudos. Just surviving was more important right now.

'Oh yes, I'm up to seeing him,' he said firmly. 'Bring him in.'

Out of the corner of his eye he saw Erin move closer to him as the nurse left.

# Chapter 49: Roseanne

It had come to her suddenly – as suddenly as the original plan had in the first case. It was what you thought about as you let go – that was what you migrated into. The last thing you thought about – where you fixed your thoughts, your energy. Fly. She'd told Erin to fly.

They thought she was completely out, unconscious, in a coma. They hadn't considered that she could control her breathing and her brain activity so well that she could make herself appear inactive whilst listening and observing carefully. The policeman, Grant, had been back – several times. He wouldn't give up. And from what he'd said to the doctor, he'd figured out who she was. The blood tests and leg x-rays had proved that. It wasn't her legs that were broken but her ribs and shoulders. *Busch-busch.* It got on her nerves but it had become as constant as the clicking and alarm sounds of the machinery they'd surrounded her with. *Busch-busch.* And it was company of a sort. The fly crawled along the side of the bedside cabinet, replete with its standard issue water jug, cardboard sputum collector and packs of dressings to mop the worst of her oozing wounds. She opened her eyes when the nurse had gone and turned her head to study it. Black cone eyes studied her in return, legs rubbing together anticipatorily, the way Erin had rubbed her hands together when she was waiting for an answer.

'I freed you,' she said to it. The legs stopped rubbing. Waiting. 'I showed you how to fly. Why are you still here?' The fly remained where it was. The leg rubbing resumed. It crawled to the edge of the cabinet, then flew away to the window and beat itself against the window pane. *Busch-busch.*

She turned her head as far as it would go, given the neck brace, and ignoring the beeps and blips that had accompanied her for the last two days, concentrated on the idea. Erin's idea. Her idea. She needed to escape again, and what better way than the plan she'd already tested out once? She could change things into other things. She could move things simply by thinking about them moving. Jay had been right – and wrong. Jay hadn't the power, only the malice – malice and madness passed on to Erin. But she could fly – yes, she knew she could fly. She'd flown out of the window with Beringer. It had only been his dead weight, clutching hysterically at her, that had pulled her down; forced her to land with him on top of her. But without him – without any fetters – she *would* fly. She would soar. Fly, Roisin, fly. She was a Lady Lazarus, time and time again. She would migrate into something better later, without Jay ever being able to follow her.

For now,

just

fly.

# Chapter 50: Grant

'Beringer has exactly the same marker?' Grant frowned.

'Yes.'

Grant thought about the MRI reports in the evidence folder. 'Will he have been brain scanned too?'

'As he has head injuries, I guess so. Why?'

'That marker – could he be the same as the women, even though he's not related?

'Well, we ultimately all come from a common gene pool in our deep and distant past, so I suppose in a way we're all related, but as for being like the two women – in what way?' Alice sounded cautious.

'Odd – weird, like them.' He paused and took a deep breath. Maybe there was no way out of this one after all? 'Supernatural weird. Listen to this.' He read her the recovered last entry from Roseanne Grey's file.

'Oh, I see. Paranormal, you mean?'

'It's the same, isn't it?'

'Well … But there's no proof, Darwin – only what Beringer claims. And he could have been …confused?'

'Maybe the shrink's off his rocker too?' Grant concluded.

'I didn't say that. I don't know.' She sounded anxious. 'It would be another mystery to solve, though – without any real way to prove it.'

'What should I write in my report then?'

'That depends whether you want me to investigate further and possibly create another mystery, or ... oh!'

'What?'

'Casey's just put a memo on my desk. Came through last week on a priority email but of course we've been on leave. Our girl's heart stopped three days ago. She was down as a DNR since tests had shown she was most likely already brain dead, so that stone has been turned over and put back down again now anyway.'

Grant hesitated. The now familiar spinning had started in his head just as Carly entered the inner office with the sour-faced receptionist from Beringer's office.

'Oh shit!' he said, as they bore down on him like two avenging angels.

'Darwin?' Alice sounded confused. 'Are you still there?'

'I've got to go, sorry.' He put the receiver down and smiled nervously. 'Ladies?'

The receptionist thrust an envelope at him. It was dated the day of Beringer's hanging accident. The flap had been opened and hung loose, a flapping tongue waiting to talk.

'I always knew there was something about her. I'm sorry, I know I shouldn't have opened it but with poor Mr Beringer in the state he was and the fact that it was his writing, I just *knew* …'

Grant took the envelope from her and eviscerated it of its contents whilst she hung over his desk, face the colour of lemon curd and mouth twisting like it tasted rancid. It contained a single sheet, hand-written on headed paper: Michael Beringer, BMBCh (Oxon), Suite 4, Boars Hill, Oxford, OX1 5JN.

*I, Michael Beringer, being of sound mind, do attest that the following conclusions made, on the basis of rigorous and thorough review, are a true record of what I have observed of my two former patients, Roseanne Grey and Erin Matthews. Should any ill befall me following the recording of these facts, this letter should be brought to the attention of the police, namely, Detective Sergeant Grant of the Thames Valley Police in the first instance*

*I've checked and checked again, and it has to be true. Erin is Roseanne and Roseanne is Erin. I've compared their two MRIs and the bone structure is identical. That can only mean that the woman who had an MRI three months ago – as Roseanne – underwent another one just under four weeks ago as Erin. They are one and the same. If I could put a long wig and about two stone onto Erin, everyone would see it too. So, what does that mean?*

*That Erin had to die in order for Roseanne to mimic Erin.*

*Why? Discussions with Erin have suggested they both feel constrained by an abusive 'personality' named Jay, devised jointly between them, and probably dating form adolescence or before. Originally, I thought both women demonstrated unusual abilities, but now of course, I understand that there is only one woman involved; Roseanne. That also means that the abilities I have witnessed so far are beyond my experience thus far. My original plan to study Erin/Roseanne and her unusual abilities will now have to be modified – maybe even abandoned – unless I can find a way to control her. The problem with that is that other aspects of my involvement with Erin/Roseanne have escalated and I'm ashamed to say I don't even seem to have any control over myself when I'm with he, let alone over her.*

*More so, I've done nothing to stop her – I've even helped her in fact – unwittingly providing the prescription drug I assume she sedated her sister with in order to cause her fatal fall, but in my defence, I don't think there is anything I can do currently except go along with her. She is too powerful. What she can do – well, it scares me. She has me trapped, like Erin – and her psychosis, which she calls 'Jay' – had her trapped and mentally and physically abused as a young woman. There's no escape for either of us, unless I can come to some accommodation with her, so that's what I'm going to try and do.*

*I've removed the evidence and placed it in the glove compartment of my car, pending a meeting with Erin (Roseanne). I am writing this in the event that meeting proves to be detrimental or dangerous to me. Call it my insurance policy. My car is parked in Tower Street, AB5 3WJ.*

Beringer's signature sprawled across the page beneath the last paragraph. Grant put the letter down on his desk and this time, willingly let his head spin as the final piece of the jigsaw completed a disturbing picture for him – one which he knew, instinctively, he'd already known as far back as the time he'd been collecting evidence of Erin's magic tricks from her kitchen. How? He didn't know, but his brain buzzed with noise like a swarm of flies were beating themselves against his skull. It had been a long journey that had spanned a short time, but was there any point in completing this story? If Erin or Roseanne – whoever she wanted to be – was dead and Beringer was comatose, where was the risk, whatever 'weird' there was to be reckoned with? And what was justice? The righting of a wrong – and there seemed to have been some major wrongs on all sides here. Who was he to judge when there were so many wrongs he was guilty of too?

He pushed the sheet of paper back in the envelope and passed it back to Carly.

'Bag and evidence that, will you, then return it to me.' He turned to the receptionist. 'And thank you for bringing it in. You'll be pleased to hear it sounds like your boss might be showing signs of recovering. We'll see if he wants to follow this through, if and when he does, but in the meantime, as this wasn't addressed to you, but to me, you say nothing about it. Understood?' She nodded mutely. 'Good, now. I was in the middle of a phone call, so if you don't mind ...'

He watched the pair of them go, then leant back in his chair and watched the two flies swoop and dive outside the window. The familiar spinning started in his head and he swooped and dived with them until he closed his eyes and this time gave in to the spinning, floating sensation, allowing the mental picture to form beyond a vague shadow. Two women, abused and abusing. Manipulative and manipulated. And something else – anger, fear, hatred, revenge, freedom. Jay – Jacinta... *Thought she was a man who could fly – or was immortal, or both... Plain mad, if you ask me... She was deranged and a danger to others. Maybe you can catch madness* Oh shit! Mad mother, mad daughters and madness of another kind too that even Beringer couldn't explain away. He'd figured it out – too late; just before the high jump, but not long enough before not to have to jump. Story of his life. But he'd jump his own way. Fly his own way. He leant forward and picked up the phone, waiting only long enough to hear the cool, calming voice of reason on the other end.

'Alice; that magic marker – I think we've had enough magic for this year. And if she's dead then who is there to prosecute? Beringer won't confess – if he makes it – and I don't want to have to go into more weird and wonderful explanations for the Super than I'm going to have to already. Roseanne Grey was unbalanced and pushed her sister out the window but her sister sounded like a nasty piece of work too from what that old woman said. Crazy family in total, in fact, since the mother died in a loony bin. Tit for tat, if you ask me, and if Beringer becomes Superman, when or if he recovers, then good luck to him after all this. Job done. Anyway, what was that you said about doing less observing and more living? You realise today is New Year's Eve?'

'I do, fresh starts and all that. That's why I wanted to get this report finished and put to bed.'

'Put to bed,' Grant said, rolling the words around his mouth appreciatively. 'Now that sounds a much better idea for a bloodhound.'

He waited, judging the feeling from the other end of the phone. She was laughing. She *was* laughing, wasn't she? 'You are laughing, aren't you?'

'Yes,' she gasped, and her amusement was now audible. 'But what are you going to do before that?'

'About what?'

'The New Year – and new starts. The Super?' she reminded him.

'Oh, that. I've got that sorted.'

'Really? It's all squared with him? No more being bumped back to uniform from the first of January? How?'

'No, none of that.' He grinned even though she couldn't see it. You could hear grins, couldn't you? Alice could, anyway.

'I'm so glad, Darwin. I'll see you later then?'

'Oh yes,' he agreed. 'In fact, I'm going to leave any minute now, if you are too?'

'Any minute now,' the amusement was replaced by a smile.

Grant put the phone down and closed the Matthews and Grey files. He took a sheet of paper from Carly's scrap pile and wrote his report. It was barely a paragraph long. Then he bundled all three files together, with the report pinned to the top of them. Roisin Liath might have escaped the long arm of the law, but natural justice had got her in the end, anyway. He tucked the files under his arm and went across to the window. The two flies had gone – maybe died already in the icy conditions. Or maybe not. They were made of sterner stuff – sixth floor windows stuff, if he was right, but for now he didn't want to think about that. He had his own jump to arrange. He made his way along the corridor to the Super's office. The PS had already gone home and Carter-Rowles' desk was empty too. So much for dedication to duty. New Year's Eve obviously relegated duty to last for even the loftiest amongst them. He placed the files in the middle of the desk, together with his resignation letter and warrant card. He pulled Maria Brakespeare's business card from his pocket.

*'We would pay you – a private job, and probably so would others in the same situation. What's more important, following rules or finding out the truth?'*

'The truth, every time,' he said aloud, smiling. 'Even if it has to take care of itself occasionally.'

So, now to break the loop and find that so highly rated unbearable lightness of being for himself.

# About the Author:

D.B. Martin is a British author, writing adult psychological thriller fiction and literary fiction as Debrah Martin, as well as YA fiction, featuring a teen detective series, under the pen name of Lily Stuart.

You can find more about her work and sign up for updates on forthcoming publications on www.debrahmartin.co.uk.

## Other books by Debrah Martin include:

**Writing as Debrah Martin:**

# Falling Awake

Some would say suffering has driven Mary mad, and the people and places she remembers all just dreams dreamt inside her insanity. But then how can her husband Joe remember them too?

Falling Awake is the story of Mary, Joe and a world populated by love, betrayal and obsession - and what it does to those who live in it.

Magic or madness? The impossible is only ever a breath away.

Just don't fall awake.

# Chained Melodies

Best friends since childhood, life takes very different courses for Will and Tom until they're thrown back together in the middle of their own individual chaos.

Surviving the terrors of war in Northern Ireland and the heartbreak of childlessness and a broken marriage, Tom learns that bravery isn't about daring death, it's about facing life. For Will, it's about being yourself – or in his case, herself, as he starts an unusual journey towards being just that; the woman, Billie.

Chained Melodies is the extraordinary story of how two men find not just courage, but self-belief and the true nature of love. *It is the winner of an Indie B.R.A.G. Medallion.*

**Writing as D.B. Martin:**

# Patchwork Man

Lawrence Juste is top of the British legal world; a paragon of justice in action...

But Lawrence Juste isn't all that he seems. Outside of the courtroom, he's another man with another past – one full of conspiracy and secrets. One that is about to catch up with him.

It's not just the blackmail note his wife leaves him just before her death, or the vengeful family he's forced to reconnect with that bring the past crashing into the present. There's someone with their own very specific agenda who's after Lawrence Juste; someone Lawrence tangled with a long time ago. Someone with a long and vindictive memory, and now they want their pound of flesh.

Patchwork Man is the first book in the Patchwork People mystery suspense trilogy, and the winner of an Indie B.R.A.G. Medallion.

# Patchwork People

The second book in the compelling Patchwork People suspense series of murder, intrigue and lethal relationships.

Previously the name in the news in UK courtrooms, now Lawrence Juste, QC, is making headlines of a different sort. Yet despite admitting to a murky history, he's still on the up. It's a PR triumph for the man with the patchwork past; until the first sinister black edged card arrives.

It's followed by a parcel of evidence that puts Lawrence right to the middle of a deceit he helped create ten years ago. Not only that, when his hated sister is found dead in his house, he's prime suspect number one. The black edged card is followed by others, and more damning evidence. Gradually Lawrence is drawn deep into a pit of conspiracy and suspense, with the certain knowledge that the dead do tell tales, and there's no escaping revenge.

# Patchwork Pieces

When Lawrence Juste QC, gentleman and liar, originally championed the case of the boy who reminded him of himself, he couldn't have known precisely how much like him the boy would turn out to be. Or that the boy's past was already as entangled in murder and betrayal as his own.

Now the wheel has turned full circle. The past is the present, the betrayed are the betrayers and only the ultimate sacrifice can save both Juste and the boy. The only question ultimately remaining, as the patchwork completes: Who will be sacrificed?

Patchwork Pieces is the final book in the Patchwork People trilogy of murder, mystery and lethal romance.

**Writing as Lily Stuart:**

# Webs

*Deadly intrigue with a ton of teenage humour thrown in... Webs is the first book in the Lily S: Teenage Detective series.*
Sixteen-year-old Lily's policeman Dad is trying to untangle a particularly nasty death and Lily's intrigued. She's even more intrigued when she proves to him it's actually murder. Perhaps she'd make a detective too? If only she could work out what would get Dad to dump awful Ange, grovel, and patch things up with Mum. Irritating isn't the word!

In retaliation, for awful Ange, Lily's mum resorts to the web for romance – the world-wide-web. Convinced she can get her parents back together, Lily resorts to her own bit of web-weaving to trip up the candidates for replacement daddy. Whilst her school friends are up to their usual tricks; Matt is alternately ignoring and chasing her. Melezz is being the worst best friend, and Jacob is up to no good with his nipple tassel pranks again, Lily's busy sleuthing. The trouble is, whilst Lily thinks she's a clever little spider, weaving clever little traps, one of her prey is smarter still – and deadly.

# Magpies

THE teenage detective is back, and looking for trouble!

Or rather trouble's looking for her. They find each other in the series of little mysteries that start cropping up as soon as Lily's back at school after her brush with death, and meets the new boy, Si. He's different, like Lily is now, with her occasional narcolepsy and frequent inclination to investigate everything. But whereas Lily watches and works things out, Si blurts it all out at the wrong time and in the wrong way. He has Tourette's.

He also has a way with rhymes; one in particular that increasingly makes sense to Lily as the mysteries mount up and a gang of drug pushers target the school and her friends with potentially lethal consequences.

One for sorrow, two for joy, three for -

But 'joy' isn't a girl's name nor the opposite of sad, and the magpies the rhyme is about aren't just black and white birds that like stealing treasure. They're far more deadly than that...